Sheila Jeffries has been writing since she was young, and has written twelve children's novels. After studying at Bath Academy of Art, Sheila spent many years teaching in UK schools. Sheila lives in Somerset where she enjoys teaching meditation and running workshops for writers.

Also by Sheila Jeffries

Solomon's Tale
Solomon's Kitten
The Boy with no Boots
Timba Comes Home
The Girl by the River
Born to be Trouble
A Cornish Orphan

Sheila Jeffries

An Orphan's Winter

**SIMON &
SCHUSTER**

London · New York · Sydney · Toronto · New Delhi

A CBS COMPANY

First published in Great Britain by Simon & Schuster UK Ltd, 2019
A CBS COMPANY

1 3 5 7 9 10 8 6 4 2

Simon & Schuster UK Ltd
1st Floor
222 Gray's Inn Road
London WC1X 8HB

Simon & Schuster Australia, Sydney
Simon & Schuster India, New Delhi

www.simonandschuster.co.uk
www.simonandschuster.com.au
www.simonandschuster.co.in

A CIP catalogue record for this book is available from the
British Library

Paperback ISBN: 978-1-4711-6529-0
eBook ISBN: 978-1-4711-6530-6

Typeset in the UK by M Rules
Printed and bound by CPI Group (UK) Ltd, Croydon, CR0 4YY

MIX
Paper from
responsible sources
FSC® C020471

To Jade

Give me my Romeo; and, when he shall die,
Take him and cut him out in little stars,
And he will make the face of heaven so fine
That all the world will be in love with night.

William Shakespeare
Romeo and Juliet

Prologue

1937, ST IVES, CORNWALL

It all began when he reached down and lifted her out of the
sea and into the brightly painted boat. He'd never done that
before. *Why now?* she thought. *Is it because I'm going away?
Does he think I'll never come back?*

His eyes looked down at her, soulful and rebellious, the
December sunlight glistening on his wet shoulders. He
seemed suddenly older than his seventeen years. Mature.
Knowing exactly what he was doing. Even the hesitation
was deliberate.

Her skin was already on fire from swimming in the sea,
diving and floating in the gold-flecked waters of St Ives Bay.
Icy cold, but it was one of the crazy, carefree things they loved
to do together. It was Christmas Eve; the winter sun held some
warmth and the sea was calm – one of those rare days when St
Ives Harbour was blessed with an echo of summer.

'What's wrong, Matt?' she asked, and his eyes turned away
to stare at the distant town across the water, its harbour,
church and cottages nestled into rocky cliffs. Once it had

been his home. But now, estranged from his family, Matt lived on his boat, *The Jenny Wren*, earning his living as an artist.

A sense of urgency darkened his eyes as he turned to the girl he loved. 'This is our secret, Lottie. The family won't understand. When you go home tonight, you mustn't tell anyone – not Mum, not Tom and definitely not Nan.'

'I'm good at keeping secrets,' Lottie reminded him. 'Don't worry, Matt, I shall tell no one.'

'Not even Morwenna?' he added.

'*Especially* not Morwenna.' Lottie touched his face, running her fingers over the hollow of his cheek. 'You know you can trust me, Matt. You're very important to me and I love you.' She smiled and watched the light flood back into his eyes. 'I know you won't come home for Christmas, so let's be quiet and enjoy our time here together.'

'Mmm – you're so intuitive, Lottie, and beautiful,' he murmured and she felt his heartbeat quicken as he pulled her close again. She let him lead her into the cabin where there were rugs and cushions. Matt was no stranger. They'd grown up in the same house after Lottie was adopted by his parents, having been rescued from a shipwreck. Through the years of conflict and poverty, their love had grown in secret like a flower bulb in the cold, dark earth, its destiny to be a flower fully open to the sun. Invisible, it had grown through the frost and the silence, and now, on Christmas Eve, it had blossomed.

To discover such compelling love at a poignant time was a gift beyond words. There would be no holding back. Lottie wanted to give herself fully to the moment. She wanted to be that flower, to experience their moment in the sun, to match the intensity of Matt's love and create a lantern of joy that would sustain them through the gloom of their upcoming separation.

Lottie was sixteen and on the brink of a life-changing trip to America to meet her birth mother, who had abandoned her when she was just four years old. It was a big, emotional journey set to begin just after Christmas. Leaving Cornwall. Leaving Nan and Jenny. Leaving Matt.

Matt was young and inexperienced, but he wasn't clumsy. He made love to her slowly, whispering kindness, asking permission. Lottie wasn't afraid. She just let go, sighing with joy as they became one being, a perfect, burning, throbbing love, rocking the boat and sending gold-lipped ripples purling across the water.

If only it could last forever.

But even the sacred time spent lying together afterwards, in blissful, healing drowsiness, seemed too brief. The sun's gold deepened into the gloom of a winter afternoon and Matt got up, put on his clothes and started the boat's engine. Lottie pulled on her dress and coat and shook her long, honey-blonde hair down her back.

Time moved on, and *The Jenny Wren* was chugging steadily into the harbour, both of them fully dressed again, ready to step ashore with no evidence of their deeper relationship on show.

Lottie felt full of a glowing radiance – and yet, in a corner of her mind, panic was beginning. Matt might disappear again, pursuing his nomadic lifestyle. She longed to stay with him. Must she choose between Matt and the shadowy memory of her birth mother?

She didn't want to go.

But she had promised.

It felt like leaving a great ocean of light to follow a spark on a journey with an unknown destination.

Chapter 1

Follow Love

Alone in the moonlight, Lottie lingered in the gateway of Hendravean, with Nan's cat, Bartholomew, warm and purring in her arms. She listened to the thud of Matt's footsteps fading as he disappeared down the darkening lane, the pain of separation hardening within her like a blade being sharpened. The glow of their lovemaking lingered on her skin, as if Matt had flung a cloak of wordless velvet around her. She wanted to race after him.

'I'm coming with you, Matt,' she'd call, and her voice would sing with happiness.

Follow love, she thought. *Follow it always.*

Matt had been resolute and relaxed about saying goodbye. Lottie searched the dying twilight for a last glimpse of him. She could no longer hear his footsteps, only the hooting of owls and the distant whisper of the waves.

Soon you'll be on that ship to America, Lottie told herself, *and there'll be no turning back.*

She needed time to think. What if she refused to go?

She sighed, remembering the way her dad, John, would look at her with bewildered hurt in his dark blue eyes. John was Lottie's birth father, and they were still getting to know one another after he'd come back into her life.

'Lottie! What are you doing out here? You'll get cold.' The door of Hendravean opened, sending a slab of light across the gravelled drive as Jenny's bright voice called into the night. A barn owl glided low across the garden.

Lottie turned and saw Jenny limping towards her and felt sad. In the old days, Jenny would have come running out, her skirt hitched, her face sweet and kind like a welcoming flower. But now she had her leg in an iron calliper and often wore a frown on her brow as she struggled to walk.

Polio is a terrible thing, Lottie thought.

The disease had put Jenny Lanroska in hospital for a year, far away from her children. Lottie knew Jenny loved her. She'd been eight years old, alone and terrified, the sole survivor of a shipwreck, when Jenny had scooped her up and carried her home, which, back then, was a tiny fisherman's cottage in the Downlong area of St Ives. They were a poor family, but Jenny and Arnie were determined to adopt Lottie.

She had a close bond with Jenny, but right now she wanted time alone to think. Time to change her mind and run after Matt. But it was too late. Jenny was there, gazing into her face with kindly concern. "Tis a big exciting trip for you after Christmas, Lottie.'

Lottie nodded. Still in her arms, Bartholomew reached up and patted her cheek with a long, furry paw.

'He's going to miss you, Lottie – and Mufty will, too.' Jenny pointed at the stable and Lottie smiled at the sight of the donkey's silvery face staring at her with bright, expectant eyes.

'I'll bet you're scared stiff,' Jenny said, slipping her arm around Lottie's shoulders. 'I would be. But don't you worry, my girl, I'll be thinking about you and praying for you every single day. Me and Nan, and Tom – we'll be counting the days 'til you come home.' She gave Lottie a searching look. 'Come on, I'll help you pack.'

Lottie gave in and let her feet plod towards the house with Jenny. Bartholomew struggled to get down from Lottie's arms, then galloped ahead of them, turning once to make sure they were following. The velvet glow floated away as if it belonged to someone else, a different Lottie who had lived and breathed in Matt's arms out on the water.

Once inside with the door firmly shut, Lottie went to see Nan, who was sitting in her favourite chair in the lounge reading an encyclopaedia, a pair of glasses perched on the end of her nose. Nan studied her with a suspicious look in her eyes. 'Exactly where have you been, Lottie?'

'Out on the boat with Matt,' Lottie said firmly, but her eyes were secretive.

'What? All this time?' Jenny asked with a surprised tone, having entered the room behind Lottie.

'I've been beside myself with worry,' Nan added, a lethal mix of frustration and caring in her eyes. 'I want to know why you're so late.'

Lottie felt her face flushing. It was the way Nan was looking at her. *She knows*, she thought, shocked. Was there some mysterious clue in the way she looked? 'We went swimming,' she said, feigning innocence.

'*Swimming*?' Nan left the word hovering in the air between them and waited.

'I need to go and pack,' Lottie said, leaving the room and walking into the hall.

Nan's eyes narrowed. 'You've been up to something, my girl.' She wagged a finger, opened her mouth, then pursed it shut, changing her mind. 'Jenny, you want to keep a closer eye on this one.'

Jenny looked down at her leg in its iron calliper. 'Well, I can't exactly go chasing after her now, can I?' she said as she slowly followed Lottie out of the lounge and into the hall. 'Besides, I don't want to be nagging her on Christmas Eve.'

Lottie turned and gave Jenny a hug. 'Oh, Jenny! Don't cry. We've got Christmas to enjoy.'

Jenny stood up straight and shook her plume of dark hair down her back. She brushed the tears away, fiercely, with a threadbare sleeve. 'I'm gonna miss you, Lottie.'

'I won't be away for long – you'll be busy looking after Mufty and the chickens – and Tom, of course.'

'Tom's a good lad.' Jenny stood hugging herself, her arms crossed and her hands rubbing her shoulders as if she were missing the comfort of having her husband Arnie there to love her.

It touched Lottie's heart. She felt both lucky and excited to be at the beginning of her relationship with Matt, while Jenny could only look back at the empty, difficult years since Arnie's tragic death. Lottie felt compassion for this brave woman who had adopted her. Yet she'd never felt able to call Jenny 'Mum', not even when her real mum was a bitter memory.

'Are you missing Arnie?' Lottie asked, kindly.

Jenny took a deep breath and shook her head. 'No – well, I do miss him, always. It isn't that. It's, well, today, Tom came home bright as a button and so happy, telling me about Matt sailing into the harbour on *The Jenny Wren*. Tom was so proud of him. I couldn't say anything and spoil it, Lottie, but it was breaking my heart. Why, when we haven't seen or heard from him all winter – all through those terrible storms I've been worrying myself sick over   why couldn't he have come home for Christmas?'

'I did ask him to,' Lottie said, concerned.

'What did he say?'

'Nothing, really. He just wants to be on his own, on his dad's boat, Jenny.'

Jenny quietly closed the door to the lounge so Nan couldn't overhear what she said next. 'Nan keeps saying that silly old rhyme to me when I mention Matt. She says, "Leave them alone and they'll come home." Honestly, if she says it to me one more time I shall scream. I've tried so hard, Lottie, to get on with her – but she's never liked Matt. I think she's glad he's not here.' Jenny spoke in a whisper. 'Tell me about Matt – if I can bear to listen – what's he like now?'

Lottie felt a radiance flood over her again, awash with words of devotion to describe her lover, but not one of them was the right one to comfort his grieving mother.

'He's tall.'

Jenny stared at her with a quizzical look. Obviously, Jenny expected her to deliver a reassuring, vivid description of Matt and his life but Lottie thought it best to say as little as possible. 'He looks like his dad now.'

Jenny gave Lottie a hug. 'I really hope it goes well for you – meeting your real mum. I hope she appreciates you. And don't you forget, Lottie: I'm your mum as well – in here,' she patted her heart with fierce, endearing love. 'In my heart, I'm your mum, for always. No matter what.'

Little does she know, Lottie thought. But there was warmth in Jenny's words, a tender message to carry with her on her journey to America.

After making love with Lottie on the boat, Matt felt crazily happy, like a bee drunk on nectar. Running down Foxglove Lane was like flying through the night, being a star on the water with other stars, sharing the euphoria. Lottie seemed to be with him in spirit, as she'd promised. He'd miss her, but he wouldn't worry – she'd be well looked after by her father.

For Matt, building his life as an artist was now a priority. Every day he must draw and paint, perfecting his technique.

He wanted to have lots of pictures to sell to the tourists when they came flocking to St Ives in the spring.

His mind was ablaze with happiness. Until he reached the harbour and remembered it was Christmas Eve – but not for him.

Wharf Road was usually strewn with with lobster pots, pilchard barrels, hungry cats and scavenging seagulls. Tonight it had been swept clean. The seagulls were hunched in rows along the rooftops, and for once there was no laughter from the Sloop Inn, no boats coming and going. It even smelled different. A spicy, Christmassy smell.

Matt's heart sank. He didn't want to get caught up in Christmas stuff.

Too late, he thought as he stood back for the procession of families converging on the slipway, carrying lanterns: little girls with red and white ribbons in their hair, boys with sprigs of holly and ivy in their caps, enormous willow baskets laden with saffron buns, gingerbread men and fudge, proudly carried by the women. In the night air, the warm, fruity aroma of freshly baked treats made Matt hungry. His stomach growled, craving the uniquely Cornish taste of a saffron bun with its plump sultanas and rich golden bread, a memory of being a child in St Ives on Christmas Eve with his family.

The ache of loneliness began, deep down, building like a thundercloud, engulfing his mind. Desolate, he sat on the harbour wall close to the assembling crowd, kicking his heels against the granite. Had he made a mistake? Blinded by happiness, he had ended up in the middle of Christmas, the very thing he wanted to avoid.

It was too dark to take the boat out. The moon was no longer silvering the water, but sat high above the town, glinting on the slate rooftops. Over the night sea, Orion was rising with one bright star shining below. The masts of boats stood upright like reeds in the lagoon-like calm of the harbour. On the slipway, the families waited, motionless, silent, gathered together in a pool of lamplight. The carol singing was about to start and Matt could see the Male Voice Choir standing ready, the conductor with his arms raised like a cormorant.

His dad, Arnie, should have been there, singing with the choir he loved. But he wasn't – he was in the cemetery above Porthmeor. Matt's throat tightened. Like many Cornish folk, the Lanroskas had been a singing family, and the music still lived in Matt, body and soul.

He needed to escape, but the carol singing started with a great burst of sound. The deep tone of the Male Voice Choir seemed to come right up from the earth, from the crystal caves and the tin mines of Cornwall where the words of Cornish carols had first been sung. As the crowd joined in, the women's sweet voices rang from the cottage walls. Matt felt like it had knocked him over. He suddenly saw himself as a small boy in that mass of singers, leaning into the comforting warmth of his mother's skirt. When she'd started to sing, he'd gazed up at her in awe, her clear soprano voice flowing over and around him, never stopping until all the hurts in his world were healed.

How had it all gone wrong? Would it ever come right again? *Not without Dad*, he thought. *Dad was the peacemaker.*

Bewildered by the way he had crashed from divine happiness into an incarcerating grief, Matt stumbled along Wharf Road and down the stone steps to where *The Jenny Wren* was moored. He climbed into the cabin and shut the door. He'd get his head down and sleep. He'd sleep until Christmas was over.

After Christmas, Lottie would be boarding the ship to America; for five long weeks she'd be away. For her, it was a dream coming true, perhaps her only chance to meet her birth mother. What if the bond was undeniably strong? Matt imagined a wealthy American mother offering Lottie a lavish lifestyle in New York. She might never come back. Matt hadn't voiced his secret fears. She'd promised to come home.

Lottie was the one person Matt trusted.

Inside the cabin he could still hear the singing. There was a pause between carols. Then something made him open the cabin door and listen with his whole mind and heart on fire. They were singing his favourite carol. He listened hard for the words he knew were coming.

> *Lo! The Eastern sages rise*
> *At a signal from the skies*
> *Brighter than the brightest gem*
> *'Tis the star of Bethlehem.*

Brighter than the brightest gem, he thought. *That's Lottie. My Lottie. It's why I love her.*

On 27th December, Jenny was alone at Hendravean. She'd managed to get up early, put the calliper on her leg and a clean apron over her dress. She'd brushed her hair until it shone, knowing she must look her best to say goodbye to Lottie and her father, John. She liked John more than she cared to admit. Flirting came naturally to Jenny and she found herself wanting to make John smile, something he didn't do very often. He was such a serious man, but not gloomy, and she liked the way he was so respectful and fatherly with Lottie. Nan had regarded him with suspicion initially, but he soon won her over, more by what he didn't say than what he did say. Nan looked forward to his visits too, relishing what she called 'intelligent conversation', usually about something far above Jenny's head.

John had hired a car to take them up to Plymouth. Nan and Tom wanted to watch them sailing off on the cruise liner, a big adventure for twelve-year-old Tom who had never been further afield than Truro.

After they'd gone, Jenny got on with feeding the chickens, grooming Mufty and leading him out to the paddock. To be in the fresh air still seemed a wonderful treat to Jenny after her year in hospital, and since being at Hendravean she'd learned a lot about the wild birds and flowers, mostly from Nan, who had a vast store of knowledge.

While she tackled the household chores, Jenny kept

glancing outside, hoping Matt might come. She mulled over what Nan had said about Lottie looking strange after being with him. She had to admit, there had been an extraordinary radiance around her, but surely it couldn't have come from Matt? Perhaps there was something Lottie wasn't telling her.

Jenny frowned. Lottie had always been honest with her – self-willed, but clear-minded and truthful. *What on earth had she been up to?*

Jenny picked up Nan's binoculars from the windowsill and studied the boats out in the bay, hoping to see *The Jenny Wren*. Would Matt still be there? And what exactly would he be doing in St Ives? She learned nothing through the binoculars. Disappointed, Jenny went out into the yard. She eyed the donkey cart and toyed with the idea of harnessing Mufty and going down to the bay herself. With her weak leg in its iron calliper, everything was twice as difficult, but the need to see Matt was overpowering and, in the end, she decided to brave the long walk down to the harbour.

At mid-morning, Jenny set off, walking stick in one hand and a basket over her arm. She'd made lunch to share with Matt, her mind buzzing with the imagined conversation they would have.

Be very, very careful, she thought.

So many times she'd tried to discipline Matt and it had gone badly wrong, getting worse as he grew older. Matt had been eleven years old when his dad, Arnie, had died, leaving Jenny alone and in desperate poverty to bring up three children. The brooding resentment in Matt's eyes had begun then. He openly blamed her for Arnie's death and he'd never forgiven her. It wasn't fair.

Walking down the lane to St Ives, Jenny relived that terrible day. It had been Lottie's birthday and she'd taken the three children to the Helston Flora Day, an event that was an inherent part of Jenny's culture. Growing up in Helston, she'd always loved taking part in the prestigious midday dance. Arnie resented her dancing with her old partner, Troy, and that night he'd stormed out, got drunk and drowned in the harbour. It haunted Jenny. She glanced up at the cemetery on the steep hillside above Porthmeor Beach and picked out the granite cross marking Arnie's grave, sad that she hadn't the strength to go up there.

She blew him a kiss and walked on – or tried to. A sudden movement up in the cemetery caught her eye. She stared. A man was sitting by Arnie's grave. A man in blue, with a fisherman's cap, sitting with his knees hunched, apparently staring at the grave. Jenny gasped. It had to be him.

'Matt!' She cupped her hands and called out.

She saw him freeze as if he'd suddenly spotted her.

They stared at each other across the cemetery, with its orderly rows of headstones and crosses.

Jenny waved. She called out again. But Matt didn't move. They were staring across a chasm of unresolved bitterness and it was only getting wider. So wide that Jenny could hardly see him as he left the cemetery, walking up the hill in long strides, away from her.

And he didn't look back.

It hurt. Like a nail being driven into tenderness. Jenny felt it going in, deep into the sacred vessel of her womb. Where she had carried him. Her firstborn. But, no, that wasn't true. Jenny doubled up and collapsed onto a bench against the wall. Her firstborn had been a little girl, perfect but stillborn. Born sleeping, the midwife had kindly said, and Jenny had begged to be allowed to hold her, with Arnie standing beside, both of them numb with grief. Never to see her daughter's eyes was so cruel. 'She'd have the eyes of an angel,' Arnie had whispered, and the words hung between them like a garland carved on a tombstone.

The eyes of an angel.

Jenny had fallen pregnant again too soon; before she'd grieved enough. Matt was born and she hadn't been ready. A boy with soulful eyes and a restless spirit, born rebellious.

In the months of poverty after Arnie's death, eleven-year-old Matt had silently tried to help, scavenging coal and wood to fuel the stove and scaling the roof to mend the storm damage. Jenny had been too exhausted to notice his efforts. Moments of empathy were lone sunbeams in an endless storm, times when she'd stared into Matt's wounded eyes and glimpsed the person he would become. Too late – everything was snatched away when Jenny was rushed into hospital with polio and the three children were sent to an orphanage. The final blow came when the cottage in Downlong was repossessed and sold.

At the time, Nan was alienated from the family by a feud, and lived a reclusive life in her isolated home, Hendravean. She and Jenny had never been friends, but when Nan discovered the unfolding tragedy, she swallowed her pride and offered them a home. Matt, at thirteen, refused to live with Nan, who he felt had always hated him. He ran away and made a life for himself as an artist.

So why do I worry about Matt? Jenny asked herself. *Why do I long to see him? Why am I breaking my heart, day in, day out?*

She loved him, despite everything.

Jenny stared at the sea, trying to calm herself. She thought of John and Lottie boarding the ship, with Nan and Tom waving an emotional goodbye. The horizon was an icy blue, the surf building out west, the swell already rocking the boats in the harbour. A storm was brewing out there in the Atlantic.

Jenny stood up, anxious to get home before the wind and rain started. But she couldn't shake off the feeling that she simply must try to see Matt. They had to talk. She couldn't let him sail off into a gathering storm and face those mighty waves. *The Jenny Wren* was old and small with only a tiny cabin. And Matt was so reckless.

With a sense of urgency, Jenny headed through the cobblestone streets, ducking under the lines of washing strung between cottages. Breathing hard, she stumbled down to the harbour, her eyes searching for Matt and his boat.

Lottie's radiance shone in her mind. Lottie and Matt were close friends now. It was important to make peace. She'd make him talk to her, make him listen, make him care.

In the bustle of a working day, it was obvious that boats were coming in, not going out, seeking a haven from the approaching storm. Jenny picked her way along Wharf Road, through the piles of freshly caught pilchards glistening as they were packed into barrels by small groups of energetic women working too fast to look up at Jenny, or the sea or sky. The shipping forecast blared out from the open door of a cottage, a calm, impassive voice warning of the impending storm.

Jenny had reached the slipway when an old familiar sound made her stop. The engine of a motorboat starting up. It had to be *The Jenny Wren* – she recognised the particular sound of its engine from happier days when Arnie would be arriving home, triumphant, from a fishing trip, a cloud of seagulls following.

Startled, she watched with a sinking heart as *The Jenny Wren* roared across the harbour, going much too fast, carving a swathe of disruptive ripples. Matt was on board, his silhouette uncannily like Arnie's, unruly hair flying as he steered the boat with astonishing skill.

'Matt!' Jenny screamed. 'Matt – wait!'

Even if he'd heard her, Matt didn't turn around, but headed for the open sea in an arc of spray.

Filled with anxiety and disappointment, Jenny watched until the boat became a diminishing dot bouncing over the waves towards Hayle.

'Please God, keep him safe,' she prayed, and headed home, limping painfully, the lunch she'd made untouched in her basket.

Chapter 2

New York

Lottie gazed down at Nan and Tom who stood on the quayside. She wished she was close enough to see the love in Nan's storm-coloured eyes, just once more, and to give Tom another hug.

'I don't want you to go, Lottie,' he'd said, openly crying and clinging to her. 'Promise me you'll come back, Lottie.'

'I promise, Tom – and I'll bring you a present – from America,' Lottie had said.

'Stop that infernal blubbering,' Nan had snapped at Tom. 'You're twelve years old, not two. Stand up straight and make Lottie proud of you.'

Tom stopped instantly and stood rigid, hardly daring to breathe in case he was ambushed by one of the huge shuddering sobs that seemed to live inside his ribcage. If it had been his mother, Jenny, telling him to stop, he would have allowed himself a tantrum. To Tom, Nan had horns and an axe like one of the Viking warriors he'd learned about in school.

The cruise ship let out an impressive noise from her siren and Lottie felt the deck rail buzz with the vibration. There was something poetic about the sound. A ship's voice. A mighty voice, reaching out across the waiting ocean, echoing through the green valleys of the Tamar River.

'America, here we come,' said her father, John De Lumen, as he gave his daughter a hug.

Lottie looked up at him and smiled. 'I'm glad you're with me, Daddy.'

As the ship pulled away from the quay, Lottie fixed her eyes on her beloved Nan and Tom, gazing at them over the frothing white wake of the ship. Nan looked like a pyramid. Unmoving, she stood with her legs planted a long way apart, a voluminous navy-blue dress covering her bulk, a coil of silver-white hair, and her weather-tanned Cornish face set in stone. It comforted Lottie to know that Nan would be standing there until the ship was a mere smudge on the horizon.

Lottie clung to the deck rail, holding on to the last glimpse of Nan, a small, dark dot of love and reliability in the fading colours of Plymouth Hoe. The ship carving through the waves was like a power source, dragging her away from everything she loved, drawing a blind of thick gauze where sea and sky blurred together, leaving nothing in between.

What if Nan dies while I'm away? Lottie thought when she could no longer see her reassuring figure standing on the quay. *I must be mad to go on this trip, to agree to meet a mother who abandoned me when I was four.*

'Lottie?' John stood patiently beside his daughter, discreetly observing her intense grief at the parting. There would be anxiety too, he imagined, considering the way Lottie had arrived in Cornwall as a shipwrecked orphan. He wished she would cry for once and let him comfort her, but Lottie only knew how not to cry. If tears came, she'd quickly brush them away and stand up even straighter. She looked up at him now with those shiny, bright knowing eyes.

'Are you okay, dear?' he asked.

'Okay? What does that mean?'

John smiled. 'It's an American word; you'll hear it a lot in New York – and in London. I guess it just hasn't reached Cornwall yet.'

'So how do I know if I'm okay when I don't know what it means exactly?'

'Okay really means you are surviving – not thriving, but surviving – something you're good at, Lottie.'

'Tell me again how you found me, Daddy – how did you know I lived in St Ives?'

John's eyes sparkled. It was something he loved to talk about. 'Well,' he began, 'I was a weekend artist. I used to come down from London to paint in Cornwall and once I discovered St Ives, I couldn't keep away. The light on the water is so special and the colours of the sea are breathtaking.

One day, I was painting at the top of Porthmeor Beach when I saw two little girls playing in the sand. It was you and Morwenna.'

'We were making a shell garden,' Lottie said, 'and Tom and Matt were building dams in the stream.'

'I wanted to paint you so much.' John looked dreamy. 'You looked so beautiful and innocent, with your lovely blonde hair tumbling round your shoulders – but it was more than that. You reminded me of the little daughter I loved and lost – Charlotte – though I reasoned it couldn't possibly be you. Then you turned and looked at me and my heart nearly stopped. I knew, I just *knew* you were Charlotte. But when I called your name you looked shocked and you ran away, all of you. I was devastated.'

'I didn't recognise you with your beard, Daddy. I only saw a photo of you when I was little – and Morwenna, well, you know what she's like. She made me think you were a threat.'

John's eyes twinkled with amusement, then darkened with sadness. 'I never saw you again on the beach. I was so upset, thinking I had frightened you. But I worked hard on the painting of you and it was the best I'd ever done. I called it *Discovering Charlotte*, and it got chosen for a big London exhibition, and two people who owned a gallery in New York bought it from me.'

'Rex and Coraline?'

'Yes – Rex and Coraline. That's where we'll be going – to see the painting and meet your mother there. It was wonderful how she walked into the gallery, saw the painting, and realised it was you. That's when Coraline gave her my address and she got in touch.'

John had told Lottie this story before, but she still relished hearing it again, and each time she listened attentively, hoping for some new detail she might have missed.

'Well, the next time I saw you after that day on the beach . . .' John lowered his voice and both of them looked serious, knowing the next bit was a painful memory, 'it was Arnie's funeral. I was on the quay painting when the procession passed by, and I was so shocked to see you three children walking so bravely behind the coffin. So tragic. My heart wept for you.'

Lottie looked at him with empathy. 'That's like . . . like crying inside,' she said intuitively.

'Like crying inside your soul,' John affirmed. Then the sparkle came back into his eyes. 'And that's when I first saw Nan. She looked majestic and powerful in her black velvet cloak. Like the Queen of St Ives.'

They both smiled.

'She's a wonderful woman, your Nan,' John said. 'I wonder what she was in her youth.'

'She never tells us,' Lottie said. 'And Nan isn't her real name, no one seems to know what it is. Even people in St Ives call her Nan. But she's very clever. She knows Latin and she loves poetry and folklore. I love her, but no one else seems to even like her. People are afraid of her.'

'How old is she?' John asked.

'No one knows. But we do know she's our great-grandmother and Arnie was her grandson. She brought him up.'

'Is that so? She really is a remarkable woman. But full of secrets.'

Warmed by the enthusiasm in her father's dark blue eyes, Lottie made herself let go of the deck rail. She let go of watching the shimmering space where Plymouth had been.

A whirling flock of seagulls had followed the ship for the first few miles and now they turned in graceful loops and spirals and headed back, vanishing into the opalescent haze. 'They've gone home,' Lottie said. 'Nan told me there's a point about ten miles out where the seagulls always turn around.'

'And is that true? Or is it Cornish folklore?'

'A bit of both,' Lottie said. 'Nan says St Ia turns the seagulls round because she won't let them get lost. But she also thinks the dolphins turn them round. She believes there's a web of life in which all the creatures of the earth look out for each other.'

'Your Nan has a rich store of knowledge,' John said. 'She hasn't shared it with me yet.'

'She won't, Daddy. Nan only tells folklore to children now, because adults laugh at her and call her a crank.' Lottie lowered her voice to a stage whisper. 'Some people have even called her a witch.'

'Is that so? Well, I wouldn't,' John said, 'and you wouldn't, would you?'

Lottie shook her head. 'Never.'

She hesitated, aware again of the great ship carrying them effortlessly into the vast and lonely ocean. Away from home and family. But a new sense of freedom began to push its way into the ache of separation. Far from home on the shining water with just the two of them, Lottie realised she could tell her father of some of the darker sides of the Lanroska family, those she usually kept to herself. There was one she felt he ought to know. About Jenny.

Lottie had noticed how much her father seemed to like Jenny. She hoped they weren't going to fall in love. John was gentle and kind and Lottie wanted him all to herself. A deeper, more secret wish hung in Lottie's heart like a tiny, fragile chrysalis: *Could my real parents be reunited in America?*

'Until recently,' she began, 'Jenny and Nan hated each other. Jenny thinks folklore is rubbish and she banned Nan from seeing the boys when they were growing up. Then, when I turned up after Arnie rescued me from the shipwreck, Nan befriended me – she is really, truly my *best* friend, even though she's old. I wasn't going to let Jenny spoil our friendship, so I used to visit Nan on my own and we had a lovely time, looking after Mufty and the chickens and the cats. I'd never been allowed any pets in my life. My real mum didn't like them, did she?'

'No – Olivia wanted nothing to do with animals,' John agreed.

The colour was back in Lottie's cheeks now, her blonde hair shining in the salty breeze, and she began to talk to John like never before, with passion in her eyes and voice. 'I loved the times I spent with Nan. She had wonderful books and we used to read together by the fire on wet days with the wind howling in the chimney. We read all through *Grimms'*

Fairy Tales and Hans Christian Andersen, and we read *Anne of Green Gables* and *Oliver Twist*, and best of all we read Nan's old books of Cornish legends. Nan taught me how to care for the animals and she let me read on the sofa with a chicken on my lap. In the summer, she took me out on the cliffs and taught me about wildflowers and herbs and birds, then she started teaching me music.'

'You were going to tell me about Nan and Jenny,' prompted John.

'Well – it was bad enough already with Nan and Jenny hating each other, but Nan blamed Jenny for Arnie's death, and then it was like open war between the two of them. Nobody told Nan when Jenny got polio and we were taken to an orphanage, but when Nan found out she made a huge effort to put things right. She rescued us and managed to make peace with Jenny. I hope they stay friends – our life would be impossible if they didn't.

'I can't do this.'

Olivia stared at her reflection in the yellowing mirror on the back of the wardrobe door. Her once beautiful complexion was plastered with thick, concealing make-up, her cheeks aglow with rouge, her lips glossed with scarlet, her pencilled eyebrows sweeping towards her ash-gold hair.

Her eyes confronted her from the mirror. She wasn't seeing the make-up. She was seeing the truth underneath. The pale cheeks. The finely etched wrinkles, not smile lines, but lines of tension and misery. Somewhere inside those solemn, desperate eyes was the sparkle John had fallen in love with, and no matter how hard she tried, Olivia couldn't seem to coax it into life.

Seducing John after all these years wasn't going to be easy. She dreaded the way he would look at her. *Dismissively.* The kindness in his dark blue eyes wouldn't be for her, but only for little Charlotte.

Little Charlotte? Olivia gave her thoughts an angry prod. Her estranged daughter wouldn't be the candid, enchanting child she had been so long ago. Olivia glanced at the sepia photograph John had sent from England. Their daughter was now a new, almost adult creature who insisted on calling herself Lottie. Not even Lottie De Lumen, but Lottie Lanroska, a Cornish name that sounded rebellious and earthy to Olivia.

I can't do this, she thought again. *I can't face the accusing glint of hurt in her eyes, asking 'Why did you abandon me, Mummy?'*

The clock ticked on mercilessly on the windowsill, against the nicotine-stained nets that screened the views of other dingy tenement flats in the haze of a New York smog. In one hour she was to meet John. Her pulse quickened at the thought. Would he take her in his arms? Would he gaze deeply into her eyes and see her, *really* see her? Or would he give her his business-as-usual look through frosted glass? Olivia had to keep reminding herself that her daughter would be there. John would be the devoted, respectable daddy in front of Charlotte. No – Lottie. Olivia picked up her keys and spoke the name aloud.

'Lottie.'

It sounded strange. Challenging.

She locked the door of her apartment. As usual, the lift wasn't working so she took the five flights of stairs, her small feet moving with swift precision. It felt like escaping from herself.

I can't do this, her thoughts insisted at each turn of the staircase. But moments later she found herself stepping into a taxi.

'Will you take me to the Rex and Coraline Art Gallery please?' she asked, and sat back cocooned against the smog, her legs crossed, her eyes hardly noticing the passing streets, her mind in a panic. She leaned forward and tapped the cab driver on the shoulder. 'On second thoughts – would you drop me at the bar on the opposite side of the road?' she requested.

'Sure.' The cabbie's eyes frowned at her from the driving mirror. 'But it's not the sort of place for a lady on her own.'

'I'm perfectly capable of taking care of myself,' Olivia snapped.

'Okay, lady,' he shrugged.

A plan hatched in Olivia's mind. She'd hide in the bar and watch for John to arrive at the gallery; she'd test how it felt to see her daughter – and see how John looked now. Had he grown a beard? Put on weight? Gone bald? Would he still have his eager, loping walk, his hard stare masking the eyes of a dreamer?

29

She could barely afford a glass of wine, but she simply had to have one. Trying to sip it slowly, Olivia sat by the window, looking through the traffic at the open doorway of the Rex and Coraline Art Gallery.

Waiting.

Remembering.

'Did I really look like that?' Lottie stood in front of her father's painting of her playing on the sand in St Ives with her best friend, Morwenna.

'To me you did.' John had his arm around his precious daughter and he gave her an affectionate squeeze. 'I wanted to capture a feeling – something deep in your heart. It spoke to me and I felt compelled to paint it.'

'What kind of feeling?' Lottie asked, her slim fingers twining into his rough artist's hand, which was on her shoulder.

John was silent for a moment, thinking. Then he said simply, 'Pain.'

'Pain?' She challenged him immediately. 'But I wasn't in pain, Daddy. I was happy.'

'Happiness doesn't come without pain,' John said, 'and it is the special task of the artist to explore its mysterious connection. It's not easy to paint a feeling because you're trying to paint the invisible.'

Lottie waited for his words to make sense in her head, which they didn't. But it didn't matter. She was here to meet her mother and the excitement was blurring everything, even the thrill of arriving in New York all the way from Cornwall.

She sighed. 'I can't really concentrate on it, Daddy. It's a lovely painting, and I like the way you've done the sea and made the waves look all shimmery and the sky so blue, but I'm too excited about meeting my mother. She is coming, isn't she?'

John frowned. 'She said she was. But this is New York. It's not always possible to be on time, especially in this kind of weather.'

'I can't wait. Look at me, Daddy, I'm shaking with excitement.'

John looked down at her, concerned. Lottie was usually so calm, taking everything in her stride. He supposed this wasn't surprising given all she had been through in her short life. He observed the ruffled hem of her blue frock was quivering, as if her knees were shaking.

'Why don't we sit down?' he suggested, and led her to one of the plush green velvet seats in the middle of the gallery. 'Just take some deep breaths, Lottie. Olivia is late, but I'm sure she'll be here soon. She wants to see you.'

Lottie nodded and sat down beside him, facing the painting. 'I do like the way you've painted Morwenna,' she said, feeling a wave of homesickness, a longing for her friend. 'She looks wild and mischievous, but doll-like – the way she is. Or was. She's grown up now and keeps on telling me she could have a baby. It's all she wants. A baby. She's not even married yet.'

John smiled. 'Has she got a young man?'

'No,' Lottie said. 'She used to make eyes at Matt, but he hates her.'

'Matt sounds like an angry young man,' John said. 'Maybe I should take him under my wing – if he'll let me.'

Lottie's eyes lit up as she remembered Matt and how he had appeared the night before she left for America. 'Matt is rebellious. He won't live with us because he blames his mum for his father's death. He survived the Cornish winter on his own, sleeping rough, and he earned enough money to buy his father's boat back. I'm proud of Matt – and he's an artist like you. Wait 'til you see his pictures of seals.' Lottie hesitated, then said what she wanted to say, her cheeks colouring a little as she spoke with passion about Matt. 'I didn't used to like Matt when we were growing up. He was horrible to me. But now he's changed – and we ... we're good, close friends.'

Her voice lost its music and faded away. She hadn't quite found the courage to say the words burning in her heart. She loved Matt. And Matt loved her. She knew he did, but it was secret.

She sighed and searched her father's eyes for understanding. John was looking at her intently, his hands clasped, the deep blue of his eyes glistening with empathy and hope. Lottie had spent most of her life without her father, but a twist of fate had brought them together and it felt as if they'd never been apart.

'Hmm ... I shall enjoy getting to know Matt. When we get back to Cornwall—' He broke off as he heard footsteps come from the far end of the gallery. 'Ah ...'

They both tensed, listening, and a look of anticipation tingled between them. Lottie felt a shiver rush up her spine. She stared at the open archway between the galleries.

Her mother! Her mother was coming.

She gasped in surprise as a beautiful, Goddess-like woman in a swinging, swishing skirt hurried briskly towards them. She had rich brown eyes and a smile wider than her face.

'That's not your mother,' John said quickly. 'It's Coraline, who owns the gallery.'

Disappointment flooded over Lottie, but she quickly regained her composure, warming to Coraline's open friendliness.

'John! It's great to see you.' Coraline grasped John's hand and held on to it. 'Isn't this a wonderful, special day? I'm so excited for you. Rex told me you were here. All the way from Cornwall – lovely Cornwall. I'm going to see it someday soon.' Without waiting for a reply, she turned her glowing eyes on to Lottie and the smile stretched even wider. 'And this is Charlotte?'

'Lottie.'

'Lottie! Okay, Lottie – what a gorgeous girl you are! I'm so pleased to meet you – the star of John's fabulous painting. How does it feel to be famous, Lottie?'

'Famous? How can I be famous?' Lottie looked bewildered.

'Aw, you're so cute.' Coraline's smile was illuminating. It was making Lottie smile too, even though she was worrying about her mother. 'It's John's painting of you that's famous. People from all over America have come to see it. The title, *Discovering Charlotte*, is so intriguing. Everyone loves a mystery.'

Coraline turned her joyful smile on John. 'There are lots of reviews. I've kept a scrapbook of them for you – you shall have it to take home.'

Lottie kept her mouth shut. She liked Coraline, but found her enthusiasm slightly alarming. She glanced at the gallery clock. Her mother was half-an-hour late. It was unnerving. Lottie felt fragile, as if her confidence had walls of glass and behind them lurked a heavy tide loaded with fear of abandonment. What if her mother didn't turn up? Suddenly she understood, with frightening clarity, what her father had meant by 'pain'. Lottie had felt that pain so young – at four years old – when her mother abandoned her, leaving her with John's mother, Granny De Lumen, and gone far away to America on a ship. Betraying her. Betraying John, who was working abroad.

If it happens again, Lottie thought grimly, *I'll hate her forever. Forever and ever. No matter what she does.*

She stared at the clock. Forty minutes. Forty-five minutes. Nearly an hour.

Leaving her father deep in conversation with Coraline, Lottie prowled along the walls, pretending to be looking at the other paintings in the gallery, none of which interested her. Except for one, a rather gloomy painting of Jesus on a donkey. Seeing the donkey reminded Lottie of home, of Mufty, far way in St Ives; the way he looked at her with those wise, hopeful eyes, the cosy warmth of his fur, the way he loved her without judgement. A hot lump of homesickness lodged in her throat. To be polite and make conversation was going to be difficult.

An hour – gone. And time, like a drain, was sucking away her hopes and dreams. All through the winter, Lottie had dreamed of this meeting with her mother. She'd imagined hugs and smiles and harmonious talks that would heal the gulf between them. She'd even dreamed of rekindling the romance between her parents, despite John's insistence that he wasn't going to let Olivia back into his life. He'd be courteous, he'd help her if he could, but she wasn't going to be his wife again.

The trip to America had been a major commitment for John, who'd had to close his new art gallery in St Ives. For Lottie, it took up almost all of the first half of the school term. Spring came early to Cornwall and it was a time she had grown to love: first the primroses and violets, then the bluebells and white bells of wild garlic, followed by the tight little buds of sea pinks and the clumps of sweetly fragrant Alexanders. Like most houses in St Ives, Nan's place had a pair of nesting seagulls on the roof, nesting jackdaws in the old pigeon holes along the barn wall, and swallows' nests on the rafters inside Mufty's stable. Standing there in the gallery, Lottie felt sad at the thought she might miss it – for nothing – for a mother who hadn't turned up.

She trudged back to where her father and Coraline were carefully wrapping the painting in layers of corrugated cardboard.

'I can see you were a boy scout,' Coraline joked, watching John tying swift and complicated knots and cutting lengths of the white string with a penknife from his pocket.

Her mother was now an hour and a half late.

Coraline noticed Lottie's disconsolate stance. 'You're disappointed, Lottie,' she said warmly. 'Perhaps your mother will be here soon. Don't give up on her.'

Lottie looked into her eyes and saw the glow of kindness there. She wished Coraline was her mother. It would be so easy and happy. But she felt too upset to speak.

'Are you all right, Lottie?' John asked, but Lottie couldn't even look up at his concerned eyes. She just wanted to go home – to St Ives.

Chapter 3

The Boy in the Barn

Far away in St Ives, Nan stood in the open door of the hay barn, an imperious glare crinkling her brow. Tom hovered beside her, brandishing a driftwood truncheon. 'I'll smash his head in, Nan, don't you worry.'

'I've never had a day's worry in my life,' Nan replied, casting a contemptuous glance at Tom's driftwood truncheon. 'That's a fat lot of good. Go and get the cricket bat from the woodshed if you feel the need of a weapon. I don't need one.'

Someone was hiding in the hay barn. Nan had sent Tom to let the chickens out in the early morning and he'd come thundering back, red-faced and bursting with importance to report hearing someone coughing inside.

Hendravean was isolated, standing alone on the cliffs overlooking Porthmeor Beach and Clodgy. Nan liked her reclusive lifestyle. Her best friends were Mufty, the donkey; Bessie and Bartholomew, the two house cats; the chickens, and the wild birds and animals. She was doing her best to adjust to a new life, having taken in Jenny and her three children. She'd taught herself to drive and had bought an Austin Seven so that she could rescue the children and bring them home to St Ives. Only Matt was missing. While Jenny grieved and worried for her eldest son, Nan was secretly glad Matt wasn't there. In her opinion, Matt was a born troublemaker and the Lanroska family were better off without him.

Nan was doing her best to build a relationship with young Tom, teaching him music and getting him involved in caring for the animals and the garden. She found him irritatingly babyish, but, unlike Matt, Tom was trustworthy. So when he told her someone was in the barn she believed him, and dragged herself out to investigate.

She and Tom stood outside the barn door, listening intently.

'Excuse me, Nan, but whoever's in there isn't going to come out if we're standing in the doorway,' Tom said sensibly, then widened his eyes and whispered, 'let's hide round the corner and keep watch.'

'Good thinking,' Nan said, impressed.

'It's what me an' Matt would do.'

'You miss him, don't you?' Nan said, detecting the wistful tone in Tom's voice.

Tom put a finger to his lips: 'Shh!'

After twenty minutes of standing in the cold wind, Nan was fed up with waiting. The chickens were clustered expectantly around her, wanting their breakfast, and Mufty was kicking the door of his stable. 'I'm not going to stand here all day, Tom. And you've got to go to school.'

'Have I *got* to?'

'Yes.'

'But who's gonna look after you and Mum, Nan? If it's a burglar in there, I could fight him and chase him off.'

'I dare say you could. But you *are* going to school, so put that cricket bat down and get yourself ready.'

Tom was going to argue but Nan's eyes fixed him with a look he hated – unquestionable, no-nonsense authority. Nan would win. She always did. But what if the person hiding in the barn was a criminal on the run from prison? Tom handed the cricket bat to Nan. 'All right then, I'll go to school. But you watch out, Nan. He might attack you.'

Nan cackled with laughter. 'Attack *me*? He wouldn't dare.' She tossed the cricket bat aside and headed for Mufty's stable, her laughter shaking her belly and ringing from the granite walls.

Halfway down the lane with his school satchel over one shoulder, Tom heard one of Nan's foghorn shouts. Alarmed, he turned to look back at Hendravean and saw a fleeing figure, dark against the morning light. He wore a small cap and raggedy clothes and he was bent double, clutching a bundle of something Tom couldn't make out. Tom watched him zig-zag through the bracken towards the Clodgy rocks until he disappeared. Who was he? Why was he desperate enough to steal? And would he come back?

Tom walked on towards school. He missed Matt, he missed Lottie and didn't want to admit he was actually scared on his own. *Two weeks, and Lottie would be back.* On his bedroom windowsill, Tom had made a timeline of pebbles. Each morning, he removed one. He was counting the days.

It's like watching someone die inside, John thought as he studied his daughter's face across the immaculate white cloth of the hotel dining table. Lottie's food lay untouched on her plate. She'd shaken her head and insisted she wasn't hungry, but John asked the waiter to bring it anyway. He'd tucked into his own generous portion of braised steak and roast herby potatoes, adding a mound of sweetcorn and peas and neat sprigs of white cauliflower, pouring copious amounts of gravy over it all.

'Won't you try even a little bit? These herby potatoes are delicious,' he said gently, not wanting to put Lottie under any pressure.

She shook her head. Her eyes stared across at the busy hotel dining room, not seeing it at all.

'What about some American ice-cream?' he asked her when the waiter came to clear the plates away.

Lottie shut her eyes and shook her head. When she opened them to the same blank stare, John noticed her cheeks were pale. 'Perhaps you should go and lie down,' he suggested.

'No, Daddy, I'll wait for you,' Lottie said politely, but her eyes still weren't looking at him. Well, they were – but they weren't seeing him.

It had gone deep, the pain of her mother not turning up. Now they were to board the ship in the morning for the voyage home. Without Olivia.

The trip of a lifetime, ruined. His daughter's trust shaken.

John was furious with his ex-wife. He'd tried to phone, but no one had answered. *How could Olivia do this to Lottie?* Oh – she could – he reflected grimly. With her track record. Maybe it would hurt Lottie more to know her than not to know her. Maybe it was for the best.

John searched Lottie's blank eyes. No, this wasn't for the best.

'It's upset you a lot, hasn't it?' he asked gently, hoping she would talk. If only she'd cry in his arms, he could smooth her hair and listen, and be her father.

Lottie shrugged. She pressed her fingers against her left temple and along her eyebrows. 'I'm sorry, Daddy, I've got a headache. A bad one.'

John knew about Lottie's headaches. They were severe and one-sided. He wished Jenny was there. She seemed to know Lottie so well. 'What does Jenny give you? An aspirin?'

'She does, but it doesn't work,' Lottie said. 'Nan gives me fennel tea and that doesn't work either. I just have to sleep it off.'

'What brings it on?' John enquired, anxious to help. Lottie squinted at him through eyes narrowed with pain. He felt sure it was emotional, but he didn't know how to say so without causing offence.

'I don't know, and Dr Tregullow doesn't either.'

'So what can I do to help you?'

Lottie managed a smile, which quickly faded. 'You're really kind, Daddy. It would help if . . .'

'If what?'

Lottie hesitated. They'd been looking forward to their last evening in New York. A jazz band was coming to the hotel and John had tried to explain his love of jazz to Lottie who had only heard Cornish sea shanties and male-voice choirs. She'd responded to his enthusiasm and his description of the way jazz players could make a saxophone and a trumpet talk to each other. 'I did want to hear the jazz band,' Lottie said, 'but . . . sorry, I really need to sleep.'

'That's okay.' John reached across the table and took her hand. It was icy cold. 'I'm so sorry about your mother's behaviour.'

Lottie held on to him, offering him the other hand as well. 'I don't care,' she declared. It was a lie, of course. How much she cared had wound itself into a tight knot of a headache.

John placed his gentle artistic hand on her brow and found her skin burning hot and clammy. 'My goodness, you've got a fever,' he said, alarmed. 'Better get you to bed right now, Lottie. Come on, I'll take you up to your room.'

'You don't need to, Daddy, I can manage,' Lottie protested, but she let him take her up in the lift and escort her to her bedroom, which was next door to his.

'Would you like me to sit with you?'

'No, Daddy – thanks, I'll be fine. You go and enjoy the jazz.'

John shook his head. 'No, Lottie, you're more important. I shall sit in my room and read, so you know I'm there. Does that help? If you get any worse, you call me straight away. Promise?'

'Promise.'

John hovered in the doorway.

'Leave me alone, Daddy. I'll just go to sleep.'

'Goodnight, Lottie.' He continued to hover, then added, 'You're very precious to me.'

She heard him unlocking his bedroom next door and the pad of his footsteps going to the window. He would be staring out, bitterly, at the New York skyline. She imagined him opening his brown leather wallet and finding the ticket he'd bought for her mother to come home with them on the ship. Her mother. What kind of a person was she? A person who could ruthlessly break the heart of a kind man, abandon a child, then write a letter begging forgiveness and pleading poverty. Manipulative.

Why do I love her? Lottie thought, sinking into the stiff, white linen sheets.

New York looked ghostly in the dim morning light, its angular skyscape half hidden in pearly grey mist. The hum of the city was something Lottie would remember. The eternal hum and the way thousands of windows winked and glimmered like the scales of a fish.

When she saw the red funnels of the ship and felt the throb of the engines, her spirits had lifted. She was going home. The Atlantic Ocean waited out there, breathing its salty breath, lifting her limp hair, cooling the lingering ache of the headache.

Going home.

Seeing Nan's dear, dependable bulk planted firmly on the quay. Climbing into the back of her battered Austin Seven, its interior covered in sand and chicken feathers. The fragrance of gorse flowers, early primroses and bracken wafting through the open windows. The light in the harbour. The softness of Mufty's fur.

Home.

But first, two weeks on the ship. Lottie marched up the gangway ahead of John, carrying her small brown suitcase with its hard corners and rusting catches. Inside were tiny presents for the family: American chocolate, pencils and rubbers with the Statue of Liberty on them. The best gift was a tiny ship in a bottle for Matt. Lottie had stood in front of it for ages, trying to decide whether she could afford it. Matt would love it and it was a gift from the heart for her secret love, a proud Cornish man with his own boat, free and alive. She hoped he would be there in the harbour when she got home.

'Shall we stand at the back and watch New York disappearing?' John said, once they had found their cabins.

'Okay.' Lottie knew he was upset about her mother. She sensed he didn't know what to say to comfort her. 'I want New York to disappear,' she added. 'It was a dream-come-true gone wrong for me.'

'It was unforgivable,' John said grimly. 'I'm furious with Olivia for not turning up. Absolutely furious. For you. How could she hurt you like that?'

'We don't know why, do we?' Lottie said as they leaned on the rails, the ship throbbing gently under their feet. People were still streaming up the gangway with suitcases. She found herself watching them, a shadow of hope hovering at the back of her mind. Would her elusive mother turn up at the last minute?

'I've still got her ticket,' John said, patting the pocket where he kept his wallet. 'What a waste of money.'

Lottie watched the anger settling in his eyes. Her father was normally calm and unruffled, and in the three years she had known him she'd never seen him angry. *What would he do if Olivia did turn up now?*

The stream of passengers boarding the ship was dwindling, the last few hurrying up the gangway, the steward checking their tickets and looking at his watch. The quayside was busy with sailors untying the fat ropes. The hope in Lottie's heart vanished with a final sting of pain. It was over. She would never see her mother again. She'd been looking forward to it so intensely.

'My mother didn't want me, did she?'

'I can't answer that question,' John said firmly. 'Nobody knows what feelings lurk in another person's heart.'

'Well, that's what is in my heart.' Lottie wanted answers. The question burned inside her, like a bonfire between her and her normal life. A fire she must walk through to get to

Nan and Mufty and beautiful St Ives. 'Did she ever want me? When I was born . . . did she love me then?'

John hesitated. 'I'm sorry to say I wasn't there, Lottie, and I regret that very much. I was working in Canada, building bridges on the railway, and she sent me a telegram. It said: BABY GIRL BORN EARLY THIS MORNING. NAMED HER CHARLOTTE. COME HOME AND SEE HER.'

Lottie's eyes widened. 'And did you?'

'I did my best – but I was the engineer, the *only* engineer, and without me work would have stopped. I was responsible for hundreds of men who were working hard to feed their families. Olivia never understood my commitment. I wrote home and sent her some money, of course, but it was weeks before I could go, and then it took another three weeks to get there. You were born on the eighth of May and I first saw you in late August.'

'Was she holding me when you first saw me?'

'No – you were in a cradle with a lace canopy, and you were truly the most beautiful thing I had ever seen in my life.' John's eyes went misty. He patted his heart. 'I loved you immediately – in here – in my beating heart. You were the most precious gift.'

Lottie soaked up this impassioned account from her father. Even though she'd heard it before, she wanted it again and again like a favourite fairy tale. Each time a new question floated to the top. 'Did you pick me up?' she asked, imagining John's powerful hands reaching into the cradle.

'I asked if I could hold you and Olivia said ... she said, "Certainly not."' His voice broke with the memory. 'She ... she said my hands were ingrained with dirt, which they were, of course – I'm an engineer, not a butler. So I gave you a finger to hold, and your tiny, magical fist curled around it and held on so tightly. You gazed up at me with dark blue, knowing eyes. I couldn't help it – I reached into the cradle and picked you up, and you were like an enchanted bundle of softness and joy. I held you to my chest and felt your strong little heart beating so fast against mine. Awesome love. Love like I'd never experienced.'

Entranced by such a comforting affirmation of love, Lottie listened, her soul in her eyes, the bustle of the ship distant like a world veiled by soft net curtains. Usually a story ended there. A happy ending, sealing it forever. But today, in the shadow of her mother's betrayal, a new question flickered its encroaching fire. 'What did my mother do then? Was she angry?'

John's smile vanished. 'I looked up at her, wanting to share my joy – and the look in her eyes was something I'll never forget, never understand, and never, ever forgive.'

'What kind of a look? Tell me, Daddy. I need to know.'

He nodded. The memory crouched in his fingers clamped together, the knuckles pearly white. 'Your mother looked at me with silent, burning rage. Unquenchable. Irreversible. It was a key moment in my life, and yours. I felt trapped between beauty and the beast.'

Shocked, Lottie was compelled to ask another question. 'What did she do next?'

'I put you down, reluctantly, in your cradle, and Olivia ripped off the little white matinée coat you were wearing and threw it at me. I'd made it dirty, she'd said. I stuffed it in my pocket and left the house with tears in my eyes. I still have it, that tiny white coat. Many times, when the loneliness of being far from home got to me, I took it out and held it close to my heart, and prayed I would find you again.'

'Oh, Daddy.' Lottie gazed at him in a wave of compassion. As she tried to find words to comfort him, she saw him stiffen and look sharply towards the quayside where a lot of shouting was going on, preparing the ship to leave. Men's voices. And another voice, oddly familiar, crying out, 'Wait, wait, I've got to get on that ship.'

A woman was running up the quay, her blonde curls bobbing.

'That's her!' John's voice turned to a business-like bark. He took out his wallet and neatly extracted Olivia's boarding pass. 'There you are, Lottie. You're going to meet your mother after all.'

Something snapped in Lottie's mind. Faced with her mother's arrival after hearing that story from John, she was plunging into a whirlpool of hostility and confusion.

Olivia was wearing a red coat, and even from a distance Lottie could see the glint of her tormented eyes sweeping the ship, and already the effect she was having on John was disturbing. He was breathing too fast. His eyes had changed from soulful honesty to an iron-cold hardness. 'I'll go down with her ticket,' he said in clipped syllables. 'You stay here.'

Lottie straightened her back and lifted her chin in defence. 'I shall go to my cabin,' she announced, 'and don't disturb me. I don't want to see her. Not now. Not *ever*! I wish I didn't have a mother.'

'Lottie! You don't mean that.'

'I do.'

Devastated, John met his daughter's determined eyes. 'I've got to go down and meet her quickly,' he said. 'Please – don't be difficult.'

'*Difficult?*' Lottie tasted the bitterness of his inappropriate word. 'I'm not being difficult, I'm being honest. *She* is the one who's being difficult. *She* ruined my life and I'm not going to let her ruin any more of it. Keep her away from me.'

John's eyes were judging Lottie, then darting back to the frantic figure of Olivia still arguing with stewards on the gangway.

She's bewitching him already, Lottie thought, furious as she got up and headed down to her cabin.

John hurried towards the gangway, Olivia's ticket in his hand. *Why, why, why did she manage to look so alluring?* Such wide eyes and a scarlet coat casting a glow on her cheeks. And why did he have a terrible feeling that he was about to fall into her trap all over again?

'*What* are you doing in there?'

Jenny froze and dropped five stitches in the jumper she was knitting for Lottie. Nan's voice blasted the sparrows out of the yard and resounded over the cliffs and into the huddled streets of St Ives.

In the split-second of silence that followed, Jenny disentangled herself from the knitting and limped to the open window. She wondered what Tom had done now to incur Nan's wrath. But it wasn't Tom. Nan loomed in the middle of the yard, a bowl of corn in one hand, her neck and shoulders rigid with rage as she stared towards Mufty's stable.

Climbing out over the door was a child. A muddle of thin legs and bony elbows, his slate-coloured clothes tattered, his small bare feet dirty and a bright trickle of blood running down one shin. Glancing at Nan with huge eyes, he scrambled over the door and fled across the yard. Despite another bellow from Nan, he didn't stop, but flung himself over the Cornish hedge, dislodging a stone and catching his jacket on a bramble.

'Don't you *ever* come here again.' Nan banged her tall walking stick on the ground. 'Insolent little guttersnipe.'

Tom came charging out of the barn door, his pounding feet scuffing up clouds of dust from the cobbled yard. 'I'll get him, Nan. He were pinching eggs.'

Nan opened her mouth to roar at Tom, and shut it again as Tom's sturdy figure sprinted across the yard, vaulted expertly over the hedge, and set off in pursuit of the fleeing boy.

'Thieving, disreputable brat,' Nan muttered and flung an arc of corn across the yard for the flock of speckled and honey-brown chickens, who began pecking it like clockwork hens.

Jenny called out from the window. 'Where did he come from, Nan?'

'No idea,' Nan said. 'He was in the hayloft door when I saw him, and his only way out was through Mufty's stable. I assume it was a boy, though his hair was long enough for a girl – and his clothes were in shreds.'

'Poor lad,' Jenny said compassionately. 'So thin. Such bony little ankles.'

Nan tutted. 'I'll give him "poor lad" if he comes here again.' She picked up a turnip that the fleeing boy had dropped in his mad dash to escape. Further along was a carrot. Obviously, whoever he was had been pinching turnips and carrots from the corner of the barn where they were stored in boxes of sand to last through the winter into spring.

Jenny pursed her lips and kept quiet. She was learning to let Nan vent her anger at the human race and its imperfections. It wasn't the only enforced lesson Jenny had battled with in the years since Arnie's death. A year in hospital with polio. A year without her three precious children, Matt and Tom, and Lottie. It was Nan who had opened her heart and her home to the troubled family, and now keeping the peace was something they worked on daily.

In her old life, Jenny would have sprinted after the poor, thin boy and probably caught him, given him a good-natured scolding followed by a hot pasty and a decent set of clothes. She hoped Tom would be kind if he managed to catch up with the mysterious boy.

They had run towards the sea, into the wild, rocky cliffs of Clodgy. Jenny started to worry. Would Tom remember the one rule she'd always drummed into them? Never chase someone towards the edge of the cliffs. At the moment the sea was wild with spring tides and a heavy swell rolling in from a trough of low pressure out in the Atlantic.

From the window, Jenny could see majestic waves, a long way apart, roaring on to Porthmeor Beach and pounding the Clodgy rocks in bursting white blossoms of spray. She could smell the salt and the sweet coconut fragrance of the gorse flowers out on the cliffs. She ached to be out there, swinging through the cobbled streets of St Ives, a shopping basket over her arm, pausing to chat with friends.

How she missed her old life.

Jenny looked down at her leg. The calliper kept her mobile, but slow and sore, and frustrated when the rest of her body wanted to dance. She missed her friends; few of them ventured up to Hendravean. They found Nan too intimidating.

An hour passed and Tom still hadn't returned. Jenny distracted herself by making a batch of Cornish heavy cake in the kitchen. Once it was in the oven, she lifted the steaming kettle from the range and made cocoa the way Nan liked it, with a dash of cream and brandy. She put the two earthenware mugs on a brass tray and hobbled out into the yard with it, putting it down on the bench against the south-facing wall where Nan liked to sit.

'Come and sit down, Nan. Cup of cocoa,' Jenny said, sitting down herself as Nan led Mufty across the yard, the donkey walking eagerly towards Jenny, his eyes shining dark out of his furry face.

'Hello, darling.' Jenny loved Mufty, and she always put a piece of carrot on the tray for him. 'Yes – this is for you.' Mufty took the carrot graciously, crunching it and nodding his head approvingly. He pressed his cheek against Jenny's shoulder and let her fondle him, running her fingers along the fluffy crest of his neck.

'He's missing Lottie,' Nan said as she sat down on the solid old bench and picked up her cocoa mug.

'We all are,' Jenny said. 'I expect they'll be on their way back by now. What an adventure for little Lottie. I hope it went well for her.'

'So do I,' Nan said, with passion. 'I hope that mother of hers turns up. She doesn't deserve Lottie.'

'I know what you mean,' Jenny said. 'Lottie is a ray of sunshine in all our lives. She was only ten when Arnie died, and she helped me so much. She did everything: the washing, the baking . . . she even mothered the boys. She's a real gem, isn't she?'

Nan nodded thoughtfully. 'Well, thank God we agree on something, Jenny.'

Jenny smiled into Nan's storm-coloured eyes, unafraid of their power. She'd learned to look beyond the glare and find the astonishing wisdom and the love that was hidden behind. 'I worry about Lottie being so far away in America,' she confided, 'meeting her real mother, after so long. I hope that woman doesn't break her heart.'

'I think she already did break her heart, from what Lottie's told me,' Nan said. 'But she's got us to come home to. We're her family now.'

'And we always will be,' Jenny said, with passion. 'I'm more of a mother to her than that selfish cow.'

Nan looked towards the house, wrinkling her nose. 'Have you got something in the oven?'

'The heavy cake!' Jenny got up and headed for the house. 'Just in time!'

Tom had been gone for over an hour, she thought in alarm as she slid the tray of sweetly scented, steaming cake out of the oven. Where was he? If only Matt was with him.

'Stop that, Jennifer!' she said aloud to herself, feeling her mind perilously near to the edge of a crumbling cliff of grief and worry. She always called herself Jennifer when she was cross with herself. 'Stop moaning and be glad for what you've got.' She took a knife and sliced the heavy cake into tempting, sugar-dusted squares.

'Who are you talking to, Mum?' Tom came into the kitchen, red-faced and endearingly solid.

'Meself,' Jenny confessed, grinning. 'Look at the state of you – you look as if you've been through a hedge backwards.'

Tom looked down at the scratches on his legs, and shrugged. 'It doesn't matter,' he said. 'I didn't catch the boy, Mum. I couldn't find him. He's got a den somewhere down under that shelf of rock.'

'Do you know him?'

'No, Mum. I never seen him before – he don't go to our school.'

'He might be a gypsy.'

Tom shook his head. 'No. They couldn't get a horse and caravan out there.'

'Well, surely he isn't living wild, is he?' Jenny asked in concern.

'I dunno. Can I have some heavy cake, Mum?'

'Don't drop crumbs everywhere.' Jenny handed him a generous slice. 'If I could walk, I'd go out there with you and look for the boy. Did you get close to him?'

'Only when he was in the hayloft. The chickens go up there and lay eggs in the hay. He'd got an egg in his hand.'

'Did he speak to you?'

'No.'

'Did you speak to him?'

'No.'

Jenny rolled her eyes. 'Well, what did he look like?'

'Like he hasn't got a mum to take care of him.' Tom bit into his slice of heavy cake. 'Can I have another slice in a paper bag, Mum? I'll take it out there for him.'

'Course you can.' Jenny quickly found a brown paper bag and popped a slice inside. 'You're good-hearted, Tom, and I'm proud of you for that.' She put a finger to her lips and whispered, 'But don't tell Nan. And don't go fighting with him.'

'I won't,' Tom promised. 'I wouldn't like to fight him, Mum. You should see his nails – like bird's claws, they are, and his toenails.'

'Really?' Jenny's eyes widened. 'Then he's on his own, poor lad. He's a wild boy.'

'Like Mowgli?'

'Like Mowgli – without the tigers.'

Chapter 4

Going Home

Lottie pressed her face against the porthole of her cabin, feeling the great ship vibrating with quiet power as it pulled away from the quay. She wanted to be up on deck with her father, watching the glimmering vista of Manhattan sliding past across the grey satin water. The sound of the ship's horn buzzed through her and vanished into the mist.

Take me home, she prayed. *Home to Nan and Jenny and Mufty and St Ives. I don't need my real mother. She breaks hearts, and I won't let her break mine.*

She decided not to look back at New York. Pressing the other cheek against the glass, she gazed forward into the glow of dawn as the ship emerged from the bank of fog. It hurt too much to imagine her mother up there on deck, flashing those manipulative eyes at John, flaunting her scarlet coat.

The last patches of sea fog drifted past the porthole and spray began to hit the glass. The golden sea turned slowly to silver, then to sage green and charcoal, a storm-flecked swell far out on the horizon.

Lottie remembered something Arnie had taught her: *When the sea is two colours, a storm is brewing.* In St Ives, the two colours were an ashen turquoise and a dark plum-purple. Here on the shores of America, the Atlantic looked stormy in a different way, heavy and metallic, as it sucked the ship out of the mist.

Lottie slumped on her narrow cabin bed and picked up the knitted toy donkey – a model of Mufty that Jenny had made for her. He felt warm and friendly, the smooth stitches and tassels kind against her fingers. She looked at the black beads of his eyes and tried to find a sentence to describe the way she was feeling, but it was too overwhelming. She retreated into a safe haven, a dreamlike memory of her last evening in St Ives with Matt.

Nobody had seen Matt all winter, and Jenny had spent hours at the window of Hendravean, breaking her heart not knowing the whereabouts of her eldest son. Their relationship had always been difficult, but Jenny loved him and wanted him back. They all wanted him back except Nan, who would only purse her lips and hold silence on the subject of Matt.

Lottie could picture him now, lean and confident in his blue-as-the-sky fisherman's smock, a sparkle in his eyes as he looked at her. 'You've grown up, Lottie,' he'd said shyly.

'You look ... lovely – really lovely.' He'd taken her hand and pressed it pensively between his rough palms, giving her that first, unexpected flare of excitement, a mysterious ache inside, an undeniable answer to the feelings of longing that she'd been trying to ignore.

She'd listened, spellbound, to Matt's story. How he'd built himself a life from nothing. From stealing his first sketchbook and pilfering food, Matt had lived rough and worked hard, developing his talent as an artist, selling his drawings to tourists. Then he'd discovered *The Jenny Wren* moored in Hayle: unwanted, derelict and sad. Seeing her as a home, Matt had set about earning enough money to buy her, restore her paintwork, make her seaworthy and learn how the engine worked.

Remembering the present she had bought Matt, Lottie opened her suitcase and pulled out the tiny ship-in-a-bottle and gazed at it in wonder, imagining Matt's face when he saw it. She sat holding it, indulging in reliving some special moments shared with Matt. After escaping from the orphanage, they had sat under the stars on the massive granite rocks of the Carn Brea. Together they had gazed at the lights of St Ives twinkling far away, sharing an unspoken sadness of seeing the lights of home so far away.

Another moment hung bright in her memory. That last evening, on *The Jenny Wren*, when Matt had looked down at her with serious eyes and touched her hair. 'I'll miss you, Lottie,' he'd said, his voice husky and intense. 'You will come back, won't you – from America?' He'd given her a hug, and Lottie found herself with her hair nestled against his chest, listening to the steady beat of his heart. In that moment, something shifted in their relationship, like the gleam on the unburnt wick of a brand-new candle, waiting for a flame.

Matt was seventeen, almost a man, startling in his resemblance to his father, and Lottie sixteen, a child-woman, woman-child, not yet understanding, but wanting, feeling that secret, unexplored fire in the pit of her belly. *Forbidden fire*, she thought.

Deep into the birth of a new daydream, Lottie jumped when someone tapped at her cabin door. She was glad she'd locked it.

'Lottie? Are you in there? I'd like to speak to you.' It was her father's calm voice, just a semitone higher than usual.

She went to the door and stood behind it.

'Is *she* with you?'

'No.'

'Promise?'

'Promise. I'm on my own, Lottie. Let me in, please.'

Sighing, Lottie opened the door, her eyes searching up and down the corridor for her mother. 'Where is she?'

'Settling into her cabin,' John said. 'We're sailing into a storm. She'll be seasick – she always is.'

Lottie glanced at the porthole and saw the crest of a wave sweeping past, trailing a plume of windblown foam.

'Can I come in?' John asked, always courteous, but with a note of resignation Lottie hadn't heard in his voice before.

'*You* can.'

There was nowhere to sit in the tiny cabin, except on Lottie's bed. Side by side they sat staring at the floor instead of looking into each other's eyes as they usually did.

'Your mother does want to see you,' John said in a dispirited tone. 'She's disappointed.'

Lottie looked at him in mutinous silence.

John straightened his back, shocked at her expression. 'This isn't like you, Lottie. I'm surprised. You're usually so sensible.'

Lottie shrugged. Only a jagged-edged silence seemed to express the antagonism she now felt towards the mother she'd longed to see.

'Talk to me. I'm trying to understand,' John said.

She clung to a stubborn silence.

'We've never had an argument, have we?' John's voice was eager and persuasive. 'It's one of the things I admire about you, Lottie.'

She raised an eyebrow.

'It's best if you meet your mother now – before the seasickness takes hold,' he said. 'In my experience, Olivia will be lying in bed for at least three days, until we reach calmer waters. She's waiting for you in her cabin.'

Lottie dug herself in, pushing her heels against the floor. Words nudged at the silence. A question. 'Why – why didn't she come?'

'To the gallery?'

'Yes.'

John didn't answer, but stroked his beard, his eyes anxious. He clasped his hands together. 'Your mother is a very complex person. It would be wrong of me to even try to explain her reasons. You must ask her yourself, Lottie.'

Lottie set her face to a hard, porcelain stare. 'I'm not going to move from this cabin.'

'You'll have to,' John pointed out, perplexed by this new stubborn version of his beautiful daughter. 'What about your meals?'

'I shall eat them at a table on my own.' A tide of sadness flowed into Lottie's life as she visualised two miserable weeks of eating alone in a crowded dining room. On the voyage to New York she'd enjoyed her meals with her father, just the two of them. The way he was so attentive, listening to her chatter, sharing fascinating bits of his life with her. John was a model parent, always courteous and encouraging. Calm. Never tetchy or critical.

'I shall miss you,' he said wisely.

Lottie bit back the words she wanted to say. Bitter words. Her father would be with her mother. Gazing into *her* eyes, patiently listening to *her* chatter. Jealousy magnified the sadness in Lottie's heart.

John stood up. 'Hating your mother is going to be complicated and painful. Loving her would be so much easier for you. I'll leave you to sort yourself out, sweetheart.' And he walked out, shutting the door quietly.

The impact of his well-chosen words burst over Lottie in a thousand pieces. John was right. She had chosen hate – and it wasn't in her nature. But having declared it, she felt as if she'd fallen into a bramble bush, and the only way out was going to be prickly.

Overwhelmed, she lay staring at the sea outside the porthole, the knitted donkey warm against her cheek. Jenny had put her love into every stitch, and Lottie could feel it there. It was something to hold onto. Jenny was far away, but close in Lottie's heart because she'd performed a simple act of love – sitting in hospital with polio, pouring her love into knitting a donkey.

For me, Lottie thought. *Jenny is my mother, my best mother. Not her. Not Olivia. Never Olivia. I'd wanted my real mother so much, and now I just want her to go away. But I haven't even spoken to her. I haven't given her a chance.*

The thought came hot with tears and she let them flow silently into the crisp linen pillow. She lay still and allowed the gift of sleep to wrap her in its embrace.

The ship steamed on, rolling a little on the swell, ever closer to the impending storm.

Lottie slept deeply, blissfully unaware that her door was not locked. She didn't hear it open and quietly close. She didn't hear the light footsteps creeping to her bed. But in her dreams she felt a presence, a mysterious butterfly warmth, a breath and a perfume.

Someone sitting beside her as she slept.

Someone who could only love when words were stripped away and, on the barest of branches, silence became a blossom.

*

From the deck of *The Jenny Wren*, Matt glanced up at Hendravean, nestled into the hill in splendid isolation. Its dormer windows had a glint of intelligence, as if the house itself was alive and on guard. He thought he might catch a glimpse of Nan or even his mum. It would be good to know they were up there and he could go into St Ives without encountering either of them. Tom would be in school, and Lottie thousands of miles away, but on her way home, he hoped. Lottie was the one person he wanted to see. Matt allowed himself a few minutes to dream about the last time he'd seen her – dressed in blue, with her golden-blonde hair rippling in the breeze. No longer a child, but a young woman with tantalising breasts and a firm, slim waist. Beautiful, but still Lottie, with her honest dark blue eyes.

He'd brought the boat down the coast from Portreath on a tranquil morning sea. *The Jenny Wren* was more than a boat. She was Matt's home, and he didn't want her stuck on the sand at low tide, tipped sideways. He wanted her afloat, so he waited for the high tide to lift her gently towards the slipway.

Coming back to St Ives was an emotional rollercoaster and Matt wasn't sure he could handle it. Even now, out on the water, the memories of his father were surfacing in his mind, shining memories dusted with the animosity he felt towards his mother, Jenny. There were happy memories, too, and Matt wanted to revisit some of those places where they had played and made dens and learned to swim.

The winter sea and sky were hazy and still, like smoked glass, the water dappled with light and reflections of boats, cottages and clouds. Matt looked at the rooftops and chimneys of St Ives, reassured to see the nests of seagulls, each with the mother bird firmly sitting on her precious eggs. Subconsciously, Matt was looking for his own two seagulls, which had nested on the roof of the cottage in Downlong where he had grown up. The pair of gulls had been like family, returning every year to the same nest, always rebuilding it with new treasures of seaweed and straw, and even strips of aubrietia plucked from cottage gardens.

Matt looked at the rings in the harbour wall, hoping it would be all right to moor the boat there. The harbour master, Ken, was standing at the top of the slipway, tapping his pipe on a stone. Matt knew him as one of his dad's many friends in St Ives; men who had proudly carried Arnie's coffin into the church on their burly shoulders. Matt called out to him and Ken turned, then froze, his eyes wide with shock.

He thinks I'm Dad, Matt thought, flattered.

The same thing had happened when he'd been to see Jenny in hospital. She'd woken up with a gasp. She'd called him 'darling', but then quickly realised and said, 'You've grown so 'andsome – so like your dad'. He'd treasured those words, but then she'd spoilt it by snapping, 'Don't you make trouble.' It had touched a raw nerve. After all he'd been through, losing his dad, surviving a time of extreme poverty, then the orphanage, Matt couldn't take any more. He'd flung some bitter words back.

'I won't make trouble. I'm leaving. And I'm not coming back.' He'd marched out of the hospital, his attitude hardening by the minute. It was the day he'd begun his life as a homeless artist.

'It's Matt,' he called to the harbour master.

'Matt?' Ken came striding down the slipway in his navy-blue overalls, his pipe in his hand. He peered at Matt suspiciously, his eyes taking in the freshly painted boat.

'Well – that's *The Jenny Wren*!' he exclaimed, and his eyes twinkled. 'That were Arnie's boat – I knew her well.' He looked again at Matt and a smile of recognition creased his weathered face. 'Aw!' he growled softly. 'If it isn't Arnie's boy. Good to see ya, Matt.'

Matt glowed. It felt so good to be welcomed, to be acknowledged, to be someone who actually belonged.

'Course you can moor *The Jenny Wren*. Anytime,' Ken said, his voice warm now, a smile creasing his old face. 'That's a spare ring there – you have that one. I'll put yer name on it, lad.'

'Thanks.'

Ken waited, lighting his pipe, while Matt secured the boat and climbed onto the slipway. ''Tis good to have you back in S'nives.' Ken looked him up and down and shook his hand with a warm dependable grasp. 'You hungry?' He didn't wait for Matt to answer, but sat down on the wooden bench against the wall and unscrewed the top of a Thermos flask. 'Hot, sweet tea,' he said, pouring the steaming liquid into two tin mugs. Next, he took an enormous flat brown bun from a paper bag. 'You have this. 'Tis a tea treat bun – my missus makes 'em for Sunday School.'

'Don't you want it?' Matt asked, gratefully sipping the syrupy tea.

'Nah – she feeds me too well already.' Ken patted his substantial paunch with a grin. 'You'll be going up Hendravean to see your mum, will you?'

Matt shrugged. Between bites of the tea treat bun, he told Ken about the orphanage and how they'd escaped. He didn't mention his devastating visit to his mum in hospital. But Ken already knew. Matt sensed it, and sensed him deliberately keeping quiet to keep the peace – something Cornishmen were good at. Exactly what his dad had been good at. Tolerance. The shrug had said it all. Ken didn't ask any more questions, but sat beside Matt in a contemplative friendliness.

When Matt had finished the huge bun and the flock of turnstones were scurrying around after the crumbs, Ken said, 'We miss your dad, Matt. Any time you want to think about training with the lifeboat crew, you're welcome – always welcome here, lad. I don't know where you're living and I won't ask – but S'nives is your home. Don't you forget that – you're one of us.'

Matt nodded gratefully. He met Ken's eyes for a brief moment of empathy before saying goodbye and walking away into St Ives, his haversack over one shoulder, packed with his sketch pads, pencils and the small black tin of Reeves watercolours. Turning his back on Hendravean, he headed for Downlong, curious to see what had happened to the terraced cottage where he, Tom and Lottie had once lived.

Lottie had told him about the artist, John De Lumen, who'd turned out to be her father, and how he had bought the cottage to use as a studio. Even so, Matt was unprepared for what he saw. Expecting a wave of nostalgia, he stood in between the lines of washing strung across the narrow street. He was stunned to see the cottage painted white, the granite walls completely covered. A beautifully painted sign was nailed over the front door.

THE DE LUMEN GALLERY.

Smart, Matt thought. He longed to go inside and see what had been done with the cramped interior where he had grown up, but a smaller notice said, GALLERY CLOSED. Of course – John De Lumen was on the ship with Lottie.

Matt peered through one of the windows, fascinated to see everything inside painted white, with lots of pictures hanging on the walls. *Boring*, he thought, compared to the ones in his sketch book.

'The gallery is closed, young man.'

The sharp voice was one Matt knew well – Maudie. She'd hounded him through his childhood, telling him off, shaming him at every opportunity, so he continued looking through the window, just to annoy her.

Maudie was not someone to be ignored. She ruled the street, and several streets beyond, and thrived on ferreting out people's darkest secrets. Matt could smell her coming close, a fusty, damp-dog sort of smell, and the particular way her shoes creaked and her maroon trench coat rustled.

Go away, he thought, but Maudie stood there, and when he didn't turn round, she started tapping the sleeve of his fisherman's smock.

'Can't you read? The gallery's closed. He's gone to New York. And I'm keeping an eye on the place.'

Ignoring her, Matt looked up at the roof. He knew how to climb in: up the drainpipe and over the roof to drop down into the backyard. He'd done it umpteen times. He braced his foot against the wall and tested the drainpipe to see if it would still take his weight.

'Oy!' Maudie poked him with her umbrella. 'Don't you try anything.'

Matt swung round and looked her in the eye. Maudie bristled. Colour spread up her frog-like neck. 'I know you!' she scolded. 'Matt Lanroska. What are you doing snooping round here? That's not your place now, is it? Is it?'

'You can't tell me what to do.'

'Oh, yes I can.' Maudie flew at him like an enraged bantam, words bursting out from ruffled feathers. 'Just 'cause you've grown into such a big fellow doesn't mean I can't tell you – someone's got to. You're a bad 'un, Matt Lanroska. Always were, always will be. And don't think you're so clever, grinning at me like that. You should be ashamed – running off and living on some grubby old boat, causing your mother so much worry. As if she hasn't got enough to think about.'

Matt wasn't good at arguments. Nothing he could say would silence Maudie anyway. He walked away with his dad's wisdom ringing in his heart.

Walk away, lad. Just let her get on with it.

But it was disappointing. He'd wanted to linger close to his old home and think. Instead, he'd collected yet another set of salt-in-the-wound rejections and unfair accusations from Maudie. Matt couldn't help it. He took everything to heart, despite his cultivated bravado. *The Jenny Wren* wasn't 'some grubby old boat'. He wanted to drag Maudie down to the harbour and make her look at the gleaming new paintwork and the homely little cabin with its well-polished windows. He wanted to tell her how he loved his solitary life out on the water under the sky. He had peace – which was more than she had. Maudie was like a storm in a barrel; she didn't know peace.

What gave her the right to attack him like that? Next she'd go boasting to her friends – 'I said to him, I said . . .'. Maudie lived in a never-ending stream of malicious gossip.

One day I'll tell her, Matt vowed.

Pulling his hat down over his eyes, he walked on, dodging and ducking under the washing, following a familiar route through Downlong to Porthmeor Beach and along the cliff path to Clodgy, his spirits lifting as he drew near to the rock stack. He planned to spend the day sketching the great weathered rocks with the startling glimpses of the deep turquoise glittering ocean and the domes of sea pinks against the light. His pictures of the place he loved would be vivid and strong.

It had been Matt's intention to stroll up The Stennack in the afternoon and meet Tom on his way home from school. But time slipped away as he became engrossed in his artwork. He sold one of the sea pink pictures to an elderly couple who were out walking. The five crisp pound notes would buy him fuel for *The Jenny Wren* and a week's meals, a bottle of cider and a thin sable-hair paintbrush for painting the curved whiskers of seals and the wiry stems of sea pink. Perfect.

Back on the deck of *The Jenny Wren*, Matt ate his supper watching an electrical storm out at sea. Lightning crackled, blindingly bright in a sky so lustrously dark that the distant seagulls twinkled like white stars against the cloud. Big peardrops of rain peppered the harbour water and pinged on the roof of the cabin. Matt moved inside and sat on his makeshift bed, enjoying the sound of rain on the roof. He found himself looking again at Hendravean and thinking about his stuff that would be stored there. Most of it was useless to him now, but there was something he passionately wanted: his dad's old cork lifejacket. Matt didn't have one, which meant he was in constant danger out at sea on the boat.

Would he dare to turn up at Nan's place and ask for it? Definitely not. He didn't need yet another storm of recriminations. No. The only way to get the lifejacket would be to act like a burglar, watch for his chance, and break in. Nan's door was never locked and rarely shut. In summer, she left it open for the swallows who nested in the rafters over the porch, and a pair of robins who had built a home in the bookshelves.

Where would the lifejacket be? In their old home, it had hung on a hook behind the scullery door, kept there so that Arnie could grab it on his way out. After he'd died, Jenny had left it there, and Matt had seen her touching it, resting her cheek against it and quietly crying. The memory sent emotions tumbling through him. Surely he had a right to claim his dad's lifejacket? He couldn't leave St Ives until he had it.

Tomorrow. He'd do it tomorrow.

The decision gathered his thoughts together under an umbrella of peace. In the thundery twilight, it felt good to fall asleep on his own bed, safe on *The Jenny Wren*, and to dream of Lottie far away on the same bright ocean, the great ship steaming on, bringing her closer – blessedly closer – to home.

Chapter 5

Intruders

Lottie's dreams of finding her birth mother had been with her constantly. She had wanted the reunion to be special and meaningful. She wanted her mother to see her as a sophisticated young woman, not the wilful child she had been. She imagined them being in perfect harmony, talking and laughing together, sharing secrets, more like sisters than mother and child.

First impressions mattered. Their first meeting should be filled with mutual respect. Lottie considered herself grown up now, in charge of her life, not to be pushed around. There would be some honest talking between them. She wanted her mother to understand the far-reaching effect her act of abandonment had caused. Olivia must be made to listen – to everything. And in return, Lottie planned to do her share of listening, if only her mother would talk candidly about her life.

In the moment of reunion, something magical would happen, like a severed nerve being reconnected. The bonding would be instant, wordless and strong. When Olivia hadn't turned up, the dream drifted away as if it were abandoning her.

She'd seen it. She'd wanted it. And it had gone.

So when Lottie awoke, her face hot and tear-stained, her hair messy, her heart full of sadness, it was a shock to realise that Olivia had crept into her cabin and was sitting on the bed. One glimpse was enough. Sensing the presence and smelling perfume, Lottie opened her eyes wide. She stared at her mother as her dreams of the perfect reunion vanished over the horizon.

The red coat was gone and Olivia wore a silver-grey cashmere dress with a low-cut neckline and a triple set of pearls against her throat. Her mother looked small and delicate with bony-white wrists, hollow cheeks and devious eyes. She smiled and reached for Lottie's hand. 'Hello, Charlotte.'

Lottie snatched it away. 'Don't touch me,' she hissed, 'and don't call me Charlotte.' She shut her eyes again.

'Aw, honey-child,' crooned Olivia. 'C'mon – don't be angry. John's been telling me how good you are.'

'Not anymore.' Lottie held her head with both hands, completely overwhelmed and desperate to escape. It was too soon. She needed time to heal and try to restore her sense of reason.

'But, honey-child, I only . . .'

Lottie clamped her hands over her ears, making her eardrums ache. 'I'm not going to listen. Go away and don't come near me.'

'We have to talk, Lottie ...'

The demons seemed to be magnifying every word that came out of her mother's mouth and using them to beat the relationship into a mound of crushed glass with thousands of winking lights, each one mocking her. Lottie felt that trust was destroyed and could never be rebuilt. Not with her mother sitting there so calmly.

Maybe Lottie Lanroska was an illusion, she thought, regressed in an instant to being a four-year-old trusting little girl in a velvet dress. When her mother had abandoned her, the sense of betrayal had fallen into her mind like an unexploded bomb. The explosion had waited all those years, years of nodding and smiling and managing. It had waited for Olivia, and her smooth, detonating words.

Lottie sat up and pushed a hank of tangled blonde hair away from her brow. She faced Olivia with hostility in her eyes. 'Will you *go away*, please – leave me alone. This is *my* cabin.' She moved her face closer and closer to Olivia. 'Will you just *go* – if you don't, I will have to – to ...' She saw herself running wildly along the corridors and staircases of the ship, up and up until she could breathe the briny air of the Atlantic, and hold on tightly to the deck rail. 'If you don't go – I might ... might find a way of disappearing. *Forever.*'

Olivia raised her eyebrows. 'My goodness, Charlotte, you are a drama queen.'

Lottie jumped to her feet, grabbed the knitted donkey from her pillow and fled from the cabin. But when she reached the final staircase leading to the deck, a rope was stretched across it, and a steward stood there guarding it. 'Sorry, madam, you can't go on deck at the moment. We are sailing into a storm.'

That evening, Lottie went to the dining room and spoke to the Italian waiter who, she knew, had a soft spot for her. She smiled up at him, straight-backed and confident, her hair swept back from her face and tied with a cerise satin ribbon.

'Would you please find me a table for one?' she asked. 'I wish to sit on my own for the rest of the journey.'

He gave a little bow. 'Of course, madam.' His inquisitive eyes studied her with interest. He led her to a small table tucked into a corner. 'I bring you cutlery,' he said, and swiftly organised a place setting for her, adding a beautifully folded napkin.

The dining room was nearly empty and people were only just beginning to arrive for dinner. Lottie studied the menu and ordered lemon sole with mashed potato, carrots and peas. She waited tensely for the moment her father would walk in with Olivia.

Alienating herself wasn't making Lottie happy. She felt worse. Self-conscious. Angry. There was a fine line between feeling proud and feeling ridiculous. Trying to prove she was independent and grown up. But actually it was an open act of hate towards her mother. Such a lonely thing to do.

She expected a confrontation, but there wasn't one. As he walked in with Olivia, her father acknowledged Lottie with a courteous nod and padded past without stopping. Out of the corner of her eye, she watched him pull out Olivia's chair for her, and Olivia gave her a tiny, apologetic wave. Like most of the women in the posh dining room, her mother sparkled with jewellery, a silver bangle and earrings that looked like diamonds. She'd added lipstick and rouge. John looked oddly subservient and subdued.

It didn't feel right. Lottie ate her meal without tasting it, trying hard to divert her thoughts to the beautiful time with Matt. Her first time as a woman. Lottie looked down at her young breasts under the crimson dress Jenny had lent her for the trip. It had subtle ruffles of pleated taffeta around the bodice and sleeves and the kind of swirly skirt that Jenny loved. Lottie felt good in it. She tried to imagine Matt sitting opposite her in an evening suit with a collar and tie. It didn't work. She could only visualise Matt in his worn blue clothes, balanced on *The Jenny Wren*, tall and lean against the sea, turning to look at her in that heart-stopping way, Matt leading her into the cabin, gentle, purposeful . . .

Her dream was interrupted by Olivia's ringing laugh. Lottie overheard the conversation she was having with the Italian waiter. 'Do excuse my daughter, Charlotte. She's only sixteen.'

The waiter raised his hands in the air. 'Ah! I too have a daughter who is sixteen – such a difficult age. We in Italy call it the silly age.'

They whispered something, glancing over at Lottie, and Olivia laughed again, her earrings swinging, her red mouth wide open, eyes flashing at John who was watching her attentively. Too attentively.

The laughter was caustic, a strong abrasive chemical burning into Lottie's dreams. She stopped eating, her throat aching with loneliness. Even her father was steadfastly ignoring her, and it hurt. She couldn't swallow another mouthful. Pushing her plate away, she sashayed out of the dining room and downstairs to her cabin where she locked the door.

How could she stand two whole weeks of this? She longed for her father to come to her cabin and talk to her kindly. What if he abandoned her now when she needed him most?

The ship ploughed on into the storm, dipping and rolling. Somewhere in the corridor outside her cabin, an empty bottle was rolling, pausing, then hitting the wall and rolling the other way. A door left open was slamming rhythmically, and all over the ship smaller objects were rattling, clinking or crashing. The hiss of the sea echoed down from the storm-washed deck as if rehearsing how it would rush and surge through the innards of the ship. Underlying the cacophony was a low-pitched, moaning sound, sinister like the buzz of a hornet in a bedroom.

Lottie had been told this ship was very safe. It couldn't sink. It had weathered countless storms. Unsinkable.

Like *Titanic*!

On her own in the cabin, Lottie began to feel scared, especially when she watched the porthole, which was underwater one minute and full of sky the next.

It was an unwelcome dollop of fear to add to her already overloaded mind. She felt far away from everyone she loved, and the person she most wanted was Jenny. Jenny was brave, bright and sensible.

Why did I do this? Lottie thought. *Why put myself through all this torment when the people who really love me are right there in St Ives?*

She was pleased to hear a tap at her door and John's voice, 'Lottie? I'm on my own. I want to reassure you.'

She let him in and once more they sat together on the cabin bed. John took her hand and sandwiched it firmly between his peaceful hands. 'You must be terrified,' he said, 'after being shipwrecked yourself.'

Lottie took some deep breaths. She looked into his steady eyes and began to feel better. John didn't push her to talk, but held on to her firmly. 'It will be all right,' he kept saying. 'The storm will pass. You just hold on to me. I'll be your anchor.'

Back in St. Ives, Nan hauled herself up into the hayloft. She knew she wasn't supposed to go up ladders, but she was determined to catch the wild boy who'd continued to steal eggs, turnips and anything else he could grab.

He'd even been coming in the dark. On the previous night, Bartholomew had sat on the windowsill of Nan's bedroom, like a sentry, the twitch of his whiskers silhouetted against the moonlit sky, his fur bushed out. He was growling like a dog, his neck moving as he watched what was going on in the yard.

Wide awake, Nan had observed him from her bed, and had finally got up. With Bartholomew now purring and growling at the same time, she'd seen the shadow of the boy, and her heart pounded with anger. He'd streaked across the yard and out of the gate, clutching his booty in a bundle of tied rag. Too late to catch him now. Nan made the decision to hide herself in the hay barn and confront the little thief.

Tom was in school and Jenny had gone down into St Ives to buy fish and bread. Knowing Jenny, she was likely to be down there chatting to friends, or in the harbour hopelessly searching for Matt and his boat. Nan didn't mind. It gave her time on her own to do something reckless or ridiculous. She chuckled to herself as she climbed the ladder. 'There's life in the old bird yet,' she said aloud.

Reaching the top, she crawled into the sweet-smelling hayloft and stood up at the third attempt. The hay bales had once been neatly stacked. Now they were all over the place. Tom and two of his friends had been playing up there, building dens.

'Little toads,' Nan tutted.

She found a place in the corner where someone had made a bedroom from the hay bales. It looked cosy and, she suspected, the same someone had been sleeping there. A perfect cosy refuge for a wild boy on a rainy night. A wisp of compassion came over Nan, but quickly drifted on.

The hayloft door was a granite archway, open to the sky and with a sheer drop down to the yard below. Swallows dived in and out at breathtaking speed, twisting and circling as they fed the first batch of fledglings in their cup-shaped nest in the rafters. Nan could see the row of black and white faces and open beaks peeping over the edge of the nest and it made her smile.

In the back wall was a neat hole in the stonework, which had once been a tiny window. A good spyhole. Nan sat down close to it, wedging herself between the stacks of hay bales, well hidden from anyone venturing up the ladder. She heard the chickens coming up the ladder, clucking as they hopped from rung to rung.

Nan sat quietly, watching the house and the open gateway through the hole. The wild boy usually came around mid-morning. He must have watched from somewhere nearby to make sure no one was outside.

Today he'd get a shock.

Nan relished the chance to give him a fright. One encounter with her would make sure he never, *ever* came back.

It would be just her bad luck if he didn't come today. After about an hour, Nan's patience was running short. The fragrance of the sweet meadow hay was heavy and she was drowsy. She sat up straighter and listened to the distant sigh of the sea. Then ... footsteps.

Nan tensed. It wasn't Jenny, but they weren't the kind of footsteps the wild boy would make either. These were slow, deliberate footsteps. Boots on gravel. Nan couldn't think of anyone who might visit her that day. It spooked her, especially when the sparrows flew up from the yard with a burr of wings.

She struggled to her feet and peered out of the hole. She saw him immediately. A strange man creeping round the side of the house, bent double, below the level of the windowsills as if he didn't want to be seen. Horrified, Nan watched him sneak into the back door, which was open.

Heart pounding, she went to the ladder, lay on the floor and slid backwards, clutching at the hay-covered edges of ancient floorboards, her feet feeling for the rungs of the ladder.

Be quiet, be quiet, she kept thinking, but she wheezed and groaned with the effort and the fright of lowering herself onto the creaking ladder. *I might have a stroke*, she thought, looking at her purple hands clinging to the ladder. And she thought about the man inside her home, eyeing her treasures. What about her money at the bottom of an earthenware rice jar in the kitchen?

Someone in St Ives had been burgled that very week. She'd heard it in the bakery. He'd taken jewellery, silver and cash from a box on top of a wardrobe. He hadn't been caught.

'I should have got a dog. I knew I should have,' Nan panted, reaching the bottom of the ladder and unhooking her skirt from where it was caught on a nail.

Trembling from the effort, she seized the cricket bat Tom had left propped in a corner. Holding it with both hands, she took a deep, empowering breath and strutted towards the house with sweat trickling out of her hair.

As she crossed the yard, Nan's mind flickered with folklore and legend. The Cornish tales of giants hurling boulders at each other and carving chasms in the granite with the power of their voice. St Michael the Archangel, with his sword of light. By the time Nan reached the front door she had worked herself into a rage that infused the cricket bat with supernatural powers.

Where was he?

She listened.

Trying not to wheeze, she crept towards the kitchen, hearing him moving bottles and jars. Next he was in the broom cupboard. Kicking the old tea chests and stumbling over boots and dustbin lids.

Got him! Nan thought. She squared her shoulders. It would be some weedy little man. Some pathetic little runt. She hoped she wouldn't have to kill him.

'GET OUT OF MY HOUSE!' Nan bellowed and the man fell over something metal. It sounded like a particular copper coal scuttle that had a way of trapping your foot in the handle. 'OUT!' she whacked the cricket bat against the doorpost, scattering flakes of paint onto the floor.

She filled the doorway and the man swung round in the dimly lit cupboard, the whites of his eyes gleaming. And Nan had the shock of her life.

'It's *you!*' she thundered and her eyes narrowed to unforgiving slits. 'Come out of that cupboard and don't you *dare* run away. You are going to face up to something for once in your life.'

The cricket bat fell to the floor and she stood back to let him come out of the cupboard into the light. He was taller than she was. He wore the faded blue clothes of a fisherman. He held out his hands to her, palms upward, strong fingers, every crease ingrained with oil or paint. He had long eyelashes and – those eyes. Those soulful eyes.

It shook Nan. Even though she'd been told by Jenny and Lottie how Matt resembled his father, she was unprepared for it. She needed to generate fury in order to deal with him.

'What the hell are you doing here?' she demanded, trying to locate the insolent little boy she had once known. She hurled insults at him, unable to stop. 'You devious brat. The black sheep of the Lanroska family. How *dare* you break into my home. My God, I could have killed you with that cricket bat – and I wish I had. You're nothing but trouble – the devil's child, that's what you are.'

Matt didn't hang his head as he used to do when he was a child. He didn't look shocked or hurt. He seemed self-assured and sceptical. In control.

Nan licked the spittle from her lips. Bartholomew trotted into the kitchen with his tail up. His golden eyes looked from one to the other and chose Matt, wrapping his front paws around his leg and gazing up at him. A smile came into Matt's eyes and he reached down with his big hands and picked the cat up.

An angry flush spread up Nan's cheeks as she restrained herself from saying, 'Don't you dare touch my cat.'

Bartholomew pressed himself against Matt's heart, purring and stretching up to kiss his face. Nan shut her eyes and pinched the bridge of her nose as if she had a headache. She could hear Matt breathing and Bartholomew purring, and the seagulls screaming down in the harbour. She was beyond words, suddenly silenced by a memory. Bartholomew used to do exactly that to Arnie.

'You don't look well, Nan,' Matt said.

His voice had broken since Nan had last seen him. She managed to open her eyes and look into his without hurling another insult.

'You'd better sit down, Nan,' he said and, with the lightest touch on her arm, he led her into the lounge to her favourite chair, the cat still draped over his shoulder. 'You're a bad colour. Shall I get you a glass of water?'

Nan shook her head. She lowered herself into the chair and looked up at him. 'You sit down too. I want an explanation. Why break into my house, Matt? Why? Why not knock on the door and tell me what you want?' She pulled a stalk of hay out of her hair and wound it round her index finger.

Matt looked at her calmly and Nan observed the way he was responding to the love Bartholomew was still lavishly giving him. 'You never liked me,' Matt said, the words coming from deep down in his soul, 'and I didn't think you would listen.'

Nan shut her eyes again. Then she said, 'I'm here now and I'm listening. Why are you here? Stealing, I suppose. You do realise you could end up in a borstal? That's where they send boys like you.'

'You're still not listening,' Matt said.

'Yes, I am.'

'No, Nan, you're not. You're accusing me and you're judging me and you're threatening me. That's not listening.'

'All right. Point taken. I'll be quiet.' Nan pursed her mouth and waited, her eyes impatient. When Matt didn't respond immediately, she pointed a finger at him. 'I hope you realise there's been a bedroom waiting for you upstairs – and meals on the table. You should be living here, helping the family, Matt – we need a strong young man like you. Your mother has been to hell and back with polio, and you've caused her endless worry, just disappearing without a word, not even a letter – nothing.'

Matt's face hardened. 'What's the use of trying to talk to you?' He put Bartholomew down and stood up, towering over Nan. 'I'll take what I want and go. Mum never wanted me and neither did you. And don't worry, I won't take any of your precious stuff – or hers. All I want is what my dad would have given me – his lifejacket. I need it 'cause I'm living on his boat.'

He went back to the broom cupboard and took Arnie's cork lifejacket from its peg.

Nan picked up a book and pretended to read, hoping Matt would just go. She wanted peace. At any price.

But Matt came back into the lounge, the lifejacket over his arm. Seeing it brought tears to Nan's eyes. She shook her head, now too upset to argue.

Matt hovered, looking at her, and Bartholomew sat between them on the floor, his tail twitching. Nan knew she hadn't listened, but she felt too weary to try again. She'd given up on Matt long ago – hadn't she? Why did she keep getting it wrong? She looked up at him, hoping her silence would speak for her.

'You look after yourself, Nan. And look after Tom.' Matt's voice had an odd blend of arrogance and kindness. 'I'll look after Lottie,' he added cheekily, striding purposefully out of the house, across the yard and down through the flower-filled lane towards the sparkling sea.

Exhausted and upset, Nan watched him go, her mind overloaded with a new threat.

What did Matt mean by saying he would look after Lottie?

Chapter 6

A Cry in the Night

On the other side of the storm, the Atlantic Ocean was tranquil, the air still. No land was visible; the horizon a vast porcelain bowl, its rim sharp against a peachy sky.

Lottie hadn't seen Olivia for three days. Her mother stayed in bed, terribly seasick and wanting to be left alone.

On that peaceful morning, Lottie loved being up on deck with her father, sitting on one of the roomy wooden seats, watching the ocean for dolphins and the flying fish that she found captivating. Earlier they'd seen a pod of killer whales close to the ship, their black and white faces bursting out of the water as if they could see her up there on the ship. Orcas, John called them. She loved to hear their haunting, high-pitched cry, a strange, musical language incomprehensible to humans.

'Matt would love to see them,' Lottie said. 'Do they ever come to Cornwall?'

'I don't know. Maybe he will see them from his little boat. He's got a lonely life, hasn't he?'

'He likes it,' Lottie said. 'When we get home you must meet him, Daddy. He wants to show you his paintings.'

'Hmm ... Well, yes, I'd like to see them.' John spoke courteously, but there was a discreet frown on his brow. 'I'm interested, of course, but everything I've heard about Matt so far has been negative. He's something of a challenging character, isn't he?'

'No, it's not true,' Lottie said passionately. Her cheeks flushed. 'He's not the bad boy of the family like people say he is. No one understands him. But I do – and honestly, Daddy, Matt is a secret angel. Jenny and Nan are so down on him. I wish I could make them see how wonderful he is. He's brave and clever and he's my ...' The word 'lover' burned on her lips and Lottie stopped speaking, her hot cheeks and bright eyes giving her away.

John looked at her sharply. Had she said too much? Ever anxious to put things right, Lottie knew she must honour the pledge of secrecy she and Matt had made. She couldn't think of a single person in her life who would understand, except her friend Morwenna, but Morwenna would gossip. Lottie wanted justice for Matt. And she wanted something they could never have – freedom to love. She sighed. 'I wish I wasn't sixteen.'

'Why's that?'

'Because being sixteen is like a disease. Everyone keeps saying I'm too young for this and too young for that – but I feel old. Sometimes I feel older than Jenny.'

'Well, you'll soon be seventeen,' John said. 'The eighth of May, isn't it? I think you'll be very surprised at what I'm planning to give you, Lottie.'

'Ooh, what?'

'It's a secret. But I shall have to go to London to fetch it.' John's eyes twinkled. Then his expression changed. 'Ah – here's your mother, up and dressed at last.'

Lottie stiffened. Olivia glided along the deck towards them in her red coat, an exotic mohair scarf tucked around her neck.

John sat up attentively. 'What a *lovely* scarf.'

Lottie bristled, remembering how annoyed he had been when Olivia didn't show up at the gallery, yet he was charm personified. As he stood up to welcome her, John turned to look at Lottie and his face shone with intense, expectant love. Lottie melted. She let her angry feelings slip away like cold pebbles. *Give her a chance. I'm sixteen, not six.*

'Good to see you up and about,' John said, and kissed Olivia on the cheek. 'Come and join us. It's a beautiful morning.'

'Hello there, John – and Charlotte, how lovely you look.'

'Lottie.'

'Okay – Lottie – forgive my absence. I've been so ill and sick. I think I'm dehydrated.'

Lottie sat tensely, mesmerised by her mother's eyes. They studied each other, both searching. Searching for love. For understanding. For strength to cross the long, iron bridge of separation and blame. Years ago, there had been confidence and fun in Olivia's expression, but now

Lottie saw only a desperate loneliness lurking beyond the painted image. She wanted to go on looking, but Olivia broke the spell first, as if the level of spiritual contact was unsustainable for her.

'It's been a long time,' she said, her voice rough and tired.

'Twelve years,' Lottie said, and added firmly, 'but I'm grown up now and I hope we can be friends.'

Olivia nodded. She seemed to change gear then, pasting a vivacious smile on her thin face. She flashed a set of scarlet fingernails at Lottie. 'How do you like my nail varnish, honey-child?'

'It ... it's okay,' Lottie managed to say and caught a discreet gleam of amusement in her father's eyes.

'We can paint your nails for you later if you like?' Olivia said, leaning so close that Lottie could feel her breath.

'I think she's too young,' John said.

'Aw, you're never too young to look pretty,' Olivia gushed. 'I did my feet as well.' She slipped her shoes off and wiggled a set of scarlet toenails on bony white feet. Lottie eyed the discarded snakeskin shoes with their high heels and longed to try them on.

Olivia seemed to read her mind. 'Wanna try my shoes on, hon? Go on – you can.'

Lottie shook her head vigorously. *Why am I still sitting here?* she thought, and started to get up, suddenly aware of a stabbing pain low down in her right side. Her father put a gentle, restraining hand on her shoulder. 'Lottie, please,' he pleaded, and she met his eyes in silence. 'Remember how much you wanted this.'

'Excuse me. I need to be on my own for a few minutes,' Lottie said. 'I've got a tummy pain. I'll be back d'reckly.'

'*D'reckly*? What on earth does that mean?' Olivia asked as she walked away, and Lottie heard John's answer. 'It's a Cornish way of saying, "in a minute".'

It hurt to hear Olivia laughing. The sound of it cut into her unopened box of bad memories. That laugh. Always *her* laughing. Lottie couldn't remember laughing with her, not the way she did with Jenny. In the first four years of her life, when she had lived with her mother in a substantial townhouse in Swansea, Lottie remembered *the laugh* and how much it had hurt. Olivia had constantly laughed *at* her, not *with* her. Laughed at her falls and her failures, her ideas and her dreams. What kind of mother did that?

Lottie walked alongside the deck rail to the front of the ship. She leaned over. It was a long way down.

John's words stayed with her: *Remember how much you wanted this*. She appreciated his quiet wisdom. She could hardly forget how her dream of going to America to find her birth mother had overshadowed her thoughts for years. It had blotted out the sun. Everything she loved and enjoyed had gone streaming past and she'd only half lived. Her childhood was over. She'd let it slip away. But now her womanhood had begun, glorious and unannounced, with Matt's lovemaking. It had eclipsed her dream of America and her mother along with it.

What she wanted now was a way out of the secret, for both of them. But right in front of her, barring the way, was a solid wall of well-meaning adults. None of them could accept that inside every child was an adult, and instead of taking painful years to evolve, that adult could emerge in a sudden burst of glory. Emerge and fly – until its wings were clipped, 'for its own good'.

It wasn't Olivia's fault. The thought dawned in a glare of light. Olivia was a relic from long ago. The nail varnish and shoes had been her frivolous but pathetic attempt to re-engage with her lost child. Why punish her? She must take the wisdom John was offering her so courteously. Give her mother a chance. It wouldn't be *that* difficult, would it?

Lottie made her decision, standing at the magnificent bow of the ship. She'd go back, hold her head high and try to be kind.

She stood back from the deck rail, a breeze rippling through her hair, a nagging pain in her side. She frowned, rubbing the place where it hurt, low down in her tummy. It was happening more and more. Lottie tried to ignore it as she walked back to John and Olivia.

Why wasn't she happy about having both of her birth parents in her life again? She supposed, since her childhood was virtually over, it didn't matter that much. Did it? But the nagging pain was getting worse, giving her a sick feeling and a sense of urgency. She must put things right, say what she had to say, try to make peace with her mother – and then worry about the pain.

*

Jenny lay awake, hearing the sounds of morning, the seagulls out on the cliffs, and a lone song thrush in Nan's garden.

But Jenny was listening to a sound that didn't belong out on those wild rocky cliffs. It disturbed her so deeply that she got out of bed to lean on the windowsill in the glow of dawn and listen intently. Would it come again or was she dreaming?

She heard it again. Crying. Somewhere out on the cliffs. It wasn't a seabird or a lamb. It sounded like a child. Jenny decided it must be coming from somewhere down in the town and waited to hear the predictable mother's voice dealing with it. But the cry went on and on in a kind of rhythm, high-pitched but weak, and it was coming from the cliffs. It gave Jenny goosebumps. The more she listened, the more the cry sounded like words "Elp. 'Elp me.'

The clock in the tower of St Ia's church struck eight. Jenny knew the tide was coming in.

She listened again, spooked when she realised the cry had stopped. A flock of seagulls passed high up over the house, circling and screaming, the whole flock moving as one, moving on over the town. When they had gone, she heard the cry again. ''Elp. 'Elp me.' Just once. Then silence.

If only Arnie had been with her. He would have been out there in seconds, surefooted and swift, running over the rocky ground towards the sea. Jenny started to cry with frustration as she pulled on her clothes and wrestled with the buckles on her iron leg. It was hard to get them right, and she was so slow.

She stood at the bottom of the stairs, banging her stick on the banister and calling Tom. He emerged, tousled and sleepy. 'What's the matter, Mum?'

'It's an emergency. Get dressed quick and come with me. Someone's crying for help out on the cliffs.'

Tom looked down at her, scratching his head. 'It might be the wild boy!'

'It might be – so be quick. I need you with me, Tom. I'll start walking.'

She heard Tom's feet running along the landing. Then Nan's bedroom door opened. 'What in heaven's name is going on? What a commotion.' Nan filled the doorway in her voluminous white nightdress. 'That boy's feet sound like an entire regiment of soldiers.'

'It's an emergency, Nan. We're going out to Clodgy. Someone's crying for help out there.'

Nan tutted. 'Doubtless some ill-informed emmet.'

'Back soon, I hope,' Jenny said, and struggled out into the cold morning.

Walking on uneven ground was difficult for her, but she set off, leaning heavily on her stout walking stick. It wasn't long before Tom caught up with her, red-faced and alert. He'd had the presence of mind to bring the old red and white lifebelt with its coil of rope, which he wore looped over one shoulder. He looked solid and reliable, Jenny thought proudly. And where was Matt when she needed him?

No one had seen Matt for days and the boat was no longer in the harbour. Jenny only knew what Lottie had told her:

Matt lived on *The Jenny Wren* and he was further up the coast at Portreath.

'Are you all right, Mum?' Tom asked, glancing at her iron leg.

'Course I am,' Jenny said, 'and you've got your jumper on inside out.'

Tom shrugged. 'Let's stop and listen.'

The winding path came to an end and they were on the cushiony green turf of the cliffs. It was quiet except for the waves.

'I can't hear anything,' Tom said. 'What was it you heard, Mum?'

'A cry for help. It went on and on then suddenly it stopped. Then I heard it again, but weaker. It came from over there.' Jenny pointed to the stretch of rocky cliff beyond Clodgy Point, where the rough path led up to an even wilder, rockier headland and on for six miles towards Zennor. 'We should call out.'

Jenny cupped her hand around her mouth and shouted in her clear voice, 'Hello, anyone out there? We're here to help you. Hello?'

Tom shouted too. Then they listened.

When the cry came again on the wind, Jenny's heart leapt. 'We're coming to help you. Where are you?'

The cry came again, louder and stronger.

Tom and Jenny looked at each other. Jenny was aware that Tom's sharp young mind was better than her own, his hearing more sensitive, and he had intimate knowledge of the rocky cliffs where he and Matt had played.

'Mum,' he whispered, 'if it is the wild boy and he sees us, he'll be scared. He'll hide, even if he's in trouble, 'cause of the stealing he's been doing.'

Jenny nodded. 'We won't hurt you,' she called. 'Where are you?'

The cry came again, louder.

'I can guess where he is,' Tom said, 'but you can't get down there with your leg, Mum. You stay up here.'

Jenny followed him along the path, which wound steeply around a high stack of rocks and down again over a trickling stream. Below was a secluded cove of storm-washed sand, with dramatic dark stacks of rock and mirror-like pools with mops of seaweed.

'There he is!' Tom shouted.

'Oh my goodness – no!' Jenny gasped, shocked to see a small, crumpled figure clinging to a rock which was completely surrounded by speeding white water. 'He's cut off. And there's a hell of a tide. What are we gonna do?'

The boy looked up at them, terrified. Tom shouted down to him. 'Don't be scared. We'll get you out of there.'

'We won't hurt you,' Jenny yelled. 'We're here to help.'

The boy's face changed a little, as if he was crying.

'I can get to him, Mum. You stay up here,' Tom said.

Panic flung itself around Jenny like a scarf in the wind. She grabbed a handful of Tom's inside-out jumper. '*No*, Tom. No! I can't lose you as well.'

'Let go, Mum. I can do it. I know I can. Matt and me used to swim in that cove.'

'But not in a tide like this. Look at it! Have some sense, Tom. Think about your dad. He wouldn't have let you.'

As she spoke, an enormous wave towered and pounced, sending a storm of hard spray flying over the clinging boy who began to wail in terror.

'That would knock you off your feet and suck you under, Tom,' Jenny gabbled. Her fingers dug into his arm. 'You know I'm right.'

He stared at her, and to her great relief, he nodded slowly. 'Mum – at least let me climb down and throw him the lifebelt. It could save his life if a wave knocks him off the rock.'

'Promise you won't go in.'

'Promise.'

Jenny let go of him. 'Be quick then. Come straight back up, then you have to run like the wind back to Nan's place and phone the coastguard. You can go quicker than me. I'll stay here and try to reassure him – poor little scrap. Where on earth are his parents?'

It was hard to let Tom go down there, but she did. Wringing her hands and praying out loud, Jenny watched him climb down, leaving her standing helplessly. Looking at the level of the water, she reckoned it would be about thirty minutes before it reached the ledge that the boy was clinging onto. Her heart went out to him. He must be icy-cold and exhausted.

Tom was down on the sand trying to throw the lifebelt, timing it between waves. At the third attempt he managed to land it on the ledge.

'Put it over your head,' he yelled, and for one perilous moment the boy let go of the rock and quickly pulled the lifebelt over himself. 'Keep holding on,' Tom yelled. 'You've got to hold on while I get the coastguard. My mum will stay and watch you.'

Breathing hard, Tom scrambled back to Jenny. She gave him a quick hug. 'Go on – run and phone the coastguard.'

Jenny watched him go, then she went as close to the edge as she dared. It wasn't a sheer drop, but a very steep slope, sculpted with granite and domes of sea pink. She sat down on a rock where the boy could see her and, hopefully, could hear her voice.

'When you're rescued, you can come home with me and Tom,' she called, 'and we'll give you a hot dinner and some warm, dry clothes. You can stay with us as long as you need to. You're never going to sleep in the wild again, not if I've got anything to do with it. You can rest and get better and tell us where you came from.'

Jenny knew the boy was listening by the way his eyes were fixed on her. He seemed calmer after a few minutes, but the tide was rising, the danger increasing as it did so, and still no one came to help. *Surely Tom has made the phone call?* she thought. What if Nan decided to be awkward?

Jenny had run out of prayers and things to say to the poor, thin, shivering boy. So she decided to sing. In her clear soprano voice, she began with the fisherman's hymn:

Eternal Father, strong to save,
Whose arm hath bound the restless wave,
Who bidd'st the mighty ocean deep
Its own appointed limits keep;
Oh, hear us when we cry to Thee,
For those in peril on the sea!

Jenny felt the thud of footsteps even before she heard them. Overjoyed, she turned to see three young, strong Cornishmen pounding along the coastal path. She waved with both arms. Her prayer had been answered and Tom, wonderful Tom, was following at a distance, running his hardest, striving to keep up. Jenny gulped. All three men had been Arnie's friends, members of the lifeboat crew, lean and fit, compassionate, ready to down tools and rescue anyone in danger. She felt their power as they ran towards her.

'Where is he, Jen?'

'Down there,' she pointed to the boy who was looking up at them, wide-eyed and afraid.

The three men, Alf, Keiran and Bryn, went bounding down the steep rocky cliff, surefooted as goats. 'There's a boat coming round d'reckly,' Alf called to Jenny. 'Keep Tom up there with you.'

Tom was only too glad to collapse on the turf next to Jenny's rock. Gasping for breath and sweating, he quickly sat up to watch the rescue.

It happened in minutes.

'Oh, thank God. Thank God. They've got him safe,' Jenny

cried, her hands clasped tightly together. She'd never felt so proud that she belonged to Cornwall, to these brave, strong, unassuming men. 'And thank you, Arnie,' she whispered, convinced he had been there in spirit.

Keiran and Bryn carried the boy out of the sea between them, talking to him all the time. The boy wasn't answering. He looked dazed, and even from the clifftop Jenny could see him shivering violently. She took off her red woollen shawl ready to wrap him up. Bryn carried him up the cliff to Jenny.

'Give him here,' she said, 'on me lap.' Bryn hesitated for a moment, eyeing Jenny's iron leg, then he tenderly placed the dripping wet boy on her lap. She quickly wrapped the shawl around him, holding him close. 'I'm Jenny,' she said, 'and I'll take care of you. What's your name?'

The boy grunted a reply that sounded like 'Worn'.

'Worn?' Jenny looked at Tom for help.

'He said Warren, Mum.'

Bryn sat down on the turf, water streaming from his clothes. He gazed caringly into the boy's face. 'Are you hurt anywhere? Any broken bones or bruises?'

Warren shook his head.

'Been living rough, have you?' Bryn asked, looking at the boy's sore feet. When there was no response, he said, 'Are you sure there was no one with you? No one else in the sea, is there?'

Warren shook his head again.

'You go home with Jenny — she'll look after you. Won't you, Jen?'

'Course I will.'

'My mum's the *best*,' Tom said proudly, 'but she can't walk too well. She had polio.'

'Don't worry, I'll carry young Warren back to your Nan's place,' Bryn said. 'Hold onto him for a minute, Jen, while I tip the water outa me boots.'

Warren clung to Jenny, closing his eyes as the warmth seeped into him. Jenny leaned her cheek against his wet dark hair, feeling a rush of maternal love for this lost boy who weighed almost nothing and seemed content to just lean against her in silence. It reminded her of the day she had carried Lottie home, cold and shocked, from the shipwreck.

A line from Arnie's funeral service came to her: 'The Lord gives and the Lord takes away.' *I've been given another child – a boy*, she thought, overwhelmed with sudden joy. *Perhaps I could adopt Warren. We'll see how it goes – and how Nan reacts. It's meant to be.* Jenny kept the thoughts to herself. Reluctantly, she let Bryn take him from her, still wrapped in the shawl, leaving a cold, wet emptiness soaking through her dress.

Another thought came, flaring from within her soul like a burst of light, a warm lantern showing her the path her life must take. Despite her iron leg, caring for this lost boy was something she could do.

Nan was waiting in the doorway, a blanket over her arm. Seeing her, Warren struggled to escape.

'No, no,' he wailed, 'let me go.' He kicked and wriggled but Bryn held on to him firmly.

'Let me have him, Bryn.' Jenny held out her arms and

took the terrified child, his small, thin body trembling with fear and exhaustion. 'It's all right,' she told him. 'That's only Nan. She won't blame you for the stealing. You couldn't help it. Forget about it and let us help you.'

Warren met her eyes and leaned against her again, slipping a thin arm around her neck, his fingers lost in her hair. The wave of maternal love swept over her again. She tucked her dream away in a corner of her mind where it was safe from Nan, reminding herself that, without Nan, she and her family would be homeless.

Nan was trying to be kind, but even as she handed Jenny the blanket, she said, 'You do realise he can't stay here?'

Jenny nodded. 'Let's just get through today, then worry about tomorrow.'

Chapter 7

A Secret Gift

'Only a few more days and Lottie will be home,' Jenny said, stirring a bowl of cake mix at Nan's kitchen table. Warren sat watching her, wide-eyed and silent, clutching a blue paper bag with sultanas in it. Tom sat next to him holding a bag of currants.

Warren now looked less like an elf and more like a boy, clean and bright-faced, but silent. They still knew nothing about him except his name, his age – ten – and that he might have come from Zennor, further west.

'Lottie was just the same after the shipwreck,' Jenny said. 'We couldn't get a word out of her, but once she did start talking she never stopped.'

Jenny didn't question Warren about his life. He'd talk when he was ready, she reasoned. Obviously some terrible tragedy had befallen him, something that had driven him to try to survive on his own at ten years of age. She'd given him a set of clothes Tom had worn at the age of six and he'd allowed her to cut his nails and his hair. Tom seemed to be enjoying his new status as the big brother; he was kind and friendly to Warren, explaining everything, playing games with him and even mediating with Nan.

Jenny knew she must call the welfare people and try to find Warren's folks, but she kept putting it off. She wanted Warren to settle down and see what family life *should* be like. So far, Nan had kept her distance from the strange boy. The fact that Warren was so quiet made it easier for her to unbend a little and accept him. She even allowed him to brush Mufty, a great honour in Nan's world.

To Jenny's surprise, Nan said something complimentary when the boys had gone to bed. 'I must say, Jenny, how much I admire your ability to be a mother. It's something I wasn't aware of until now.'

A compliment indeed from Nan. Jenny glowed. 'I love it, Nan – and it's the only thing I'm good at.'

'Well, they're very lucky children. I wish I'd had a parent like you,' Nan said. 'I was petrified of both my parents.'

Would this be the moment to tell Nan her plans to adopt Warren? Jenny was tempted, but she didn't want to rock the boat, especially with Lottie and John coming home on Saturday.

Jenny stared out of the window and was surprised to see the postman pedalling into the drive of Hendravean. 'What's he doing here at this time of day?'

Nan looked out of the window. She stiffened. 'Oh dear. It's a telegram, Jenny. He's got a yellow envelope.' She waddled to the front door and took the envelope from the postman.

'I hope it's not bad news,' he said, doffing his cap to Nan. 'And I've got to wait and see if you want to send a reply.'

Nan looked very serious as she handed the envelope to Jenny. 'You open it.'

Jenny pulled out the folded yellow paper and read the words aloud, horrified:

LOTTIE VERY SERIOUSLY ILL IN SHIP'S HOSPITAL. ARRANGED FOR AMBULANCE TO MEET SHIP WHEN ARRIVES PLYMOUTH AND TRANSFER TO DERRIFORD HOSPITAL. PRAY TO GOD THEY CAN SAVE HER LIFE. JOHN

'Oh, Nan – how awful. What could be wrong with her?' Jenny closed her eyes in horror. All she could hear in her head were those words – again.

The Lord gives – and the Lord takes away.

'Not Lottie!' she wept. 'Please, God, don't take our Lottie away.'

Lottie lay stretched out between the crisp white sheets of the ship's hospital. She drifted in and out of consciousness, aware of her father's constant presence beside her, holding her hand. A few times she felt she was floating away, up to the ceiling, and once she seemed to be outside, high above the ship, looking down at the sunlit deck and the foaming wake. She could see through everything, as if the entire ship was made of glass, and she saw herself lying there like a ragdoll in the hospital bed.

John's hand was an anchor. The resonance of his voice felt comforting, like the blaze of a fire on a cold day. He wasn't going to let her float away. He wanted her to stay and he was putting power and light into his intention, like a lantern to guide her home through the dark ocean twilight.

In a rare moment of clarity, she asked John where Olivia was. He was silent. Lottie managed to open her eyes and observed that he looked upset. 'Daddy? Where's my mother? Does she know I'm ill?'

'Oh yes – she knows.' John's eyes darkened. 'She's worried about you, of course, darling, but she won't come in. She can't stand hospitals.'

Detecting bitterness in his voice, Lottie gave his hand a squeeze. Her eyes wouldn't stay open and she spiralled back into darkness. 'It doesn't matter, Daddy. I just want Jenny – and Nan – so much.'

His words echoed into the tunnel where she was floating. 'It won't be long now. The sea is calm and we're almost at the end of our journey. Nan will be waiting for you on the quay.'

Lottie felt a hot teardrop trickle down into the starched pillow. Questions whirled in her mind and she hadn't the energy to voice them. One particular dark thought hung over her like a black umbrella: was her mother going to abandon her all over again? She'd tried to reassure John by saying it didn't matter, but it did matter – it did.

Before Lottie fell ill, John and Olivia had been getting on well. Laughing a lot, gazing at each other. That had changed a few days ago at the dining table. The pain in Lottie's side had been getting steadily worse and she felt too nauseous to eat. She'd pushed her plate away.

'I'm sorry, Daddy – and Mother – I can't eat this. I've got a really bad stomach ache. I need to go and lie down.'

John's face had shown immediate concern, but before he could speak, Olivia rolled her eyes. 'Oh, for goodness sake, Charlotte, you were forever doing this when you were a child. Surely you're not *still* having these convenient stomach aches?' Olivia turned to John, her bony fingers waving expressively. 'Ignore it, John. Believe me, it's attention-seeking.'

Wordless frustration filled Lottie's heart. The glint in Olivia's eyes was sharp and merciless. John put down his knife and fork. He fixed Olivia with an icy glare. 'You come with me, Lottie,' he said, his arm around her shoulders. 'I think it's time for the ship's doctor to look at you. You're deathly pale.'

Lottie could hardly walk as he led her away, his arm supporting her. 'It hurts. It really hurts,' she whispered, almost in tears from the pain.

'I'll be in the bar later, John,' Olivia called after them as she reached across the table and poured herself another glass of red wine.

Lottie was rigid with fright as she let the ship's doctor examine her.

'How brave are you, Lottie?' he asked when he'd finished.

'*Very* brave,' John said. 'She survived a shipwreck.'

Lottie didn't feel brave. She felt terrified and held John's hand tightly as the doctor explained that she must have an operation – immediately.

'Can't it wait until we get to Plymouth?' John asked.

'Absolutely not. If it's delayed, even by an hour, the appendix could burst and cause peritonitis, which is nasty – and . . .' he lowered his voice . . . 'life-threatening.'

'*Life-threatening?*' Lottie's mouth went dry. 'But I'm only sixteen, and . . .' She thought of Matt. She saw the beauty of their last evening together, with the sun and moon on the water. The velvet cloak. The love.

She dug deep, and found bright threads of courage. She lifted her chin and met the doctor's kindly eyes. 'I'm perfectly capable of facing an operation if it will make me well. Just tell me what I have to do.'

John held her hand. He looked at her in awe and closed his eyes for a few seconds. 'I'm proud of you.' His knees trembled.

'It's okay, Daddy,' Lottie said. 'The only way out of it is through it. I'll be okay.'

Hours later, her father was tucking the knitted donkey close to her cheek on the pillow. Touching it gratefully, Lottie could see Jenny's warm, bright eyes and feel her love in every stitch.

John stayed beside her, day and night, and when the doctors and nurses came, he stepped outside the curtain but continued to tell her he was there.

'Just a little pinprick, dear,' the nurse would say, but the big injections into her leg hurt even more than the tightly bandaged wound across her tummy. The slightest movement sent pain raging through every nerve in her body. She hadn't the strength to cry. Next came a second huge injection of a painkiller, which gave her blessed relief. Profound and fathomless sleep soon followed, lowering her down to the floor of the ocean, far below the ship, into a shadowed, indigo cavern, undisturbed by dreams.

Hours later, rising again into consciousness, her thoughts were vivid. The dreams brought her to the nets of sunlight on the surface of the sea, always in St Ives Bay, and then Matt appeared. She saw the gleaming new paint of *The Jenny Wren*, and saw his smile, his long legs and his confidence. Matt was the way out of the dream. Matt was the future, if only she could get there.

Lottie opened her eyes and searched through the nets of light until she found her father sleeping in the chair by her bed, his hand still gripping hers. She gave it a tiny squeeze and John woke up instantly. He smiled. 'You're awake, Lottie!'

They gazed at each other.

'Is there anything you want?' John asked.

'I want to go home – to St Ives.'

'You will, darling, very soon. You shall see the sun and the moon rise over the water. I know that's what you love,'

John said. He took his leather wallet from the inner pocket of his jacket and fumbled inside it, withdrawing a seashell, a pretty limpet with rays of orange, white and brown. He put it into Lottie's hand and closed her fingers around it. 'Hold this, Lottie,' he said, his voice husky with emotion. 'It's from Porthmeor Beach. I picked it up from the shell garden you were making with Morwenna the very first time I saw you – the day I started painting *Discovering Charlotte*, because I knew I'd found you. I've carried it with me all these years. Hold it, and remember the beach. That's what I do.'

'Thank you, Daddy.' Lottie closed her eyes, her fingers exploring the texture of the limpet shell, its rough, conical outer surface, and its smooth, cool inner side. Immediately, she heard the surf and the sand martins, and saw the lovely face of her friend Morwenna. She felt the arms of St Ives Bay all around her like a hug.

'John ... *John*! Will you please come out here?' Olivia hovered at the door of the ward. 'I *must* speak to you.'

Annoyed, John let go of Lottie's hand. He smoothed a strand of her blonde hair back from her sleeping face and whispered, 'I'm going out just for a minute, my angel. Back soon.'

His legs were stiff from the hours of sitting. Olivia's eyes were huge and red-rimmed. A sour tang of alcohol clung around her. 'Come to the bar with me,' she drawled. 'It's only up those stairs.'

'Certainly not,' John said, his voice icy. 'I'm not going anywhere. What is it, Olivia?'

She sank onto one of the leather chairs, which were bolted to the wall. 'Then sit down with me, John.'

'No. I'd prefer to stand. What do you want to say? Say it quickly, please.'

'Aw, don't be huffy with me, John,' she whined. 'I need to explain why I can't go in and see Charlotte. I hate hospitals. The smell – and the illness – makes me giddy. I've been on my own on this ship for three days, John – I need some company. It's a big ordeal for me, moving back to England, especially to this place you're so obsessed with.'

She paused. John listened silently, watching her nervous fingers clawing at the sleeves of her cashmere cardigan.

'Don't look at me like that, John. We were getting on so well – weren't we?'

He didn't answer.

'Charlotte will be okay for a few hours – she's got all those nurses and doctors around her. I feel lost on this ship. I've left my home in New York – I . . .'

'Be *quiet*.' John's eyes were firm and steely. 'Don't you even want to know how Lottie is?'

'Sure I do. But—'

'She's very ill,' he barked, 'and the least you could do, Olivia, is come in and see her. She's asked for you.'

Olivia's eyes softened. 'You can give her my love, but I can't, and *won't*, go in there. I have a phobia. You have to understand that, and so does Charlotte. Don't glare at me like that, John, it's so mean.' Her fingers were in her hair now, twiddling and tugging at its silver-blonde tresses. 'I've made such an effort. For *you*, John. I hoped we—'

'*Stop!*' John felt something snap inside his mind. 'If you were hoping we would get back together – so was I, until now. Forget it, Olivia. If you can't be a mother to Lottie when she needs you, honestly, dear, I'd rather stay on my own in Cornwall.'

Olivia wailed. 'But ... where am I going to go? I thought you'd take care of me because of what we once had.'

John shook his head. He put his hand into the inner pocket of his jacket and took out a key. 'This is the key to my London apartment. You can stay there until you find somewhere to live. That's the best I can do for you. I'm going back to look after Lottie.'

He gave her one long, hard stare and walked away firmly, ignoring her cries. *I'm better off without her,* he thought, *and so is Lottie. Thank God I've realised that now.*

His footsteps were lighter as he padded back to Lottie's bedside.

'How long before we get to Plymouth?' Lottie asked.

'A few hours,' John said.

'Only hours – not days?' A sudden radiance shone in Lottie's pale face. 'I'm looking forward to it so much, Daddy.' She thought of Nan waiting on the quay and it was like a tonic. If only she could get up, get dressed in the new

American frock John had bought her, and stand in the front of the ship, waving.

John looked very serious. He glanced up at the doctor who had come through the curtain when he'd heard Lottie talking. They nodded at each other in silence. It was time to tell the truth.

'Now then, young Lottie.' The doctor sat down on the bed and took her hand. 'I'm afraid you won't be going home to St Ives just yet. An ambulance will be waiting for you on the quay and it will take you straight to Derriford Hospital in Plymouth. It's an excellent hospital – they can give you the treatment you need to make you better.'

Lottie stared at him. 'But it won't take long – will it?'

The doctor looked over his glasses, his eyes grave. 'A few weeks, Lottie.'

A cold gust of shock knocked the joy out of Lottie's heart. Her pulse began to race. 'No!' she cried, and tears of disappointment meandered across her cheeks and dripped onto the crisp white pillow.

'Oh, darling.' Her father was there, his arms around her instantly.

'I wanted *so much* to go home – to St Ives,' Lottie wept bitterly, the deep sobs hurting the wound on her tummy, making her cry harder. 'I wanted to see Jenny and Nan. They can make me better. I know they can. Oh, please – please let me go home.'

The doctor felt her pulse and shook his head. 'You must keep calm, Lottie, you're very ill.'

'But why? What's wrong with me?' Lottie asked, on the verge of hysteria. 'I'm terrified of having polio like Jenny.'

John held onto her firmly. 'You haven't got polio, I promise, darling – and you will see Jenny. I shall bring her to Plymouth myself. Now take some deep breaths and listen to what the doctor is trying to tell you.'

His calm, strong voice steadied her a little. She didn't understand why she couldn't sit up and have a proper conversation.

'We have tried to explain this to you, Lottie,' the doctor began, 'but you've been very . . . sleepy because of the drugs you are having. Do you remember being brought in here? Do you remember what I told you then? You were in terrible pain, weren't you?'

'Yes,' Lottie whispered. 'You said it was appendicitis and I had to have an operation. I don't remember much after that except waking up, and the pain had gone – but I felt dizzy and my whole body felt as if it was on fire.'

'Well – what a good description,' the doctor said. 'We removed your appendix, but it was badly infected and what you have now is peritonitis. It's a horrid, painful infection in your tummy. We're doing our best to stop it spreading. We're giving you an antibiotic – but your body is like a battleground. That's why you have to just lie still and let it fight. The antibiotic will win if you let it.'

Lottie managed to listen in silence, feeling great waves of drowsiness driving her down into the indigo cavern again. All she could say was, 'But I want to go home.'

'You will go home, but not until you're better. Derriford Hospital is much better equipped than what we've got here on the ship. This is very basic. They've got clever young doctors and all sorts of new medicines and therapies. I'm confident they will make you completely better, Lottie.'

Lottie lay back on the pillow trying to believe him, her eyes closing. She felt her father's hand on her brow. 'She's going again,' he said, and kissed her gently. 'Sleep tight, my darling girl. I'm here. I won't leave you.'

His constant, reliable love was her lifeline. She fell into a deep sleep, with Jenny's knitted donkey in one hand and John's firm grasp in the other one.

Hours later, she awoke to the triumphant blare of the ship's siren.

'We're docking in Plymouth Hoe now,' John said. 'I went up to have a look – Nan is standing on the quayside.'

Lottie felt a change in herself, an aura of peace billowing around her. Nan was there, waiting for her. And Nan was like home. Like the whole of St Ives packed into her reassuring presence.

A nurse and two porters came bustling up to Lottie's bed with a stretcher covered in a cosy red blanket. 'Come on, young lady, you're a VIP,' the porter said cheerily. 'You're going to be first off the ship.'

Lottie smiled and tried to sit up. 'I'm going to stay awake and wave to Nan so she'll know I'm all right.'

*

Olivia walked away from Plymouth Hoe feeling utterly desolate. She'd tried so hard to rekindle the fragile relationship she'd once had with her daughter. It hadn't worked. Charlotte had been unbelievably hostile from the start. Icily polite, but hostile. To be rejected was bad enough, but it was ten times worse to be rejected by a daughter who was intelligent, articulate and beautiful. Olivia had looked forward to feeling proud, feeling loved, feeling like somebody of worth. She'd imagined a wedding in the not too distant future, her own supremely elegant outfit already planned. Charlotte must marry money, of course. A rich man's only son and heir, clean-shaven and accomplished.

She regretted not turning up at the gallery. Of course, Charlotte had overreacted. John had been cold towards Olivia, courteously accepting her explanation, but secretly judging her. Why couldn't he understand? He knew what a battle she'd had with alcohol. Didn't he realise what an effort it was for her just to stay sober and come out to meet them?

Olivia was still in love with John. In her opinion, he'd never given their marriage a chance, going off abroad on long-term engineering projects, leaving her alone and stuck at home with a baby. Now he fancied himself as an artist! In some poky little fishing port in Cornwall. But if he would only unbend and give her a chance, she could get used to it. There had been moments when she felt he still found her attractive, and she'd done her utmost to seduce him without seeming to do so. The trouble was, John was totally besotted with Charlotte – obsessed with her, Olivia thought, and pangs of jealousy had been added to the mix.

The romantic cruise she'd expected turned out to be a nightmare. First the seasickness. Then Charlotte's stubborn rejection of her, then the illness, which meant she hardly saw John again for the rest of the voyage. He really was fanatical about Charlotte. Olivia had almost wished it was herself lying there, getting all the attention.

Arriving in Plymouth was the final straw. The way that mountain of a woman in her scruffy old dress had looked her up and down with her storm-coloured eyes. 'Oh, so *you're* the mother, are you?' Nan had said scathingly and added, 'Better late than never, I suppose.'

Nan had been all over Charlotte, calling her 'our Lottie' and hugging her for so long that the stretcher-bearers had to ask her to move. Nan and John seemed to have forgotten Olivia was there as they fussed over 'Lottie' and saw her being loaded into the ambulance. Oliva ran forward to say goodbye, but Charlotte hadn't even noticed her. Both John and Nan had been allowed to travel inside the ambulance.

'But I'm her *mother*,' Olivia pleaded. 'I should go with her.'

'I'm sorry, madam, we have no more room.' The doors were slammed shut, the ambulance drove away with its bell ringing, and Olivia was left there, devastated and alone.

John hadn't even said goodbye.

Legally I am still Charlotte's mother, Olivia thought angrily. *I should find a lawyer and insist she comes to live with me in London – it's my right.*

She turned her back on Plymouth Hoe and walked into the town, carrying her suitcase, holding back her tears. Dealing with the immediate crisis was priority. She needed somewhere to stay – a cheap guest house. She eyed the big church in the middle of the busy town, tempted to go in and find a sympathetic young vicar.

She stopped in front of a chemist. In the window were bottles of calamine lotion, pots of Pond's Cold Cream, Mason Pearson hairbrushes – and brown glass bottles of aspirin. One hundred aspirin tablets! All she needed was a bottle of wine to go with them.

John would be sorry he'd ignored her.

Warren began to talk now that Nan had gone to Plymouth, but his speech was hesitant and difficult to understand, and Jenny relied on Tom to interpret. For some reason, Tom knew exactly what Warren was trying to say. Jenny didn't ask him questions, but chatted brightly to him and let him follow her as she hobbled around.

'Wuzzatfer?' he asked, looking at her with bright, enquiring eyes.

Jenny looked at Tom.

'He wants to know what your iron leg is for,' Tom said.

Jenny was at the kitchen table making pastry, rolling it and flouring it. 'I used to have a normal leg like yours,' she explained, 'but one terrible day I got very ill with polio. I went to hospital.'

'Wuzzat?'

'Hospital – it's a big, big house with lots of windows and doors, and inside are lots of beds where you can rest if you're not very well. There are clever doctors and kind nurses who make you better.' Jenny took care to look into Warren's eyes when she talked to him. She figured he hadn't had that kind of nurturing attention in his life.

'That's where our Lottie is right now,' Tom said.

'You wait 'til you meet Lottie,' Jenny said to Warren. 'You'll like her.'

'She's got golden hair,' Tom said, 'and I'm learning to play a song for her on me squeeze-box. Shall I show you?'

Warren nodded and the two of them ran upstairs to Tom's bedroom. Jenny began to cut the pastry into tart-sized circles, smiling as she heard Tom struggling through the notes on his piano accordion, then playing the other tunes he knew. She figured Warren would soon get fed up with Tom's halting recital.

But Warren did something so surprising that Jenny almost dropped the tray of jam tarts she was putting in the oven.

'I didn't say you could have it.' Tom looked hot and flustered as he followed Warren downstairs. 'Nan said I wasn't to let me friends mess with it.'

'Warren is more than a friend. Let him have a go,' Jenny said, mindful of the light in Warren's eyes and the sudden flush on his cheeks. She started singing 'Trelawny' as she cleaned the table.

Warren gave her one of his rare smiles. His eyes danced with a devilish glint and he sat down on the stairs, the piano accordion strapped around his thin shoulders. He looked at Jenny so piercingly that she couldn't look away. Then with one confident chord and a tap of his foot, Warren launched into playing 'Trelawny'.

Jenny stood, open-mouthed, a cloth in her hand. Warren wasn't stumbling along like Tom did. He came alive, the music pouring from his bony little fingers, note perfect, his foot tapping, rocking the old wooden staircase and making the plates ring on the dresser.

Was this the same whimpering little scrap of a boy who'd been stealing eggs and turnips, a boy rescued from the sea and carried home, a pathetic bundle in Jenny's shawl?

'Warren! That's incredible,' Jenny gasped when he'd played the final chord with a flourish. 'How did . . .'

Grinning wickedly at Jenny, Warren paused to take a breath, then plunged into 'The Ash Grove', playing it with sensitivity and joy. Next came 'My Grandfather's Clock' and 'Scarborough Fair'. He played on and on, the music burning in him like a fire, as if the boy and the piano accordion were one, its keys and buttons glittering in a shaft of sunlight. While he was playing, the chickens paraded into the house and settled into Nan's armchair, and the two cats sat mesmerised at Warren's feet, their golden eyes dancing as they watched his flying fingers.

Finally, Warren stopped and there was a silence as the music left the house and drifted across the land to the sea.

'Cor, you are *good*,' Tom said, in awe.

'Well, thank you, Warren – I really enjoyed that,' Jenny smiled. 'Made me want to dance.'

Warren looked at her as if he could tell how much dancing meant to Jenny. He unhitched the strap and gave the piano accordion back to Tom. Then he did something even more surprising. He gave Jenny a hug. She felt the fast beating of his heart against her dress.

'How did you learn to play like that?' Jenny asked.

Warren shrugged. 'Just did.'

'You wait 'til Nan hears you play,' Tom said.

Warren frowned. He shook his head firmly. 'Won't play fer 'er.'

'You don't have to,' Jenny said warmly. 'Just play when you want to, eh?'

She sent the boys outside to brush Mufty and lead him out to the paddock. Then she sat down with a cup of tea and both cats on her lap. She understood only too well why Warren wouldn't play for Nan. He was petrified of her. Since Nan had gone to Plymouth to meet the ship, Warren had begun to relax a bit, and Jenny was careful not to put any kind of pressure on him. The unexpected hug had been a gesture of gratitude and trust – in her.

His musical talent was exciting. Jenny would have loved to share it with Nan, but she respected the fact that it was a secret jewel belonging to Warren. He would only share it when he felt confident and loved.

So far, Nan had only managed to tolerate Warren. In particular, his poor speech annoyed her and at first she'd been openly critical, coming out with scathing comments.

The moment after Warren's arrival, Nan had fired a question at him. 'Where on earth are your parents, boy?'

'Gun.'

'Gun?'

'No – gun.'

'That's not an answer, boy. That's a monosyllabic grunt.'

Warren had shrivelled under Nan's imperious glare and Jenny had confronted her, hands on hips, a spark of indignance in her eyes. 'Give him a chance, Nan. He's doing his best and I won't have you intimidating him. It's counterproductive and if you can't say anything kind, you should keep your mouth *shut*.'

Everyone had held their breath. For a moment, it was like the old days when Nan and Jenny were deadly enemies. The colour of rage had spread up Nan's neck and into her jaw, but she'd kept quiet.

Since then, Nan had kept her distance from Warren and, sensing the difficulty she was having, Jenny said no more, but got on with her task of mothering this poor lost boy. It was precarious. Every day, Jenny expected an ultimatum from Nan, declaring Warren had to leave.

The crisis with Lottie distracted them both, but it gave Jenny a chance to have Warren to herself and, with Tom's help, it was going well. Surely if Nan knew of his musical gift, she would be more inclined to let him stay. Jenny wasn't going to tell her. No. She'd set something up so that Nan 'accidentally' heard him playing.

She kept an eye on the boys, pleased to see Mufty standing still and enjoying the attention. The donkey was shedding his thick winter coat and the boys were combing out tufts of silvery brown fluff, leaving it to blow across the yard.

Worrying about Lottie, Jenny stayed within hobbling distance of the phone. When it rang, she was ready and picked it up quickly. 'Hello, Jenny here.'

It was John, calling from Derriford Hospital. Breathless with anxiety, Jenny was glad to hear his calm voice.

'Relax, Jenny. Lottie is getting better. These new antibiotics they've got seem to be working. Her temperature is normal at last and she even managed breakfast this morning.'

'Oh, thank goodness, John. I've been so worried.'

'Well, it was touch and go when she first arrived here,' John said, 'but now they say she is stable and should make a full recovery.'

'Aw, bless her. We miss her so much.'

'Nan has been wonderful – just wonderful. She's a rock, isn't she? She sat with Lottie for hours, talking to her even when she was asleep, telling her stories from Cornish folklore – I quite enjoyed them myself. And she talked about flowers. I felt Nan was actually drawing the life back into Lottie. She's a powerful old lady – very powerful.'

Jenny nodded. 'Don't I know it!'

'I've booked her into a guest house near the hospital,' John continued. 'She wants to stay until she can bring Lottie home.'

'What about Lottie's birth mother? Where's she?'

John hesitated. 'I'm afraid it didn't work out too well, as I told you, and Olivia has disappeared into Plymouth. I've no idea where she is, Jen. But I did give her a key to my London apartment – she likes London, and she can stay there until she makes up her mind what to do, if she ever does.'

'Won't she want to come to St Ives and see Lottie?'

'She might, yes. But I'm not going to be responsible for her, Jenny.'

Chapter 8

A Bottle of Aspirin

Lottie opened the train window with its thick leather strap.

'Be careful. You'll get a smut in your eye,' Nan said, but Lottie didn't care. The wind from the sea was blowing the train's plume of white steam away towards the land. Lottie wanted to savour every moment of the homecoming. As the St Ives train sped across Lelant Saltings, she felt as if she were flying. Flying home like a swallow, an intense ache of joy in her throat, aching harder with everything she saw on the familiar ten-minute journey. The flocks of seabirds over the Saltings, the sand dunes of Hayle Bay, Godrevy Lighthouse. Nothing had changed. Shining waves curling across pale sand. The wooded headland of Carrack Gladden with memories of the wishing well and the nut grove. The whistle of the engine as it burst under the bridge and into St Ives Station.

Home.

The bay was busy with fishing boats. She hoped one of them would be *The Jenny Wren* with Matt on board.

'Does Matt know I've been ill?' Lottie asked Nan.

'Probably not. We haven't seen him for a while,' Nan said, struggling to get up as the train came to a halt.

John lifted their cases down from the string luggage rack. 'Come on, Lottie, home sweet home!' he said, seeing her still at the window. 'And guess who's waiting on the platform?'

Jenny and Lottie hurried towards each other, both unable to run, Jenny with her iron leg and Lottie still with a sore tummy. Jenny held her arms out. 'Hello, my bird!' and Lottie melted into the warm hug, both of them crying with joy. 'How I've missed you,' Jenny murmured, holding Lottie tightly. 'My little girl.'

Jenny still made her feel as if she were about eight years old, but Lottie didn't mind. There was something nurturing and cocoon-like about being someone's little girl. She wondered what Jenny would say if she found out about her secret love with Matt. *It must remain a secret*, Lottie thought. *Jenny would go absolutely crazy – and Nan – and even my father. They'd never understand.*

Tom was there with Jenny, a wide smile on his face. Lottie gave him a hug. 'I've got you a present, Tom. You can have it when we get home.'

'I hope it's something he can share with Warren.' Jenny looked around. 'Where is he? Where's he gone, Tom?'

'He's behind you,' Tom said, 'hiding.'

Nan tutted and got a warning frown from Jenny.

'Hello, Warren.' Lottie peeped round at him and Warren looked up at her shyly. Nan had given Lottie a graphic description of Warren. 'He looks like a drowned rabbit and his speech is abysmal,' she'd said, and added, 'Jenny is mothering him, but I'd call it *smothering*.'

Lottie saw something different in Warren's eyes. Sadness, but strength too. Abandoned. Surviving. Familiar territory for Lottie. She squatted down and looked into his face. 'I was rescued from the sea like you.' There was a spark of recognition, which quickly faded as John led them to a lofty, dark green Model T taxi that was to take them up to Hendravean.

'Won't you come with us, John?' Jenny said. 'I've made pasties.'

John looked at her and Lottie noticed how bright his eyes became. She could see he was drawn to Jenny. 'Thanks, but no,' he said. 'I must go home and open the gallery. You know where I am if you need anything.' A secret smile passed between them and Lottie saw Nan raise an eyebrow as John kissed Jenny on the cheek. A business-like kiss. Then he turned his attention to his daughter. 'I'll see you soon, Lottie. You go on getting better. Lots of rest – and no school for two weeks.'

'Bye, Daddy, and thanks – for everything.'

'I'm sorry it didn't work out with Olivia,' John said. 'I'm sure she'll turn up in St Ives one day, but in the meantime we must just get on with our lives.'

Lottie went straight to see Mufty when they arrived. The donkey trotted across the paddock to her.

'A great honour,' Nan said. 'Donkeys will never trot when they can walk.' Mufty leaned his head against Lottie and stayed there while she fondled his furry ears and pressed her cheek against the top of his head.

'*Ibrushdun*,' Warren said. '*Smoletin*.'

'He helped me brush him,' Tom translated, 'and he says Mufty's moulting.'

'You did a good job,' Lottie said. She smiled into Warren's sad eyes and he reached out and touched a strand of her honey-blonde hair.

'Our Lottie taught me to read,' Tom said, 'and she'll teach you too, Warren, if you want.'

Lottie looked over the paddock hedge and she could see a haze of blue from the bluebells growing in the bracken, and in the thick grasses near the sea were clouds of sea pink, trefoil and red sheep sorrel.

'There's so much I want to do,' she sighed, 'but I'm really tired.'

'You look tired,' Jenny observed. 'Why not go and lie down on your bed?'

'I've had enough of bed.'

'Well, take a rug and lie under the apple tree. I'll come with you. I want to hear all about America.'

Lottie felt blissfully happy stretched out with a blanket under Nan's apple tree, which was in a sheltered part of the garden. She wanted to forget the trip to America. She closed her eyes and dreamed of Matt, instead.

She opened her eyes, feeling rested and grateful. Jenny

was on the rug next to her, lying on her tummy, a reassuring glow of love in her amber-brown eyes.

Jenny wanted to hear Lottie's version of the meeting with Olivia. 'How did it go – with your birth mother?' she asked, and quickly added, 'You don't have to tell me, Lottie, if you don't want to.'

'Oh, I do want to tell you,' Lottie said. 'I hate her.'

Jenny looked at her for a long time. 'I've never heard you say that about anyone. How did that happen? You were so looking forward to meeting her.'

'I was deluded,' Lottie said. 'I built her up in my memory from all the good things I could remember because I wanted it to be true. I couldn't bear to believe she never wanted me. She only wanted a model child, like a sort of trophy. When it came to looking after me, she didn't. I just don't understand her, Jen. She let my father spend so much money for us to go out there. I was excited going to the gallery to meet her and she didn't turn up. It was going to be the best day of my whole life, meeting her after years of wishing and dreaming.'

Jenny nodded. 'That was cruel. Did she have a reason?'

'Daddy tried to defend her. He went on his own to see her and she told him a sob story – she couldn't make up her mind whether to see me or not so instead she went and got drunk. She seemed to have no consideration, no awareness of how I might feel. I thought my birth mother was a bright, interesting person, not a selfish old drunk.' Lottie began to speak faster and faster, the words tumbling out of her. 'I'm

130

never going to be like her. She's selfish, selfish, *selfish* and I
hate her.'

'Aw, Lottie,' Jenny looked at with caring love. 'That's hard
for you to bear.'

'You'd never be like that,' Lottie said fiercely.

'I hope not,' Jenny said, 'but I'm no angel!'

'To me you are. I love you, Jenny – and I loved Arnie too.
Thank you for adopting me.'

Jenny looked pleased. 'And what about your tummy? Is it
better now?'

'Much better, almost back to normal. But I've got a
horrible scar.'

'It will fade,' Jenny said, and grinned mischievously. 'It's
a good job you're not old enough to be worrying about
boyfriends.'

If only you knew, Lottie thought, and changed the subject.
'Are you going to adopt Warren?'

'Well – yes, if I can,' Jenny said. 'I haven't told the welfare
about him yet. I wanted him to settle down and have a bit
of peace. Tom's been so good with him. It's not fair on Nan,
but she's tolerating Warren. I want her to hear him playing
the piano accordion because he's astonishing, and she might
take more of an interest in him then, but Warren is petrified
of her. I've got to set it up so that he doesn't know she's
listening.'

'We'll think of a way,' Lottie said.

'But don't tell Nan.'

'I won't.'

'What do you think about me adopting Warren?'

'I think he'd be a lucky boy. You should adopt him if he wants to stay, Jenny. It's what you're good at – being a mum.'

'So why did I fail so miserably with Matt?'

'I don't think you did. Matt is just . . . Matt.'

Jenny looked gloomy. 'I lost my first baby – she was a little girl. Arnie and I were heartbroken.'

'What happened?' Lottie asked, not quite understanding how a baby could be 'lost'.

'She was born dead – stillborn, they call it.'

'But why?'

'They didn't tell us – I don't think they knew the reason. They just took her away – and she was perfect.'

Lottie put her arm around Jenny's shoulders. 'That's so sad. I didn't know babies could be born dead.'

Jenny looked at her thoughtfully. 'I don't suppose you know how a baby is born, do you?'

'Not really – only from what Morwenna told me. She watched her little sister being born and it sounded awful. Her mum was screaming.'

'Well, don't let it frighten you, Lottie. Morwenna does exaggerate everything, doesn't she?' Jenny was looking intently at her. 'If you want to know anything, Lottie, you must ask me – not Morwenna. I'll tell you the truth.'

Lottie nodded. There was something she wanted to ask – but not yet. Her period was late and the doctor in Derriford Hospital had told her it was because she'd been so ill. 'It will come right,' he'd said. 'You might miss one, or even two, but your monthly cycle will return eventually.'

'Promise?' Jenny said, and when Lottie didn't answer, her expression changed and she asked, 'Is there something? Lottie?'

Lottie felt cornered. 'I don't want to talk about it.'

'Well, you're only young. Plenty of time yet,' Jenny said, looking directly into Lottie's eyes.

Jenny was still looking at her searchingly. Time to change the subject.

'What about Olivia? I don't want her to come to St Ives, ever. I don't want to live with her, Jenny, *ever*.'

Jenny rubbed her hands together. 'Don't you worry. I can deal with her!'

'You're not welcome here.' Jenny stood on the doorstep of Hendravean, her hands covered in flour.

'Oh, but let me explain who I am,' Olivia said, her eyes sweeping over Jenny and pausing a bit too long on the iron leg. 'I'm Charlotte's mother. Her *real* mother.'

'Who's Charlotte?'

'I think you know that,' Olivia said smoothly. 'My daughter – Charlotte De Lumen – she lives here with you, doesn't she?'

'There's no one called Charlotte here.'

'Well, Lottie, then, if you must call her such a common name.'

'It's the name Lottie has chosen for herself. Lottie Lanroska.'

'What a pity you have encouraged her to choose a name

like that. It sounds like a circus act. It won't help her get on in life.'

'It's a perfectly good traditional Cornish name,' Jenny hissed, struggling to control the sparks of antagonism gathering in her mind. 'I'm Jenny Lanroska and proud of it, I'll have you know. My husband, Arnie Lanroska, was a wonderful man – brave, strong, kind and clever – and a respected member of the RNLI lifeboat crew.'

'Aw, how sweet.'

'*Sweet*?' Jenny thought Olivia was being sarcastic. She stepped outside and closed the front door behind her. She pushed her face closer to Olivia's thickly powdered mask. A faint smell of wine hung in the air around her and the inner corners of Olivia's eyes looked red and sore. She noted the blonde hair, wavy like Lottie's but thinner and limp, dragged back from a face very similar to Lottie's, but the mouth was tense and unsmiling, the eyes had no light. In fact, they were so dark that Jenny thought it impossible she had a soul. 'What do you mean, sweet?'

'Aw, don't take it the wrong way. I just meant to compliment you on the way you defend your poor husband,' Olivia said with a faint tinge of sincerity. 'It's the way we talk in New York. I'm getting used to England again – and Cornwall is so quaint.'

Jenny stood looking at her, hands on hips, trying to reason with the exasperation Olivia evoked in her. This woman had abandoned four-year-old Lottie, broken John's heart, and now had the cheek to turn up, uninvited, at the home Lottie loved.

'Is Charlotte here?' Olivia asked. 'Is she better? She was so dreadfully ill, you know.'

'I *do* know. Lottie's not here. She's out with a friend.'

'I wanted to see her. And – I think we need to talk, don't we, Jenny? Couldn't we go indoors and sit down?'

Jenny was alone at Hendravean. Nan was out selling herbs and posies from Mufty's cart, the boys were playing in the hay barn, and Lottie was either with John or with Morwenna. If she asked Olivia in, Jenny wasn't sure she could handle it.

I'm that angry, I might start chucking saucepans, she thought.

Olivia looked at her pleadingly. 'Couldn't I use your bathroom, Jenny – please?' she begged, inching towards the door. 'And I need to take some aspirin. All I want is a glass of water. You can't deny me that, surely? I've never done anything to you. We ought to be friends, surely, for Charlotte's sake. I promise if you just let me use the bathroom and give me a glass of water to take my aspirin, I'll go.'

Jenny sighed. 'Oh, come on then. Anyway, I'm burning me scones standing here.' She opened the door and the swallows came bombing out. 'Oops,' Jenny said, 'I forgot about this lot. We have to keep the door open for them – they've got a nest in the rafters.'

Olivia gasped. 'Birds! Nesting *inside*?'

'We've got a robin's nest as well,' Jenny said, seizing a chance to wind Olivia up, 'in between two chutney jars on the shelf this year. Last year they were in the bookshelves.'

Ducking her head, Olivia followed Jenny through the hall, eyeing the high shelves stacked with Nan's bottled pears and homemade chutneys. The male robin supervised her from the shelf, a territorial gleam in his eye.

'The bathroom is first left at the top of the stairs,' Jenny said, 'and do mind the chickens don't peck your ankles,' she added wickedly; even though the chickens were actually outside, there were plenty of feathers lying around.

Leaving Olivia to brave the stairs, Jenny limped into the kitchen and flung the oven door open to rescue a tray of slightly burned scones. She filled a glass with tap water and slammed it on the table for Olivia and her aspirin. Manipulative. That's what Olivia was. She'd wormed her way in.

A few minutes later, a wild-eyed Olivia came creeping into the kitchen. 'I've never been in a place like this,' she said, staring at the cornucopia of Nan's kitchen. 'What are these bunches of dead leaves hanging from the beams?'

'Herbs. We grow our own and dry them,' Jenny said proudly. 'And there's your glass of water.'

'Thank you.'

Olivia sat down gingerly and opened the snakeskin handbag she carried. Jenny was horrified when she took out a brown bottle labelled '100 Aspirin'. 'Whatever do you want a gurt bottle like that for? Surely you don't get a hundred headaches, do you?'

Oliva tipped the bottle, releasing a pile of white tablets into the palm of her hand. She carefully counted out two, then tipped the pile back into the bottle.

'That lot could kill you, Olivia,' Jenny said, using her name for the first time.

Oliva smiled sweetly. 'Yes, I know. That's why I carry them with me.'

She's insane, Jenny thought, and finally the two women had eye contact over the tray of burnt scones.

Was this woman for real? Was she really Lottie's mother? What exactly was the demon lurking behind those dark eyes? Fear. It had to be fear. It had floated to the surface after Olivia's cryptic words. Jenny felt herself cooling down. She'd been prepared for a cat-fight, but not such an emotionally precarious opponent. She reached out and touched Olivia's arm. It felt brittle. 'What did you want to talk about?' she asked in a kinder voice.

'My daughter.' Olivia's voice went husky.

'Lottie,' Jenny said firmly.

'Okay, Lottie.' Despite being invited to talk, Olivia went quiet, her scarlet fingernails tapping the scrubbed pine table. 'I'm . . . I'm so sad that she hates me now. She hates me, Jenny. What can I do?'

Jenny felt immediate empathy. 'My son, Matt – he's seventeen too – and he hates me. I know how it feels. Believe me, I do.'

'We're quits then.' Olivia's eyes swam with tears and she fished out an embroidered hanky from the snakeskin bag and dabbed her cheeks with it, smearing the heavy layer of powder. Under the powder, her skin was deathly white and as the powder washed away, it uncovered the circles of shadow under her eyes. 'Instead of fighting, we could be friends – support each other.'

137

Jenny nodded slowly. 'We could. But that depends on what your intentions are.'

'I am Lottie's birth mother,' Olivia said, still clutching the bottle of aspirin, turning it over and over, top to tail on the table, the tablets inside rattling. 'I carried her. I gave birth to her. She was a beautiful baby, just beautiful. I did love her, and – I want her back, I guess.'

Jenny shut her eyes and made herself listen to Olivia's tale of woe, knowing that for Lottie's sake she must try to understand. Those white aspirin tablets being tipped over and over in the glass bottle chilled Jenny.

What if she swallows a handful? she thought in alarm.

'It would be lovely to have a mother and daughter friendship now she's growing up – shopping for clothes, doing our nails, seeing movies together. She's missing so much stuck down here in a place like this. I want to take her to live in London where she'd meet people and—'

'She meets people down here.' Jenny felt her face flame and the words she'd been holding back sizzled in the air between them. 'As for you carrying her – I carried Lottie when she was eight years old, soaking wet, cold and terrified after my Arnie rescued her from a shipwreck, risking his own life. I carried her through the wind and the rain to our cottage. I took off her wet clothes by the fire and we were horrified – *horrified* – to see the terrible scars on her little back. You didn't know that, did you?'

'No.' Olivia was wide-eyed and trembling.

'She'd been beaten. Cruelly beaten by a man in an

orphanage who was supposed to be caring for her. Where were you? Go on, tell me, where were you, Olivia?'

Olivia trembled and shook her head violently, unable to answer.

'In America with your fancy man – the man you broke John's heart for, the man you abandoned your little girl for.' Jenny reached out and grabbed Olivia's arm as she tried to get up. 'Oh no you don't. You're gonna sit here and listen to this, 'cause it's the truth. Do you know why Lottie was on that ship? Do you? She ran away from the orphanage – eight years old she was, a little blonde angel who never hurt anyone, and she stowed away on a cargo ship. Why? Why, Olivia? Look at me. Why?'

'I don't know,' Olivia whispered, terrified of Jenny's passion.

'Because Lottie thought the ship was going to America. She thought she was going to end up in America and that she would find you – her mother. That's what she wanted, Olivia. But the ship was wrecked here on Porthmeor. She ended up with us and we've loved her and looked after her – the whole town loves her. She belongs here now.' Tears ran down Jenny's face but her eyes hammered the words into Olivia like nails. She pushed her face closer. 'So don't you come here and think you can take our Lottie away, madam, because the whole town will rise up against you. If you want Lottie so much you should *ask* her, not tell her – *ask* her what she wants to do – and respect the choice she makes.'

Jenny sat back, drained, looking at the wreckage of Olivia, still clutching the bottle of aspirin. In one swift movement,

Jenny whipped the bottle away from her. Olivia cried out and clawed at the air, but Jenny struggled to her feet, lifted the iron lid of the stove and threw the bottle and its contents into the fire.

She went back to Olivia and sat close, holding her the way she would hold a child. 'I just saved your life,' she said, with quiet love. 'I hope we can still be friends.'

Chapter 9

Searching for Matt

Unbeknown to Jenny, Lottie was spending a lot of her time searching for Matt. No one had seen him, not even the harbour master, Ken, who kept a kindly eye on Lottie. She was known and liked by most of the locals, especially those who knew her story and understood what she had been through. There was much gossip when John had turned out to be her father – it seemed like a story with a happy ending. At first, John had been regarded with suspicion, but gradually people were talking to him, liking his quiet ways and forgiving him for having painted a granite cottage dazzling white and turning it into a gallery.

Two days were left of Lottie's sick leave from school. Longing to see Matt, she often sat at the end of Smeaton's Pier on the sun-baked granite, watching every incoming boat. Why didn't Matt come? Was he all right? Both Nan and Jenny seemed to have forgotten about him, except in the occasional doom-laden prediction: he'd get in trouble with the boat, he'd get caught stealing and be sent to a borstal. Lottie talked to her father about it.

'Does he steal?' John asked.

'Only when he's desperate,' Lottie said. 'He doesn't steal for fun.'

'And what would he be desperate for?'

'Food mostly – and maybe fuel for the boat.'

'Jenny would be told if he'd been sent to a borstal,' John said, 'so it couldn't happen without her knowing.'

'He might lie about his age.'

'Hmm – well, the police have clever ways of finding out the truth,' John said. 'I don't like to see you breaking your heart over him, Lottie. I know he's your brother, but he's chosen his life.'

'I suppose so.'

'He's settled in Portreath, hasn't he? It's not too far away. Why not go there? Nan would take you, wouldn't she?'

Lottie shook her head. 'Nan hates Matt.'

Leaving her father attending to customers in the gallery, she walked back to the harbour, thinking about how it would feel to return to school on the following Monday. She didn't have to go back. She could leave, like Morwenna had done, and earn some money.

And live with Matt.

Why have I changed so much? Lottie sat on the harbour wall, gazing at the water. Today it was tranquil, with gently waving reflections and silver lips of light unfolding like smiles along the flare path of the sun. It was the middle of March, summer on the horizon. A time to be free. A time to dream.

Lottie knew she was bright. She'd worked hard at school, but her education had been badly disrupted. The teacher, David Merryn, had offered her the chance to join the elite college class, but was she too far behind to catch up with the class? Nan, Jenny and her father had encouraged her to work hard and try for a place at college. *Make something of your life*, they'd all said. Right now the only thing Lottie wanted to make was a nest. Like the two seagulls on the roof of the Downlong cottage. They mated for life, came back every year contented and regal, devoted to each other, so sure of what they had to do next. Raise a family.

Raise a family. The thought fell from the sky like fruit from a tree. A fruit to be eaten and savoured. *I want to be a mother*, Lottie thought. It was a dream beyond all dreams. Powerful. But still so far away. If only time would disappear. She wanted a life that wasn't controlled by age, a life dominated by adults forever saying, 'You're too *young*', and sometimes, 'You're too *old*.' There was a very hazy line between being a child and being an adult, over which she had no control. Then there was the option of rebellion, which was what Matt had chosen.

Deep in thought, Lottie squealed in fright when someone crept up behind her and put a pair of rough hands over her eyes. 'Guess who!'

Her pulse quickened when she recognised the soft

huskiness of the voice. She turned, laughing. 'Matt!' He towered over her, unrefined and earthy against the noontime sky. His hair stuck out from under his cap, his eyes devouring her with the same deep hunger as she'd been feeling.

He sat down. 'Are you better, Lottie? Tom told me how ill you were.'

'I had peritonitis – but I'm okay now.'

Lottie felt herself tingling deep down from the intensity of his gaze.

'You look like a beautiful seashell,' he said quietly, reaching out to take her hand. He glanced around furtively. No one was there on the end of the pier except a pair of herring gulls perched on a coil of rope.

Lottie smiled. She noticed how the fine hairs on his arms glistened a brassy colour in the sunshine. She waited.

'I'd love to kiss you,' Matt said, 'but when we're here in St Ives we've got to be brother and sister.'

'Of course. I've kept our secret, Matt. Have you?'

'Yeah. It's in here,' he patted his heart.

'Where's the boat?' Lottie asked.

'She's in Portreath. I came by train. I can't do too many long trips in *The Jenny Wren*. It's cheaper by train and I've found a way to walk up through the woods to Camborne from the North Cliffs. You'd love it, and Tom would. I've been drawing some of the old trees – there's an ancient beech tree that is twisted like a rope. The trunk is wide and underneath is a thick carpet of red-gold leaves. It's so quiet in there. I really want to take you there, Lottie.'

'For a picnic – like we used to have with Nan?'

'Well, yeah, but just for us. Just you and me. Don't you dare bring Nan!' Matt grinned. 'We could go now, but it's a long walk. Are you back to normal or still a bit delicate?'

'I do get tired, and my tummy hurts from the operation. I haven't been swimming yet.'

'We could walk through the woods towards Carbis Bay,' Matt said. 'No one knows us down that end of St Ives.'

Lottie noticed his other hand was delving into the canvas haversack he carried over his shoulder. 'What's in there?' she asked, hearing a crackle of paper.

Matt's eyes sparkled. 'I missed you,' he said, and his tanned cheeks flushed with sudden awkwardness. 'I – I wanted to make you something special, Lottie, to remind you how . . . how much I love you.' He thrust a parcel into her hands, something carefully wrapped in a brown paper bread-bag and tied together with a frayed bootlace.

'Ooh, Matt! Whatever is it?' Lottie fingered the mysterious package, her eyes and lips wide open with surprise. 'How kind of you.'

'I made it for you,' Matt said, and he went all fidgety with excitement as she undid the bootlace. 'From driftwood.'

Lottie gasped in surprise. 'A boat!' She extracted the model boat from the bag and squealed. 'It's *The Jenny Wren*! Oh, Matt – it's just perfect. I can't believe you *made* this for me.'

Matt looked pleased. 'Took me a while,' he said modestly. Lottie could see by the look in his eyes how much it meant to him. She examined it closely, marvelling at the detail and the way he'd painted it so beautifully. 'I can't think how you made it. It's exquisite, Matt. I shall keep it forever and ever. I *love* it.' She stood on tiptoe and kissed the hollow of his cheek. She felt him catch fire at the touch of her lips. The longing swept through both of them like a blaze of light. Then he stepped back. 'Brother and sister,' Matt whispered, and grinned. He took a deep breath and blew it out slowly. 'Best calm down.'

Lottie gave a little quiver of happiness. The velvet cloak was still there. So much to look forward to. She grinned back, impishly. 'Okay. I've got a tiny present for you too – from New York. I'll give it to you when we get back to Hendravean. Let's go for that walk first.'

They looked at each other, both wanting time together away from anyone who might gossip.

'Did you come specially to see me?' Lottie asked.

But before Matt could answer a voice called out, 'Charlotte!' and Olivia came tapping down the pier in her snakeskin shoes. She was waving and smiling.

'What's the matter?' Matt asked, shocked to see resentment appear on Lottie's face.

'*She* is my birth mother,' Lottie hissed, aware that her own smile had turned quickly to a glare. Olivia couldn't have chosen a worse moment. Damn her. Lottie wanted Matt to herself.

'You look as if you want to kill her,' Matt said, intrigued.

'I do,' Lottie mouthed.

Matt frowned as Olivia wove her way to them between the piles of lobster pots and nets. 'I should go,' he said.

Lottie hung onto his arm. '*No*, Matt. We're going to the woods. I'll just try to be polite to her, then we'll go.'

'Well, hello, Charlotte. How lucky to see you here.' Olivia's smile glittered with artificial optimism.

'Lottie.'

'Okay, Lottie, then.' Olivia tried to kiss her daughter, but Lottie twisted neatly out of reach. 'Aw, don't be so huffy, honey-child – and who's your handsome friend?' Her eyes raked over Matt.

'Matt,' Lottie said and turned her head to look up at him. He looked down at her, one eyebrow raised.

Olivia held out an eager hand. 'Well, how lovely to meet you, Matt. Are you a fisherman?' She held onto his hand far too long.

'No. An artist.'

'Ooh,' she breathed, 'an artist. I'm interested in art. What do you paint?'

'Pictures.'

She laughed. 'Pictures of what?'

'Wind-sculpted granite.'

Olivia looked at Lottie for clarification but Lottie stayed silent, hostile, resenting every word gushing from Olivia's painted mouth.

'How interesting, Matt – but tell me please, what exactly is granite?'

'Rock – like this one.' Matt patted the warm stone of the harbour wall. 'It's what most of St Ives is built from.'

'But wind-sculpted? I don't understand,' Olivia said, fluttering her eyelashes at Matt. 'You'll have to show me. Where is your work hung?'

'Nowhere. It's in a cupboard on my boat.'

Oliva gasped. 'You have a boat? A real boat? But you're so young. Can we go and see it, and look at your pictures? I'd love that, and Charlotte . . .'

'*Lottie.*'

'Okay, *Lottie* wants me to see your work, don't you, honey-child?'

Lottie wanted to scream. Matt stood awkwardly, shifting from one foot to the other, trying to understand this woman from America who was different from everyone he'd ever met.

'No, not right now.' Lottie lifted her chin, letting her hair slip down her back. She lifted her bust, aware suddenly of her new woman power. Matt was looking at her admiringly, and he gave her a secret wink that made her heart miss a beat.

'But Charlotte . . .'

'*Lottie.*'

'When we were on the ship, Lottie, you told me about Matt and his wonderful drawings, and – no – let me finish . . .' Olivia held up a bony hand, its palm blue and white against the sea, 'when you were talking about Matt, you had fire in your eyes and your cheeks went rosy – you were so proud of him. So why can't I see his pictures?'

'I was actually talking to my father,' Lottie said, pronouncing every syllable with perfect diction, something that came naturally to her when she was annoyed. 'You just happened to be sitting there.'

In the heat of her anger, she was aware of Matt's appraising eyes. Was he wishing they were lying together in the cosy cabin of *The Jenny Wren*, far out on the water? His gaze was roving over her, lingering on her breasts, returning to meet her dark blue eyes, meeting fire with fire. It pushed her beyond the bright edge of anger into an urge to giggle.

Olivia caught the smirk that passed between them. The corners of her painted mouth turned down and the hollows deepened in her cheeks. 'You're being so mean to me. I am your mother, I'm not well and I've made a big effort to come here to St Ives to spend time with you.' Her voice became high-pitched and indignant. 'I want to come with you now and see Matt's pictures. I can come with you, surely – it won't take long.'

'No, Mother, you can't,' Lottie said. 'Matt's pictures are in Portreath, which is about fifteen miles away. Matt and I are going for a walk.'

'Well, I can come with you,' Olivia looked appealingly at Matt.

He gave her an assertive stare. 'No. You can't come. Lottie needs some peace.' He slipped a long arm around Lottie's shoulders. 'She's had a hard time and I'm taking her for a quiet walk along the cliffs. And don't try to follow us – you'll soon come to grief in those shoes. Come on, Lottie.'

Matt took her hand, tucking her fingers reassuringly into his, and Lottie walked beside him, her nose in the air.

Olivia wasn't going to give up. She scuttled beside them, like a crab, her face turned to focus on Lottie. 'You'll have to change your attitude, my girl. I hope you realise why I'm down here in this fishy little backwater. I'll be going back to London shortly, and you, Charlotte, will be coming with me. I've seen a solicitor and it will all be made legal. I'm doing this for you. I'm enrolling you at a good college in London and we can live very comfortably in John's apartment.'

Panic swept around Lottie like a whirlwind. Her skin chilled and she felt dizzy. The three of them were at the harbour end of Smeaton's Pier. 'You've gone deathly pale,' Matt said, and steered her towards a seat. She leaned against him, taking deep breaths the way she'd learned to do in hospital. Olivia tried to sit next to her, but Lottie pushed her away. She sat cocooned in Matt's arms while he demolished Olivia with a few well-chosen words.

'That's not gonna happen,' she heard him say confidently. 'I was there when my parents signed the legal adoption certificate. I know where it is too. Lottie was legally adopted by my mum and dad, to last until she's twenty-one. So back off. We don't want you here in St Ives. Leave Lottie alone, madam, or you'll have me to reckon with.'

'What's happened to Lottie? She should be back by now.' Jenny leaned on the yard gate, watching the lane, hoping to see Lottie's blonde mane bobbing along between the hedges. Lottie was usually punctual and reliable. Where could she be?

It was six o'clock, the air fluttering with blossom petals and birdsong, the sea a blade of bright silver in the distance. The table in the kitchen was laid for high tea, a meal they all enjoyed together. Hunks of home-baked bread with butter, slices of pink ham, cold boiled eggs, crunchy lettuce and radishes from the garden, homemade flapjacks and a spicy Nelson cake. Fresh fruit wasn't available in March, so Nan had opened an enormous jar of bottled pears. It was the kind of meal where everyone helped themselves and ate at their own pace. It was Lottie's favourite meal. Where was she?

'We'd better start without her.' Jenny went back into the kitchen. 'Come on, boys.' Tom and Warren sat down, with Nan at the head of the table. Always wide-eyed in the presence of so much food, Warren looked at Jenny. 'You can help yourself – *slowly*, Warren. The food's not going to fly away.' It had been a battle, getting him to understand that it was possible to eat without grabbing and stuffing.

'I'll put some aside for Lottie,' Jenny said eventually, and she took Lottie's empty plate and arranged a selection of food on it for her. She covered it with another plate and left it on the table.

'Me and Warren could run down and look for her,' Tom said eagerly. 'We've finished our tea, Nan.'

'No, Tom – thank you – you've got school tomorrow and I don't want the two of you running wild before bed.'

'You should telephone John,' Nan said. 'Lottie might be down there with him.' She clapped her hands and looked piercingly at the boys. 'It's getting late. You two lads go and put the chickens to bed. Make sure you count them. If one is missing, check the tops of the hedges where they like to roost. They must all be inside at night or the fox will get them. You can bring Mufty in and make sure he's got water.' Her eyes twinkled unexpectedly. 'If you manage to do all that without fuss, I might tell you a bedtime story.'

'*The White Horse of Porthgwidden*. Please, Nan?' Tom pleaded.

'That's not a bedtime story,' objected Jenny. 'That's a scary old legend.'

'I like it,' Tom said, 'and Warren hasn't heard it.'

'Go on and do the chickens then,' Nan said, 'or I'll do them and you can wash the dishes instead.' Then she tutted and rolled her eyes as Warren overturned his chair in the rush to get outside.

'Warren actually smiled at you, Nan,' Jenny said as they cleared the table. 'I think he's beginning to trust you.'

Nan cackled with laughter. 'I wouldn't trust me if I were him.'

'But we are all getting on better, aren't we?' Jenny said.

'I am finding Tom a remarkably wholesome little boy,' Nan admitted, 'but Warren is unbelievably uncouth and I don't know how you have the patience with him.'

'It's called love,' Jenny said.

'But how can you love such a wimpish apology for a human being?'

'He can't help it, Nan. He's not had any education. It's as

if no one has ever talked to him, so he hasn't learned to talk. He does like music.'

'Does he?' Nan looked interested. 'Well, music is language – language without words, so it's universally communicative.'

Jenny longed to tell her about Warren's amazing gift for playing the piano accordion, but she held back. She'd work out a way of getting him to play again and surprise Nan. It would work better that way.

Nan glanced out of the window and stiffened. 'Well, look who's coming across the yard. I'll leave you to deal with *him*, Jenny. I shall retire to my armchair with a book.'

Jenny limped to the window. Who did Nan mean by '*him*', using such a derogatory tone?

She squealed, excited to see Matt, with Lottie by his side, talking to the boys who had Mufty between them.

Did she dare go out? She feared Matt would go skulking off when he saw her. How long since she'd been close to her firstborn son? Years, she thought, when Matt had unexpectedly turned up to see her in hospital and it had gone horribly wrong. Jenny's heart began to beat unreasonably fast.

She made a decision. Instead of rushing out there, she'd sit down, pick up her knitting and watch and wait from her chair.

The talking out in the yard seemed to go on forever. Matt squatted down to talk to Warren. Lottie looked pensive as if something was wrong. She stayed close to Matt, really close, and Jenny found that surprising. When they did finally come into the house, they both looked uncannily serious.

Jenny looked up from her knitting, hardly knowing what best to say.

'How are you, Mum?' Matt asked, and his eyes looked steady and strong. But there was a shadow. *It's me,* Jenny thought, *I'm the shadow.*

Matt and Lottie sat down at the table. Jenny frowned. 'So you've come home,' she said, looking directly at Matt.

'Just for a visit,' he said. His voice had deepened, and he had a gingery fuzz of a beard. *Ginger?* Jenny thought. *Why is it ginger?* She put down her knitting. Whatever she said would be wrong. Silence didn't come naturally to Jenny.

'We want to ask you something,' Matt said.

'Go on then. What?'

They looked at each other.

'I would like to go for a holiday,' Lottie said.

'A holiday!'

'With Matt. On *The Jenny Wren*. Just for a few days. Please let me go, Jenny.'

'But – what exactly do you mean by a holiday? I've never had a holiday in me whole life.'

'Matt has got the boat moored at Portreath.' Lottie's dark blue eyes shone with excitement. 'We want to explore the North Cliffs. You can walk to the woods.'

'Sounds lovely,' Jenny said, 'but who's going to go with you? I can't, 'cause of me leg. What about John?'

'Daddy is busy with the gallery,' Lottie said firmly. 'We want to go on our own.'

Jenny looked sceptical. 'Where are you going to sleep?'

'On the boat. Matt does.'

'In that tiny cabin? The two of you?'

'Why not?' Matt said. 'I can sleep on deck under the stars and Lottie can have the cabin.'

Jenny paused to think. Something didn't ring true. Matt and Lottie hadn't even been friends when they were growing up in the Downlong cottage. Why were they suddenly so close?

Nan looked up from her book. 'Over my dead body,' she said, in a voice that would freeze a bonfire. She directed the icicles at Matt. 'Don't you *dare* try and drag Lottie down into your feckless, deplorable lifestyle. Or you'll both end up in a borstal.'

'Nan!' Lottie's eyes blazed, unafraid, stung by the injustice. 'That's not fair. Matt works hard and you haven't even seen his pictures. Why do you hate him so much when he hasn't done anything wrong? It's pure prejudice.'

Jenny saw Matt squeeze Lottie's hand in gratitude. She felt caught in the crossfire, glad of Nan's support but hurt by her ruthless condemnation of Matt. Her firstborn son whose eyes were brave and proud and . . . lost. She ached to hug him. But knew he'd push her away.

Tom and Warren came into the kitchen, bright-faced, just as Nan directed her storm-coloured glare at Lottie's indignant face.

'How dare you speak to me like that, you impudent little madam. After all I've done for you – and your family. I could have turned my back and let you all end up in the workhouse.

155

It's been hellishly difficult for me, sharing my home, and there are times when I wish I'd never suggested it.'

Nan paused for a fit of coughing, her freckled old hands gripping the chair. The coughing seemed to ignite another explosion of pent-up fury – at Lottie. 'The hours and hours I've spent with you – teaching you, reading with you, sitting in Plymouth Hospital with you – and now you speak to me like that, Lottie. I could cry. I could bloody well cry. Time wasted. I feel like telling you to leave this house – the lot of you.' She picked up her walking stick and banged it on the floor in a crescendo of rage.

No one moved until a horrible silence fell. Then there was a crash as Warren again overturned his chair and fled, his footsteps pelting through the hall and out.

'Nan . . .' Jenny dared to go close, 'you'll make yourself ill. Please try to calm down.' She put a hand on Nan's shoulder. 'You're shaking. And burning hot.'

Nan looked directly at Matt. 'You're the one who should go. We were all doing fine until you turned up.'

Matt feigned innocence. 'I'm just sitting here. I'm not doing any harm.' He gave Nan a look loaded with insolence.

'Stop it, Matt,' Jenny said. 'You'll make Nan ill.'

'How?' he challenged.

'Because she's old, and when you're old, anger is bad for you.' She kept a hand on Nan's shoulder, trying to calm her. She looked at Lottie. 'We don't want anything to happen to Nan, do we?'

Lottie shook her head. Obviously Nan's words had

touched her heart and she was feeling guilty. 'I'm sorry, Nan,' she muttered.

'I'm glad to hear it,' Nan said, 'because I love you dearly, child.' She held out an arm and Lottie went to her and became a child again, the child Nan wanted her to be. Lottie had crossed back over the bridge, away from Matt and into the security of the family. Jenny glowered at Matt who was left sitting on his own in an arrogant stance.

Matt is bad for Lottie, she thought, and sensed he wanted a fight. He'd got the familiar challenging smirk on his almost adult face.

'Why has it got to be like this, Matt?' she asked. 'I wanted to see you so much.'

'I haven't done anything wrong.'

'Yes, you have, Matt. You're influencing Lottie – trying to make her talk like you talk. Don't think I don't know.'

'Oh yeah – I grew up being made to think you knew everything. But I know a few things too – like why my dad got drunk and drowned in the harbour.'

Jenny drew her breath in sharply, tasting the hatred Matt was sending her. She felt defeated by it. Whatever she said he would shoot it down. The meeting she'd longed for was cruelly widening the gulf between them.

She opened her mouth to give him a good scolding, but something was happening down in the harbour at that very moment, as if the hand of God had cracked a whip and torn them apart.

The walls of the cottages, the rocks, and even the air

itself cracked and trembled with an almighty reverberating boom, and shockwaves sped out in rings across the sea to distant beaches and cliffs. Before the seagulls could rise and scream above the town, there was a second boom; the same, but louder and more urgent in the stunned, awakened air.

'The maroon!' cried Jenny. 'That's the call-out maroon for the lifeboat. A ship is in trouble out there.' To Jenny, it meant a surge of grief. *Arnie*. At the sound of the maroon, he'd grab his lifejacket and run, no matter what he was doing, to join the RNLI lifeboat crew.

She looked at Matt and saw him transform from an insolent boy to a man who cared about saving lives. As if to honour his father's courageous spirit, Matt was on his feet.

'I'm gone,' he said, and ran, his feet slamming through the hall, thudding like a heartbeat merging with the landscape as he headed towards the harbour.

'You've no business going down there,' Jenny yelled after him.

'He has,' Lottie said, with quiet pride. 'He's a trainee member of the crew.'

Lottie went outside to lean on the garden wall, a lump in her throat as she thought of Matt and watched the sea. One by one, the others came out to join her, first Jenny, then Warren and Tom, and finally Nan. 'I haven't even given him his present,' Lottie said, thinking of the tiny ship in a bottle still in its paper bag upstairs.

The call-out maroon, the lifeboat and its brave crew

touched something deep and unifying in the whole family, and in the town of St Ives. Every cottage door was open, everyone outside, their wordless prayers radiating out across the bay like the silent, shining petals of a lotus.

Chapter 10

Truant

Playing truant from school turned out to be the only solution to Lottie's craving for time with Matt. It was a show passing of time – change to May as referenced later in the chapter. morning, much too nice to be spending it shut up in a classroom. With both Tom and Warren at home with chickenpox, there was no one to tell Jenny of Lottie's absence from school.

A stolen day felt like a luxury version of a normal day, its colours vivid, its fragrance intoxicating, the skylarks and the song thrushes singing forever, the bees humming from deep inside the bells of foxgloves. Lottie skipped and sang on her way down the lane between billows of wild flowers, pink campion, stitchwort and fumitory. The bluebells were almost over, their seed heads nodding between the red sheep sorrel and horsetail grasses.

At the bottom of the lane, Lottie paused to hide her school satchel, which was heavy with books, in a dry hollow under an ancient hawthorn tree. She pushed it under the roots and covered it with dry leaves, having first extracted her lunch pack. At one o'clock in the morning, she'd crept downstairs and hastily made a thick sandwich and wrapped it in greaseproof paper, adding two slabs of flapjack. It fitted neatly in the large pocket of her apron.

She stopped at St Ia's Well and from her cupped hands drank deeply from its bright, refreshing water. Then she leaned on the sea wall above Porthmeor Beach, smiling at the sight of families of seagulls in the shallow edge of the shining water, teaching their speckled young how to wash and preen their feathers. *Free, free, free as a bird, free as a bird for a day*, she thought, and skipped on past the cemetery and the gas works, and along the cobbled streets of Downlong.

Matt was waiting on *The Jenny Wren* at the foot of the stone steps and the moment he spotted her, Lottie saw him change, as if a light in his head had been suddenly switched on. Lottie waved, and he nodded back. The Lanroska men didn't wave. Waving was for girls. The Lanroska men gave a curt nod of acknowledgement, always with a glint in the eyes – a glint of intention, or amusement, or scepticism, or resentment, or love. The glint was like a seed pod with a neatly packed repertoire of feelings.

The way Matt looked at her made Lottie feel a change in herself, her footsteps feather-light, her hair gossamer soft, her skin velvety. Like a dove flying home.

'You came!' His lips brushed her cheek as he helped her step onto the boat. His breath tickled her ear. 'Until we're out of the harbour,' he whispered. His fingertips touched the satin ribbon in her hair, the briefest of gestures, like the nod, but to Lottie it felt as if the ribbon itself had come alive, sending minute pulses of shock through her.

'Are we going to Portreath?' Lottie asked.

'No.' Matt pointed to Godrevy Lighthouse. 'There's white water out there and a swell building. Ken warned me not to try it – you have to go a long way out to sea to avoid Godrevy – that's what the lighthouse is there for. I'll be going back when the sea is calm and I've got plenty of time.' He turned and looked deep into her eyes, reaching her soul. 'I won't take any risks with you on board, Lottie – you are very precious.'

Lottie smiled. 'We can go round to Carbis Bay and walk to the wishing well.'

Matt nodded. 'Yep. No one knows us up there.'

They both had happy memories of the walk through the nut grove to the secluded well on Carrack Gladden. Nan had taken them for picnics and told them the legend of the Maiden's Tears and the fern cave in the cliffs below where the rare Maidenhair Fern grew, watered by the tears she had wept for her lover who had been swept out to sea. It was a love story, now more poignant to both of them.

'I feel blissfully happy,' Lottie said, lifting her face to the sun, the salty breeze tangling her hair as the boat picked up speed. She looked down into the water and saw shoals of tiny, bright green eels, which the fishermen called sandies. The water was glass–clear and she could see the sand eels' pixie-like faces, their slender bodies quivering and rippling in perfect unison.

The day unfurled before her: lying in each other's arms, so happy, wanting nothing more; walking the path over Carrack Gladden, the bracken waist-high, the luminous sunlight filtering through young hazel leaves, and out in the open, the butterflies bobbing over cushions of white campion and yellow trefoil; a picnic by the trickling well water; watching the flocks of gannets diving out over the sea.

A perfect diamond of a day.

Back in St Ives, Olivia walked smartly up The Stennack looking for the school. A few local women glanced at her curiously, but she ignored them. Today her resemblance to Lottie was striking, her hair loose and swinging down her back as she walked. It wasn't just her American clothes that set her apart, but the haunted look of someone whose endless searching finds only emptiness.

The beautifully built granite school was easy to find. Olivia stood looking at it, fascinated to find a school that looked like a cottage. The playground was empty except for a few seagulls and jackdaws parading around. Faint echoes of times tables being chanted came from within. Olivia pushed the heavy door open and went inside, expecting to find a headmaster's office where she would knock on the door. Instead she found herself in a classroom with a number of children, heads down, pencils busy. It looked like the top class – so where was Charlotte?

The teacher had his back to her, writing vigorously with squeaking chalk on the blackboard.

'Sir. Sir! A lady . . .' one of the boys called out, and David Merryn turned, his eyes locking onto hers.

'Good morning. I'm Mrs Olivia De Lumen and I've come to collect my daughter, Charlotte.'

'Ah, yes, well, let's step outside for a minute, shall we?' David Merryn brushed past her. 'Excuse me.' He opened a door and led her into a small office, leaving the classroom door ajar. She noticed his grey threadbare suit had a sheen from too much ironing. It made his legs look like planks. His clothes smelled of chalk.

The busy pencils had stopped in mid-air and the children's faces turned to scrutinise Olivia. One of the girls cupped her hands around her mouth and whispered to the rest of them, 'That's Lottie's American mum.'

David Merryn barked like a dog at a window. 'Turn round and get on with your work. How dare you all stare like that?'

'So where is Charlotte?' Olivia asked. She wondered if David Merryn was married. If not, he'd be quite a catch, even with his plank-like legs.

'We don't know her as Charlotte. To us, she is Lottie Lanroska, and is legally so, I believe.'

Olivia rolled her eyes. 'Okay – Lottie. I have this battle with her every time we meet. She'll have to get over it when she lives with me.'

David Merryn raised his eyebrows, sending deep furrows

over his brow and into his receding hairline. He made no comment but waited, his eyes suspicious.

'I was hoping to take her with me right now,' Olivia said. 'I have two tickets for the train journey to London, Paddington. So – where is she?'

'Lottie is not in school today. We don't know why she's away but her brother has chickenpox so I imagine her mother is keeping her at home. Perhaps she has it too.'

'Oh no!' Olivia smoothed a skein of hair back from her brow. 'May I sit down? I've not been well and I'm not used to walking, especially over these dreadful cobbles.'

'Of course, yes – sit down.' He steered her to two battered chairs against the wall and sat next to her, a mask of courteous concern covering the suspicion in his eyes. He crossed his legs, his foot tapping the air impatiently in a shiny brown brogue.

Olivia took some deep breaths and dabbed her eyes with a lace-edged hanky. 'I can't believe I've got to walk all the way up to that place where she lives. Have you been there? They have chickens running in and out of the house. And the foster mother – Jenny – she has an iron leg. I know she can't help it, but . . .'

'Yes, I do know Jenny,' David Merryn said briskly, 'and I knew her husband, Arnie. They are good, kind parents – and the grandmother is very well educated. Lottie clearly adores her.'

'But I am her birth mother. She belongs with me, don't you think? She will do much better in London. I can get her into a good college and give her a chance to have a career – I don't want her to end up packing fish, which is what most of the young women seem to be doing down here.'

David Merryn's foot was going faster and faster. He seemed deep in thought, irritated by Olivia and anxious about his class of children. 'This is not for me to discuss,' he said. 'You must talk to the Lanroskas about it – and talk to Lottie. And – excuse me saying so – you must also *listen* to Lottie. She's very intelligent. She knows exactly what she wants. I've got great confidence in Lottie and she's working hard to catch up after missing so much school. She will get the chance to go to college here in Cornwall with her friends.'

Olivia was so fragile that her whole life could be ruined by a single comment. A wave of depression surged over her, sweeping away her efforts at being optimistic, turning her credibility into the lace-like foam on the fringe of an incoming tide that would vanish into the sand.

'You're all against me,' she said, her eyes tracing the knots in the polished wooden floor. She didn't want to look at David Merryn anymore, whether he was married or not.

'I can't comment on that remark,' he said, and stood up. 'I really can't help you, Mrs . . .'

'De Lumen. Olivia De Lumen.'

'I have a class to teach, Mrs De Lumen, and I must go back to them.' He held out a chalky dispassionate hand. 'As Lottie isn't here, you should leave now, please.'

'I'm sorry. I'm feeling so ill.'

'I sympathise. But what would you like me to do?'

Olivia battled with the reply, not speaking it aloud, but

locking it into the overflowing hell of her mind. It said, *Want me. I want someone to want me. In body and soul.* She let the words corkscrew away down the same old drain. It was almost full. Ready to start welling up and brimming over. Everyone was so cruel. Even here in England. Why was everyone so cruel to her? She hadn't any friends. Not one. She thought about the bottle of aspirin and how Jenny had been strong enough to chuck it in the fire. But Jenny had spoken to her kindly. It was a friend like Jenny she needed.

'I must return to my class,' David Merryn said. 'Will you please leave – quietly. Good morning.'

Out of the corner of her eye, Olivia watched the plank-like legs disappear into his classroom. Vanishing. Like everything else in her life. If only she could vanish too. Evaporate. Become a lustrous silver cloud drifting above the tantalising world. It should be possible. But first she needed a drink.

Maybe a glass or two of wine would give her the courage to go up to Hendravean and see Jenny – and Charlotte.

'You're not really going to live in London with your birth mother, are you?' Matt asked, his eyes searching Lottie's as they sat by the wishing well on Carrack Gladden.

'Definitely not,' Lottie said. 'She can't make me. You were right about my adoption being legal. Jenny showed me the document.'

'So what are you planning to do now you're old enough to leave school?'

'I'm not going to leave. Mr Merryn wants me in the higher class. In September there will be only five of us: Natalie, Karenza, Morgan, James and me. If I work hard and catch up for the time I missed, I can go to college.'

'What for?'

'I could learn to be a secretary or a journalist – or even a school teacher.'

'You'd be good at that,' Matt said. 'I remember you teaching Tom to read when we were little.'

'I shouldn't have played truant today. I'll have to work twice as hard. But . . .' she slipped her fingers over the back of Matt's hand, 'it's been worth it.'

Matt nodded. 'I should be working too. I've got to keep drawing and selling. It's hard. I have to keep *The Jenny Wren* afloat and in good condition, and make enough to buy food. I don't get free meals like you do at home. It's hard – really hard.'

Lottie traced the bones in the back of his hand, enjoying the texture of his tanned skin, and the fuzz of sun-bleached hairs along his forearm. For a moment they were both silent, watching her small, pale hand exploring his large one. 'You could come home, Matt. Jenny does want you to.'

'Never,' Matt said. 'Don't think I haven't wanted to. I have. But I'd want our real home back – the way it was when Dad was alive.' His voice trembled. 'I still miss him. Do you?'

Lottie leaned her head against his shoulder. His shirt was damp from being used as a towel after their swim. 'I do miss Arnie, even though I've got my real daddy now.' She looked up into Matt's grieving eyes. 'Let's sit quiet and think about him, Matt – keep him alive in our memory.'

They held each other, this time in a peaceful way. Lottie listened to his heart beating so slowly, like a wheel ponderously turning their memories of Arnie, as if the sorrow was a great golden hayfield needing to be raked and aired in the sunshine.

'We feel like one person,' Lottie said, 'don't we?'

'Yep,' Matt whispered and she sensed him soaking up the peace, not wanting to talk.

'But we felt like one person on the boat when we ...' Lottie lowered her voice, 'when we made love, and our hearts were beating madly. We were flying like two birds with beating wings, wings you can hear if you listen.'

Matt kissed the top of her head and she felt his breath in her hair. 'Go on talking to me, Lottie. Hearing you talk is like filling an empty space in my heart.'

'Love isn't just a madly beating heart,' she said. 'Love is sharing stillness and peace together, like we're doing now.'

'That's why you'd be a good teacher,' Matt murmured into her hair, ''cause no one ever teaches peace, do they? All I ever remember learning was how to fight.'

'How did you learn to make love?' Lottie asked. 'You're so good at it – like Romeo in *Romeo and Juliet*. You make me feel as if my bones are made of velvet, and you make my whole body sing – even my toes are singing. I've never felt so wonderful.'

She heard the smile in his voice as he said, 'I used to

listen – when Dad was alive. At night I'd lie in bed, wide awake, and listen to them talking and laughing. I heard every word when I was a little boy – I was a horrible little boy, always in trouble, but I used to lie in bed, and sit in school, dreaming of being like a prince and finding my princess, and she looked just like you. Listening to Mum and Dad, the happiness used to come through the walls, and I realised love was something worth fighting for.' He pulled her closer. 'Stay with me, Lottie. Let's never be apart.'

'Let's make a wish – in the wishing well.' Lottie sat up and fished in the pocket of her apron.

'What are those for?' Matt laughed as she extracted two bent pins.

'Nan told me – and she was deadly serious – that when you make a wish in this particular well, you must drop a bent pin in the water.'

'But why a bent pin?'

'Well, according to Nan, a bent pin means you are prepared to bend the rules.'

'I like that!'

'Believing in magic is bending the rules, so when the fairies find a bent pin, they can make your wish come true.'

'So where are all these fairies running round with bent pins? You don't believe Nan's tales do you, Lottie?'

'Nan's tales are like oyster shells. Each one has a magical pearl of truth inside.'

Matt looked stunned at her description. He allowed the scepticism to leave his mind for a suspended moment as they dropped the bent pins into the bright water and made a silent wish.

'I think our wishes were the same,' Lottie said, 'but we mustn't speak them.'

They ate lunch watching a pod of dolphins playing out in the bay. Drowsy in the afternoon sun, they fell asleep on cushions of turf, with curls of bracken and lofty spires of foxglove towering over them against a sky of powder blue.

The sound of waves and skylarks melted into their dreams, and the fierce May sun burned down on Lottie's face as she lay blissfully with her head in the hollow of Matt's shoulder. To sleep pressed tightly into the warmth of another being had a profoundly tranquillising effect on her. She felt safe and recharged with love as if it was permeating her body for all time, like crystals in the granite. She didn't want to wake up, just to stay there with her arm stretched over Matt's taut young body, his breathing soothingly rhythmic.

Lottie made an effort to synchronise her own breath with his, wanting to feel them breathing as one being. A hypnotic peacefulness rolled her consciousness down and down into a dream that waited, fathoms deep, below the sky, below the waves, below the sun's dazzle.

In her dream she was breathing with Matt and they were diving down through green translucence into deep, dark purple waters. And there on the ocean floor, lying in the sand, was an oyster shell. It wasn't just any old random shell. She knew immediately it was special. It was waiting there for her, and it was the shell she had told Matt about, the shell with the pearl of truth, wrapped in the iridescent layers of legend.

With her hair streaming, she swam down towards it, her hands outstretched. The minute she touched it, the oyster shell began to open, and Matt detached his long limbs from her, letting her go, making her hold her breath until her lungs were on fire. Without him she felt stressed and responsible, compelled to stay and watch the oyster shell struggling to open.

Lottie forced herself to stay down there until, in a moment of glory, the shell finally burst open, and inside its luminous cavern lay a shining pearl. She picked it up and held it against her heart as she swam up and up until she surfaced through the nets of sunlight. Clutching the precious pearl, she swam to *The Jenny Wren* where Matt was sitting with his head in his hands.

'It's okay, Matt,' she said, and she put the shining pearl into his hand. They both stared at it with the utmost joy. It was then that they heard Arnie's voice. It came from the sea all around them. Lottie cried out in fright. 'Where are you, Arnie?' and he answered immediately, 'I'm in the pearl. Look after me. I'm very small.'

Suddenly, she snapped back into consciousness, and the colours around her looked earthy and heavy after the iridescence of the oyster shell in her dream.

Matt was awake, holding her, his face a mix of amusement and concern. 'You were dreaming, Lottie. You cried out.'

She tried to tell the dream to Matt but all he said was, 'Your face is red as a strawberry.'

Then, across the bay came the distant chimes of the church clock. 'Oh no!' Lottie was horrified. 'It can't be four o'clock already! There's no way I can get home in time for Jenny to think I've been to school – I'm in terrible trouble.'

'Momter,' Warren mumbled.

'That's right – a thermometer,' Jenny said, before she tucked it under Warren's armpit. 'Hold it tight and we'll count to sixty. Then it will tell me what your temperature is.'

'Wuzzat?'

'Temperature? It means how hot you are.'

Warren looked wizened lying on the sofa, his face flushed, his eyelids heavy. He gazed at Jenny constantly, his eyes following her every movement. 'Dogs do that,' Nan said. 'It's anxiety.'

Jenny thought of Nan's words as she made a glass of rosehip cordial for Warren. She had no one to ask except Nan, and Nan was often crabby and uncommunicative, tossing out crumbs of wisdom and walking away. Jenny missed her neighbour Millie who had lived next door to their old home in Downlong. Millie had a wonderful way with children and she'd mothered Lottie and Tom, even Jenny. Matt had been difficult but Millie understood how to handle him, finding the good bits of his complex personality and building his confidence. When Millie had left St Ives to live in Penzance with her sister, it had been like a bereavement.

Millie would know exactly how to treat Warren. *If only I could find her*, Jenny thought, a plan hatching in her mind.

Warren took the glass of cordial eagerly and downed it in noisy gulps, his eyes still watching Jenny.

'You sound like the tide coming in,' she said, but Warren didn't smile. Humour was lost on him, even gentle humour. *What could have happened to make a ten-year-old boy so deadly serious?* Jenny wondered. The only time Warren came alive was when he played the piano accordion, but despite Jenny's efforts to encourage him, Warren refused to pick it up again, even if Tom left it lying on the sofa. He eyed it, and crept round it in a deliberate circle. Then Nan would come in and bellow, '*What* is that instrument doing there?'

Right now, Warren had a fever, and it was difficult to know how best to look after him. Jenny glanced at the clock. Lottie would read Warren a story and help him settle down. It was five o'clock. Where was she? Jenny felt annoyed but not worried. Lottie would be with her father or Morwenna.

She left Warren dozing on the sofa and worked in the kitchen, hoping to spot Lottie coming up the lane, her school bag heavy with books.

Since her illness, Lottie had come home from school pale-faced and serious. The long school day seemed to be draining her. So when Lottie finally came swinging in, her nose and cheeks a fiery pink from the sun, Jenny looked at her suspiciously. It wasn't just the sunburn. It was that strange radiance again, a glow all around her, and in her eyes both a light and a shadow.

Jenny trusted Lottie – didn't she? 'Where've you been, my

girl?' She found herself pursuing the shadow. Evasiveness —
deep in the eyes. 'How come you've caught the sun?'

'I went to sleep at lunch time.'

'What? In the playground?'

Lottie looked at her silently.

'So . . . how long do you get for lunch?'

'Half an hour.'

'You couldn't have burned like that in half an hour,' Jenny
frowned. 'Your nose is already peeling.' She opened the
heavy oak door to the medicine cupboard, which was a stone
cubbyhole to keep the remedies cool. 'Calamine lotion is
what you need.' She gave the bottle a vigorous shake, opened
it and dabbed some of the pink lotion on Lottie's blistered
skin with a piece of cotton wool.

Lottie shook her head. 'I don't want it on my face, Jenny.
It looks unspeakably disgusting.'

'You sound like Nan!' Jenny teased. 'Let it dry and it
will take the fire out of your sunburn.' She tried to make
eye contact but Lottie wouldn't look at her. 'You'd better
tell me where you've been today. I hope you haven't been
playing truant.'

Lottie lifted her chin. 'I don't want to talk about it,' she
said airily. 'I've got homework to do.'

'I was hoping you'd read Warren a story.'

Lottie sighed. 'Okay — on one condition,' she said. 'I'll
read Warren a story if you stop interrogating me, Jenny. I'm
not a child.'

Jenny blew her cheeks out. 'All right, madam, but I'll be

watching you,' she threatened. 'This had better not have anything to do with Matt.'

Guilt flickered in Lottie's eyes. 'I said I don't want to talk about it.'

'I understand that – but, Lottie, you are all right, aren't you?'

'Perfect, thank you.'

'And you'd tell me if anything *bad* happened to you?'

'I might. Or I might not.'

Jenny stared at her, a wad of cotton wool still in her hand. Lottie could be infuriatingly stubborn. She was looking at Jenny now and the mysterious radiance was still there, illuminating a very assertive, adult stare.

I suppose I'll have to let her be, Jenny thought.

Chapter 11

Unthinkable

Lottie stared at Morwenna in horror. 'That's not true – is it?'

The two girls were sitting on the warm sand at the top of Porthmeor Beach. Above their heads the sand martins flitted to and fro, feeding their young, their nests in cosy holes at the top of the sandy cliff.

'It is true, Lottie. Cross my heart,' Morwenna insisted, her eyes soft and truthful. 'My mum explained it to me after she told me off for lying in the grass with Bennie Jenkins. We were only kissing, but she didn't believe me.'

'Nobody's told me,' Lottie said.

'Well, you haven't got a proper mum, have you?'

'What do you mean?'

'Jenny's got her leg in an iron – and that lady from America doesn't look after you, does she? Even if she is your real mum. And as for Nan – she's a dragon in an apron; everyone's scared stiff of her.'

Lottie tried to digest her friend's tactless honesty. At any other time it might have made her angry, but so great was her need to understand Morwenna's shocking revelations about how babies were made that she bypassed the anger and let it run beside her like a barking dog. The feelings inside her were building storm waves foaming with curiosity, disbelief and panic.

'Come and talk to my mum if you don't believe me, Lottie. She said you could,' Morwenna reminded her.

'No, I couldn't. She'd gossip.'

'No, she wouldn't.'

'She would.'

Morwenna looked hurt. 'My mum's rough an' ready, but she's kind to me – and she tells me anything I need to know.'

Lottie stared at her friend. Morwenna sat in the soft white sand, her legs tucked under the heavy drapes of her only dress, which had once been red but was now a threadbare russet colour, sun-bleached along the folds and frayed around the hem. It was too small for her now, the fabric straining over her breasts, but Lottie couldn't remember her wearing anything else. Morwenna had two aprons, both made from old bed sheets, and she went to work in the bakery in her brother's boots. She never wore a new hair ribbon so Lottie had given her a new cerise pink one from America. Morwenna loved it too much to ever take it off, and it was looking tatty.

'My American mother has gone to London for a while – thank goodness,' Lottie said, 'but I've got my father now and he's kind to me.'

Morwenna snorted. 'But he's a man, and you can't talk to men about periods and babies. And if he's kind, you watch out, Lottie – he might interfere with you.'

'What do you mean – interfere?'

Morwenna gave her a pitying look. 'He's a pervert, Lottie, it's time someone told you.'

'He is *not* a pervert.' Lottie clenched her hands together to stop herself from slapping Morwenna. She wasn't actually sure what a pervert was, except that it was something bad and secretive, something horribly alive in the catacombs of shame.

'He is, Lottie – everyone knows. He stands in his gallery doorway leering at all the women – and he paints women with no clothes on.'

'He is *not*,' Lottie said, furious with Morwenna. 'How dare you insult my father!'

Morwenna pumped herself up, towering in the sand like a territorial blackbird. 'Don't shout at me, Lottie. I'm your friend and I'm trying to tell you a few home truths. You're too innocent.'

'I am not.'

'Yes, you are. I know you study books and all that, but you still don't know things that really matter.'

'What things?'

'Like how babies are made.'

Blinding tears of rage ran down Lottie's cheeks. She hardly heard what her friend was saying now. Morwenna's flagrant accusation against her father, her gentle father who'd been so kind to her, had stung. How could he be a 'pervert'? And how could her best friend say something so insensitive?

'Aw, don't cry, Lottie.' Morwenna leaned over to give her a hug.

'Don't touch me.' Lottie twisted out of reach, her mouth pursed, her mind struggling with the enormous worry that must be kept secret. She and Matt had promised each other. Secret love. Like Romeo and Juliet. Love forever trapped. What would happen when its delicate eggshell cracked open? *I am the shell*, Lottie thought, *and my best friend is smashing it*.

Morwenna's eyes became insolent and glinting with confidence, as if she held all the cards in a game.

'Anyway, it's true what I told you,' Morwenna tossed her mane of tangled hair, 'about babies. And it's true your dad's a pervert – so stop being so hoity-toity.'

The eggshell trembled. Lottie jumped to her feet. 'I hate you, Morwenna Bartle,' she screamed, 'and I'll never speak to you again.'

'Oh yes you will,' Morwenna teased. She climbed to her feet. ''Cause I'm the only friend you've got, and if you're doing what I think you're doing out on that boat with Matt, you're heading for trouble and you're gonna need me, d'you hear?' she yelled as Lottie turned to walk away. 'Don't say I didn't warn you. You're heading for trouble and you'll end up an outcast.'

Lottie ploughed her way across the sun-baked sand, Morwenna's words flying after her like wasps. Scarily true. 'You're gonna need me, Lottie Lanroska. See if you don't, Miss Hoity Toity.'

Lottie didn't look back. Gnawing at the edges of her fury was a doom-laden suspicion that Morwenna was right. If the unthinkable happened, Morwenna and her mum would be her only friends. She'd lose everything: Jenny, Nan, her home, her education. Her future.

Only Matt would stand by her. Wouldn't he?

Lottie didn't feel like going home. She couldn't bear to see her father – or anyone. She didn't even want to go to the harbour and see if *The Jenny Wren* was there.

She stumbled along the rocky path around the island. Surf was breaking on dark, wet rocks in rising fans of spray, the drops whiter than snow against a sea of peacock blue. Halfway along the track was a massive boulder of granite, bearded with sage-green lichen. Tufts of white sea campion and red stonecrop grew in its cracks, and a lone seagull was there, just sitting, eyeing people.

Lottie leaned against the rock, alone like the seagull, her entire life passing before her in a useless pageant.

Had she and Matt made a baby? Was it, even now, growing inside her? She put her hands over her tummy. It felt normal except for the scar from her operation, which was still a bit tender.

As the anger subsided, Morwenna's words flew through her mind, rippling like a banner. Morwenna told lies, but only when she was in trouble. Denial-type lies. She didn't, and *couldn't*, fantasise. She was Lottie's best friend. Her eyes had shone with honesty and concern when she was telling Lottie how babies were conceived.

I was wrong not to listen, Lottie thought, annoyed with herself. *She's right – I was being hoity-toity.*

Lottie sat facing the sea, her back against the warm rock. She picked at the seed heads of grasses, tearing the bleached ripe seeds from their stalks. It wasn't something she normally did. Watching the seeds trickle from her hands, seeing them cluster on patches of bare soil seemed to be a lesson she had never learned: their mysterious inner power to grow and reproduce.

I am the earth, she thought, *and Matt is the seed. Matt gave me a seed. Well, he might have. And he didn't mean to. Because neither of us knew.*

Each thought seared into her, burning her mind and all the books in there, the stories and the poetry. *We were so young when we lost our family. Matt was eleven and I was ten when everything was snatched away. Arnie died. Jenny got polio. And we were imprisoned in that orphanage where we worked like slaves and learned nothing except how to survive.*

Miss Poltair had masterminded the girls' part of the orphanage. She was cruel and cold, stout and unsmiling. Joyless. Lottie did remember her giving the girls a talk about menstruation and how to manage it. The girls had sat rigid, hardly breathing. Menstruation was made to sound like a monthly punishment for being female. Babies were not mentioned, and neither were men.

Lottie sighed. Somewhere between menstruation and romantic literature, a vital truth had been missed.

*

'I'm not a childminder,' Nan said, 'especially for *that*.' She jerked her thumb at Warren who was finishing his breakfast, his eyes wary in the presence of Nan.

'Please, Nan. Just this once,' Jenny pleaded. 'I'm taking Lottie to the doctor. Warren's not well enough to go to school yet.'

Nan frowned. She picked up Lottie's plate, which had an untouched slice of buttered toast on it. 'Lottie's all right, isn't she? Why take her to the doctor?'

'Because all last week she was like this,' Jenny explained, 'refusing to eat her breakfast. She says she feels sick, but she still went to school. If it was only the odd day I wouldn't be concerned, but she's been sick every morning for a whole week, and she's getting worse. We can't take any risks, Nan, not after the illness she had on the ship. Better safe than sorry.'

'And where is she now?' Nan asked.

'In the bathroom. You should have seen her, Nan. She went white and just ran upstairs. She can't stop being sick.'

'Hmm.' Nan narrowed her eyes in silence.

'He won't be any trouble – will you, Warren?' Jenny said, and Warren shook his head. 'You don't need to do anything except keep an eye on him, Nan.'

Nan agreed reluctantly. She felt irritable around Warren and only gave in for Lottie's sake. In her opinion, Lottie's sickness could be fixed with ginger tea. And as for Warren, Nan found him infuriatingly gauche and uncommunicative. She marvelled at Jenny's patience with him and had to admit that progress had been made. But what was behind Warren's fathomless eyes, Nan had no idea, and her attempts to find out had been a waste of time. Warren remained stubbornly unresponsive and Nan resented him being there, another mouth to feed and a drain on Jenny's energy. It had been hard enough for her to get used to sharing her home with Jenny. Without her, Nan would have handed Warren to the welfare officer.

She stood in the open doorway and watched them go down the lane, Lottie white-faced and unwilling, Jenny limping along determinedly. Once they had disappeared from view, Nan made herself a bowl of porridge with a swirl of honey. Warren sat hunched on the deep windowsill, his chin on his knees, his eyes studying a flock of yellowhammers flying over the gorse flowers. Or was he staring out at the Clodgy rocks, remembering his time of living wild?

Nan made no attempt to talk to him, but she couldn't help sensing the loneliness within the strange boy. Surely he had a family somewhere. Whoever they were, Nan felt angry with them and began mentally rehearsing what she would say to them if they bothered to turn up. Annoyed that Jenny had made no effort to trace his parents, Nan began to think she should take matters into her own hands. A bit of private research. A few discreet trips out in the car. What if she drove around some of the villages and asked questions? And, why not take Warren with her? Maybe he would recognise a place where he'd lived.

Warren was looking at her anxiously, appearing to sense her thoughts. Nan finished her porridge, struggled to her feet and began clearing the table. Lottie or Tom would have jumped up and helped her, she reflected. They were good kids. *Thanks to Jenny*, Nan thought, begrudgingly. But Warren didn't do anything, nor did he seem inclined to do anything. He just sat. Like a little old man. *A grumpy gnome*, Nan thought mischievously.

It seemed odd to be marooned with a boy who wouldn't or couldn't talk. Words were no good, so how could she communicate with him? How could she reach that spark of intelligence in his eyes? Nan believed everything happened for a reason. Was this time alone with Warren a celestial masterplan to encourage her to engage with him? *If I opened my mouth, it would frighten Warren to death*, Nan thought, so she kept it shut. But music talks to the soul without words; maybe she could reach Warren with music . . .

Nan began to hum, beginning with 'The Ash Grove', and when she glanced at Warren, there was a subtle change, as if the soul of him had suddenly arrived to take over the grumpy gnome.

In her youth, Nan had been a music teacher and an opera singer. She had sung the role of Brünnhilde in Wagner's *The Ring of the Nibelungs*, and had taken solo parts in many concerts. Her sequinned dresses, now much too small, hung silent in a fusty wardrobe in the attic, glittering weakly from the occasional sunbeam venturing through a crack in the door. She longed to sing again, and did so only when she was alone.

Nan went on humming 'The Ash Grove' and variations on it, adding a bit of finger-tapping on saucepan lids and cake tins. She pretended Warren wasn't there. This was Nan on her own having fun.

When she started humming 'Scarborough Fair', Warren moved. Quiet as a rabbit on his bare feet, he darted into the hall and up the stairs.

Nan pretended not to notice, but went on humming, half listening to what Warren might be doing up there. She sat down in her chair, encouraged by Bartholomew, who jumped onto her lap and spread himself out, his sumptuous paws reaching up towards her face. He seemed determined to keep her still, his purring adding a kind of rhythm to the humming. Nan chuckled to herself. It was a long time since she and Bartholomew had made music together.

She heard Warren plodding downstairs, moving carefully for once instead of hurtling down. *What is he up to?* Nan wondered. Then he appeared shyly in the doorway with Tom's piano-accordion strapped around his small body.

The eagerness and sparkle in Warren's eyes, and the touch of Bartholomew's paws on her neck, restrained Nan from shouting at him for daring to help himself to that instrument. To shout at a child in such a fragile moment would have been like killing a butterfly. So Nan held herself and waited, bewitched by the engaging smile on Warren's wizened face as he began to play, hesitantly at first, then swept away by the music.

He played 'The Ash Grove', then 'Scarborough Fair' and 'Trelawny'. On and on he played, filling the house with music as Nan sat spellbound, tears of joy pouring down her wrinkled cheeks. After all the grand operas and concerts Nan had done in her life, the exotic venues, the sequinned gowns, the passion and the applause, Warren's unexpected performance was reconnecting her with the very roots of music.

Humility was a rare feeling for Nan, but it tugged at her now, seeing this homeless, inarticulate boy, the piano-accordion covering most of his body, his bony knees on the edge of the chair, his little face shining with joy. With all her defences down, Nan bonded with him forever.

'You'll go on to school, will you?' Jenny asked, relieved to see Lottie looking more at ease when she came out of Dr Tregullow's surgery.

'Yes, I'll go to school.'

'Tell them why you're late.'

'Okay, Jenny.'

'What did he say?' Jenny searched Lottie's face for clues.

She shrugged. 'Nothing much. He said I was healthy and normal.'

Jenny frowned. 'Oh good. Though I can't say I agree with that.'

Lottie sighed. '*Must* you interrogate me? I just want to go to school and catch up on what I've missed.'

'Go on then – you go.' Jenny gave Lottie a hug. 'See you later.' She watched from the waiting-room window as Lottie ran up The Stennack towards the school.

Dr Tregullow popped his head round the surgery door and invited her in for a chat. Jenny went, hoping for more information than Lottie had given her.

She sat down on a leather chair – everything in the consulting room seemed to be leather, even the surface of the doctor's vast desk. He wore a tweed jacket with leather buttons, with leather patches sewn over the elbows. A pigskin doctor's bag stood half open on the desk and horse harnesses hung on the walls, dark old bridles and heavy black straps covered in horse brasses.

'So how's that leg getting on?' Dr Tregullow enquired, looking at Jenny's iron calliper.

'I'm managing, thank you,' Jenny said, 'but what about our Lottie? What exactly is wrong with her?'

The doctor looked over the rim of a pair of round glasses. 'Nothing to worry about, Mrs Lanroska. In my experience, girls of her age are often inexplicably sick, and frankly it's all in the mind. Young Lottie's had a lot of upheaval this last year and she's facing the dreaded exams.'

'I don't agree with you,' Jenny dared to say. 'She's never been sick like this – sick one minute and going to school the next. I worry about the peritonitis coming back.'

'No. She's clear of that, I can assure you. However . . .' Dr Tregullow dipped a gleaming fountain pen into a bottle of Quink, keeping Jenny in suspense as he flicked the tiny silver lever, releasing it slowly to allow the ink to fill the rubber tube inside. Then he made a mess with it, dropping blots onto his leather desk and mopping it up with a tartan hanky. 'Dratted thing.' He wrote something on a pad of paper.

'Are you writing a prescription?' Jenny asked, hoping for a magic potion in a dark bottle which would stop Lottie being sick.

'No. There's nothing I can give her today. I'm just making a note of her symptoms.'

'But what if she goes on being sick? It's been every day this last week.'

'I don't think we should jump to conclusions,' he said. 'If it continues, then bring her back for further examination.'

'So you didn't examine her tummy?'

'No. She didn't want me to so I didn't force the issue. She seemed nervous and jumpy. Given her age and the fact that her periods still haven't returned after her illness, I think it may be hormonal moodiness, if you understand what I mean.'

'Oh I do, yes.'

'Keep an eye on her, and don't be cross with her for being sick. I'm sure it will resolve itself one way or another. Is there any chance she doesn't want to go to school? Deep down, I mean. She bottles it up, doesn't she?'

'No, she likes school and she wants to study.' Jenny remembered the sunny day when Lottie had played truant. She wasn't going to tell the doctor that.

'Has she got friends?'

'Oh yes – she's thick as thieves with Morwenna Bartle and I'm not happy about it. Morwenna is a bad girl, don't you think?'

'I can't comment on another patient, I'm afraid.'

Jenny left the surgery feeling frustrated. It had been a waste of time. She wanted answers. Doctors were a pompous bunch, in her opinion, especially this one who hadn't got a family of his own. She felt even more worried. Who could she talk to? If only Millie were there.

It was raining as she limped down The Stennack and she didn't feel like getting soaked on the long walk home. She decided to go and see John. She wound her way through the narrow alleyways and bumped into Maudie Tripconey, who was coming out of the bakery. Jenny said good morning and tried to walk on but Maudie homed in on her. "Ow's yer leg?' she asked, trying to be nice.

'It's a nuisance,' Jenny said, 'but at least I can walk.'

'Hmm.' Maudie filled the space in front of her between a parked car and the wall. Her eyes glittered. 'That girl of yours, you want to watch her,' she warned.

'Lottie?'

'Yes, Lottie. She goes off with your boy, Matt, on his boat. And, believe me . . .' Maudie lowered her voice and pushed her pug-like face close to Jenny, 'they'm up to no good, those two. You watch out. Lottie's a nice girl, I like her – everyone does. But that boy, great tall thing, he were always trouble, weren't he? He'll lead her into trouble – trouble you don't want, I'm tellin' you.'

'Don't you criticise my family, Maudie. Mind your own business,' Jenny fired back, tossing her head. 'Excuse me, I haven't got time for this.' She squeezed past Maudie.

'You'll wish you'd listened to me, Jenny Lanroska,' Maudie called after her. 'I'm trying to warn you, but you can't see it, oh no. You go on then – too good to talk to me now you live in that posh house up there.'

It was hard to look dignified with an iron leg. By the time Jenny reached John's gallery, her face was flushed with the worry. *Interfering old bat*, she muttered to herself. *And she pongs to high heaven.*

John was busy painting in his studio, his smock covered in colour. The smell of turpentine and oil paint was somehow calming, as was his greeting.

'Jenny! What a nice surprise!' John put his brushes down, his eyes calm and bright as he gazed at her. 'Your hair is sparkling!' he breathed. 'And your face is glowing. You look so beautiful – like a rose in the rain.'

'Why, thank you, John. I haven't had a compliment like that since I was a girl,' Jenny said coyly. She took a step back, thinking John was too close. His eyes continued appraising her. 'Can I sit down for a minute, please?' she asked. 'I'm worn out.'

'Of course, my dear.'

There was only one chair in his studio, a Lloyd Loom cane chair painted green. It was piled high with sketch pads and books. He picked it all up in an armful and dumped it on the paint-spattered floor. 'Would you like a cup of coffee?' he asked.

'Coffee? I don't know – never tasted it.'

'You'll like it,' John assured her. 'It won't take a minute. I've got an electric kettle now.'

'All right – I'd like to try it.' Jenny tried to relax as John went into the kitchen. If only he knew how hard it was for her to be there in the studio, the very cottage that had been her home. She felt nostalgic and tried to distract herself by gazing around at the paintings on the wall, embarrassed to see one of a woman with no clothes on. Jenny tried not to look at it, but the woman's face was familiar. *Olivia!* He'd painted her in the nude. Was John still in love with his ex-wife, Jenny wondered. She couldn't stop looking at it. The eyes were so compelling.

'Don't take any notice of that one,' John said. 'I painted it years ago, before Lottie was born.'

'Has Lottie seen it?'

'Yes. She doesn't like it, but at her age she wouldn't, would she? No. She sits with her back to it when she comes here.' John put two mugs of steaming coffee on an upturned fish crate. 'I've added some brown sugar to yours.'

Jenny sipped the unfamiliar coffee. 'Mmm, it's lovely.'

John sat close to her on a kitchen chair and they talked about Lottie. Why Jenny had taken her to the doctor and how she was getting on at school. 'I've got high hopes for her,' John said, proudly. 'She's a bright girl – she's sure to get into college. I wouldn't want her to end up packing fish.'

'She won't,' Jenny said firmly. 'She'll have a career. I'm proud of her too and so is Nan.'

'You should be proud of young Matt too,' John said. 'Did you know Lottie brought him to see me?'

'No,' Jenny said, surprised. 'Lottie's getting increasingly secretive.'

'Well, I liked Matt a lot,' John said. 'He ought to have a career. He's a gifted artist, you know. He brought his sketches to show me – in fact, he asked if I would store them here for him. He was worried about them getting wet in the boat so I told him I would. I might even frame a few for him and put them on the wall. He's a brave young fellow and I'd like to help him.'

Jenny gulped. It was hard to admit she hadn't even seen Matt's pictures, especially to John, who was looking at her with concern.

'You look upset, my dear,' he said gently.

Jenny couldn't speak. A bit of kindness from John and she'd fall apart. She didn't want him to see her weakness; she wanted him to have confidence in her as Lottie's adoptive mother. She must be strong and cheerful. Not weepy and needy.

'Would you like to see Matt's work?' John said, instinctively rescuing her.

Jenny nodded. 'I'd love to.'

John opened a wide shallow drawer under the worktop and took out a homemade cardboard folder. Even seeing his name, *Matt Lanroska*, beautifully inscribed on the front made Jenny worse. Usually she was in control and able to laugh and chat convincingly when she felt terrible, but now, with John's kind face hovering over Matt's folder, her strength seemed to have deserted her. She felt vulnerable and weepy. And John had noticed. She could tell from the way he kept peering at her, with kindness in his dark blue eyes, so like Lottie's. Jenny held herself still and quiet as he opened the folder.

'I was moved by his story,' John said. 'He'd no money so he started out with just two pencils, an HB and a 2B. These are the first ones he did at Carn Brea.'

Jenny felt her eyes widening. 'They're marvellous!' she managed to say, fascinated by the way Matt had boldly sketched the great granite boulders and used them to frame bits of the distant landscape, exquisite little cameos of tiny tin mines, cottages and trees.

'They get better,' John said, pleased at her reaction. 'These next ones were done on the beach at Portreath.'

'Oh, look at that!' Jenny breathed, marvelling at his swirly drawings of seals and sea caves. The seals' eyes seemed to stare off the page, so real, so peaceful, and so . . . motherly. More motherly than she had been. She managed to speak the word aloud: 'Motherly'. The feel of it on her tongue was velvety and reproachful. She held up her hand. 'Don't show me any more. I must go home.' She tried to stand up and leave in a dignified manner.

'Jenny!' The tender way he said her name in a low, kindly voice was both healing and disempowering. She sat down again and John's arm was around her shoulders, his hand patting gently, and she let him pull her in closer, her head resting on the cool thick cotton of his smock, smelling the oil paint, hearing the slow, calm beat of his heart. 'I know how it hurts to lose a child.' He kept repeating it, like a mantra, and it somehow simplified everything, gave her freedom to cry and time to recover.

Eventually she felt peace returning, as if John's steady heartbeat had restored her. She detached herself, found her hanky and dried the tears from her hot cheeks. 'I'm sorry, I . . .'

'Don't apologise.' John faced her squarely, a hand on each of her shoulders, compelling her to meet his eyes. 'You've been a wonderful mother, Jenny. Wonderful. I know that from Lottie, and I can see it for myself. Matt does love you – deep down, he does – and he'll come back to you in time. Just hold the faith and believe in him. He's a young man now and young men are full of feelings they can't handle. He'll come back – believe me – and it's not your fault. You be proud of who you are, Jenny.'

'I . . . don't know who I am anymore.' Jenny looked down at her iron leg.

'You're a beacon of love and courage,' John said, and she felt the power of him, the stability, and the passion in his gaze as he said, 'You're everyone's mother, Jenny. And you're full of children.'

It seemed an odd thing to say. But Jenny loved it. The words went straight to her heart and stayed with her. She sighed. 'You've made me feel better, John. Thanks.' She wanted to kiss him, but held back. 'I can look at the rest of Matt's pictures now. Then I simply must go. I left Nan minding Warren so goodness knows what I'll find when I get back.' She grinned, feeling more like herself.

Half an hour later she set off on the long walk home, her iron leg lighter, her mind free of torment. She loved the image John had given her. It sang in her heart.

Chapter 12

Warren

'I don't think we can manage.'

Nan's face was serious as she gathered the family around the kitchen table on the first day of the children's long summer break from school. Between her freckled hands was the money box, a battered red OXO tin with a lid. She prised it open and showed them the stash of coins inside. Pennies and halfpennies, threepenny bits, sixpences and shillings, a few florins and half-crowns.

'Cor – we can have ice creams!' Tom said, and Jenny gave his leg a smack under the table. 'Ow.' He glared at her indignantly.

'Don't you dare even speak,' Jenny hissed. 'Listen to Nan. This is deadly serious.'

Nan fired a glint of approval at her across the table. She burrowed under the coins and extracted a few ten-shilling notes and pound notes. 'This looks like a lot,' she said, 'but it's got to feed five people *and* buy corn for the chickens *and* pay the milkman *and* buy shoes if anyone needs them.'

'I do. Mine are pinching,' Tom said, 'and Warren does too.'

'Shush.' This time he got a fierce poke from Jenny and a steely glare from Nan.

Lottie sat quietly next to Jenny. She and Jenny had done it all before. Poverty. Burning the chairs to keep warm. A bad time they both wanted to forget. It was different now, for Lottie anyway. Her father would buy her shoes and meals if needed, though she didn't think it would be right or tactful to say so.

She still couldn't help feeling sad, even though her morning sickness had disappeared, she'd finished her exams and she felt well and energetic. It was July, and the first hazy blue morning of the summer holidays should have been a joyful time of freedom, with long days of swimming and picnics stretching ahead. Carefree days.

Warren sat leaning on Jenny, looking at Nan with anxious eyes. But he was better. Since Nan had taken him under her wing, he'd gained confidence, still refusing point-blank to go to school, but thriving at home with Nan's music lessons and stories, and Jenny's patient, loving efforts to teach him to talk.

'The only money we have is what I earn from Mufty's cart,' Nan said. 'The tourists are flocking into St Ives now and I can't make enough things to sell. Jenny is knitting hats, but now you children must help me too – think of things you can make and sell. We've got to all pull together. Otherwise, come the winter, there'll be no money in this tin.'

Everyone looked gloomy.

'You can buzz off now.' Nan put the lid back on the OXO tin. 'I'll expect you to come back at tea time with some ideas.'

'But Nan, my mother is coming tomorrow. I'm supposed to spend time with her,' Lottie said.

'Pick her brains,' Jenny said. 'She must know how to make something.'

Lottie frowned. 'She won't understand why we need to.'

'Then tell her,' Nan said, picking up her flower basket, scissors and raffia. 'I shall be in the garden. You could come and help me, Lottie, couldn't you?'

'Okay.' Lottie relished the thought of spending time with Nan in amongst the lavender heads and the montbretia and marigolds. She loved to stand under the massive spires of echium and hear the bees working away inside its blue flowers. Even taller were the dracaena palm trees with their great trusses of creamy white flowers, their heady perfume making the air deliciously fragrant. The tropical garden was Nan's pride and joy. It grew in its own microclimate, in a hollow sheltered from the sea winds by an arc of thick tamarisk and cypress trees. Enormous succulents grew there with crimson-black rosettes of shiny leaves, and in the south-facing, sun-baked rockery grew masses of daisy-like flowers in the hottest colours, tumbling down over the rocks. It was a perfect place to hide and dream on a hot afternoon.

Olivia can wait, Lottie thought. She suspected Nan knew she didn't want to see her birth mother and had deliberately led her into the tropical garden to lift her spirits. Jenny would deal with her, Lottie thought confidently. She had gone into the kitchen to make biscuits, with Tom helping her. They'd pack them in little squares of butter muslin tied with scraps of bright ribbon for Nan to sell.

Everyone was busy and no one noticed Warren slipping away in his bare feet, his shoes hanging around his neck from the knotted laces. Despite the hot sun, he wore his cap and jacket and over one shoulder carried the piano-accordion, its keys and pearly buttons glinting in the sun as he lugged it down Foxglove Lane towards the town.

Hearing the brisk trot-trot of the milkman's pony and the jingle of glass bottles, Warren darted through a gap in the stone hedge and hid there, enjoying the morning sun on his face. While he waited for the milkman to come back down the lane from Hendravean, Warren set about putting his shoes on. Jenny had given him an old pair of Tom's and he wasn't used to them. All his life he'd gone barefoot or worn plimsolls, and the leather shoes made a lot of noise when he ran. Hearing his own footsteps, loud and important, was something new, and Warren wasn't sure it suited him.

He brushed the grit from between his toes and pulled on the grey socks Jenny had given him too. Wearing socks was also a new, luxurious experience, for he'd never had a pair, even in winter. The feel of them was soothing, like damp sand. He shivered with pleasure as his feet slid easily into the shoes, then he struggled to tie the laces. Today he wanted to look smart, and he wanted his feet to be cushioned for the long walk. He thought about hitching a lift on the milk cart, but he didn't like the milkman's eyebrows. Crows' wings they were. Always angry.

Once the milk cart had gone, Warren picked up the piano-accordion, hung it around his bony chest, and set off again. He glanced back a few times but no one was following.

In his loud shoes, he marched along Fish Street and down to the busy harbour. An enormous heap of pilchards glittered on the quayside, some of them still squirming and alive, a circle of women gossiping and laughing as they packed the freshly caught fish into barrels. None of them noticed Warren and neither did the group of artists setting up their easels along Wharf Road. He marched on determinedly, past the church and the lifeboat house, past Pedn Olva point where, according to Nan, the rocks were different. *Blue Elvan*, she'd said, but the rocks didn't look blue.

At last he came to the granite steps that led up to the railway station. Climbing them with the weight of the piano-accordion was hard, but he managed it. A train was coming. He heard the whistle of it coming through the wooded cliffs of Carbis Bay and he felt excited. The station was busy with people in clean clothes waiting on the platform and others hurrying to catch the train.

Pleased with himself, Warren found a niche in the sunny rock face close to the entrance gate. He sat down, took off his cap, turned it over and put it on the ground at his feet. Then he opened the bellows of the piano-accordion and played a long, breathy chord. Heads turned as people walked by, gazing in astonishment at the tiny, raggedy boy half hidden behind the beautiful, shimmering instrument with its black and white keys and mother of pearl buttons, the bellows creasing and stretching as he began to play. First 'Trelawny', then 'The Skye Boat Song' and 'Greensleeves'. A few tourists actually clapped and it wasn't long before a lady in a flowery dress opened her shiny handbag and threw a silver shilling into Warren's cap. He rewarded her with the wild, engaging smile that came from doing what he loved, there in the morning sun, and getting paid for it.

The gathering pile of coins winking in the sun inside his cap added fire and energy to the music. His small fingers flew, his body shook with the rhythm and his normally pale face glowed with joy. Inspired, he played his repertoire of tunes over and over again, adding new ones as he remembered them. Between trains it was quieter with fewer people and Warren took short breaks, gathering the coins from his cap into the pockets of his jacket and putting the cap out again, empty.

The station porter eyed him from a distance but didn't intervene. Live and let live was a deeply Cornish attitude encrypted into his character. He didn't know where this bony little boy had come from, or even if he was allowed to be there, but the tourists were loving it.

Warren was thrilled when a plump and portly lady threw half a crown into his cap. He thanked her with his brightest smile.

'Aw, bless 'im,' he heard her say to her friend. 'He's all knees and elbows.'

By mid-morning, Warren found he simply couldn't play any more. His arms ached and his fingers were weak and shaky. He was too hot and savagely thirsty. The long walk back to Hendravean was daunting. He climbed to his feet and stretched, searching around for the nearest tap. There wasn't one. He looked at the neat row of red fire buckets on the station platform and made his way towards them.

'Oy!' The station porter was watching him. 'Don't you drink that, boy. The water's been in them buckets since Christmas! Thirsty, are you?'

Warren nodded.

'Wait there – I'll get you a mug of water.' He looked at Warren kindly. 'Don't be scared, I ain't gonna tell you off. Enjoyed your music, I did. Lovely. Made me morning, it did. You wait there. Don't go runnin' off now.'

Reassured, Warren stood, trembling a little, the piano-accordion at his feet. He watched the porter's rotund figure go into the back door of the ticket office and emerge with a white tin mug full to the brim with clean water. It felt like a gift from the gods. Warren took the mug, the enamel deliciously cool against his hands, and drank it down. Jenny had taught him how to say thank you. It was two words. Not one. Not 'Ku', but two words, with a smile. He decided to try it out on the porter.

'Th ... th ... thank – you.' It was such an effort that he forgot the smile, but the porter looked pleased.

"Ope to see you again one day.'

Warren picked up the piano-accordion and hung it over his shoulder for the walk home. It felt heavier than ever, and the four pockets of his jacket were weighed down and bulging with money. One had a hole in it and Warren could feel the coins working their way through and accumulating inside the lining of his jacket. Exhausted by two hours of performing in the hot sun, he trudged homeward, longing to lie in the dappled shade of the pear trees and rest. Several times he paused, thinking he just couldn't walk another step, then dragged himself on with his heavy load. Picturing Nan's face when he tipped the money out of his pockets and onto the table was what kept him plodding determinedly on.

Nan was hard to please, but Warren passionately wanted her to accept him. He wanted her to treat him the way she treated Lottie, reading stories and explaining the secrets of flowers and animals. At first he'd hated her for being so cold and contemptuous towards him, but gradually it had changed as he witnessed her love of magic and her tenderness towards birds and animals. He reckoned it was humans Nan didn't like, especially him. Then he'd made her cry just by playing music. The way the tears glistened on her aged skin and the way she suddenly looked vulnerable was something Warren would never forget. The bond forged between them in those moments was precious.

Jenny had explained to him how Nan had given up her solitary life and shared her home and everything in it with them when they might have been homeless. When he saw

Nan holding the money tin and asking for help, Warren knew he could quickly make some cash by busking. He'd done plenty of busking in his short life, though never on his own. It had been scary, sneaking downstairs with the piano-accordion, but he wasn't stealing it, Warren reasoned. He was borrowing it.

As he trudged up the lane, hungry and exhausted, he dreamed of the way he would scoop the money out of his pockets. It was a lot. He didn't know how much exactly, but it was more than Nan had in the OXO tin. It would fix things. It would make Jenny smile, and Lottie, and Tom. Smiling at him.

It would be a transformational moment, boosting his confidence, establishing him as a worthy member of the family he had grown to love.

Tired as he was, Warren walked on up the lane with a happy heart. Until, with no warning, it all changed.

First there was a smell, an old remembered stink of nicotine, beer and sweat. Then a shadow on the lane, overtaking him on soundless feet, and a fist coming out of nowhere, punching him on the side of his head, hurting his ear, knocking him to the ground. The piano-accordion crashed onto the tarmac, his stash of hard-earned money spinning and tumbling into the lane. He tried to escape by wriggling out of his jacket but the man caught him in an even harder grip, leaving the jacket lying in the grass.

It was over. Warren's dream of happiness, his life with Jenny, Lottie and Tom, his chance with Nan, his safe haven. Gone in an instant. Too exhausted to fight, too terrified to shout, Warren crumpled, whimpering as he was dragged away and hurled into the back of a covered wagon waiting behind the hedge. Nan's piano-accordion rang and rattled, dumped beside him on the dirty floor. His jacket with the precious hoard of money was left behind, his little hands tied cruelly together with a rope, cutting and scorching his skin.

With his eyes glistening, the man climbed into the driver's seat and cracked a whip in the air, making the pony set off at a brisk trot down Foxglove Lane.

'I'll go and look for him, Mum, don't you worry.' Tom looked solid and reassuring as he helped Jenny wrap the biscuits they had made. The first batch was already in a box on Mufty's cart, along with the herb and flower posies Lottie had made. She and Nan were on their way down to the town to sell their wares. It was the holiday season and there were tourists everywhere.

'You look out for Warren,' Jenny had said, but Lottie was on edge and hardly seemed to register what Jenny was asking, and Nan didn't seem bothered about Warren. Jenny felt she was the only one who cared about him.

Then Tom discovered the piano-accordion was missing.

'He *can't* have taken it — surely not,' Jenny said. 'It's so heavy and cumbersome.'

'But he can play, Mum. He's good. Gooder than me,' Tom said.

'*Better* than you he certainly is, and we don't know who taught him. Has he told you?'

Tom shook his head. 'No.'

'Are you sure he didn't tell you anything – about what he was planning to do today? He seemed worried about Nan's money talk,' Jenny said. 'But he sat there listening. Then he just – vanished. Tom, he must have said something to you. Come on, think.'

'I dunno.' Tom's brow puckered. He hesitated.

'Come on, Tom, you *must* tell me, even if it seems unimportant.'

'He did say he used to go and play music in the street – with his dad. "Uskin", he called it.'

'*Uskin*? Oh, *busking*. That makes sense, Tom. So what happened to his dad, I wonder?'

'Warren hates him,' Tom said. 'And he's scared of him. That's why he lived wild.'

Jenny stared at him. 'I wish you'd told me that before.'

Tom shrugged. 'Didn't matter, did it?'

'Of course it did.'

'Why?'

'Don't be so tiresome,' Jenny snapped. 'Go and look for him, will you please? And talk to people. Ask if anyone's seen him.'

Tom sighed. 'I wanted to play with me friends.'

'Tom, Warren is missing. Don't you care?'

A sullen silence hung between them.

'Tom?'

'No,' he said bluntly. 'He's not my brother, is he? I just put up with him, Mum.'

'Just *go*!' Jenny turned away, angry at Tom's honesty. She saw it as resentment. It raised another issue: had she neglected Tom and favoured Warren? Was Tom jealous? Was she making the same mistakes she'd made with Matt?

Overwhelmed and annoyed with herself, Jenny felt weary and wanted some peace. Her leg ached and she wanted to lie down on the sofa.

I'm useless, she thought, watching Tom stomping across the yard. In her pre-polio days she would have been down there energetically searching for Warren. Talking to friends. Sharing the burden. Again she found herself longing for Millie. If only she could find her.

The summer afternoon seemed endless. Jenny wandered around the perimeter of Hendravean, half hoping to find Warren hiding somewhere. The air shimmered with heat and the wings of bees, and the sea was a tranquil green–glass lagoon, the tide rising like well water, silver-lipped and clear. The church clock struck five with timeless resonance.

And still Warren had not returned.

Jenny could see Mufty's cart coming slowly up the lane. Had they found Warren and brought him home? Jenny hobbled to meet them at the gate. Tom was there, helping Nan to push the cart up the slope to help the patient donkey.

'No sign of Warren, Mum. Is he back?' Tom called.

She shook her head, disappointed. It seemed so final. Warren had gone. He wasn't coming back. Jenny knew it.

Nan's face was serious. 'We've lost Lottie as well,' she said. 'She's gone out with Matt on the boat. I tried to stop her, but she'd set her heart on going and she's worked hard helping me all day. I couldn't say no.' She handed Mufty's reins to Tom. 'Can you sort Mufty out, please? Unhitch him, take his harness off and rub him down – and give him a drink.'

'Right. Can do.' Always pleased to be trusted with a major task, Tom took Mufty away, his hand on the tired donkey's fuzzy neck.

Nan patted the leather bag she wore over her shoulder and it jingled impressively. 'We sold all the biscuits – and lots of posies. It's been a good day.'

'Not for me it hasn't,' Jenny said. 'I'm worried sick about Warren. He hasn't come back, Nan. Something's happened to him. I know it has.'

Nan looked at her searchingly. 'You look very tired, Jenny, and upset – I can see that. Now . . . I did hear something about Warren. That woman – Morwenna's mother, Cora Bartle – came over to speak to me and she said she saw Warren busking outside the station, and he had a pile of money in his cap. Cheeky little toad. With my piano accordion.'

'Oh, Nan – he must have been doing it to help you, after what you said this morning. He took it all to heart, Nan, I watched his face. So where is he now?'

'Cora said he'd gone by mid-morning. She tried to ask him what he was up to, but you know what the boy's like. You can't have a conversation with him. My guess is he'll come home when the money runs out.'

209

'No, Nan. Warren wouldn't know how to go into a shop and ask for something. He's a sitting target for some opportunist crook. Buskers get robbed all the time. And with his talent someone might have kidnapped him or robbed him on his way home and left him injured somewhere.' The worries poured out of Jenny and she fought to control her frantic tears. 'We've got to do something, Nan, before dark.'

Nan hesitated. Then she said, 'I believe Warren belongs to the travelling folk – the Romany gypsies. I like the real, genuine Romanies, and when they're in St Ives I make it my business to talk to them. At first they tried to ignore me, but when they saw Mufty's cart and realised I was hawking my wares, some of the women would sit and talk to me. They're fascinating people, remarkably wise, and intuitive too.'

'I was brought up to keep well away from them,' Jenny said, uneasy.

'Well, you should open your mind if you want to help Warren. What if he's one of them?'

Jenny nodded thoughtfully. 'The fair is down there right now – on the island as usual.'

'The Fair folk are not Romanies,' Nan said, 'but I did hear about a Romany woman marrying one of them. I hear all sorts of tales from the travelling folk, Jenny. I haven't told you this but I went off in the car one day and drove around some of the villages, trying to find out if anyone knew of a boy like Warren.'

Jenny stared at her. 'I never know what you're up to, Nan,' she teased.

Nan's eyes twinkled. 'I'm a devious old crone,' she cackled with laughter, 'but life is never dull.'

'But we must take some action,' Jenny said. 'I'm going to ring the police.'

'Go on then – do it now. I agree with you,' Nan said, 'but I don't want them up here with those great dogs they've got, upsetting the chickens and the cats. I won't have dogs galloping all over my vegetable garden. They've got paws like African lions.'

Jenny bit back a sarcastic retort and headed indoors for the phone. At least Nan agreed with her.

There were no dogs or sirens. The search for Warren began with the local bobby on a bike puffing up Foxglove Lane in the heat, a pencil and notebook in his pocket and a mildly sceptical glint in his eyes when Jenny tried to explain how a wild boy who couldn't talk had come to live with her, despite her iron leg, despite her being a widow. And how this ten-year-old 'wild boy' had the grit and the confidence to steal a piano-accordion with mother-of-pearl buttons and go busking.

Lottie took Matt's hand and stepped aboard *The Jenny Wren*, both of them longing to be out on the water, away from prying eyes and gossip. It was weeks since they'd seen each other because of Lottie's end of year exams. If she did well, she would be offered a place in the college class from September, and she wanted it with all her heart, knowing she had the support of her father and Nan. Jenny was less enthusiastic, but Lottie understood it was an attitude rooted in her by her upbringing.

'How did you get on?' Matt asked her. 'In your exams?'

'I don't know yet. We get told by a letter in a few weeks' time. But I think I did okay. I found the questions easy and I wrote lots – and I enjoyed the Shakespeare. We did *Romeo and Juliet*.'

Matt grinned. 'That's a love story, isn't it?'

'Yes – star-crossed lovers, like us.'

'What do you mean, star-crossed?'

'Everyone was against them. Their families were at war with each other and they tried to keep them apart.'

Lottie gazed up at Matt. His tanned skin had a glaze of salt and his hair stuck out in sun-bleached tufts from under the rim of his navy fisherman's cap. His dark eyes glowed, his gaze never leaving her face. 'And Romeo was just like you,' Lottie added.

Standing close to him had lit the flame between them as if it had a flickering life of its own. 'Let's get away from St Ives. Out on the water.'

Matt started the engine and turned *The Jenny Wren* to the west, into the blaze of sunlight on the water, leaving an arrow of foam as he pushed her faster and faster. To Matt, speed was an expression of an emotion too big for words. Joy, fury, rebellion, and now love. Only speed came close to the intensity of those feelings.

Lottie sat beside him, adoringly, her hair streaming, her lips parted, giving little squeals of excitement. As they sailed west into the balmy evening, Lottie felt her worries flying away, detaching themselves from her one by one, leaving her alive and free. The resolutions she'd made after the talk with Morwenna unravelled and let go of her like ribbons in the wind.

She'd resolved to talk to Matt about how babies were made.

She'd planned to warn him about the consequences of their lovemaking.

She'd tried to tell herself to say no. No, we can't do it anymore. No, we can't. We mustn't. It has to stop.

And now her mind was cutting those ribbons, leaving them fluttering far away.

She felt the love, even as they sat together, fully clothed on the speeding boat. They were one bird. One bird of paradise.

She couldn't say no. It was too beautiful.

Chapter 13

A Crack of Sunlight

Jenny felt she couldn't take any more. Losing Warren was bad enough, but now Lottie hadn't come home. It was nine o'clock, twilight on a summer evening, a lone star shining over the sea, not a breath of wind. Nan went to bed, exhausted, and so did Tom. Jenny was left alone, sitting on the doorstep, stunned by the emptiness of the night. Was she the only one who cared about Warren? She felt abandoned, even by the cats. Bessie slept on Tom's bed and Bartholomew always followed Nan upstairs. A barn owl circled, turning its black eyes to look at Jenny each time it floated by on silent wings.

When the phone rang, Jenny nearly fell off the doorstep. She scrambled up and hobbled into the hall to answer it, her heart pounding with hope and fear. 'Hello. This is Jenny.'

'Hello, Jenny dear.' John's calm voice was very welcome.

'Oh – John. What is it?'

'It's Lottie. She's quite all right, don't worry. But she won't be back tonight. You know she's with Matt on the boat – don't you?'

'Yes, Nan told me.'

'I was having a pint in The Sloop,' John said, 'and Ken came looking for me. Matt sent a message with one of the fishermen to say they have decided to stay out there on the boat. It's a lovely calm night.'

Jenny battled with relief and anger. She didn't want to vent her feelings on John. 'Lottie did ask me, weeks ago, if she could have a little holiday and stay on the boat with Matt. Nan and I both said no and she didn't mention it again – but she's a strong-willed girl, isn't she?'

'She certainly is. I had a taste of it on the ship,' John said. 'But is it such a bad thing? She's young and she's been studying so diligently, and it will do her good, a little adventure – and spending time with Matt. He seems very capable to me.'

Jenny managed to stop herself from snorting.

'You've gone quiet,' John said, his voice kind. 'Are you not happy about it?'

Breathe, Jenny thought. *Pull yourself together and breathe. You are not going to rant down the phone at John.*

'Jenny?'

'Yes, I'm still here.'

'You're upset, my dear, I can tell. Shall I come over?'

'No, John, it's nice of you, but it's late. Nan's gone to bed and so has Tom. I was sitting on the doorstep, worrying.'

'Jenny, I've got a bicycle, with a light, believe it or not. I can be with you in ten minutes,' John said firmly. 'Put the phone down and make some cocoa. I'm on my way. No argument.' There was a click and Jenny was left looking at a silent phone.

Don't panic. Make cocoa.

At least she knew where Lottie was. She went inside to the kitchen where the gas light was still burning. She tried to make cocoa. Overwhelming, powerful feelings streamed through her mind as if trying to funnel through a bottleneck. A voice echoed in her head. She'd lost Matt, now Warren was missing, and Lottie had finally rebelled and taken charge of her life, today of all days.

She stood in the window, stirring the earthenware cocoa teapot, the steam chocolatey and mildly comforting. John arrived just as a giant moon was rising over the sea. Sitting bolt upright and pedalling vigorously, he swept into the yard, the yellowy shaft of the bicycle's light attracting a flurry of summer moths. He skidded to a halt and dismounted expertly, propping the bicycle against the porch and pausing to remove the ankle clips from his trousers.

'Come in, John. The door's open.'

He came into the kitchen, his face glowing boyishly from the exercise, his eyes attentive and serious.

Jenny felt better immediately. 'It's nice of you to come, John.' She smiled, determined to be cheerful and pretend she was coping when she wasn't. 'I expect you've had a busy day, have you?'

'Moderately,' he said. 'Is that cocoa in the brown teapot? *Mmm*, lovely – and biscuits!'

'Homemade this morning by me and Tom.' Jenny offered him the plate. 'Nan sold the lot from Mufty's cart – but we saved the broken ones for ourselves. Mind you, I think Tom might have broken a few accidentally-on-purpose!'

'They're delicious.' He crunched one, silent for a moment as he enjoyed the taste. 'Melt in the mouth, don't they? Well done, my dear, you're such an accomplished woman.'

Jenny's eyes rounded. She wasn't used to being complimented on such a basic skill as making biscuits. John's steady gaze was encouraging and calming. She actually began to feel human again in his presence. Human and in control.

'Tell me about Warren,' he said. 'Tom said he'd gone missing. Could he have gone back to his family?'

'I doubt that,' Jenny replied. 'He's never told me anything, partly because his speech is so bad, but he told Tom he hated his father. I think he's had a hard time, to put it mildly. It isn't that he can't talk – he's never been allowed to. He's a bundle of nerves. But when he plays the piano-accordion he comes alive. He's really astonishing. It made Nan cry when she heard him.'

'Really?'

'Morwenna's mother, Cora Bartle, told Nan she saw Warren busking outside the station. The truth is, John, Warren is deeply sensitive, not tough like he appears to be.

This morning Nan told us how difficult it is getting enough money to live. She was fine on her own, but she took us lot in, and Warren. It was good of her. She's used up all her savings and the only money she gets, for the five of us, comes from what she earns from selling herbs and hats and stuff from Mufty's cart. By rights, Matt should be here now he's left school – he should be in a job and contributing to the family. That's partly why she's so angry with him.'

Jenny paused, moved by the concern in John's eyes. His cocoa lay untouched on the table and he sat listening to her with the whole of his being, his hands clasped under his chin. 'I think Warren took it all to heart,' Jenny continued. 'I think he was busking to make some money for Nan. I mean, what a brave thing for a ten-year-old to do – and he had to lug the heavy piano-accordion all the way to the station on this hot day. I worry that . . . maybe he just couldn't make it home, poor little scrap.'

John nodded in silent empathy.

'I've told the police. The constable came up here and wrote down everything I said. He asked if we'd searched the barns and the waysides nearby, but of course we have. Anyway, if Warren was nearby he'd come home.'

'There are a few policemen around, more than usual,' John said. 'They were searching the island with a dog.'

'The trouble is, John, even if they find him, the Welfare will be up here in the morning asking questions, and . . . and . . . accusing me of neglect. Then they'll look at me iron leg and tell me I'm not fit to foster a child.'

'Surely not!' John looked shocked.

'Oh yes. They could take Warren away, even if he didn't want to go.'

'But you've been wonderful to him, Jen. Anyone can see that. Warren doesn't say much, but he loves you. It's in his eyes. He gazes at you all the time.'

'And I love him too. We've tried so hard to accept him the way he is – like, he won't go to school. He just won't. And if he did, they wouldn't cope with him. So we're teaching him at home, me and Tom – Tom's been good to him, and so has Lottie. She's an angel, John. She reads to him and explains things so beautifully. And recently Nan has got involved, helping him with music and ordinary life skills like gardening and caring for animals.' Jenny sighed bitterly. 'But Welfare don't seem to care about any of that. They'll blame me for not sending him to school. They'll blame me for everything, even for not having a husband.'

John reached out and took her hands. 'I shall speak for you, Jenny. All you have to do is ring me when they arrive and I shall drop everything and come up here.'

'They won't listen.'

'Oh, I think they will. I've dealt with a lot of awkward, upset people in my life, Jenny. And I believe in you. You're a gem, a real gem.'

Jenny felt tears welling.

'You know Lottie adores you,' John said passionately. 'You've been a real rock in her life.'

'I've told her I love her no matter what,' Jenny said, and

in her heart she wondered whether she could possibly keep that promise if it came to the test.

'It's a beautiful summer night,' John said. 'Why don't we take our cocoa outside and look at the moonlight on the sea? Moonlight is so calming.'

Jenny let him steer her outside and they sat close, side by side. 'Let's just be quiet together,' John said, 'and be peaceful.'

The reflection of the moon in the water stretched for miles across the bay, the dark hills beyond studded with clusters of light from cottages and villages far away, the lights dim and sallow compared to the intense white silverness of the moon.

Like John and Jenny, Matt and Lottie sat close, the boat hardly moving on the phosphorescence of a calm night sea. Nearby, a flock of Manx shearwaters burbled and piped as they dived and fished, and when the beam from Godrevy Lighthouse swept the sea, their smooth bellies gleamed like pearls. The western sky retained a blush of rose and overhead the colour of night was blueberry, the summer stars twinkling, some bold and bright, others infinitesimal like dust.

'I can see Cygnus,' Matt said. 'See it? Like a gurt cross in the sky. It's supposed to be a swan.'

'Arnie taught us about the stars, didn't he?' Lottie leaned against him, her face upturned to the night. 'And Nan told me the legend – it's a great swan flying across the heavens that has come from the Cosmic Egg, the brightest star in its tail. It represents the birth of a new world, and when a baby is born you must hold it up to the stars and sing out its name to the heavens.'

'You don't believe all that stuff do you, Lottie?'

Lottie pondered how to answer. Matt stared up at the universe, the moonlight sketching him like a charcoal drawing, the light through his beard and the texture of his skin, the curl of an eyelash and the sun-bleached tips of his hair. She remembered how adamantly Jenny had denied the truth of Nan's folklore tales, pouncing on the boys if they dared mention it.

'I don't think believing is the right word,' she said eventually. 'I think folklore and legends are to be enjoyed – and wondered about. But it's like a secret code, Matt. Truth is in there somewhere, in disguise, if you can find it.'

'Yeah, well, that's a good way of looking at it.' Matt's voice sounded wistful. 'I was never allowed to even think about it. Mum terrorised Tom and me.' He launched into a comical falsetto imitation of Jenny's ferocious attacks on folklore, making Lottie giggle. 'But now, since I've been drawing, I'm discovering parts of my mind I never knew I had. Now I'm away from home I can dream, and sometimes I come close to painting my dreams. Haven't done it yet, but it will come. Your father's an interesting person, Lottie. D'you know what he said to me after he'd looked at my pictures?'

'What?'

'He said something I'll never forget. He said when you begin to dream, and paint your dreams, it will be a key moment in your life, a breakthrough. He said don't work too hard or try too hard because your dreams need time and space. Don't brick them up.' Matt clicked his fingers and looked at her with bright, excited eyes. 'That's what he said. Don't spend your life bricking up your dreams.'

'He hasn't always been like that,' Lottie said. 'He told me how hard he worked at being an engineer when in his heart he wanted to be an artist.'

'You're lucky to have him, Lottie, aren't you? I think he's inspiring, and ... different.'

Lottie smiled. She was happy, out on the water with Matt, with *The Jenny Wren* keeping them afloat, dry and warm on the cold salty sea. She listened for a few minutes to the Manx shearwaters, their sleek bodies making little plops and splashes as they dived. She kept looking at the stars of Cygnus and thinking about the legend. It would be so beautiful to hold a baby up to the stars. She was waiting for the right moment to talk to Matt, tentatively, about babies. It was so fragile. Matt was fragile. She didn't want to test his reaction and get it wrong. She knew only too well that she could lose everything.

Enjoy it, while you can. Love your life, she told herself. *Don't waste a single moment of this enchanted night.*

She felt Matt's fingers in her hair, combing it, his touch going deeper, finding the back of her neck, her scalp, burrowing into her thick hair with his sensitive hands until he cradled her head, pulling her closer, into their magic circle where their eyes gazed deeply into each other and, long before the velvet fire began to burn, they had already made love; spiritual love in the looking, and the knowing, and the brave new world of finding the point of infinity where twin souls meet.

It was midnight when John left Hendravean, pedalling along the lane under the stars, the moon now a tiny disc high in the sky. Spending time with Jenny had warmed his heart and made him feel young again. He sensed Jenny was wary and still committed to Arnie. She wasn't ready for a relationship. But she liked him and he allowed himself to believe she needed him.

John was glad Olivia had decided not to come to St Ives again. She seemed to have settled in London. He'd given her the use of his apartment – temporarily, he hoped. He never wanted to return to city life after living in St Ives and finding his beautiful, clever daughter. What a joy it would be to guide and nurture Lottie as she worked through college and into a career. He glowed with pride as he imagined her future.

The lane was in shadow with ghostly silhouettes of fern and foxglove against the stars, and the soporific fragrance of meadowsweet. The moon was no longer reflected in the sea but on the slate rooftops of St Ives. John wanted to gaze at it, but he needed to focus on the road ahead in the limited yellowy light on the front of his bicycle.

Something caught his eye. A coin lying at the side of the road. A shilling.

He stopped and picked it up. Hmm – lucky! Then he

noticed another, and another, and yet more coins deep down in the long grass of a gateway.

How odd, he thought.

John propped the bicycle against the hedge, unclipped the lamp from the handlebars and shone it around, gathering the money quickly, finding some of it by touch. The more he found, the more puzzled he became.

Something had happened here. It spooked him a little.

'Hello,' he called, and shone the light around. 'Is anyone there?' He ventured through the gap in the hedge, noticing some fresh wheel ruts in the turf. No one was there. A crumpled mound of fabric lay at the base of the hedge. It looked like a sack.

Goosebumps prickled along John's arms. He touched the fabric, then picked it up gingerly. A jacket. A little boy's jacket. And it was oddly heavy as if the pockets were full of pebbles, or marbles – or *money*. John slid his hand inside one of them and felt the cold coins. Then it struck him. Warren's jacket. Stuffed with the money from his busking.

With only the fading bicycle lamp to search with, John felt overwhelmed. Moved by the little jacket, he wanted Jenny to see it before the police got involved. He looked up at Hendravean. The downstairs light was still on. Leaving his bicycle in the lane he jogged back there, holding the jacket against him, wishing it were Warren he'd found, not just his jacket.

Jenny was still on the doorstep.

'It's only me, Jenny, don't be alarmed.' John hurried towards her, breathing hard.

'What happened?' she asked, her eyes big in the moonlight. 'Did you fall off your bike?'

'No. I've found Warren's jacket – and it's full of cash, Jenny. It is his, isn't it?'

Jenny gave a cry and took the threadbare jacket, cuddling it against her face. 'Yes, it's his.' Her eyes widened as she felt the weight of the coins. 'Oh, John – poor Warren. He'd have been so proud to bring it home to Nan after doing the busking all on his own. He'd have loved it. I can't bear to think about it. Oh John . . .'

John held her and they clung together, the jacket between them, both silent, sharing a wordless anguish.

'What could have happened to him?' Jenny whispered.

John pulled himself together and became suddenly business-like. 'We must telephone the police, immediately. Warren could be lying somewhere – hurt. It's no good waiting until morning. He could be . . .'

They stared at each other in horror.

'You make the phone call, John, please,' Jenny said. 'I couldn't talk to them. They'd better care . . .'

She stood in the moonlit garden hugging Warren's jacket while John reached the hall telephone in a few brisk strides. 'It needs your urgent attention, sergeant,' she heard him say. 'We need lights and a search party or that boy could die.'

Nan appeared at the top of the stairs in the voluminous white gown she wore in bed. 'What the hell is going on down there?' she boomed. 'I can't sleep in my own bed.'

Jenny put her finger to her lips. 'Shh.'

'Don't you shush me! *What* is going on? Is there a fire?'

'No, but will you come downstairs, Nan?' Jenny said, trying to keep her voice calm. Calm, like John. 'There's something you've got to see.'

'At this unearthly hour?'

'Yes.' *Come on, Nan, don't be awkward*, she prayed, still clutching Warren's little jacket. Nan had to see it. Jenny hoped it would touch her heart.

Still talking to the police, John didn't move from the phone. Only his eyes moved, fixing Nan with an unwavering, autocratic stare. She clamped her mouth shut and began to come down in her bare feet, the stairs creaking as she clung to the banister. Bartholomew sat at the top, meowing. He waited until Nan was safely down, then descended at a fast trot with his tail up.

John put the phone down and turned to face them. 'A police car is on its way now with two policemen. They're bringing searchlights and a dog. And a second car will come over from Penzance.' He turned to Nan, his expression softening respectfully. 'Excuse me, Nan, invading your home at this time of night. Would you come and sit down and we'll explain what's happening.' Escorted by Bartholomew, he steered Nan into the kitchen and Jenny followed.

The three of them sat round the kitchen table with Nan at the head. Jenny put the jacket on the table. She smoothed it lovingly, her voice breaking as she said, 'Nan – this is

Warren's little jacket. John found it in the lane – and it's full of money. Feel the weight of it.'

Nan's mouth stayed clamped and anger flared briefly in her eyes. She took the jacket in both hands and suddenly began to shake with emotion.

'He was nearly home, Nan. He was bringing the money he earned from busking, and he must have been so looking forward to giving it to you. It looks like he was attacked or kidnapped in the lane, poor little mite.'

Nan looked at the passion in Jenny's eyes and remembered how her own eyes had welled with tears when she'd heard Warren playing.

'He wanted to please you so much, Nan. He wanted you to have this money. I know he doesn't talk but he's got a heart.'

Nan shut her eyes and nodded. 'Pray to God they find him.'

In the morning, the cobbled streets of St Ives rang with music and rumbled with the scrape of cartwheels and heavy horses pulling wagons stacked high with colourful timber and bunting. Behind the horse wagons a few lorries roared slowly along, their loads strapped down under tarpaulins. Each wagon bore a multi-coloured placard. One said CAROUSEL, another HELTER-SKELTER, others TOMBOLA, ROLL-A-PENNY and COCONUT SHY. As the procession entered the town, clog dancers and Morris men danced between the wagons with bells on their socks. Musicians sat high up on the front of the wagons playing piano-accordions, violins and banjos.

The town welcomed the funfair with the flag of St Piran flying from garden gates and windows and, instead of washing, there was bunting strung across the streets. Many smaller funfairs and circuses came throughout the summer, setting up on the wide grassy space at the foot of the island. This one was the biggest and the best – The Harvest Fair – and there would be market stalls and local produce: Cornish butter and cream, candyfloss, fudge and toffee apples.

Hidden in the back of one of the wagons, Warren lay curled up on the floor, his hands still tied together, his head aching from the blow. Alternately waking and sleeping, he kept quiet, knowing what would happen if he cried or called out, or kicked at the sides of the wagon.

His dad would never let him go – he would have to escape. But that couldn't happen until he'd somehow earned his dad's trust again. It meant long, miserable weeks of pretending to be good, never daring to ask for anything, even for time in the sunshine. It would go on until he was grown up and big enough to fight back. That time seemed far away, but worth thinking about. Good things had happened in his life. Like Jenny holding him close like a mother. Jenny teaching him to talk.

Warren made up his mind to carry on, listening and learning, and teach himself to talk. Music wasn't enough. To have a life worth living he must talk. Like Lottie. Warren was in awe of Lottie and the way she talked and read stories to him. He thought he might be in love with Lottie. She inspired him, and just thinking about her as he huddled on the grubby floor of the wagon lifted his spirits. Then there was Tom. Warren had never had a friend, and Tom had been a true friend. Tom had played with him and hadn't teased him. Tom had been patient and understanding – and fun. Everyone in the Lanroska family had given Warren a life. Even Nan. Even Mufty and the cats had given him limitless, unconditional love.

He stared at a slender crack of sunlight blazing into the gloom of the green tarpaulin. The short time he'd been with the Lanroskas seemed longer than the rest of his young life, and it shone as brightly as that crack of sunlight. And he hadn't told them. Jenny had patiently taught him to say thank you, but he hadn't said it to her. He had to go back.

Escape or die, he thought desperately. *Escape or die*.

Why live on the floor in the dark, in the fear, in the anger? Why live like that when you could love and be loved?

For three days and nights, Warren huddled there, alone, listening to the raucous sound of the funfair, the laughter, the screams from the helter-skelter. Then night, and the soothing, eternal roar of the surf. Then morning. Dawn, and the symphony of seagulls. Then people walking past.

And no one called his name.

On the fourth day, the funfair was dismantled and loaded noisily onto the lorries and wagons. Heading up country for the winter, so they said. The procession formed up, this time without the musicians and dancers, and rolled back up the hill and out of St Ives, perhaps never to return.

Chapter 14

A Tiny Heartbeat

'Time to say goodbye,' Matt said, helping Lottie off the boat and onto the slipway. He'd taken her for one last trip on that September morning.

Unexpectedly tearful, Lottie looked into his eyes, searching desperately for a way in. She still hadn't told him – and now it was too late.

He grinned, his face glowing from the sea, sun and happiness, but the rain now starting to fall on his fisherman's hat and on the tufts of sun-bleached hair, and on his shoulders the drops sparkled and darkened as they soaked into the thick blue cotton.

The long summer holiday was over and school would be starting again. Lottie was hoping for a place in the college class, but she would have to work hard to catch up with the studies she had missed.

Matt looked at Lottie's silent, desperate face in alarm. 'What's the matter?'

She shook her head dumbly.

'Lottie?'

'I need to talk to you about . . . something,' she murmured, and her voice sounded strange. Not her usual confident self. It sounded apologetic and nervous.

'What, now?' Matt looked puzzled. 'Can't it wait? There's a swell building and I've got to get back to Portreath.'

'Couldn't you stay in St Ives for the night?'

'No. I've got to earn some cash,' Matt said. 'You're okay, aren't you? We've had a whole day together. We'll talk next time.'

She shook her head again.

'Come on – smile at me, Lottie.'

'I don't have to smile. I need to talk to you.'

'You're in a mood.'

'It's not a mood, Matt. It's really, really important – and you're the one who asked me what's wrong.'

A heavy wave lifted the boat and swept on, the raindrops peppering the surface of the water. A low wind blew the loose sand up the slipway.

'You should have said something before. Why leave it 'til the last minute?'

Lottie felt mutinous. She hadn't meant it to be like this. Both of them standing on the slipway getting soaked, and Matt shifting from one foot to the other, eyeing the sea and accusing her of being in a mood. She lifted her chin.

'Forget it, Matt.' She shook the raindrops out of her hair and walked away without looking back.

'Bye, Lottie,' he called after her.

It wasn't the way she wanted to say goodbye. His last look had been one of impatience. A man-of-the-world-who-had-to-work look. Not the Romeo look. But they loved each other, it was just the world getting in the way. She wasn't going to be pathetic and clingy like Olivia.

Lottie walked briskly until she was out of sight of the harbour.

Who could I talk to? I've got two mothers, she thought, *and I can't talk to either of them.*

School was starting on Monday and she couldn't go on like this. It had been a wonderful summer. Now it was time to face the truth.

She headed up The Stennack to Dr Tregullow's surgery, went in and sat on one of the hard leather chairs in the waiting room, planning what she would say.

She was last in the queue and when Dr Tregullow popped his head round the door to say 'Next, please', he looked surprised. 'Are you here on your own, Lottie?'

'Yes.'

'Where's your mother?'

'She's busy at home.'

'Does she know you're here, young lady?'

'No . . .'

He raised his eyebrows. 'Then I ought to say no, I won't see you. It's not my policy to see a girl of your age without her mother. '

Lottie looked at him desperately. 'Please, please see me. Can't you bend the rules just this once? I *have* to see a doctor, and it's private. I don't want you to tell anyone.'

'Well, well, well.' Dr Tregullow looked at her over the top of his glasses. 'What have you been up to?'

'Please – it's urgent.'

He sighed. 'All right. Come on in.'

She sat on an even harder leather chair, waiting while he inspected her notes from a brown cardboard folder. 'Ah – last time you were here it was sickness.' He folded his hands together and looked at her shrewdly. 'So what is it this time?'

Lottie took a deep breath. 'Can you – can you tell if I'm going to have a baby?'

He tutted. 'Oh dear. Well, yes, of course I can.'

'But please – *please* don't tell Jenny ...'

'I presume you've had sexual intercourse?'

Lottie frowned. Sexual intercourse? It sounded so boring and clinical. Nothing like the lovemaking she'd had with Matt. Was it really so unromantic? 'Yes,' she managed to say, and felt herself blushing with embarrassment.

'How long ago?'

'Yesterday.'

He tutted again. 'But how long has it been going on? When was the first time?'

'In December.'

'And was that the only time? Or were there more?'

'There were more.'

'In which month?'

'Regularly – since May.'

'Hmm. I am surprised, I must admit.' Dr Tregullow tweaked the end of his waxed moustache. 'There is a test I could do, but it involves sending a urine sample to the laboratory. It's long-winded and expensive.'

'We couldn't afford it,' Lottie said, thinking she couldn't possibly expect her father to pay for *that*.

Dr Tregullow shut his eyes and nodded. 'I've known you since you were rescued from the shipwreck, young Lottie, and I know what you and your adoptive family have been through.'

'Is there another way?' Lottie asked.

'It depends how far along you are. Was there a particular time when you thought something had changed? When, perhaps you felt different after sexual intercourse?'

Lottie closed her eyes. It came to her instantly. That day by the wishing well on Carrack Gladden – when she'd had the dream. She looked into the doctor's eyes. Would he understand?

'Yes – it might have been the thirty-first of May.'

The doctor counted the months on his fingers. 'June, July, August, September. Hmm – you could be far enough along for me to be able to tell. I will need to examine your tummy. Will you lie on the couch, please? I'll be very gentle, don't worry.'

There was no going back. She undressed and lay down on the cold leather couch. An absurd thought came into her mind. The leather had once been skin, the skin of a cow or

234

a pig. It was barbaric, expecting a young woman who was nervous and embarrassed to lie on the cold, well-polished skin of a dead animal. Her knees trembled.

Dr Tregullow loomed over her, his head emerging from an immaculate collar, an apparition of nostrils, skin pores and a waxed moustache. Lottie felt she couldn't bear him near her, but she made herself keep still as his big hands pressed and probed her tummy. Her mind screamed *Stop* and she tried to distract herself by turning her eyes away from his florid face. She found herself staring into the glassy eyes of a stuffed fox who was mounted on a plaque on the wall.

At last, he lifted his hands, his eyes grave and stern. 'I'll just have a listen,' he said, and reached for his stethoscope. 'This might feel a bit cold, but I have to hold it on your abdomen for a minute. All right?'

She nodded the tiniest of nods. It was nearly over, but getting scarier by the moment. She watched his face for clues as he listened intently, and suddenly an extraordinary light flooded his eyes. 'Ah!' he exclaimed. 'I have a heartbeat.'

Lottie's mouth fell open. 'My heart's not down there!'

He smiled. 'Indeed it's not.' He put the stethoscope down. 'Get up now, Lottie, and put your clothes on —we'll have a little chat.'

Lottie's hands shook and her whole body quivered as she quickly got dressed and sat down on the chair. To her surprise, the doctor picked up his own grand leather chair, carried it round from behind the desk, put it next to her and sat down. She stared at him anxiously. He looked different, like a benevolent grandpa about to read a story.

'You're a brave, intelligent young lady, Lottie,' he said, his voice very quiet, 'and I want you to listen carefully to what I'm going to say and, whatever happens in the future, please remember it. Remember it always.'

She nodded, wide-eyed and afraid.

'As a doctor, I have done this hundreds of times, and when I hear a baby's strong, fast heartbeat, it moves me deeply.' His voice went quieter and quieter and he took her hand in a kindly grasp, compelling her to listen. 'I want to tell you this in a certain way.' He paused and his old eyes smiled into hers. 'Every baby is a miracle, and a tiny baby who wants to live is growing inside you now. It's still very small at the moment, but if you could see it you would marvel at its perfection. It has tiny, perfect fingers and toes, and a sweet little face. It's sleeping and growing – maybe it's thinking and dreaming, we don't know. But its tiny heart is beating and it wants to live and it wants you to be its mother, Lottie.' He squeezed her hand, then let it go. 'Always remember that, whatever happens – and don't let anyone bully you into a wrong decision. This little one has chosen you. You are going to be a mother, Lottie.'

She sat, stunned, frightened, yet appreciating the way this leathery old doctor with his waxed moustache had spoken directly to her soul in a language she understood: the language of poetry.

'I will do everything I can to help you, Lottie,' he assured her. 'What about the father? Do you know who it is?'

'I do, but it's a secret.'

'Does he know?'

'No.' Lottie pictured Matt, so carefree and alive on his boat. The beautiful hours of love they had shared. Love that had made a baby. She remembered the dream she'd had about the pearl in the oyster shell.

'You must tell him – or I will, if you'd like me to.'

'No,' Lottie shook her head. 'Not yet – I need time to think about it.'

'And you *must* tell your mother, Lottie.'

'Which one?' she asked, with a trace of irony.

'Jenny, of course. I know how much she loves you.'

'She – she'll go crazy. I shan't tell her.'

'You won't be able to hide it, Lottie. I think you know that.'

'Please – *please* don't tell her,' Lottie pleaded, her eyes filling with tears. 'Please.'

Dr Tregullow looked at her steadily. 'You think it through, Lottie. I won't say anything just yet, but eventually Jenny will have to know – sooner rather than later. She may be angry at first, that's only to be expected, but she will need time to get used to the idea, and time to plan; with you, I hope, not against you.'

'I should go now.' Lottie stood up and squared her shoulders, flicking her blonde hair away from her face. 'I'm perfectly capable of being a mother. And why shouldn't I? It's my life.'

*

'Here he is again,' Nan remarked, seeing John arriving in the pouring rain on his bike.

'Who?' Jenny asked, busy with a skein of red wool looped over the backs of two chairs. She went on winding it into a manageable ball.

'John,' Nan said. She eyed Jenny suspiciously. 'It must be you he wants to see, or doesn't he know Lottie's gone to school?'

Jenny was still missing Warren. The police had told her she must accept the likelihood that he belonged to the travelling fair folk and had found his family again. They'd seen children like him before, they'd said. A witness had seen the horse-drawn wagon coming down Foxglove Lane and the police had been to the fairground when they were packing up and been told that, yes, a man called Leo had been to fetch his boy, and the boy was all right. Jenny didn't believe them, but there was nothing she could do legally if Warren was with his father.

Jenny was so upset that she hardly noticed Lottie and Tom. She left Warren's bedroom exactly as it was and, with Nan's agreement, the little jacket was hung in his wardrobe, the money still in its pockets.

'That's Warren's money. We won't touch it,' she declared. 'He earned it and if he ever comes back here, he can have it.' Everyone agreed it was fair. Nan had chosen not to tell the police about the piano-accordion. She didn't want Warren branded as a thief. 'I'd have happily given it to him,' she said, sadly. 'With his talent he deserves it.

But he'll come back, Jenny, I feel sure he will – when he gets the chance.'

On that wet morning, both women were glad to see John arriving and Jenny limped to the door to greet him, her eyes bright again.

'Hang your coat by the stove, John,' she said. 'Here, let me take it. You're soaking wet. Shall I make tea? Or would you like some Bovril?'

'Bovril would be nice.' John leaned against the stove, steaming gently. 'I did come for a reason. I've got an idea to share with you, Jenny, and Nan of course.' He looked at Nan fondly and her eyes twinkled a little. 'Has Lottie gone to school?'

'Yes, and Tom.'

'I wondered if Lottie was all right?' John said.

'I think she is. Why?'

'That woman – Maudie, in the long maroon trench coat; she told me Lottie was in Dr Tregullow's surgery the other day. I expect you were with her, Jenny.'

Jenny and Nan looked at each other. 'Surely not,' Jenny said. 'I wouldn't let her go on her own to the doctor. That can't be right, John.'

'Maudie's gossip knows no boundaries,' Nan said with contempt.

'I thought it was odd.' John frowned thoughtfully. 'Has she been unwell?'

'No – in fact she seems to be thriving. She's even putting on weight. Isn't she, Nan?'

'Oh, it's just puppy fat at her age,' Nan said. 'She was keen to get back to school and be in the college class. She's going to do well, especially at English. You must be so proud of her, John.'

'I am.'

'When she gets home from school, I'll ask her about the doctor.' Jenny handed him an enamel mug of steaming Bovril. 'You get this down you, John. The only problem with Bovril is you can't have rum in it!'

'Thanks.' He gave her a heart-stopping grin and watched as she made two mugs of Camp Coffee, beating some cream into them and adding a dash of rum to Nan's mug.

Nan doesn't miss much, Jenny thought, seeing the shrewd expression on the old lady's face. Nan had noticed the way John was gazing at her.

'What was the idea you had, John?'

He looked thoughtful for a minute, both hands wrapped around his mug. Outside, the rain pelted down and water streamed over the blocked guttering like a bead curtain. 'I need some help in the gallery,' John said. 'It's going well, but I'd like to be out and about doing some new paintings, especially now I've got the bike. So I'm thinking of employing someone part-time to man the gallery.' He looked at Jenny. 'Would you like the job?'

'Me?'

'Yes – you, Jenny. I'd be ... honoured if you'd think about it.'

'Ooh, I'd love to do it,' Jenny said, excited. 'I couldn't man it for you, but I could woman it.' She raised a clenched fist.

'You could indeed,' he laughed. 'I'd pay you, of course. We can talk about hours and pay – but the job's yours if you want it, Jenny.'

'Even with me iron leg?'

'Even with your iron leg.'

'How would you feel about me having a job, Nan?' Jenny asked. 'It would give us an income.'

'I'd be delighted,' Nan said warmly. Then she chuckled. 'It would give me some peace and quiet!'

'I was expecting something better from you, Lottie.' David Merryn frowned at Lottie's English book. 'You've only done two lines.'

Lottie looked up at his disappointed face. 'Sorry,' she mumbled.

'I'm afraid "sorry" won't do. You've wasted an hour. What were you doing?'

Lottie shrugged and stayed quiet.

'Daydreaming, I suppose. Is that it?'

'Perhaps . . .'

'Perhaps! This isn't like you, Lottie. Is something wrong?'

'No.'

'Then how about staying behind after school and doing it?'

Lottie looked at him beseechingly. 'Please, Mr Merryn, don't make me stay behind. I'll take my book home and do it if you like, but I can't possibly stay after school. I promise I'll do it at home.'

He sighed. 'All right, just this once. But if you want to be in the college class, it needs your full attention. Try and concentrate please, we're starting *Hamlet* next lesson and it's a very exciting play, full of wisdom and pathos. I think you'll like it.'

Lottie had been looking forward to the new school year when she would be in the elite college class with five other students. David Merryn was to take them for English, and a new teacher, Miss Polkenna, for everything else. She seemed cold and unfriendly and Lottie had taken an instant dislike to her in their first lessons that morning. She missed Morwenna and didn't feel drawn to any of the other students.

Dr Tregullow's words haunted her. She wished she'd written them down. She needed a script for when she was brave enough to tell Jenny. It had to be Jenny first. She couldn't bear the thought of telling her father, when he was so proud of her. She feared losing him. And Nan. But Jenny would understand. Jenny had pledged to love her no matter what. So telling Jenny was the key. But if only she had those words the old doctor had spoken. They'd been wise and poetic, like Shakespeare. She'd wasted her favourite lesson – English – trying to memorise them. Perhaps she would go back after school and ask him to remind her.

Morwenna's words also kept echoing in her mind: *You're heading for trouble, Lottie, and you're gonna need me . . . Come and talk to my mum.*

Lottie had met Morwenna's mother a few times and found her alarmingly outspoken and earthy – too ready to laugh, and her laugh was disgustingly infectious. She wore exceptionally scarlet lipstick and jet black beads and earrings. Lottie was slightly afraid of her. She pondered the possibility of going to see her after school.

Lottie desperately wanted to keep her baby a secret. Dr Tregullow's words had encapsulated the way she intuitively felt about the tiny person growing inside her. A miracle. She wanted to keep it as a miracle. She wished she could go off and live alone on a secret island, have her baby and bring it up in a magical world where there was no poverty, no prejudice and no gossip.

'Lottie!' David Merryn interrupted her thoughts. 'Pay attention. This is important.' He tapped the blackboard where he had written something for them to copy and memorise. 'This is a famous quotation from *Hamlet*. Copy it down, please, and learn it tonight. I shall test you tomorrow and we shall discuss what it means.'

> *To be, or not to be, that is the question:*
> *Whether 'tis nobler in the mind to suffer*
> *The slings and arrows of outrageous fortune,*
> *Or to take arms against a sea of troubles,*
> *And by opposing end them.*

Lottie knew immediately what it meant, and it seemed tailor-made for her. *Or to take arms against a sea of troubles*, she thought, *and by opposing end them.*

That's exactly what I have to do.

At the end of the first week back at school she found herself heading for Morwenna's place, a terraced granite cottage facing the narrow street and with the back high above the sea, so close that in stormy weather the waves splattered Morwenna's bedroom window with spray. Lottie felt apprehensive knocking on the door. Was she doing the right thing? It didn't feel good.

'Hello, Lottie. What you doing 'ere?' Cora Bartle opened the door with a cigarette hanging from one side of her mouth. 'Well, come in then – Morwenna's 'avin' her tea.'

Lottie followed Cora's thick calves through to the back where Morwenna was finishing a dish of trifle, silhouetted against the salt-encrusted window panes. 'Aw, Lottie! I thought you weren't speaking to me.'

'Sorry,' Lottie said, and meant it, glad to be with her friend again.

'Want some trifle?' Cora said. 'Go on, it's lovely. Spoil yourself. You look as if you need to.'

'Do I?'

'Yeah – you do.' Cora dished out some trifle anyway and peered shrewdly into Lottie's face. 'What's the matter, dearie?'

Lottie glanced at Morwenna's concerned eyes and suddenly she could only whisper. 'You were right. And I do ... need ... your help.'

Morwenna gasped. 'Aw, blimey ... no ... you're not – are you, Lottie?'

Lottie nodded. She slumped onto a chair, put her head down on the table and began to shiver and shake, taking great gasps of air. She heard Morwenna whisper to her mum. 'He's got her up the spout.'

'Who has? I'll kill the bastard,' Cora hissed.

'Matt. Bloody Matt.'

Lottie felt deeply offended, hearing them describe Matt so ruthlessly. But she couldn't take any notice. There were bigger issues to think about.

'Go on, darling. You have a cry,' Cora said kindly. 'These won't be the last tears you shed, believe me.'

'Who said you were pregnant?' Morwenna asked.

'Dr Tregullow.'

'So it's true?'

'Yes. He listened to my baby's heartbeat.' Lottie kept her head down, great sobs shaking her body, while Morwenna and her mum held her in a caring hug, one each side. She felt intense gratitude for their warmth and non-judgemental kindness. They held onto her until she managed to stop sobbing and sit up. She wanted to repeat Dr Tregullow's poetic words. She tried to dredge them up.

'A baby is a miracle ' she began, but Cora shot her down immediately.

'That's a load of rubbish. Babies scream and they stink, and you have to change their nappy and feed the little buggers.' Cora's eyes matched the jet beads around her throat. 'When is it due, Lottie? Did he say?'

'In February.'

'You can get rid of it, girl. I'll help you,' Cora said. 'I know a few tricks. And I know a woman who does it on the sly.'

Lottie stared at her in horror.

'Have you told Jenny yet?' Cora asked.

'No.'

'Good. Then you can get rid of it and she'll never know.'

'But . . .'

'I won't tell her, Lottie. And I can take you to this woman – she lives in Hayle – and we'll look after you afterwards, won't we, 'Wenna?'

'Mum!' Morwenna looked embarrassed.

Lottie felt sick and cold. She thought carefully about how to reply, how to say something polite but meaningful to Cora. How had Morwenna survived, she wondered. And yet she'd felt so moved by the warm, forgiving friendliness radiating from both Cora and Morwenna. If the devil himself knocked on their door, he'd be given a dish of trifle and a hug.

Cora didn't wait for a reply, but turned on Morwenna. 'Well, I dunno why you're looking shocked. That's what I'd do if you got a bun in the oven, don't you forget it. Any road up, Lottie came here for my down-to-earth advice and I've given it to her. Isn't that right, Lottie?'

Lottie stared out at the sea. It was rough, flecked with white crests of breaking waves, the wind whisking and spinning the foam. Was Matt out there somewhere? Was he safe?

'She's clammed up now.' Cora looked at Morwenna. 'What did I say?'

'Lottie's like that, Mum. She takes ages thinking what to say.'

Lottie smiled at Morwenna. 'Thanks.' She studied the bright, expectant glint of Cora's black eyes and said, 'Thanks for your advice, but I wouldn't dream of killing my child or abandoning it. My child is loved and wanted and no one is going to stop me being its mother.'

Cora looked flummoxed. She shook her head as if Lottie were a lost cause. 'That's very magnanimous, dearie, but you are in for a *very* hard time. Don't say I didn't warn you. Your family will throw you out – you wait and see. And where are you gonna go then? Eh?'

'I've said all I'm going to say.'

Cora rolled her eyes. She lit another cigarette, letting the smoke drift over the trifle. 'Well, I haven't. Someone's gotta tell you straight, girl. Do you realise how fat you'll get? Like this.' Cora picked up a cushion and stuffed it inside her cardigan, did the buttons up and paraded around the room. 'You can't hide. You won't be able to go to school. No one will give you a job. You'll be driven out of St Ives – not by me, but by all them holier-than-thou gossips. And after it's born it'll be ten times worse.' She paused to chuck the cushion back on the sofa. 'And Matt isn't gonna support you, is he? How can he? Does he know?'

'No.'

'Well, you wait, he'll run a mile when you tell him. Believe me, most men don't want to know – and he won't. You mark my words, Lottie, he'll bugger off on that boat and you'll never see him again.' She held up her hand as Lottie tried to interrupt. 'I know you don't like what I'm telling you, but I'm doing you a favour. I hope you listen to me, 'cause if you don't, your life is gonna be ruined, and all your dreams with it, Lottie. You'll lose everything. You've got to get rid of it. Come on, eat your trifle.'

Eat trifle? After that? Lottie shut her eyes. She wished she could shut her ears as well. She wished she'd never gone there. Cora was such a straight-talker.

You haven't given me advice, Lottie thought, *you've crucified me*. She picked up her school bag. 'I must go home. I've got homework to do.'

She walked away with one hand over her tummy. 'I hope you weren't listening, little one,' she murmured, and headed home, her hair streaming back, her face cold in the wind from the approaching storm.

Chapter 15

Denial

After the meeting with Cora, Lottie needed some breathing space. She retreated into denial, trying to go on living her happy life as if nothing had happened. She threw herself into her schoolwork, and into the intensive September harvest time at Hendravean. At weekends, she and Tom worked tirelessly in Nan's abundant garden, picking pears and crab apples and blackberries, and the entire kitchen, scullery and beyond, steamed with fruity clouds that migrated into the hall like a weather front over the Atlantic.

Nan joked that it would be raining over the stairs before they had finished. She became a fearsome sight, engulfed in her huge fruit apron of heavy linen. It smelled like old marmalade, and generations of stains twisted and turned, layer upon layer, like an abstract painting.

'When you've finished with that apron, I'll cut it into squares and frame them,' John remarked on one of his visits. 'The London Tate Gallery would love it.' And Nan had cackled with laughter as she stirred a great cauldron of bubbling chutney with energetic, fruit-stained arms. Nan had never been happier than she was now, sharing the good feeling of stocking up for the winter. Lottie enjoyed the ambience of what seemed to be a golden time. She didn't want to spoil Nan's obvious contentment, or Jenny's euphoria at having a job at John's gallery.

Lottie felt very close to Nan, especially when they shared the poetry she had to learn and analyse for homework. To have Nan sitting beside her, encouraging her and adding bits of her own knowledge, made the work a magical journey. Nan was proud of her, and so was Jenny. Surely they would continue to love and support her when they knew about the baby?

September passed in its 'mellow fruitfulness', and at last Matt's boat came in to St Ives on a quiet sea, a day when rainbows appeared and disappeared as the mist of showers crossed the sea.

'You've worked hard enough, Lottie,' Nan said. 'I know you want to go out on the boat with Matt. You go and have a lovely day.'

If only she knew, Lottie thought, pleased to have Nan's blessing on her Saturday morning. The raw power of Cora's prediction – *Your family will throw you out* – had begun to fade as Lottie's life was cushioned by love, beauty and abundance.

Lottie felt good as she walked down to the harbour, wearing the frock her father had bought her in New York. It had been too big then, but now it was perfect. Its loose style was comfortable and there would be room for the bump to grow. She loved the fabric, which shimmered with turquoise, emerald and white, with ruffles around the swirly skirt and neckline. John had chosen it because it resembled the colours of the Cornish sea. Her honey-blonde hair looked soft and exotic against the lovely dress and she'd done it the way Matt liked it, the front strands tied back with a green ribbon.

Lottie hoped today would be the time to tell Matt about the baby. She wouldn't tell him straight away. She'd wait for the right moment – and she'd tell him in the language of poetry. The miracle and the tiny heartbeat. She wanted Matt to feel good. She wanted him to love the little person who was curled up inside her womb.

But when she reached *The Jenny Wren*, Matt wasn't there. Usually he was standing on the boat, watching and waiting for her to arrive. She always loved the moment when he caught sight of her and gave her the curt Lanroska nod, and as she drew close she could see his eyes full of light.

Where is he?

Slightly deflated, Lottie sat on the sea-worn timber of the slipway, arranging her skirt nicely over her legs. She put the picnic basket down, glad that it had a lid strapped over the food as a few seagulls were eyeing it hopefully.

Wharf Road was busy with women packing and selling fish, artists with their easels, Saturday shoppers with baskets, and local children playing. As she watched them, Lottie thought about Warren and wondered where he was. She'd enjoyed reading him stories, seeing his face light up, and teaching him to talk.

At last she spotted Matt's rangy figure weaving through the crowd at the far end of the quay. She waved, but he didn't wave back, and Lottie immediately sensed something was wrong. Normally Matt walked in a leisurely, rather insolent way, his eyes challenging everyone he met. Now he walked in angry strides, his head down. Perhaps he hadn't seen her. Something must have happened. Had he stolen something and got caught?

He came pounding down the slipway, his face flushed, his eyes wild. 'Get in the boat,' he said roughly. He didn't even look at her. Lottie froze. 'Well, don't just sit there in your posh frock. I've got to get out of here.'

'What's wrong?' Lottie asked, upset at the way he was treating her.

'Just *get in*.' Matt pulled the boat in closer and vaulted in. He turned and held out his hand. 'Are you coming or not?'

'Matt!' Lottie glared at him. 'If you continue to speak to me like that, I shall take the picnic and go home.'

Matt crumpled. 'Please, Lottie, I don't mean to upset you. I'd die if I lost you.' He rubbed his shoulder and as he turned, Lottie noticed a dark bruise on the side of his face. It was bleeding a little into his hair, as if it had only just happened. 'We have to talk about this.' He touched the bruise gingerly, his hand shaking.

'You're hurt, Matt.' Lottie swung herself into the boat. She tried to dab at the blood with her small hanky but Matt moved her arm away, gripping it firmly. 'You're trembling, Matt. What happened?'

He looked down at her, his eyes full of pain. 'I'll tell you.' He glanced anxiously at Wharf Road as if someone were chasing him. 'But let's get away, out on the water. You sit down – and hold tight, Lottie.' He started the motor and steered the boat skilfully through the harbour, too fast, making Lottie gasp and cling on with both hands, the bow wave rocking the other boats, raising a few shouts of protest. But Matt didn't seem to care.

Lottie was terrified, not only for herself but for the tiny person growing within her. Could her baby hear the savage roar of the engine? Could it feel her anxiety at the way the boat was ripping through the calm water, rocking and bouncing? Matt had never done this before. He'd always been careful and considerate when she was with him. She shut her eyes and struggled to stay calm, images of the shipwreck haunting her. Then the storm on the way back from America, the way her father had held her so caringly.

Out in the bay, *The Jenny Wren* came to a halt. Matt cut the engine and a tranquil circle of silence spread out around them in ripples of chalky blue and silver.

'Are you okay?' Matt sat down, his knees hunched, his body still, as if the burst of speed had dispersed his anger into the ocean.

Lottie couldn't reply. She looked down at her dress, which was now damp from the spray, and wished she hadn't worn it. She reached out for a hug and they held each other. Lottie waited for Matt to start talking and when he did, she took both his hands in hers and looked into his troubled eyes.

'I do love you, Lottie,' he said in a low, husky voice, 'and I don't want to lose you. You're truly the most precious thing in my life. But I need you to be honest with me.'

'I always am.'

'You're not going to like this, Lottie, but you have to know. This morning I was here early and I went up to the gallery to give John some more of my drawings. I was feeling good. But when I walked past Morwenna's place, her mother was standing outside her door smoking and talking to her friend. She came across the road and started screaming at me – she was right in my face. She kept on and on saying she hated bastards like me because of what I've done to you. So I laughed at her. I said, "Get off me, you mad woman," and I told her I hadn't done anything to you and I didn't know what she was on about – and she yelled, "Ask Lottie – go on – ask her."'

Lottie listened, horrified. Why had she trusted Cora? 'Did she actually *say* what you were supposed to have done?'

'No. She wouldn't shut up and people were coming out of their doors to see what was going on – like they always do around here. I laughed at her and called her Crazy Daisy and she went mad. She went into her house and grabbed a frying pan and threw it at me. It really hurt. I thought she'd broken my jaw.'

'How dreadful! What did you do then?' Lottie asked.

'I kept telling her I didn't know what she was accusing me of. I felt like throttling her with my bare hands, Lottie, but I managed to walk away without touching her. She threw all sorts of things after me – shoes, saucepans. It was hard, but I just walked away. I thought of Dad and how that's what he would have done. And that Maudie woman was there as well, gloating. But Cora Bartle really got to me, Lottie. I hate those women. What gives them the right to attack me like that in my own home town?'

'Oh, Matt.' Lottie slipped her arm around his shoulders.

'I mean – I haven't done anything, have I? What exactly is she blaming me *for*? And why did she keep saying, "Ask Lottie"? Do you know why?'

Lottie shut her eyes. There was no avoiding it now. Matt must be told. The language of poetry wasn't going to work. He was looking at her so intently, with darkly wounded eyes. He needed the plain truth – no frills. She let go of his hands and placed hers over her tummy.

Help me, she thought. *Little one, little star – help me.*

'Lottie? What did Cora mean? Tell me.'

'Cora shouldn't have blamed you, Matt. It wasn't something you did on your own. We did it together. We made love and it was beautiful. Our love has made a baby.'

Matt frowned and drew his lips back into a horrified snarl.

She waited, but he didn't speak so she said, 'Our baby – yes, *our* baby – is a miracle. It has a tiny heartbeat, a sweet little face, perfect fingers and toes. It wants to live and it wants us to be its parents.'

Matt went pale, the bruise already darkening to a florid purple over his cheek. 'A ... baby?' he spluttered. 'But ... we're young lovers, Lottie – we're too young to have a baby.'

Lottie tried to speak gently and quietly, infusing her voice with a sense of magic, the way Nan did when she was telling a legend. 'I'm a woman, Matt, not a girl. I have monthly periods like every woman does. Don't you know that?'

Matt shook his head. He spoke in a hoarse whisper. 'No – no, I didn't. I might have heard about it, but I didn't know what they were, and nobody's told me. Dad would have explained it, but he's gone and he'll never come back. I don't talk to Mum and I couldn't possibly ask her anything like that – she'd go mad, like Cora Bartle.' A single tear rolled down his bruised cheek. 'I've lived like this, on my own, since we escaped from the orphanage. It's been hard, Lottie – yeah, I know I chose to do it, but no one knows how hard it is. And I've got no one to talk to. Ken, maybe, but not about things like that – or your dad, John. I really like him but I've only just met him. Who else is there? I could have talked to Grandad Vic but he just went off, didn't he? He lives in Newlyn.' He gazed out at the sea. 'He always liked me. He stuck up for me and gave me advice. I miss him, Lottie.' Another tear caught a glint of sun as it rolled down his cheek. 'When we lost Dad, we lost everything, didn't we?'

Lottie nodded, still holding his hands, rubbing the rough texture of his skin with her small thumb.

'We lost ... *everything*,' Matt repeated. 'Our dad, our grandad, our home. And when we were dragged off to the orphanage, I even lost you, Lottie, and it made me understand how much I loved you. Everything I've tried to do – finding *The Jenny Wren* and restoring her, doing the drawings to make some money – has been for *us*, Lottie, and when you told me you loved me too, it was suddenly like my whole life had changed and I had a reason to go on living.' He stopped talking and let his eyes gaze at her steadily.

'Listen, Matt – don't speak, just listen, please.' She looked at him with a bright, compelling gaze. 'Yes, we lost everything, but now we've been given a miracle of life, a tiny, perfect baby, a secret star that came through our beautiful lovemaking. It came through you and into me, and it wants to live, it wants us to be its parents. It will bring laughter and happiness into our world. I am carrying it, keeping it safe and warm.' She patted her tummy. 'And Dr Tregullow could hear its fast little heartbeat in there.'

'But ...'

'No – listen, Matt,' Lottie spoke with all the intensity she could muster. 'Both of us, you and me, have had broken childhoods, and this little person will be *our* family. I don't know why but I feel it's a girl, and she will look a bit like me and a bit like you, and even a bit like your dad. He always wanted a little girl.'

'But, Lottie, this is a *baby*, not an angel with wings. And babies are horrible. They scream day and night. I remember when Tom was born. He was awful. Mum was worn out – and babies smell; the whole house stinks for years.'

'You sound like Cora Bartle!' Lottie felt annoyed. Her plan had failed.

'I do not!'

'Cora's attitude upset me. She painted a sordid, miserable picture of motherhood. She even said the family would throw me out.'

'So you did tell Cora Bartle – why tell her, of all people, Lottie?'

'I needed some down-to-earth advice, and like you I felt . . .'

Matt interrupted her, angry now. 'So what was her down-to-earth advice? Attack me in the street and shout it all over St Ives? You might have told me first.'

'I did try to tell you that day on the boat, but you wouldn't listen.'

'Well, how was I to know it was something so . . . so *devastating*?' Matt snatched his hand away from hers and clenched it into a fist. 'You betrayed me, like all women do.'

'I did not!'

'Yes, you did – and don't glare at me, Lottie. It hurts. How did you think I'd feel, having her yelling at me? Eh?'

'I didn't know she was going to.'

'So what else did Cora Wonderful Bartle advise?' Matt snarled.

'She said I should keep it a secret and she offered to help me get rid of it.' Lottie's voice became a whine of pain.

'Get rid of it? What the heck does that mean?'

'I don't know.'

'Oh – you don't know!'

'Don't be horrible to me, Matt,' Lottie spoke quietly, but her eyes blazed. 'I don't know because I don't *want* to know. I wouldn't dream of killing our child – *our child*, Matt. I intend to let it live, let it be born into a loving, caring family, and that includes you. You'll be its father, Matt. Think about it. But if I have to, I'll do it on my own.'

Matt clenched his hands into his hair. He hunched his back and rocked forward. 'I can't take this,' he growled. 'Just leave me alone to sort my head out.'

'Oh, Matt,' Lottie tried to give him a hug.

'Get off me.' He pushed her away. 'Leave me alone. Give me a chance to think, will you?'

Lottie went cold. She looked at the distant shore. 'Okay, then will you please take me back to the harbour? It's too far to swim.'

Matt continued to rock and growl. She remembered how he'd been as a child. Angry. He'd sit hunched on the stairs, chucking a ball at the front door, endlessly.

Sadness clawed at her heart. His attitude, his rough disregard of her feelings – was this the same Matt who made love with her so tenderly? Was it really *love*? Or was it something he could switch off when she needed support?

The brilliance of the day burned at the edges, the shimmering sunlight and the calm sea reduced to a distant blob of light. Surely the love of her life wasn't going to abandon her?

He started the boat's engine. 'Hold tight,' he said, grim-faced. Without looking at her again he headed for the harbour. The tide was ebbing so he pulled the boat in at the bottom of the stone steps leading up to Smeaton's Pier. 'Well, there you are. You can go,' he growled.

A sense of finality swept over Lottie. Shocked at his ruthless, uncaring behaviour, she sat frozen. 'Matt – Matt, please – don't be so cruel.'

'I did what you wanted – brought you ashore. So just go.'

'But, Matt . . .'

'*Go!*'

Numbly, she climbed out of the boat onto the granite steps. He revved the engine and left in a curve of flying spray. Lottie felt hollow inside.

Cora's words rattled in her mind: *When you tell him, he'll run a mile.*

Matt had gone. Without saying goodbye, without looking back. Lottie stumbled up the steps with only one thought hammering away in her mind: her life was over.

'I've had a lovely day,' Jenny said, her face glowing with happiness as John returned from his outdoor painting time, his easel tucked under his arm. 'I sold three paintings, John! Two of yours and one of Matt's.'

'Oh, well done, that is good news.' John stood gazing at her. 'It must be your pretty face.'

Jenny flushed. 'And I met interesting people, mostly from up-country. Some of them do speak funny, but I rather enjoy listening to a different accent. I've put the money in the drawer, where you showed me – and I put Matt's money in an envelope. He and Lottie must have had a wonderful day out on the boat. What about you, John? How did the sketching go?'

'Pretty well. I walked inland up to Trencrom and did some drawings of the quoit.'

'Come on – show me,' Jenny said, wanting to encourage him.

John opened his sketch pad and showed her his pencil drawings of the giant granite dolmen said to be a burial chamber.

'I've been up there a few times,' Jenny said. 'It's quite a climb, isn't it? I couldn't do it now.'

'Have you mastered the electric kettle yet?' John asked.

Jenny grinned. 'Is that your way of asking me to make coffee?'

'Yes, please.' John shut the gallery door and put the CLOSED sign up. 'I won't lock it in case Lottie comes by on her way home. She often does.'

For a moment they both stared at *Discovering Charlotte*, the painting John had done of nine-year-old Lottie playing on the beach with Morwenna. It had pride of place in the gallery. He'd never sell it, John promised. It would be an heirloom to be handed down through the family.

'She was such a beautiful child,' he mused. 'It's good to have the memory. She's growing up so fast.'

'She went out this morning in the posh frock you bought her in New York. She looked stunning in it. Maybe it's time to do another painting of her, John, don't you think?'

John's dark blue eyes shone. 'Well, actually Jenny, it's you I'd like to paint.'

'Me? Whatever for?'

'Because you're beautiful, Jenny. Beautiful and strong, and you have a radiance about you today.'

'Have I?'

'But exactly how to paint such radiance is something I haven't worked out yet. Perhaps I should just enjoy it instead.' He reached out and touched her face, his eyes holding hers in a stare loaded with intention. Jenny held her breath, her lips parted. His fingers moved over her cheekbone and softly down to trace the shape of her mouth, lingering for a moment to stroke the centre of her top lip.

Jenny felt herself melting. She knew he wouldn't want her to be stiff and resistant and thinking of Arnie. John would want her soft and pliable and passionate. He wanted her to want him. And she did.

'You're lovely,' he breathed, his feet shuffling closer, pulling her gently in until she felt the full length of him against her. She reached up to touch his face, watching the light in his eyes, the loneliness and the longing, the letting go as he finally kissed her.

Jenny's spirits soared. She felt weightless and free. 'Shall we go upstairs?' he murmured.

'Lock the door,' she whispered. It wouldn't do to have Lottie walking in on their lovemaking.

*

On that still, warm day, thundery showers were building over the sea, peppering the tranquil water with fat drops of rain. Alone at Hendravean, Nan fetched Mufty in from the paddock. Donkeys hated getting wet so she wanted him inside with a haynet stuffed with sweet meadow hay and a luxurious bed of crisp golden straw. It took Nan an hour to settle him in, heaving barrowloads of straw across the yard and then shaking it out with a pitchfork. She struggled up the ladder into the hayloft, filled Mufty's net and rolled it down. The hay dust made her wheeze and cough. She dragged herself back to the house and brewed a mug of hot black tea, the steam from it easing her breathing.

Nan fell asleep in her chair and awoke at noon feeling rested, enjoying her time alone. The struggle to look after Mufty made her reflect with gratitude on the work Tom and Lottie did on a daily basis. They were willing and quick, looking after Mufty and the chickens, bringing in wood and coal for the range. It was good to have them around. Her decision to take them in had been hard, but it had brought blessings into her life.

Sharing the harvest meant a lot to Nan, and she'd enjoyed every minute. Instead of facing winter on her own, she was looking forward to cosy evenings by the fire, helping Lottie with her studying, telling stories and legends in the flickering firelight.

Jenny's job in the gallery had been a welcome bonus too, easing their finances and giving Nan some peace. Nan often found herself thinking of Warren. Where was he? Was he all right? How sad that he'd gone just as she was getting to know him. Did he still have the piano-accordion? It was an heirloom, having belonged to Nan's father, and she would have liked it back. But it was only a thing, Nan reasoned. Nothing mattered as much as Warren's life. Sometimes she went into his room and touched the little jacket, and so did Jenny. Nan intended to go off in the car one day and try to find him, but there never seemed to be a day when she had enough energy and strength.

Between showers, the noon sun was balmy, warming the cottage walls and coaxing bees and butterflies out to feast on nectar from the mass of blue Michaelmas daisies, the wide-open marigolds and sunflowers. Nan went outside to potter in the garden, pausing to check Mufty on the way. She looked over the stable door and was astonished to see the donkey lying down in the straw with Lottie curled up against his shoulder, fast asleep, still wearing her posh frock. Bartholomew was there too, nestled close to Lottie, his paws stretched over her heart. Nan could hear him purring. She opened her mouth to ask what in heaven's name was going on, and shut it again when the cat gave her a slit-eyed stare. Best not to disturb them.

Nan leaned on the door and Mufty looked up at her with liquid eyes, his soft grey muzzle resting on Lottie's hip. Both cat and donkey looked blissed out. But Lottie didn't. She was deeply asleep but there was a frown on her brow and her cheeks looked drawn and smudged as if she'd been crying. Her dress was splayed out on the straw, its colours glimmering in the dim interior of the stable.

Nan knew immediately that something terribly upsetting had happened to Lottie. It would be Matt's fault, of course, Nan decided.

Hailstones bombed down from a cloud with violet edges racing over the sun. A chilled wind blew low across the yard. Nan glanced at the sea and noticed surf breaking over Godrevy and white horses tossing far out beyond the bay. It confirmed what Nan had heard on the shipping forecast: a storm was out there in the Atlantic. She turned and went indoors to find a blanket, and emerged with a thick tartan rug. Moving furtively, Nan eased the stable door open and covered Lottie's sleeping form with the warm rug. Mufty didn't move and neither did Bartholomew.

Let her sleep, Nan thought, *and when she wakes she will tell me what's happened.*

Her mind went back to the time Jenny took Lottie to the doctor because of her constant sickness. Now Lottie had been to Dr Tregullow on her own and had refused to tell Jenny why. Nan tried to dismiss the suspicion building up inside her.

Surely not Lottie? But the thought just wouldn't go away. *I'll find out*, Nan told herself.

Nan went back to the house and rummaged in a drawer for her pendulum, which was a small pebble with a hole in it, threaded onto the end of a piece of string. She crept back to the stable, pleased to see Lottie still fast asleep.

'You stay quiet,' she whispered to Mufty, and the donkey did as he was told, keeping still as Nan came in and closed the door. She didn't want Lottie to wake up and ask what she was doing.

She held the pendulum directly over Lottie's womb, steadied the string so that it hung motionless, and then waited, her heart beating faster as she asked a question from her mind. It began to stir, then it spun round positively. *Yes.*

Nan's heart raced with shock. She asked another question. 'Is it a boy?'

No.

Then: 'Is it a girl?'

Yes.

'I knew it,' Nan thought, and her legs began to tremble. She wound the string around the pebble and pushed it into her apron pocket. This poor child is pregnant. So young.

Nan drew a kiss in the air with her finger. 'Sleep well, precious one, little mother.'

Lottie didn't stir. Nan left the stable and shuffled back to the house where she sat in her chair, shaking with emotion, her mind replaying something that had happened in her own life. A secret she'd never told.

Chapter 16

The Last Happy Day

There would be no more revelations, Lottie decided, when she woke up in Mufty's stable. Her arms and legs itched from the straw and the first thing she spotted when she opened her eyes was Bartholomew's golden-eyed cat face very close, his expression radiating concern. She felt he wanted to know if she was okay so she said, 'Thank you, darling cat. I might never be happy again, but I can manage. Providing nothing else goes wrong.'

Bartholomew got up and stretched, then leapt down into the yard, the tip of his fluffy tail disappearing over the door.

Mufty was fidgeting and she sensed he wanted to stand up. She wondered what the time was. Late afternoon, judging by the mellow gold of the sunlight. Mufty must have stayed lying down for her benefit. Lottie gave him a hug.

'You helped me so much, Mufty.'

They both stood up, Mufty having a good shake, and Lottie brushing the bits of straw from her dress. Everything hurt. Even seeing the flowers on the fringe of Nan's garden. Even the butterflies.

She put both hands over her womb. 'Don't worry, little one, little star. I am strong. I shall carry you and be your mum forever. I will never abandon you.'

With that empowering thought, Lottie walked towards the house and each footstep brought an affirmation: *I can still walk, I can still feel the warmth of the sun, I can still be a mother. A secret mother. Without Matt.* She turned back to pick up the tartan rug. Someone must have loved her enough to put it over her. Nan. Nan, her rock. Lottie folded it and carried it inside.

'Ah, there you are,' Nan said, deftly crimping the edges of the pasties she was making, her freckled old hands covered in flour. She asked no questions, and for that Lottie was grateful.

'I'm going upstairs to study,' Lottie said, and Nan gave her an approving nod.

Lottie trailed upstairs thinking of Matt. He was having a bad day. He'd get over it, wouldn't he? She was glad she'd walked away and left him to sort himself out.

She opened her school bag and took out *Romeo and Juliet*. It fell open at some of Juliet's meaningful words:

> *Give me my Romeo; and, when he shall die,*
> *Take him and cut him out in little stars,*
> *And he will make the face of heaven so fine*
> *That all the world will be in love with night.*

It was exactly how she felt about Matt. Stunned, she sat reading it over and over. Matt could do no wrong. She loved and adored him. Why hadn't she told him that?

He'd abandoned her without looking back. Where would he go? What did he intend to do?

A vivid memory came to her – of the night Arnie left. She'd been nine years old, and awake, listening to the row he was having with Jenny. The sound of his footsteps thudding down towards the sea was unforgettable. She'd leaned out of the window and tasted the easterly wind, heard it driving waves into the harbour. She'd gone downstairs and told Jenny.

'We should go out and get him,' she'd said. And Jenny had said no – he'd be all right. But Arnie never came back. Matt closely resembled him, especially today: his face strong, his eyes wounded.

Abandonment and bereavement were twins. If Matt had truly abandoned her, then Lottie would deal with it like grief. She stared out at the sea, *Romeo and Juliet* open on her lap. Surf was breaking over Godrevy and under a lustrous thundercloud the sea was flecked with the white crests of waves, the wind ripping and twisting them into plumes of spray.

Was he out there trying to get back to Portreath? Would *The Jenny Wren* cope with such a wind-whipped tide?

Lottie sat on her bed, surrounded by books but not looking at any of them. Could she really study with a broken heart? Could she eat and chat to people as if nothing had happened? She would have to try.

Telling Cora and telling Matt had been disastrous. Right now, Lottie didn't feel strong enough to tell anyone else. She needed time to reclaim her true conviction that being a mother was beautiful and important. Mothers should fight for their children. She would fight. She would fight everybody and anybody who opposed her right to love and keep her child, and for the child's right to have its own true mother.

There were three more people she had to tell: Jenny, Nan and her father. Olivia didn't count. Olivia was out of the way in London and Lottie didn't care if she never saw her again. It occurred to Lottie that telling each of the three individually would only prolong the agony. Why not tell them all at once? Choose a good, happy moment when they were together. Instead of three ordeals, she'd only have one.

Lottie sighed. Everything was going to be twice as difficult with a broken heart. She felt more vulnerable than ever before, as if the slightest thing would make her cry.

With the books untouched around her, she sat watching the golden evening melt into twilight. She jumped when her bedroom door opened and Tom came in.

'Supper's ready,' he said, 'and Mum's got a surprise. Why are you sitting in the dark, Lottie?' He didn't wait for an answer but thudded down the stairs, leaving her door wide open. Lottie didn't want a surprise. It sounded like a threat when her heart was broken. She wrapped a shawl around herself and went down into the warm, steamy kitchen.

'Here you are, Lottie.' Jenny put a plate in front of her with one of Nan's pasties on it. The crust was golden-brown and flaky and the pasty was longer than her plate. It was one of Nan's specials with the meat and vegetables at one end, and spiced apple and sultanas at the other. Dinner and pudding all in one. Both ends had a rock-hard knob of pastry.

'So you could drop it down a tin mine,' Nan said, and she cackled with laughter.

Everyone looks happy, Lottie thought, *and I've got a broken heart.*

Jenny sparkled. Her skin glowed and her eyes were bright. 'I've got a surprise,' she said, beaming. 'We're having a day out tomorrow. John is taking us to Penzance. And there's an island there, with a castle on top – St Michael's Mount. You can walk to it at low tide along the causeway.'

'Aw, Mum, I always wanted to do that,' Tom said, his cheeks full of pasty.

'Isn't it exciting, Lottie?' Jenny said, looking at her with wide, magnetic eyes. 'You'll come, won't you? John wants you to – and Tom. He said we've worked hard and we deserved a day out, as a family.'

Lottie hadn't yet bitten into her pasty. It felt like a hot water bottle in her cold hands.

'All five of us,' Jenny added happily.

Five and a half, Lottie thought, and felt yet another ache in her throat.

Jenny looked at her suspiciously. 'Is something wrong, Lottie? Aren't you well? You've been so quiet.'

'I'm okay.'

Nan gave her a knowing look, but tactfully changed the subject. 'When we've had supper, I *might* be persuaded to tell you the legend of St Michael's Mount, *and*,' she added, seeing Jenny rolling her eyes, 'even Jenny will like this one as it's based on a true story.'

'Oh, go on then, Nan,' Jenny said. 'A bit of silly magic might do us good.'

Nobody moved from the table as Nan prepared herself for telling the story, first cleaning her hands on her napkin, then sitting perfectly still with her eyes closed, creating tension without even trying. When she opened them, she had a captive audience. It lifted Lottie.

'Cor, look at THAT,' Tom yelled. 'A real castle – on an island!'

Jenny and John smiled at each other, enjoying Tom's excitement as the train steamed into the great curve of Mount's Bay, the sea and sky china blue and the mystic island of St Michael's Mount floating like a tall ship in the shimmering light.

Even Lottie, who had been quiet all the way, stood at the window with Tom, thrilled to see the fairy tale island. 'You know what Nan would say if she was here?' she remarked.

'What?' Jenny asked.

'She'd say, "O Magnum Mysterium",' Lottie said. 'It's Latin, and she's always saying it.'

Nan had chosen to stay at home. She'd seen the Mount many times and someone had to look after Mufty and the chickens. Lottie's plan to break her news to all three of them at an auspicious moment didn't seem likely to happen. Jenny and John looked so happy, and Tom's enthusiasm was infectious. Why spoil their lovely day? Lottie almost felt like a child again, an echo of being carefree, and it was pleasant.

There's magic in the air, she thought, and it wasn't only coming from St Michael's Mount. It was coming from Jenny and John too. Lottie had never seen her usually serious father smile and laugh so much. The way he kept looking at Jenny, looking *after* her, and Jenny was enjoying it. She remembered how she'd once hoped John would fall in love with Olivia again. She was glad he hadn't. John falling in love with Jenny would have been Lottie's perfect dream, if only she were still a child. But she wasn't. She was a mother in waiting.

John paid for a cab to take them to Marazion where they spent the first hour watching the tide slowly ebbing to reveal the cobbled causeway leading to the island. While they waited, Lottie and Tom collected some of the pebbles studded into the wet sand, tiny jewel-like stones in myriad colours, quite different from the black pebbles of Porthmeor Beach. The shells were different too. Instead of limpets and blue mussel shells, there were neat little spirals of bright yellow, amber and cream, and delicate fan-like shells in pink, orange and white.

'She's still a child at heart,' John said, as he sat on a rock with Jenny, watching Lottie gathering shells.

'She is,' Jenny agreed, 'but something's wrong with her, John. She doesn't look right, does she?'

273

'Hmm. I worry about the illness she had. It's left a shadow,' John said. 'Before I took her to New York, she was confident and optimistic, wasn't she? Now she often looks as if she's carrying a secret burden.'

'It's Matt,' Jenny said. 'I wish she wasn't so obsessed with him and his boat. He's always been the troublemaker, I'm afraid.'

'I like him. He's a fine, brave young man.'

'I don't see him like that at all.'

'When I look at him, I see a young man who desperately misses his father,' John said, thoughtfully. 'I hope, as time goes on, I can take him under my wing. He does talk to me about art.'

Tom was on the causeway. 'It's nearly uncovered,' he yelled. 'I'm going over. Come on, Lottie.'

Lottie followed him, stepping over the wet cobbles. Life would be so wonderfully simple if she could just follow Tom and be a child again.

'Do you think you can manage to walk the causeway?' John asked.

'Course I can,' Jenny said. 'Forget about me iron leg. I'm going to enjoy this.'

'We can always catch a boat back,' John said, taking her arm, 'and the slower we go, the more beauty we will see. I love these ancient stones, all different-coloured granite. When they're wet and in the sunshine they're quite gorgeous. I think I shall be down here painting before long. Perhaps I'll bring young Matt with me.'

The walk to St Michael's Mount was unforgettable, with clear, shallow water on either side of the cobbled causeway. Mops of wine-coloured seaweed flounced in the waves, leaving lush curls of it deposited on the pale sand, entangled with white cuttlefish and driftwood. Ahead of them, the island towered out of the sea. There was a harbour with a terrace of cottages along the quayside. Enormous crags of granite and mysterious pine woods led up to the castle walls.

'Nan says there's a tropical garden on the other side of the island,' Jenny said. 'She said flowers grow out of the cracks in the rock; not wild flowers but some kind of multi-coloured daisies, and they come from Africa.'

'Osteospermums,' John said.

Jenny laughed. 'Osteo-who? That's a mouthful, isn't it?'

Tom and Lottie were already on the island, exploring the harbour. Jenny welcomed the chance to sit down on a sunny bench with John and gaze across the sea to Penzance. 'Wish I'd brought a picnic.'

John had a gold watch on a chain in his top pocket. He took it out and listened to hear if it was ticking. 'We've got about three hours,' he said, 'and before we catch the train home, I'd like to treat you all to fish and chips.'

'We've never had fish and chips,' Jenny said.

'The fish is covered in crunchy batter. It's delicious. You put salt and vinegar on it and eat it out of newspaper. It doesn't taste the same if you put it on a plate.'

Jenny looked at him with round eyes. 'I'm having a wonderful time, John – thank you.' She gave him a quick kiss and saw the spark leap in his eyes. She wagged a finger. 'Better not get too cuddly, had we? Here's Lottie.'

Lottie was walking slowly towards them, her blonde hair swinging down her back. 'She looks deadly serious,' John said. 'I wonder what she's thinking about.'

Lottie was considering whether now might be the time to tell them, here in the sunshine on the peaceful island. The thought wouldn't leave her alone.

But when she saw Jenny kiss John and saw how happy they looked, she couldn't do it. She just couldn't.

Matt had gone to ground like a wounded fox. He'd intended to sail back to Portreath, but realised the boat was low on fuel and the only option was to return to St Ives. He couldn't face seeing anyone so he sailed in quietly, moored the boat and crept into the cabin. He drew the curtains over the windows and lay down on his bed, a row of brown velvet cushions from a discarded sofa, and two fusty grey rugs he'd bought for sixpence at a jumble sale. His pillow was clean and comforting, made for him by Lottie, a simple patchwork of sea and sky with white stitched-on clouds and a stitched-on boat like *The Jenny Wren*. Matt pressed the cool cotton against his face, his fingers touching the neat stitches she had made.

As soon as Lottie had gone, he'd wanted her back. But the way she was, not pregnant and irritable, like Jenny had been. He didn't want her torn apart by birth pains and worn out and scruffy with the demands of a screaming baby. In his mind, his Lottie had gone forever. He'd lost the beautiful girl he worshipped and adored. It had sabotaged his dream of a future: a home in St Ives with Lottie.

Matt felt cheated. He felt their youth had been snatched away. And to make it worse, Lottie seemed to have a relaxed attitude towards it.

The future he had looked forward to for so long was ruined.

What was he supposed to do about this baby? He was the father, and that was an overwhelming thought. Matt remembered his own father, Arnie, and how calmly he'd coped with the disruption when Tom was born. Arnie had loved his family. Matt desperately needed to talk to him. Going up to the cemetery and sitting by the grave was the only option, but he'd tried it before and came away feeling even more desolate. Arnie wasn't there, and never would be.

But Grandad was still alive. Why not go down to Newlyn and talk to him?

Matt reached into a cupboard and took out his map. Newlyn wasn't too far. He compared the distance with Portreath. It was further and probably more hazardous.

I'll go while the sea is calm, Matt thought. His need to talk to his grandfather was overpowering. Grandad Vic was kindly and wise, and since he wasn't in St Ives he wouldn't be adding to the gossip.

Matt looked at the picnic basket Lottie had left behind. There was enough food in there to sustain him for a while. He grabbed the empty fuel cans and headed for the garage, going a long way round to avoid Cora Bartle's place. He was annoyed to find the garage closed. Early closing day on a Saturday and closed all day on Sunday.

He couldn't leave St Ives until Monday morning. It added another load to his overburdened mind.

Matt returned to the boat in long strides and flung the two empty cans onto the deck. He crawled into the cabin, picked up his sketchbook and hurled it into a corner, its pages fluttering like a dying bird.

Nothing mattered anymore.

He'd lost Lottie. He didn't want to draw or eat or do anything. He wanted today and tomorrow to disappear, to melt away under the sun or get washed away by the tide. The bruise on his face ached and Cora's words clung round him like barbed wire.

Half listening, half hoping Lottie might come, he lay down and sleep became his only sanctuary.

He'd never felt so utterly alone.

Lottie began to think there never would be a right time to tell her family about the baby. Their day in Penzance was drawing to a close and Jenny looked happier than Lottie had ever seen her. The three of them were sitting on a bench near the railway station, waiting for John to bring the parcels of fish and chips.

'I wish we could come here every day,' Tom said. 'I had the best time ever and I want to come again and bring Matt. Matt would like it, wouldn't he, Lottie?'

Lottie managed a nod. 'Yep.' Then she went on staring out to sea.

'Are you all right, Lottie?' Jenny asked.

She nodded again. She met Jenny's eyes. It might have slipped out then if something else hadn't happened first.

A voice called out, 'Jenny!' and a small, round woman came waddling up to them, her face crinkled with a sunray smile.

Jenny gave a scream of delight. 'Millie! Oh, Millie – I was hoping we might see you.'

'I wasn't expecting to see you – what a lovely surprise,' Millie said. 'And this is Tom! How you've grown!' She turned her sunray smile on Lottie. 'And Lottie! Well, you've grown up – quite the young lady now.' Their eyes met and a question hovered in Millie's eyes.

She knows, Lottie thought, panicking. She folded her arms and tried to divert Millie from coming out with an unfortunate remark. 'I've still got the doll you knitted me on the night of the shipwreck!'

'You were a lost little girl,' Millie said, 'but you were lovely, my darling, and you're still lovely, bless your heart. Now where's Matt?'

'Matt's left home,' Jenny said, tight-lipped.

'He lives on Arnie's boat,' Lottie explained, 'and he's an artist. He paints pictures and sells them.'

'Does he now?' Millie looked down at Jenny's iron leg. 'What happened to your leg, Jen?'

'Polio,' Jenny said, and Millie sat down beside her. There was so much to talk about. Lottie sat quietly thinking about Matt, while Jenny related the long story to Millie who listened attentively and with compassion. By the time John arrived with the fish and chips, Millie knew the whole story of how the children had gone to the orphanage, and that they all now lived with Nan.

Jenny did most of the talking and introduced her to John. Millie shook his hand and beamed. She looked at Jenny enquiringly and Jenny gave her a coquettish wink. Millie's smile stretched even wider. 'Ooh, he's handsome – aren't you the lucky one?'

Millie and Jenny seemed like sisters who understood each other long before words tried to make sense of thought. They'd been next-door neighbours, together through thick and thin, helping each other with the washing, the child-rearing, the poverty and the mopping up after storms, not just weather storms but storms in the family. They sat close together, automatically sharing Jenny's fish and chips with no need for an agreement.

Jenny talked and talked, and she'd just got started on Warren when John tapped his watch. 'We ought to be heading for the station now.'

'Behave!' Jenny snapped at Tom who had made a ball from his fish and chip paper and was playing football with it.

Lottie took one last look at St Michael's Mount, fixing its enchantment into her memory. For something had happened to her on the Mount. While Tom had played and climbed, she'd sat very still, and a lady dressed in grey had hovered close to her. She'd had clothes stitched from the mist and fog, clothes that swirled in the breeze, clothes with no edges, the fabric fusing into the sunlight. Her hair was ash-blonde with tendrils floating outwards as if she was under water. She'd blinked her grey pebble eyes and moved her slender fingers down her body to touch the bulge where a secret child lay curled asleep.

She's like me, Lottie had thought, startled. *She's carrying a tiny baby.*

The grey lady's eyes had darkened, and sadness rippled through her hair and clothes.

Suddenly, she'd turned and wildly jumped from the high rock.

A scream had echoed in Lottie's mind as the grey lady fell towards the sea. Eerily, there was no splash but only a fusion, a melting of those gossamer-grey clothes into the crisp air around St Michael's Mount, and a great sword of light shimmered as it pierced the waters of the bay.

Had she been dreaming? Or had it really happened? And what did it mean? Nan would know. Lottie could hardly wait to get home and tell her. She had seen a grey lady who had disappeared into a pillar of light.

'Come on, Lottie – we're catching the train now.' Jenny tutted and smiled at Millie. 'She's a daydreamer, our Lottie.'

Millie waddled briskly into the station with them. It breathed with steam and noise from the steam engine that had been shunted, turned around and reversed onto the waiting brown and cream carriages.

Millie was scribbling something in a red memo notebook. She tore out two pages and gave one to Jenny. 'My address – and I've got a telephone now. You can ring me up for a chat.' She waited until they were about to board the train, then stood squarely in front of Lottie. She looked directly into her eyes and handed her the other page.

'That's so you'll know where I am, darling, if ever you need me. You can come and stay if you want. I'll always love you, little Lottie. Don't you forget that, darling, and God bless you.' Millie gave her hand a tight squeeze. Then her eyes filled with tears and she let go. 'Go on, get on the train!'

Lottie leaned out of the window watching Millie's dumpy figure getting smaller and smaller, waving as the train steamed out and was soon rattling along the curve of the bay, a last glimpse of St Michael's Mount floating in the evening light.

Nan was asleep in her chair when they arrived home in the cool of an autumn twilight. Bartholomew was draped over the back of the chair like a lion in a tree, his furry white chin resting on top of Nan's head.

'I'll see you in the morning, Jenny,' John said, 'at the gallery – will you come?'

'Yes, I'll be there,' Jenny replied. She grabbed Tom who looked ready to wake Nan. 'You say thank you to John for such a lovely day. We all enjoyed it, John, and I hope you did.'

'I did.' John smiled at the three sun-kissed faces looking at him. He ruffled Tom's hair and gave Lottie a peck on the cheek. 'Have a good day at school tomorrow, my dear. You're doing so well.'

If only you knew, Lottie thought, closely followed by yet another compelling prompt. *Tell them. Tell them now.* The chance might not come again.

She hesitated. She was surrounded by happiness. It glowed in the air.

Bartholomew was purring. John and Jenny were gazing raptly at one another. Tom was tipping out his paper bag of shells and pebbles onto the table. She couldn't spoil it. So Lottie kept quiet, a decision she was to bitterly regret the very next morning.

Chapter 17

A Mother's Fury

The book of legends waited on Nan's table, the gold-rimmed pages glistening as Jenny lit the gaslights. Nan woke up with a jump, dislodging Bartholomew. Tom was beaming at her, his cupped hands full of shells. Temporarily bewildered, she looked around at everyone. 'You're back already. I must have fallen asleep.'

'Come on, Tom, don't monopolise Nan. You've got school in the morning. Bedtime now.'

'But Mum . . .'

'*Bed.*'

Tom pouted at Jenny's fierce expression.

'We'll look at those interesting shells tomorrow,' Nan promised, and Tom trudged unwillingly up the stairs.

'He'll be asleep before his head touches the pillow,' Jenny said. 'He hasn't stopped all day.' She limped into the kitchen to make a pot of tea.

Alone with Nan, Lottie said, 'I saw a grey lady, Nan.'

Nan sat bolt upright. 'A grey lady!' She reached for the book with the gold-rimmed pages. 'Tell me about her.'

'She – she wasn't real, Nan. Well, she was, and she wasn't, if you know what I mean.'

'Oh, I do,' Nan said. 'Go on.'

'Her clothes were filmy and drifting around her, and everything was grey, except for her hair and the whites of her eyes. She looked straight at me, Nan, trying to tell me something. Then she flung herself off the high rock. It was strange, really strange because there wasn't a splash. She somehow disappeared into a pillar of light.'

Nan's eyes opened very wide. 'A pillar of light? What exactly do you mean?'

'I don't know. It may have been the sun blazing on the sea, but to me it looked like a great sword of light.'

Nan seemed to stop breathing, her storm-coloured eyes fixed on Lottie. 'It's happened,' she wheezed. 'I knew it would. I knew it.' She reached out and took Lottie's hand. 'You sit down – sit on the pouffe, close to me – and tell me more.'

Together they sat with the book tingling between them, as they'd done many times before. Sharing the magic. Sharing Cornwall's ancient, mystic folklore. It had always been fun. Now it was deadly serious.

'My goodness – the hairs on the back of my neck are standing up,' Nan said.

'I wasn't sure whether I was dreaming it,' Lottie said, 'but it seems brighter and more detailed in my memory. She wasn't evil, Nan. She was lovely, but *sad*, so very sad. That's why she jumped, and why she chose me to share her feelings.'

'And what were the feelings?'

'Sadness.'

'Yes, but why? Do you know?'

'Because she was . . .' Lottie hesitated, wanting to use the word *pregnant* but, well, it wasn't Nan's kind of word. 'She had a secret baby growing inside her – like a miracle.'

Nan closed her eyes and nodded.

'That's all I know,' Lottie said. 'I don't know why she jumped.'

'I do.' Nan opened her eyes and looked intently at Lottie. 'I've read the legend of the grey lady many times. She was beautiful, and the secret child was a love child. The grey lady worked in the castle and fell in love with one of the manservants. But he betrayed her. When she told him about the secret child, he denied being the father, turned his back and left her to fend for herself.'

'So is that why she threw herself off the cliff?'

'Yes.' Nan pursed her lips.

'I wouldn't do that,' Lottie said, sensing Nan's disapproval.

'I'm glad to hear it,' Nan said. 'The story has a special meaning to me, but we won't go into it just now.' Her eyes went dreamy and she glanced at the framed sepia photograph of the Lanroska family on the wall. She towered over them all, her hair piled high. She was slimmer then, with a haughty posture, dressed in an ornate, high-collared gown. Her son, Vic, stood beside her, square and proud

286

with a neat moustache, and below them Arnie and Jenny sat on a velvet sofa, Jenny with a baby on her lap who must have been Matt. No one ever dared to ask where Nan's husband was.

Lottie kept quiet, watching Nan looking at the photograph. She was beginning to feel tearful again. The day in Penzance had been a distraction, but now she was facing a night of heartbreak when her mind would go over and over Matt's ruthless behaviour.

Ruthless, uncaring and selfish.

Yet she still loved him and wanted him back. How could she make him listen? How could she make him care? And how on earth could she go to school tomorrow and study while love and anger crossed swords in her mind and a tiny child slept in her womb?

Jenny brought the tea in on a tray. 'You're glaring at me, Nan,' she observed. 'Did I interrupt something?'

'Yes, so you might as well hear it,' Nan said bluntly, and turned to Lottie. 'The pillar of light you saw – how long did it last?'

'Just seconds,' Lottie said, 'and then it vanished and the grey lady had gone.'

'What you saw was the sword of the Archangel,' Nan said. 'The sword of light used by St Michael, the Archangel, to protect a soul in danger. It's been seen before on St Michael's Mount.'

'So who is the soul in danger?' Lottie asked and the answer came to her instantly. Matt. She deemed it wiser not to say so.

'Kindly stop rolling your eyes like that, Jenny,' Nan said in a dictatorial tone. 'I know you don't like folklore but that doesn't give you the right to rubbish it for other people.'

'Well, don't fill Lottie's head with your mumbo jumbo,' Jenny fired back. 'She's got enough to worry about with school tomorrow.'

'She certainly has got a lot to worry about,' Nan said. 'More than she's telling us.'

The air trembled with unspoken words.

Lottie picked up her mug. 'I'm going to bed.' She gave them each a kiss on the cheek. 'Goodnight.'

Jenny smiled at her fondly. 'Goodnight, dear girl. Sleep tight.'

'Sweet dreams,' Nan said with a touch of irony.

'Do you think you could take this down to Matt?' John asked when Jenny arrived at the gallery. 'I noticed his boat was there early this morning when I was walking. There's ten pounds in this envelope – his picture money – and I'm sure he'll be glad of it.'

Jenny nodded. 'Course I will.'

John handed her the envelope, his eyes looking at her caringly. 'I thought it might be a good way for you to make contact with him. I know things are difficult. Would you like me to come with you?'

'No, thanks. I'll be fine.' Jenny set off, trying not to limp. Both her legs were painful from the walk across the causeway and she felt exhausted and irritable. Nan had been tetchy, and Tom didn't want to go to school. He'd got blisters on his feet and Jenny had felt draconian about making him go. But Lottie had gone silently, which made Jenny worry. Lottie wasn't often so silent and withdrawn, and she had shadows under her eyes. What could be wrong with her?

John had no idea how difficult things were with Matt, and Jenny made light of it, not wanting to drag him into her family problems. Secretly, Jenny had high hopes of her relationship with John. He made her feel like a woman again and she knew he was serious. He wasn't the sort of man to have a meaningless flirtation. She wanted him to see her at her best so she made an effort with her work at the gallery, enjoying welcoming tourists and she was delighted to find she was quite good at persuading them to buy a picture.

Once she reached the harbour, she could see *The Jenny Wren* moored in a quiet corner. The cabin curtains were drawn so Matt must be still asleep. Jenny felt nervous about seeing him. The money would be welcome, but would *she* be welcome? First she must negotiate the granite steps with her iron leg and her walking stick. They were wet and slippery and there was no handrail, only the rough ridges of the granite wall to hold. Clinging to the stone with her fingertips, she edged down, her back against the wall, remembering how confidently she used to skip down and leap onto the boat when Arnie was there. She stood at the foot of the steps, realising she couldn't possibly climb onto the boat without help.

'Matt!' she called, trying to sound friendly. 'Are you awake? It's Mum.'

He wouldn't be expecting her.

When there was no response, she reached out with her stick and tapped on the cabin roof. 'Matt. Will you come out, please? I've got some money for you – from John.'

The boat twitched and rocked. The cabin door opened and Matt emerged, looking wild and savage. 'What do you want?' he growled.

'John sold two of your pictures. I've got ten pounds for you. Can I come aboard?'

'I suppose you'll have to.'

'Help me then. I've got an iron leg – or hadn't you noticed?'

Matt held out a begrudging hand. Jenny took it and gulped with the realisation that it was many years since she had held her son's hand. Safe in the boat, she looked up at him and gasped in horror when she saw the bruise down the side of his face. 'Matt! Your face – what happened?' She tried to sound gentle when her instinct was to accuse him of fighting. He towered over her, making her feel small and dainty.

'You don't need to know,' he said curtly.

Jenny gazed up at him, a mother's passion in her eyes and in her response. 'Yes, I *do*, Matt. Whether you like it or not, I'm your mother and I care about you. Not a day's gone by without me praying for you and worrying about you and wishing you'd come home. One day when you're a parent yourself, you'll understand how much you love your kids. It's a powerful love that lasts forever, and sometimes it hurts worse than any pain in your body. So you tell me what happened, Matt, because I'm not leaving this boat until you do.'

Jenny sat down firmly on *The Jenny Wren*'s blue painted seat and looked at him expectantly.

Matt softened. He sat down with a thud, folded his arms, stretched his long legs across the deck and tried to look arrogant. Jenny believed she'd got through to him at last. But she'd only get this one chance.

Please God, where are you? she prayed. *Help me get this right for once. Otherwise I'm going to lose my son forever.*

Instinct told her Matt was actually glad she was there. She made her voice quiet. 'What happened to your face?'

He managed a shrug, looked at her from under those long eyelashes and said, 'Morwenna's mother, Cora Bartle – she threw a frying pan at me in the street.'

'That's appalling.' Jenny was instantly furious. 'Why would she do that?'

'I did nothing to her. I was just walking past her house minding my own business.'

'Cora Bartle – she's usually all right. I get on with her,' Jenny said. 'Mind you, I wouldn't like to upset her. Matt, I'm going to confront her. I could kill her for doing that to my boy.'

'I'm not exactly a boy now, Mum.'

'No, you're a big handsome guy like your dad,' Jenny said. 'Every time I look at you, I see Arnie. It pulls at my heartstrings.'

'Thanks.' Matt looked pleased and the ghost of a smile passed over his face.

It was going well. Jenny began to feel hopeful. She and Matt were talking, quietly, and he was looking at her as if he needed a mother.

'Don't get into a cat fight with Cora Bartle, Mum,' he pleaded. 'Stay out of it or you'll get hurt.'

'I'm hurt anyway. A bit more won't make much difference.'

'I know I'm not the kind of son you wanted,' Matt said, and for a moment he emerged from the hard shell of arrogance, 'but I was doing well, living like this, on my own. I work hard at the drawings and I really want to be an artist, like John.'

'You like John, do you?'

'Yeah, I do. He's a good guy.'

An interval of warmth and light glowed between them, a rare sense of togetherness.

Ring the bells in heaven, God, Jenny thought, *we're actually smiling at each other!* Her heart told her to walk away at this point and leave it pleasant, but she needed to know why Cora Bartle had attacked her son.

'Have you put anything on that awful bruise?' she asked.

'I haven't got anything. Don't let Nan near me – she'll come at me with a big spoonful of marigold oil,' he grinned.

Jenny handed him the envelope containing his money. 'I'd better go, Matt. I've got a job now in John's gallery – four mornings a week. It's been really good talking to you.'

Matt nodded. He glanced at her briefly then stared at the floor, his eyes black and desperate.

'I will speak to Cora Bartle,' Jenny said. 'She mustn't get away with it.'

'No, Mum, don't,' he said fiercely. 'Please.'

'Why not? I'm a fighter, Matt. I fight for my family.'

Matt regressed to looking wild and savage. 'I don't want you to.'

'Well, I'm going to unless you tell me why not.'

Matt held his head with both hands, his elbows on his knees. He began to rock to and fro. 'The truth is, Mum . . .' A great sob escaped from him and his back heaved. 'I've lost Lottie.'

'What do you mean?'

Matt just rocked and muttered. 'What am I gonna *do*?'

'Tell me – please.' Jenny tried to touch his hunched back but he shook her off.

'Hasn't she told you, Mum?'

'No, but I know something's wrong with her.'

'Oh, God.' Matt looked at her with black desperate eyes. He took a deep breath. 'Lottie's having a baby. And it's mine.'

Jenny froze. She felt like a bomb about to explode. It was unstoppable. In the seconds before detonation, Matt added, 'I didn't force her, Mum. We've been lovers since last December.'

Jenny screamed and clenched her fists. She wanted to hit him with the burning passion of an enraged mum. What stopped her was his use of the word *lovers*. Her raging mind couldn't sort out exactly why it had made a difference. All she could see was the ruin of her family. The shame, the gossip, the merciless prejudice.

The consequences.

She let go of a torrent of words, her arms crossed, her fists digging into her own shoulders. 'You've *ruined* our family. Everything we've tried to build. Haven't we been through enough without you doing this? You've ruined Lottie's life. You've ruined Tom's life. And Nan's. And you've ruined your own life. Oh, you'll pay for this, by God you will. We'll be driven out of St Ives. Just when things were going well for us – and ... and John won't want me now, or Lottie. How could you do it, Matt? How *could* you?'

Matt hesitated. Then he said the worst possible thing. 'Mum, you just don't understand what it's like to be in love.'

Jenny narrowed her eyes. 'You *rat* – and Lottie's just as bad. After all I've done for her. Wait 'til I get my hands on her, the deceitful, precocious little whore.' She stood up. 'Help me off this boat.'

Matt did as she asked, towering over her, offering a strong, suntanned arm, and looking at her with frightened, soulful eyes.

She didn't try to say goodbye.

She didn't look back.

She didn't go to the gallery where John would be waiting for her.

Jenny headed up through the town without looking at anyone, carrying her burning rage in dignified silence up The Stennack and towards the school.

Lottie always enjoyed the English lesson with David Merryn. Even today, the poetry they were studying held her attention. It was a poem by William Wordsworth and it spoke to her soul.

'Will you read these lines aloud for us, Lottie?' David Merryn asked.

Lottie stood up and read the extract in her clear, expressive voice.

> *Our birth is but a sleep and a forgetting:*
> *The Soul that riseth with us, our life's Star,*
> *Hath had elsewhere its setting,*
> *And cometh from afar . . .*

'Beautifully read, thank you,' David Merryn said. 'What do you think it means, Lottie?'

Lottie was considering how to answer when there was a scuffle of footsteps and the tap of a stick approaching the door. It flew open with a crash and Jenny barged in, her face white with fury.

'Mrs Lanroska – please – you are disturbing my class!' David Merryn protested.

'It won't take a minute,' Jenny said. 'I want my daughter outside, right now, please.'

Lottie dropped the poetry book she'd been reading. She looked at Jenny in alarm. 'But . . .'

'Don't you dare argue.' Jenny hobbled over the wooden floor. She clenched her fist around Lottie's slim wrist and held it viciously. 'You come with me right now, you wanton little trollop,' she hissed. 'I'm taking you to the doctor. Come on.'

Shocked, Lottie stumbled after her. 'You're hurting my wrist.'

'Mrs Lanroska, I must protest at . . .'

Jenny threw David Merryn a contemptuous glare. 'Don't you dare intervene, and don't criticise me when you don't know what it's about.'

'I've a shrewd idea.' He reached the door before she did and blocked it with a wiry arm. 'Please let go of Lottie. She doesn't have to be dragged. And – please – bring her back here. She's my best student and I don't want to see her hurt.'

Jenny snorted. She let go of Lottie's wrist. 'Come with me – *now* – or I will drag you, *madam*.'

Lottie looked at David Merryn gratefully. She felt vulnerable and frightened. The bedrock of her life was crumbling. Jenny had never treated her like this before.

'Who told you?' she asked, expecting it to be Cora Bartle.

'Matt,' Jenny hissed, 'and I'm not discussing it in the street. The surgery's not far so just walk with me as if everything is normal.' She pursed her lips and walked on. 'And we're not discussing it in the waiting room either.'

Lottie bit back the words she wanted to say. She walked meekly behind Jenny, rubbing her wrist, indignant at how suddenly the person who had rescued her and loved her as a daughter could turn into an enemy.

She remembered how Jenny had lost her temper so easily in the past, even with Arnie. Usually when she felt powerless. She'd flare up and later regret it, calm down and apologise. Once she'd told Lottie she got in a rage because she loved too much and cared too much. It helped her to understand, but it didn't ease the shock and hurt Lottie now felt at being suddenly criminalised.

In the doctor's waiting room, Jenny sat, poker-faced, having an inane conversation about the weather with another woman who was sitting on the row of brown leather chairs.

'Storm coming in tonight.'

'So they say.'

''Tis calm at the moment.'

'But you never know, do you? What with autumn coming on.'

'Next, please.'

They all shifted sideways to the next chair as the weather woman went into the surgery. Jenny sat white-faced and rigid. She didn't look at Lottie once.

'Come on,' she said curtly when their turn came, 'and no telling lies.'

Dr Tregullow looked different when Jenny was there. He hardly glanced at Lottie, even though she searched his old eyes for a trace of the wisdom he had shared with her. The script he'd given her was rapidly losing its power. Tarnished by Cora Bartle, ignored by Matt, it had no chance with Jenny in her present mood.

Lottie sat calmly next to her, thinking things couldn't get any worse than they already were so she might as well stay calm for the sake of the tiny baby.

'You look upset, Mrs Lanroska,' Dr Tregullow observed.

The kindness in his voice made Jenny break down. 'I've just found out that Lottie is pregnant, Doctor. Can you please confirm whether it's true? Because if it is, it's ruined our lives.'

'Indeed I can. I examined her myself.'

'You did *what*?' Jenny cried. 'Why wasn't I told?'

'I promised Lottie I wouldn't tell you. She wanted to tell you herself.'

Jenny turned on Lottie. 'So why didn't you tell me, you dirty little whore?'

'There's no need for that,' Dr Tregullow said calmly.

'*Why*?' Jenny pushed her face close to Lottie.

'I was waiting for the right moment.'

'The right moment! There is never a right moment to tell me something like this, you devious little madam.' She swung back to Dr Tregullow, her face contorted with fury. 'It's been going on under my nose, Doctor . . .' Jenny ranted and raged as if she'd never stop. Dr Tregullow clasped his well-scrubbed hands and listened dutifully. He glanced at the clock and then briefly at Lottie. It had been twenty minutes and Jenny was wrung out like a rag.

'I've heard everything you've said, Mrs Lanroska,' the doctor said, 'and if you go on like this, my dear, believe me

you will end up in hospital again. Furthermore – no, listen!'
He held up his hand as she tried to protest. 'I suggest you
turn around and look at Lottie. She is remarkably composed,
given the circumstances. She's an intelligent, responsible
young lady and she is going to be a mother. Have you asked
her how she feels about that?'

'No,' Jenny shook her head.

'Then look at her, please, and I shall ask her.'

Jenny managed to look at Lottie, her gaze red–rimmed and
quivering, and Lottie stared back. The bond of love was still
there. Surely Jenny wasn't going to break it?

'How do you feel, Lottie, about being a mother?' Dr
Tregullow asked.

'I love my baby,' Lottie said. 'It's like the pearl in an oyster.
I love my baby – no matter what.'

Jenny's mouth fell open and some of the hardness in her
eyes melted.

The doctor was watching her very intently. In a quiet,
compelling voice he said, 'I suggest to you, Jennifer, that
this baby is a love–child, not a bastard. He or she is also
your grandchild and, if Lottie doesn't mind undressing and
hopping on the couch, we are going to listen to its heartbeat.'

While Lottie quickly undressed behind a screen, Dr
Tregullow looked sternly at Jenny. 'You really must pull
yourself together. Remember how it feels to be young and
in love –and pregnant. And it's not the baby's fault.'

While Jenny stood defensively, arms folded, mouth set in
a stubborn line, he moved the cold disc over Lottie's bump.

'Ah, I have it.' His old eyes lit up and the magic was back. He handed the ear pieces to Jenny. 'Now you have a listen.'

Jenny almost threw the stethoscope back at him. Stepping across the bridge from rage into wonder was too risky for her. 'Don't try to manipulate me.'

She returned to the brown leather chair and sat down, her back very straight. 'I want to know what you're going to do about this, Dr Tregullow. I don't care who you are, I know my rights and you deliberately deceived me and apparently encouraged my daughter to go ahead with this unfortunate pregnancy. It was your duty as a doctor to tell me. I want something done about it. Otherwise I shall find another doctor.'

Dr Tregullow gave Lottie an apologetic look. 'You wait in the waiting room. I'll do the best I can to help you.'

Lottie got dressed. Hearing the heartbeat had filled her with wonder and she felt suddenly strong, strong enough to march down to the harbour and find Matt. Jenny had seen him earlier. Perhaps he'd had a change of heart and sailed back in to St Ives and was waiting to see her.

There was no one else in the waiting room. Lottie put her ear to the surgery door and strained to hear what was being said. She heard Jenny's clear voice saying, 'I want a termination.'

'You know I can't arrange that. It's against the law.'

'Even for a seventeen-year-old girl?'

'I'm afraid so. But there are other options, like adoption — there are couples desperate for a child. The adoption agencies are very good – very discreet – and they take the baby straightaway.'

Appalled, Lottie went outside into the street. She'd thought of Jenny as her best friend and her adoptive mother. Jenny had always loved her, supported her and passionately defended her. Jenny was the one person who, she'd *thought*, would understand how much it meant to her to keep her baby. Jenny loved children and didn't care about the gossip. Now Jenny had turned on her, called her a dirty little whore, and she was in there with Dr Tregullow working out a masterplan of how to get rid of *her* baby. Could this really be the same Jenny who had taken Warren in and been so kind to him?

Lottie felt hurt and bewildered. She couldn't rely on Jenny any more.

She had some big decisions to make, with only minutes before Jenny came out of the surgery. Lottie felt she couldn't let it happen. She must take immediate action to save her baby's life. And it meant leaving everything and everyone she loved.

Lottie broke into a run, her shoes tapping. It didn't help that St Ives was at its best, the blue air warm and still, the sea sparkling, and Matt's boat was in the harbour. It didn't help to look up at Hendravean, its gabled windows facing the bay, and wonder if Nan was in the garden.

First a broken heart, and now a broken life.

She must take a bold leap of faith. Like the grey lady.

Chapter 18

Far From Home

Nan dragged herself upstairs. Bartholomew followed her and so did two of the chickens. They all came to a halt outside Lottie's bedroom.

Despite feeling sure Lottie wasn't in there, Nan knocked at the door. Bartholomew meowed and when Nan pushed the door open, he trotted in with his tail up, jumped onto Lottie's neatly made bed and lay there, dough-punching her pillow with his furry paws. The knitted donkey, which was usually on the bed, wasn't there and Nan couldn't see it anywhere. She opened the drawer where Lottie kept her ironed hankies and a folded set of underwear and socks.

Empty.

She opened the wardrobe. A few items hung there forlornly, dresses and a pinafore Lottie had outgrown. Nan looked for the pale blue bag with the wide shoulder strap, but it had gone.

A chill crawled over Nan. She looked at the books Lottie had loved and left on the shelf, their spines upright. *Black Beauty. Heidi. Anne of Green Gables. The Wind in the Willows.* Only the slim copy of *Hiawatha,* which Nan had given her for Christmas, was gone. Books were too heavy to carry.

Nan opened Lottie's trinket box. The blue lapis lazuli beads were gone and the gold bracelet John had given her. Nan shut the lid with a heavy hand. Her eyes searched the room and saw a piece of notepaper neatly folded into four. Her fingers trembled as she picked it up, took it to the window and read the hastily scribbled, poignant note.

To Nan,
I was happy here at Hendravean. I will always remember you, Nan, thank you for everything. I will always love you.
Lottie

Nan sat down on the bed. She put her fingers over Lottie's signature and prayed in the silence of her soul. She accepted that there was nothing she could do to get Lottie back. Love and let go. Leave them alone and they'll come home.

Easy to say, Nan thought, *but harder to do. This time I've got it wrong. I should have talked to Lottie as soon as I discovered she was pregnant. She needed my support and I let her down.*

The silence filled with Bartholomew's purring as he sought to comfort Nan, giving her his warmth and love. Until now, it had always been enough. The love of her pets and the beauty of her flowers had sustained Nan through the years. She'd never needed people. People had been an intrusion. Except for Lottie. Lottie was a magical, inspiring creature in Nan's life.

Recently, Nan had noticed a heaviness about Lottie. She moved differently, plodding instead of floating. She glowed rather than sparkled. There was a new depth to her personality. Nan stared out at the sky over the distant hills. Where would Lottie have gone? Surely not to live on the boat with Matt? That wouldn't work. So young. So alone.

Like me, Nan thought, *like I once was.*

The walls of Hendravean had guarded Nan's secret until it had almost disappeared into the granite, into the cracks in the dark oak timbers, into the subsoil of the garden. Respectability, softened only by the fringe of little love nests in the eaves, sparrows and swallows, wild bees and bats, which Nan allowed and protected. A network of life in which she was happily entangled. Easier to love than people.

Nan knew without being told that Lottie was in love with Matt, and she'd kept quiet about it. Jenny was so volatile, in Nan's opinion. She sighed resignedly when she heard the sounds from downstairs, the iron leg and the stick clonking through the hall, the doors banging as Jenny arrived home and searched the rooms. Then the commotion of her chasing the chickens off the stairs.

'Are you up there? Nan? Lottie?' she called.

'I am,' Nan responded. 'I am sitting on Lottie's bed.'

'Is she there?'

'No.'

'Do you know where she is?'

'No.'

'I'm worn out,' Jenny called. 'I need to sit down before I fall down.'

Nan lumbered downstairs and found Jenny lying on the sofa looking utterly wrung out. An aura of defeat clung around her and her eyes were red-rimmed and puffy.

'Have you been drinking?' Nan asked.

'No! Trust you to think the worst of me.'

'I shall ignore that assumption.' Nan sat down beside Jenny, the sofa springs creaking from her weight. 'What's the matter?'

'Nan – it's Lottie.'

Nan looked at her silently.

Jenny took a deep breath. 'You're not going to like this, but the little minx has got herself pregnant.'

Nan closed her eyes and nodded.

Jenny looked at her, wild-eyed. 'Surely you didn't know, did you?'

'Not officially. I guessed – and I dowsed.'

'Dowsed!'

'Never mind that. How did you find out?'

'Matt told me. I gave him a good scolding – and Lottie. I took her out of school and had the doctor look at her.'

'It must have been a shock for Lottie.'

'Oh no, she knew. She's been keeping it from us. Would you believe she told Cora Bartle instead of me? I am furious with her, Nan. She's *ruined* her life, and *ruined* our family.'

Nan shut her eyes and pinched the top of her nose. 'It all sounds horribly familiar.'

'What do you mean?'

Nan shook her head. 'Now is not the time to dig up the past. Suffice to say I know exactly what Lottie is going through, Jenny. Let's not be too hard on her, and Matt must take his share of the blame.'

Jenny snorted. 'Pigs might fly.'

'Does John know?' Nan asked.

'I don't think so. He'll be devastated – and, well, it's like the end of everything, Nan. The end of our happy life and we've worked so hard at it, haven't we?' Jenny leaned back on the sofa, her eyes awash with tears, and she let them flow, appearing to have no energy or will to fight them.

Nan took her hand and held it firmly. 'You need to calm down – and so do I. Things are not always as bad as they seem.'

'I'll lose my job at the gallery,' Jenny sobbed. 'John won't want *me* around, will he.'

'You don't know that. Give the man a chance.'

The fight had gone out of Jenny and with it the light. Nan couldn't help remembering how vibrant and happy she'd been only twenty-four hours earlier after their day in Penzance. It was hard to know what to say. She looked down at Jenny's iron leg and noticed the skin was bruised and blistered from too much vigorous walking. 'Would you like me to put something on your leg? It looks painful.'

306

Jenny shook her head. 'No, thanks. Forget about me leg. I want to know where Lottie is. Do you know?'

Nan sighed. She'd have to tell the truth. 'No, I don't know, but she's packed a bag and gone. She left me a note.' Nan took the folded paper from her pocket and handed it to Jenny. 'I was working in the tropical garden all day and she must have come and gone without me knowing. She's taken her clothes and the knitted donkey and her jewellery in the American bag.'

Jenny stared at Lottie's note. 'She never left *me* a note.'

'I wonder why that could be,' Nan said, with more than a hint of sarcasm.

Worse was to come. Neither of them had noticed Tom in the doorway hearing every word. Placid, reliable Tom who'd always helped and defended his mum, standing there now with hatred burning in his eyes.

'I know why Lottie's gone,' he said. 'It's your bad temper, Mum. I saw you dragging Lottie out of school, shouting and calling her names. She ain't done *nothing*. You drove Matt away. Now you've driven Lottie away with your horrible temper. Lottie might never come back. And next time it'll be me, Mum. Just wait 'til I'm old enough and I'm getting out of here too.'

He slammed his school bag against the wall. It burst open and marbles rolled everywhere.

'Out of the mouths of babes,' said Nan wearily. She raised her eyebrows at Tom. 'Are you going to pick those up?'

Red-faced and muttering, Tom gathered up the marbles. 'And are you going to apologise to your mother?'

'I'm not sorry.' Tom glared bullishly at Jenny. 'Lottie's having a baby, isn't she?'

'How did you know?' Jenny asked.

''Cause it's all over school. Everyone knows now 'cause everyone heard you yelling at her.' Tom pushed his hair out of his eyes. 'I don't understand it, Mum. Lottie's not bad, she's good. So what's wrong with having a baby? You had me and Matt.'

Jenny couldn't take any more. Tom's unexpected burst of rebellion had sucked the last glimmer of light from her eyes. Nan would have preferred to distance herself from the conflict, but she sensed Tom had a lot more to say and painful questions to ask.

In one way, she was pleased to see him showing a bit of fire in defence of Lottie.

'I agree with you, Tom,' she said, 'but now is a bad time. Your mother is extremely upset and exhausted. Remember how you felt when she was in hospital? She's going to end up there again if she's not allowed to rest and recover from this terrible day. And it won't be Truro Hospital, Tom, it will be Bodmin.'

'Bodmin?' Tom looked guilty. 'That's the loony bin.'

'No.' Nan spoke quietly and firmly. 'It's a hospital for people who are upset and tired from worrying about their families. So leave your mother alone, Tom. You and I can have a talk later about how you feel. Right now, we all need some peace and a cup of tea.' She helped Jenny swing her legs onto the sofa. 'You close your eyes and have a little sleep. It'll do you good.'

Jenny nodded. 'Thanks, Nan.' She sank into the cushion, her face faintly blue-tinged and pale.

'I don't like the look of her. She's had enough,' Nan said, and turned a demanding stare on Tom. 'Now – are you going to make the tea or make the peace?'

'I dunno how to make peace.'

'Watch Bartholomew,' Nan said as the cat flowed in like a weightless cloud and settled himself over Jenny's heart, his loud purring filling the room, bringing with it a feeling of fireside warmth and peace.

'He wouldn't care if your mother had robbed a bank,' Nan said. 'It's unconditional love – exactly what Jenny needs.'

At John's apartment in London, Olivia scurried around in a frenzy of cleaning and tidying. She seized armfuls of clothes from where she'd flung them, over the backs of chairs and on the floor, and put them on hangers or into drawers. She disentangled a heap of shoes and handbags and put them in an orderly line, accidentally knocking over a half-empty bottle of red wine that was in the heap.

Swigging what remained in the bottle, she slouched into the kitchen to find a cloth and stood contemplating the stack of unwashed dishes in the sink. *Better tackle those first.*

She opened the bow-fronted refrigerator and surveyed the contents. Half a bottle of milk, a few eggs and a wedge of hard yellow cheese wrapped in greaseproof paper. She would need to go shopping and do some baking.

It really was inconsiderate of John to spring this on her at such short notice. He'd telephoned at midday, his voice curt and business-like, to say he was bringing Charlotte – no, *Lottie* – to London. The train took about six hours, so it would be dark when they arrived.

The longing to be in London instead of New York had been unfulfilled, and Olivia soon discovered she felt just as bad, if not worse, than in America. Her life was lonely, her health precarious. Her dreams of being reunited with her daughter and of seducing John had come to nothing.

Thanks to that Cornish family Lottie was so attached to.

The powerful grandmother with those scathing eyes. The insolent boyfriend who lived on a boat. And Jenny! Olivia had felt drawn to her. Jenny was everything she was not. Olivia saw her as the perfect friend, someone she could respect and learn from. Lottie's attitude had been a huge disappointment, a snub of the worst kind. Alcohol was the only solace for Olivia. John had told her to get a job, find her own flat and build a life. He was still sending her money to help her get on her feet, but she'd spent it all on alcohol and clothes.

She had six hours to restore John's flat to its previous pristine condition, and she must have a scented bath, do her hair and nails, and find something seductive to wear. The dishes could wait.

Still procrastinating, Olivia wandered into the spare room where Lottie would sleep. The narrow iron bedstead was covered in an old army blanket with a tattered hem, and the heavy brocade curtains were dark brown. The electric light was a yellowy bulb with a grubby white shade, hanging on a twisted cord from a badly cracked ceiling. A sludgy old oil painting dangled from the picture rail on a greasy string.

Olivia sighed. It seemed a miserable, unwelcoming room for a bright young girl like Lottie. She'd take her to Portobello Road market and let her choose some fabric, but John would have to pay, of course. The idea of shopping with her daughter appealed to Olivia and she spent some time dreaming of trips to Harrods and Selfridges. Lottie couldn't go around London looking like a Cornish fishwife. She'd need elegant dresses nipped in at the waist, as well as hats, gloves and shoes. Mother and daughter stuff, at last.

The one redeeming feature of the room was the lofty sash-window, west facing, catching the evening sun and a pleasant view over one of London's elegant squares with tall plane trees, their huge, arty leaves tinged with the fires of autumn.

Olivia had no idea why Lottie suddenly wanted to come and stay with her in London. John hadn't offered any explanation. Lottie had been so hostile on the ship. What had made her change her mind? Could she be running away from something? Had something gone wrong in the Lanroska family?

The six hours flew by and when nine o'clock came, Olivia was beautifully dressed in a willowy, peacock blue frock, her hair swept up into a shining coil, like a ballerina, the way John liked her to look. She'd had a bath, painted her nails and put a dab of Eau de Cologne on her wrists, behind her ears and in her cleavage. She paced the floor, sucking peppermints to mask the tell-tale smell of wine. When at last the doorbell rang, she glided downstairs to open the front door, her pulse quickening with nervous excitement.

John met her eyes, briefly, business-like. Lottie stood beside him, her hair limp, her face unsmiling.

'Hello, honey-child. Good to see you.'

'Hello,' Lottie said flatly and looked directly into Olivia's eyes. 'First of all, my name is Lottie, not Charlotte, and not honey-child. I'm sorry it's short notice but can I please stay with you for . . . for a short while?'

'That's okay, Lottie. I said you could, didn't I? But you didn't want to. Why the change of heart?'

Lottie shrugged. 'I don't want to discuss it.' She looked at the stairs. 'Is this the way to Daddy's flat?'

Olivia rolled her eyes at John and Lottie headed up the stairs, her blue American bag over one shoulder. 'What's the matter with her?' Olivia mouthed at John.

He shook his head. 'I've no idea. She's usually so full of life, but she's hardly spoken a word since we left Cornwall. We had dinner on the train and she couldn't eat it.'

'She was like this on the ship, wasn't she?' Olivia said. 'You don't think she's ill again, do you, John?'

'She was fine yesterday. We had a lovely day out, walked over to St Michael's Mount. Even Jenny managed it with her iron leg.'

He followed Olivia upstairs and into the flat where Lottie was standing forlornly. 'I honestly haven't got a clue what's wrong with her – but something is. I'm extremely concerned about her, Olivia. Do you think you can manage her, the way she is?'

'John, she is my daughter. Of course I can manage her. I'll take her shopping, show her the sights of London. She'll soon snap out of it.'

'I'm concerned about her schoolwork,' John said. 'She was working hard in the college class and enjoying it.'

'Excuse me,' Lottie looked at both of them, her eyes blank, 'but I'm very tired and I'd like to go straight to bed. Where will I be sleeping?'

'Okay, John and I will have a quiet drink together,' Olivia said as she opened the door to the spare room. 'There you are, Lottie. It's a bit gloomy in there but I'll take you shopping for some fabric.'

'Thank you – and goodnight. Goodnight, Daddy. Thanks for bringing me.' She gave her father a kiss on the cheek and Olivia a dismissive stare.

'Wait a minute, Lottie,' John said. 'Jenny doesn't know where you are and she'll worry. Will you telephone her, please?'

'No.'

'She'll worry all night.'

'Let her.'

'Then I shall phone her,' John said firmly. 'Would you like me to give her a message?'

313

'No, thanks. I'm going to bed.'

'Would you like an aspirin, honey-child?' Olivia opened a cupboard. Bottle after bottle stood on the shelf inside, each with a white label: 100 ASPIRIN TABLETS.

'No, thanks. Please just leave me alone.' Lottie retreated into the spare room and closed the door.

John looked at Olivia, his eyes shrewd. 'Why on earth have you got so much aspirin? Are you curing the British army of headaches?'

She gave him a haughty stare. 'It's my way of making sure I have everything I need when I need it.' She opened the cupboard next to it. 'I have plenty of wine, as you can see. Why don't you choose a bottle for us to share?'

'Thanks, but no thanks, Olivia. I don't want to encourage you to drink. Especially with Lottie here. She's going to need you to be sober.'

Olivia looked miffed. 'For goodness sake, John, I was only going to have a glass.'

'I'd rather have coffee or Ovaltine if you have it. I'm tired after the journey.'

'Where are you planning to stay tonight?'

'Here, of course. It is my flat.'

Olivia leaned towards him, her graceful fingers fiddling with his tie. 'It's been a while, John, but it's time we shared a comfortable bed together, don't you think?'

She watched him turn to stone. 'Definitely not, Olivia. I'll sleep on the sofa. All I need is a rug. I intend to get the afternoon train back to Cornwall tomorrow – I have some business to attend to in London. Right now, I'm going to telephone Jenny so would you kindly make me a hot drink? *Without* alcohol.'

Olivia tossed her head angrily. 'Certainly, your *lordship*.' She tip-tapped into the kitchen and left him to make his phone call. She opened the refrigerator and reached for the willow-patterned jug hidden at the back, glad she'd remembered to empty half a bottle of wine into it earlier.

Hearing John on the phone, she drank quickly, gulping the chilled red wine directly from the jug. Wine, wonderful wine – it was the answer to everything. Loneliness. Jealousy. Anxiety. Rage. Wine would fix it.

Satisfied, Olivia slid the jug back again and eavesdropped on John's conversation.

It was brief and business-like, and when he'd finished he came into the kitchen.

'I only spoke to Nan. Jenny's gone to bed early, not well from the sound of it. Nan was relieved to know Lottie was safe – she didn't offer any explanation. She's awkward on the phone. She said we'll talk when I get back –that's all she said really. Is the kettle on?'

'Not yet.'

John looked annoyed. He picked up the kettle, took it to the sink and filled it. 'How long have these dishes been festering here, Olivia? Isn't the hot water working?'

'I was going to do them. I haven't had time.'

'Obviously.' John took his jacket off and hung it over a chair. He rolled up his sleeves, turned on the hot water tap, and tackled the disgusting pile of plates, pans and mugs, scrubbing them diligently with a brush.

Olivia sank into a chair feeling the wine beginning to take effect, blurring her loneliness, her longing and her guilt.

Lottie slept deeply and awoke at first light. She lay in the narrow bed listening to rain drumming on a variety of hard surfaces, gurgling and gushing from hundreds of pipes, making a magnificent sound. She drew the curtains and sat cross-legged on the wide window seat, fascinated by the tree canopy level with the window, the huge golden leaves and the twigs gleaming and dripping. London rain came straight down in rods of silver white, so different from Cornish rain, which always blew in at crazy angles. The lawned square below was a quiet space and beyond it the city growled with traffic, a hectic mix of horse-drawn wagons and noisy buses and lorries with grinding gears.

The sea was far away. And Matt was far away.

It hurt.

How was she going to stand it? What was she doing here in London?

Panic spun through her. Thoughts came at her like traffic and she felt marooned in the middle of a highway, vulnerable and alone, each thought louder, harder, brighter. The same ones. Relentlessly coming at her. Matt was far away. Nan, and Jenny and Mufty, and Tom, and Morwenna. St Ives Harbour. The moon on the sea. The flowers on the cliffs. The white, white waves.

Go back. Go home. You *must* go home. You can't live here in London with its black umbrellas and its vertical rain. The voice of London is stern and unforgiving.

Panic was something new to Lottie. She'd always considered herself brave and confident. But now, in a perfectly safe place, she found herself gasping for breath, dizzy, shivering, her cheek pressed against the cold glass between her and the rain. It was hard not to scream.

Terrified she might die, Lottie stumbled back to the bed and sat on it. She wrapped the army blanket tightly around her shoulders and over her knees like a tent. She held onto the knitted donkey, feeling Jenny in every stitch. Jenny when she was calm and motherly.

The *real* Jenny.

Not the Jenny who had dragged her out of school and screamed at her, called her those terrible names. Unfair, untrue, undeserved names.

The *real* Jenny who had carried her home from the shipwreck. Lottie wanted her badly. No one else would do. Not even Nan.

I was born again, Lottie thought, *when Jenny lifted me up from the sand, wrapped me tightly in her shawl and took me into her family – the Lanroska family. I was born again.*

A flutter of movement deep in her womb brought sudden peace. *Little star!* She wasn't far away. She was there. Lottie managed to slow her breathing down. The rain stopped and the window sparkled like the sea.

Lottie got back in bed, the scratchy blanket wrapped around her, the two pillows heavenly against her cheek. Her breath became steady and sleepy. She remembered her plan. On the long train journey, she'd closed her eyes and planned every detail of her future life. It was bold. But it would work. She'd make it work.

The only problem for her would be learning to tell lies.

Chapter 19

The Road to Ruin

A flicker of excitement lit up John's mind as he surfaced from sleep the next morning. He was going to buy Jenny a ring – and he intended to propose. Secretly, he believed she would accept, and Lottie would be thrilled. He even allowed himself to dream about a wedding, with Lottie as a bridesmaid and Nan in a flowery hat.

The dream had sustained him during the train journey from Cornwall, with the anxiety he felt about Lottie's uncharacteristic silence, the strange decision she had made and the look in her eyes.

Arriving at the flat had been difficult for John. It was a decent flat, comfortably furnished from his own efforts, and it hurt to see it so messy. The place felt abused and unloved, and the smell of wine had permeated the upholstery, the curtains, and even the walls with their heavy anaglypta wallpaper. John didn't want a confrontation with his ex-wife, especially with Lottie there. He felt reasonably confident that Lottie would soon return to Cornwall, and to Jenny. Hopefully they'd only had a minor upset, which the two of them would quickly forgive and forget.

Comfortable on the drop-end Chesterfield sofa, he dozed for a while, dreaming of choosing a ring for Jenny. A ruby. He thought she was definitely a ruby kind of person, and the red would be deep like a red rose. Red was for courage, and Jenny was the brightest, most courageous woman he'd ever met, and so motherly. He'd go to Hatton Garden and choose a sparkling ruby ring and take it home in a secret box. A perfect ring for his perfect woman.

Olivia was moving around in the kitchen and John was pleasantly surprised when she brought his breakfast in on a tray.

She's made an effort, he thought. *She must want something, probably money – or the moon.*

'How kind of you,' he said, eyeing the boiled egg, the crusty bread roll with butter and marmalade, and the steaming mug of strong coffee. 'Exactly what I need.'

He took the tray to the dining table in the window. Olivia sat down with him, sipping her own mug of coffee, her eyes anxious. 'Are you going to do the same for Lottie?' he asked.

'Yes, I suppose I could,' she said. 'When I've had a coffee. But while she's asleep we should talk about this, John. I'm not sure I can manage her if she's being so moody. And if she intends to stay, I want to enrol her in a good school. She must have decent clothes, too, for London. I shall need some money, of course.'

John shut his eyes for a moment. The whine of Olivia's voice was painfully familiar. He ate his breakfast mindfully, concentrating on breaking the crusty bread roll, buttering it and munching.

'Don't go silent on me, John. I mean ... look, you can't just dump Charlotte on me with no warning. I don't understand why she suddenly wants to be here when she won't even talk to me. She shuts me out. If she wants to live here then she must live by my rules. Otherwise you will have to stay here with her.'

John felt pressure rising in his head. 'That's not an option, Olivia. I have a business to run in St Ives.'

He noticed how her painted nails were digging into her arms, going deeper and deeper, leaving marks on her white skin. It was a habit that had driven him mad in the past. Remembering it was painful.

'Calm down,' he said, and that made her worse. 'Why don't you go and get Lottie's breakfast?' he suggested. 'Then we can talk to her about what she wants to do.'

Olivia sighed. She finished her coffee and went into the kitchen. John saw her open the fridge, take out a large jug and swig from it. Then she leaned against the wall, holding her head.

Wine, John thought. *At breakfast time.*

He felt a surge of anger. Something he was no longer used to dealing with. Anger belonged to the past, to those painful years of being married to Olivia, compounded by the fact that he'd idolised and admired her beauty. But her grace and sparkle were transient, like a soap bubble.

John watched her carry a breakfast tray to Lottie's bedroom. She tapped on the door, opened it and went in.

'Wakey, wakey, honey-child. Breakfast in bed!'

John smiled at the enthusiasm in her voice. He hoped Lottie would respond with a warm thank you. Instead there was a jangle of china as Olivia banged the tray down.

'Oh no!' she cried, and reappeared in the doorway, her hollow cheeks taut with shock. 'She's gone, John.'

'*Gone?*'

John got up and joined Olivia. They looked down at Lottie's neatly made bed. 'Where can she be?' Olivia wrung her hands. 'She can't go out on her own in a strange city. John, this is London, not St Ives. How am I going to cope with her? She's a liability. What am I going to do?' Olivia cried a few panicky tears. 'She'll get lost – or . . . or attacked.'

'No, she won't,' John said calmly, 'not Lottie. Believe me, Olivia, she is smart. Let's not panic. Has she left a note?'

On top of the chest of drawers was a square of folded paper, torn from a notebook. Olivia pounced on it. *Gone for a walk. Back soon. Lottie.*

She handed it to John.

'She must have sneaked out so quietly. Surely you heard her, John?'

'I did sleep heavily.'

322

'We've had nothing but trouble with this child,' Olivia moaned.

'Excuse me, I dispute that.' John's eyes hardened with indignation. 'Lottie has had nothing but trouble from us. From me, her father working abroad, and from you, abandoning her when she was only four.'

'I didn't abandon her. I left her with your mother. How was I to know she was going to die?'

John turned to stone. 'Let's not dig up the past.'

Olivia tossed her head. 'One of your favourite get-out lines. Charlotte is a devious child and when she lives with me, I shall stop this nonsense about her name. She won't be Lottie Lanroska in London. Charlotte De Lumen has a very different ring to it. And as she grows up, I shall make sure she meets some classy, eligible young men – a cut above that lanky, insolent boy she goes around with in St Ives.'

'If you mean Matt, he's a fine young man – courageous, and a gifted artist. And he's Lottie's *brother*, Olivia.'

'Not by birth.'

'No, but Lottie has grown up with him and they're good friends. She's going to miss him, and Tom and Jenny. I hope you'll be kind to her, Olivia.'

They both turned at the sound of a key in the lock, and Lottie came in, the ends of her hair curling and glistening from the rain, her eyes bright. John gave her a hug.

'Good to see you looking better,' he said warmly. He looked into her eyes and detected a secretive gleam. 'Not too wet, I hope?'

'I'm glad you gave me a key, Daddy. I borrowed your umbrella, and I—'

'Where the *hell* have you been, Charlotte? Answer me. Charlotte!' Olivia gave her a look of cold, matriarchal steel.

Lottie threw her a contemptuous glare, the light in her eyes dying as she marched into the bedroom and closed the door with a dignified click.

Jenny lay in bed with her face to the wall. Outside, the autumn sunshine glowed on cottage walls, warming the granite and drying the fishing nets spread out across the island. The cliffs beyond Hendravean were alive with bobbing butterflies feeding on the late flowers of greater knapweed, and flocks of finches pecking the seed pods of thistle and teasel. Tom had gone to school and Nan worked alone in the garden, collecting and labelling seeds into envelopes.

It was a beautiful day; a day to enjoy before the wheel of the year turned again to winter, to bitter winds, storms and hardship. But Jenny refused to get up. She'd had enough. Tom's unexpected outburst had been the last straw. Tom, who had always been dependably cuddly, imperturbable and loyal, had turned on her, removing the last shreds of hope. After Tom, there would be nothing. The family Jenny loved so fiercely had gone. Arnie, Matt, Warren, and finally Lottie.

Was Tom right? Have I driven them away?

She'd tried so hard to love and guide them. Bringing up children alone was a harrowing, exhausting task. Hiding the constant pain and inconvenience of her iron leg. Sharing

Nan's home. Despite Nan's kindness, Jenny felt beholden to her. She felt victimised and abandoned, punished by life, worn down until she no longer existed.

At lunchtime, Nan came in with a tray, a bowl of homemade soup, which smelled good, and a thick slice of fresh bread. 'Sit up, Jenny. Come on, you've got to eat something.'

Nan's voice, the clink of china and the aroma of soup seemed distant to Jenny, a world on the other side of a bank of dense fog. She needed to keep totally still and unresponsive. To move or speak would open the floodgates to a torrent of grief and despair.

'Jenny!' There was irritation in Nan's voice. 'I've never seen you like this. Are you in pain?'

'No.' Jenny's voice sounded like the moan of a storm wind.

'Are you ill or sick in some way?'

'No.'

'Then you must make an effort. Frankly, I could do with some help.'

Nan's voice floated in the distance. *Please just go away. Leave me alone*, Jenny thought.

But Nan wasn't going to. 'Jenny, will you please pull yourself together.'

She didn't move. A wisp of anger at Nan's attitude drifted by and Jenny let it go. Enough anger. *Enough*, she told herself.

Nan put the tray down and patted her on the shoulder. 'Jenny, you *must* pull yourself out of this. If you don't, I shall be obliged to call the doctor – and I'm sorry to say he will declare you mentally ill. He will send you to Bodmin, Jenny, I'm warning you, and I'm doing it for your own good. If you go on like this you will lose everything. I know you think you've lost everything already, but you haven't, Jenny, you haven't. You've got a safe home, you've got Tom, and you've got me, even if I am an old battleaxe. And there's John. He'll want to see you, won't he?'

'No!' Jenny cried. 'Don't let John near me – please.'

'Why not?'

'I can't let him see me like this.'

'Well, isn't that a good reason to sit up, eat your lunch and wash your face, Jenny, and brush your hair. That's all you need to do. John will understand, believe me. He thinks the world of you.'

'He *did*. But he won't now. I can't see him, Nan, keep him away – please. I don't want him to see me at my worst.' Jenny managed to sit up, driven by the words tumbling through her mind.

'I don't think John is a fine-weather friend.'

'But he thought I was such a good mother to Lottie.' Jenny stared at Nan with desperate eyes. 'And I've been a rotten, useless, angry witch of a mother. I've driven Lottie away – and . . . and . . . it's truly the most terrible thing I've ever done, Nan. I want her back. I love her so much. But she'll never forgive me. I let her down when she needed me the most. Oh, what am I going to do, Nan?'

Nan was sitting on the bed, looking shabby but rocklike. 'You are going to calm down, dry your eyes, and make yourself eat this lovely soup. My soup makes people feel better, believe me – try it.'

'But . . .'

'No buts. One thing at a time. You've managed to sit up. Now eat. I'll leave you to it. I need some lunch too.' Nan heaved herself up and left the room.

Jenny knew she was right. She took a deep breath, tasted the soup and discovered that she did want it, and every spoonful filled her with simple warmth and goodness. Her body felt softer and more ready to move, *wanting* to move, yet knowing it wasn't strong enough to carry the weight in her mind. To move would be to see with every step some new reminder of Lottie and Matt and Warren – and Arnie.

Jenny closed her eyes and relapsed into sleep, a sleep embossed with one thought, *I can't live like this*.

'I'll stay another night if I have to,' John said as he walked by the river with Lottie. 'I need to be sure you are all right.'

'I'll be okay, Daddy.'

'But can you handle being alone with your mother?'

'I won't be with her much. I'll be out, like we are now.' Lottie stopped to lean on the wide stone balustrade to gaze at the river. 'I didn't know the River Thames was so wide and crowded with boats. What muddy water flowing very fast – it's powerful, isn't it?'

'Oh, that's not the river's power – it's the tide,' John explained, enjoying the look of wonder on Lottie's face. For a moment she looked like herself again.

'The tide? How can the tide be in the middle of London?'

'It floods in from the North Sea twice a day, thanks to the moon.'

'The moon.' Lottie's eyes widened. 'Does it make a silver pathway on the river?'

'It might in some places, but not like it does in St Ives.'

'And the sun – does it rise over the water and make a blaze of gold?'

'No – not much,' John said, feeling her sadness and her longing already burning for the special light of St Ives shining on a clean, vast ocean, not random sparkles on a muddy river.

Lottie fell silent again, her eyes watching the swirling water, her hair burnished by the coppery sunlight of London.

John felt proud to be with her. *My daughter*, he kept thinking. If only he knew what was troubling her. What had made her so determined to come to London to be with a mother she said she hated? He remembered his brief conversation with Nan when he'd phoned to tell her they were in London. Nan had sounded unusually tense, and Jenny wouldn't come to the phone. Nan had said only one meaningful thing: 'You must talk to Lottie. She needs to tell you something.'

He led her along the embankment to a seat tucked against a wall at right angles to the river, facing the sun. 'Shall we sit down for a minute? This is my favourite place to sit in London. I've spent many hours on this seat, Lottie, drawing and thinking, sometimes reading.'

She seemed glad to sit down.

'Are you tired?' he asked.

'A bit.'

They sat in silence. He wondered how to begin to ask her what Nan had meant. Could it be something to do with Olivia?

'I will give you some advice,' he said, and Lottie looked at him in alarm. 'I've lived with your mother, and I found the best way to handle her was not to argue with her. Just say yes and no, keep calm, and do what you want anyway.'

Lottie gave him a rare smile. 'That sounds very wise – and wicked, Daddy. I'll remember it.'

'And where's the key I gave you?'

'In my bag.'

'Keep it on a string around your neck – at all times,' he warned, 'because Olivia is devious and she wants to control you. If she decides to take that key, you won't get it back.'

Lottie nodded. 'Okay.'

'And you must be careful in London if you go for walks. There are people you can't trust.'

'Daddy, I already know plenty of people at home who I can't trust.'

John gave her a searching stare, a slight frown on his brow as he detected the hurt in her dark blue eyes. For a minute she looked at him miserably, then continued to gaze at the river. 'I'm sorry to hear that, Lottie. I thought you were happy at home.'

'I was.' Her voice went low. She began twiddling a strand of her hair, winding and unwinding it.

'Was?' John asked sharply. 'So – who has let you down?'

'Morwenna, and Morwenna's mum, and ...' Lottie paused. Her voice had gone so low that John strained to hear it against the noise of London. He was aware of the tension in her as she struggled to speak.

'And who else?' he prompted, trying hard to be calm and gentle.

'Matt.'

'Matt?' John couldn't think of anything to say that wouldn't sound like a platitude. Lottie's haunted eyes told him trivia wasn't welcome. He must take her seriously. Even if it was just sibling stuff. Looking at her in silent empathy seemed to work best.

Lottie's eyes brimmed with tears, but she brushed them away and let go of another name. 'And Jenny.'

'*Jenny*?' John put his hand into his pocket and touched the small Hatton Garden box with the ruby ring inside. Was it sparkling in the dark? To him, Jenny was a person who sparkled in the dark, and the dark was his secret loneliness, his yearning for a woman in his life. Jenny was perfect. What could she have done to hurt Lottie so deeply?

'I thought you got on so well with Jenny.'

'I did.'

'So what happened, Lottie? I want to understand.'

Lottie shuddered with the memory of Jenny dragging her out of school in front of all her friends. She closed her eyes and wanted to scream. She let the feeling pass over her in the silence, then felt strong enough to speak calmly. 'If I tell you something, Daddy, will you please keep quiet and listen until I've finished?'

'Okay, my lovely, I'm listening.' John offered her his hands and she took them. Her fingertips were cold but her grip was firm. Not needy like Olivia but unconditionally strong. He remembered her as a baby, how her tiny fist had curled around his finger, claiming him for life. He mustn't let her down.

'You're going to be shocked, Daddy,' she began, 'but please – let the shock surge over you like an ocean wave; let it pass and, when the water is calm, you can try to understand.'

Startled at the intensity in those dark blue eyes, John tried to speak.

'No, Daddy, just listen, because it's hard for me to tell you this,' Lottie said. 'I'm not a child, Daddy. I'm a woman, and I'm in love – with Matt. We've been lovers since last December and like Romeo and Juliet we are star-crossed lovers. Our love has been a secret, but it's beautiful, the most beautiful thing that has ever happened to me.' Lottie began to speak with passion, and her eyes shone. 'We knew no one would understand. People think it's bad and wicked. But it isn't. How can something so sacred be wrong? How can *love* be *bad*?'

Stunned, John made himself listen, squeezing her hand just enough to let her know he was still there.

Lottie took a few deep breaths and continued. 'Matt didn't know what would happen and neither did I, although Morwenna tried to warn me and I didn't believe her. Since

Arnie died, Matt hasn't had anyone to talk to. It wasn't his fault – and now the whole town is against him. You should see the bruise on his face, Daddy. Morwenna's mum attacked him in the street – she threw a frying pan at his head when he wasn't doing anything wrong! He was just walking past her house.' Sobs of fury were breaking up Lottie's voice. She paused for breath.

Instinctively, John knew he mustn't interrupt, though he longed to say something calming. He felt her distress deeply. *Just be a rock*, he kept thinking.

Finally, she told him. 'The truth is, Daddy, I . . . I'm going to have a baby.'

John kept perfectly still, letting the shock wave wash over him as Lottie had asked. From inside the translucent curl of the wave, the blackest reactions came.

He wanted to kill Matt. He wanted to take an axe and smash *The Jenny Wren* into splinters. He waited in the tunnel as moments turned into ages. He held on, and the wave toppled and broke, surging away from him, taking his bad feelings and crashing them onto the beach where they vanished into the sand.

Lottie lifted her chin and began to talk again, this time with defiance, conviction and love. 'Dr Tregullow let me listen to her heartbeat through his stethoscope and it made me want to sing and clap my hands and dance – but Jenny wouldn't listen to it. She was so angry. I felt sad for her, Daddy. Poor Jenny. She would have loved it. She loves children and this little one will be her grandchild, and yours. It's not my baby's fault Matt and I made a mistake, is it?' Lottie paused, her eyes questioning his, and John felt himself closing down.

He managed to listen to the bright words flowing from his daughter's lips. She was speaking from the heart while his own heart was sinking into a deep crater. He wanted to tell her to stop, or at least to slow down and let him think.

'I love my baby, Daddy, and I want to be her mother, and be a good mother. I shall never abandon her or have her adopted. If I need to, I shall leave home and take her far away where I can bring her up in peace.'

A moment hovered between them, with the sounds of London filtering into the silence. Lottie took a strip of paper from her pocket and unfolded it. 'Listen to this, Daddy. It's from some poetry we were doing at school and it will be the last and most important thing I learned there – listen ...'

> *Our birth is but a sleep and a forgetting.*
> *Our soul that riseth with us, our life's star*
> *Hath had elsewhere its setting*
> *And cometh from afar.*

Lottie thrust the paper into his hand. 'You keep it and read it, Daddy, when you have doubts. I know it by heart now.' She stared into his retreating soul. 'A baby is a star sent from God. Remember that, Daddy.' Lottie closed her mouth and looked at her father with a compelling light in her eyes, a look he was to remember many times in the lonely days and nights to come.

His eyes read the words on the strip of paper. He folded it and tucked it inside his leather wallet. 'May I speak now?' he asked, and Lottie nodded. He sensed how eagerly and anxiously she was awaiting his reaction, but John was so shattered that he couldn't think what on earth to say. He admired her clear, brave vision of being a mother. But with his life experience, he could see all the pros and cons. How could he both morally support her *and* warn her of the consequences? His thoughts plummeted into a downward spiral. He'd had such high hopes for his daughter's future.

'Daddy?'

Whatever he said, he was going to lose her. How could he condone this? It was the road to ruin.

'Daddy, please, you're the last person I trust.'

'I'm sorry, Lottie, but I need time alone to think about this. You must give me a chance to recover.' He stood up and put his hands in his pockets. 'It's time I headed back to Paddington — to catch the train to Cornwall. Are you coming?'

'No.'

'Then you must go back to Olivia and try to get along with her. But come home soon, won't you, dear? You've got your rail ticket.'

'I might never come home,' Lottie said with pride.

'That would make me sad. Very sad indeed.' John wanted a quick, uncomplicated goodbye, brisk and business-like. No heartbreak. No tears. 'Goodbye now.' He gave her a peck on the cheek and walked away, his mind hammering out the words he should have said.

Days later, Lottie walked alone along the embankment, a map in her hand. She passed John's favourite seat, eyed it, and walked on, her back straight, her blonde hair coiled into an elegant bun. Her shoes tapped importantly along the pavement. Nobody smiled at her the way they did in St Ives. People stared coldly into the distance, imprisoned in stiff black overcoats and intimidating bowler hats. Only the shabbily dressed people looked at her with greedy eyes. Lottie felt wary. If she dared to smile, she'd be dragged up an alleyway. Being po-faced was a new skill she needed to master in London.

She did pause to admire the work of a pavement artist who was creating evocative pictures on the stone slabs with only a grubby OXO tin of coloured chalks. How could he bear to do such beautiful works of art when the rain would wash them away? He looked up at her with eyes like Matt's. She gulped and walked on, searching the street names high up on the buildings across the road, a tingle of excitement and dread in her mind when she saw the one she was looking for: MOUNTBERRY AVENUE.

Lottie crossed the busy road and turned into the tree-lined avenue, the crisp, copper leaves of autumn rustling around her feet. Why were the streets of London so endlessly long? Number 139 would be at the far end of this expensive-looking road. The tall houses had immaculate steps with wide banisters and pillars, tiled doorsteps and magnificent front doors winking with swirls of mullioned glass.

A flutter of movement in her womb made Lottie stop to rest for a few seconds. Discreetly she touched her growing bump with caring hands, sending the baby a message: *It's all right, little star, I know exactly what I'm doing, and it's for you.*

Moments later, number 139 loomed. Lottie's heart began to thump as she climbed the scrubbed steps under the dappled sunlight of the plane trees. Feeling small and very Cornish, she stood on the spacious doorstep and rang the bell. She heard it ringing deep in the house but there was no sound of approaching footsteps, only a spooky sense of someone already hovering inside the substantial door. It swung open, ponderously, and a man with tired eyes stood there, smartly dressed in a suit with a matching waistcoat, a rose–gold watch chain looped from his top pocket.

'Good morning,' Lottie said, looking directly into his eyes. 'I have come in response to your advertisement. My name is Miss Lanroska.' She held out her hand and he took it, his cold fingers firm and dry, his large, flat nails immaculately clean.

He looked her up and down. 'May I ask how old you are?'

'Twenty-one,' she lied.

'And when could you start?'

'Tomorrow.'

His tired eyes brightened and he opened the door wide. 'Would you like to come in? We'll have a chat about what is involved. My name is Mr Ford-Morgan.'

'Yes. Thank you.'

Lottie gave him a candid stare and stepped inside. The house smelled of cloves and old books. The walls ticked with multiple clocks and two bronze dogs with ugly faces guarded the thickly carpeted staircase.

'Come this way.'

Lottie followed Mr Ford–Morgan through the muffled silence of the house, her heart thudding with the huge lie she had told. It sat in her mind like a hungry bird, its beak gaping, its eyes glimmering. Every day, from now on, she must feed it – feed the lie and keep it safe – and she must ignore the slender echo of a voice within her, a distant, fading cry that said: *I'm too young. Too young for this – and too alone.*

Chapter 20

To Live That Day Again

John had come home from London and Jenny begged Nan not to let him see her.

'He knows about the baby,' Nan told her. 'He's shocked, of course. Aren't we all? But he wants to see you, Jenny. He's very persistent.'

'I can't see him. Please Nan, just keep him away.'

'I thought you liked him.'

'I do.'

'So what's the problem? Lottie's his daughter and he needs to talk to you about her.'

'Leave me alone, Nan.'

'Does that mean let you starve?' Nan was getting annoyed with her. Jenny feared she might do something drastic, like calling the doctor or even throwing her out. But did it matter? There was only Tom to consider now, and Tom had turned on her too. He'd meant what he said. The words rang in her heart: *Next time, Mum, it'll be me leaving.*

From her bed, Jenny heard Nan's loud voice telling John she wouldn't see him. His disappointment crept under the door like autumn fog and Jenny heard him eventually leaving.

It left a hollow space.

The days rolled on and nothing changed. The telephone didn't ring and no letters appeared. October was passing and the autumn gales stripped leaves from the hedges and blew sand into the streets. There was no word from Lottie in London.

I've lost her, Jenny thought, grief-stricken. *I've lost Lottie, and John as well. If only I could go back and live that day again. I'd be kind and motherly. But it's too late so what's the point in trying?*

But one morning, to her alarm, Jenny heard Nan starting the car and driving off, the sound of the exhaust backfiring as it lurched out of the gate and down the lane.

Where could Nan be going? Tom was in school and Jenny was lying in bed, alone at Hendravean. Nan seldom used the car and everyone, including Jenny, worried about her erratic driving. *What is she up to?*

At least it would give Jenny time to sleep in peace. She snuggled into the pillow and closed her eyes.

Nan had left the door of Jenny's downstairs bedroom ajar and it wasn't long before the two cats padded in. First came Bartholomew. He jumped onto the bed and paraded carefully up Jenny's body until he found her face. Then he sat on her shoulder, purring and peeping over to kiss her nose, tickling her cheek with his white whiskers. She couldn't help smiling and it felt strange after the days of stubbornly maintained misery.

The smile seemed to illuminate the inside of her head. Bartholomew slithered down to lie beside her, curled on the pillow, his golden eyes like two suns shining at her every time she opened her eyes. Then Bessie arrived and the two cats lay together, entwined in a heap of paws and tails. Jenny stroked them gently, aware of their silky fur and the love they were giving.

Obviously it was all part of Nan's plot to get Jenny out of bed. After the blissful interlude of purring and stroking, something suddenly startled the cats. They leapt, with bushed-out fur and bottlebrush tails, onto the windowsill and crouched there, watching the door with huge black eyes.

Spooked, Jenny sat up and swung her legs to the floor. She dragged her iron leg out from under the bed and quickly strapped it on. Wrapped in her cream shawl, she sat shivering on the bed. The cats knew when there was danger. Nan had left the front door wide open as usual.

Jenny stood up, her legs unsteady from too much time in bed. She jumped as a rumpus erupted in the hall.

Usually the chickens were clumped peacefully on the stairs in the morning. Jenny tiptoed into the hall, a shoe in one hand ready to use as a weapon. The ginger eyes of a fox confronted her. The morning sun glowed through his cream and orange ruff, a glaze of droplets misting his fur as if he'd been running in wet grass. He stood with one paw raised, his black nose twitching, his eyes unafraid, challenging and in control. While the chickens squawked and flapped, the fox looked steadily at Jenny. She could smell his musky coat.

She sensed his fire. Fire that kept him alive. She felt he despised her, saw her weakness.

Jenny brandished the shoe and yelled at him, 'Get out!' The fox threw her a contemptuous glance and fled, light as air, across the yard and over the hedge. The cats stayed on the windowsill like two porcupines and the chickens carried on squawking at full volume. Fright seemed to ripple across the floorboards and into china cupboards and cutlery drawers. The rows of chutney jars clinked and the bunches of dried lavender, rosemary and sage released a fragrant, lustrous dust into the air.

Outside, the garden looked peaceful and bright. Jenny felt drawn to go out there. Unsteady on her feet, she shuffled along, close to the wall, so preoccupied with the simple task of walking that she didn't notice John come sweeping into the yard on his bike. She was stepping out of the door just as he was walking in.

There was no place to hide.

Jenny shook her fist at the sky. 'You're at it again, God,' she hissed, and smiled at the look on John's face. 'I didn't mean you to see me, John. Not like this. I'm such a mess.'

'Oh, Jenny,' John spoke her name with immense tenderness. He held out his arms. 'Darling.' Again, the word was loaded with nurturing warmth. To be spoken to with such tenderness in the middle of so much stress was like being wrapped in layer upon layer of goose down.

'Don't run away from me. Don't hide from me,' he pleaded, not touching her but standing close with his arms held out in welcome.

It's a long time since I felt welcome on this earth, she thought.

She allowed him to hold her, and it felt sweet and sustaining, like the first sip from a mug of Ovaltine.

'I'm sorry, John – about the gallery. I let you down,' Jenny mumbled. 'And I'm so, so sorry about Lottie. I let her down when she needed me. I'm horrible, John. Don't get close to me. I've got a bad, fiery temper and I'm no good to anyone.'

'Jenny!' he breathed, making her name sound like a healing mantra. 'Jenny.'

'Even Tom doesn't . . .' Jenny stopped herself. She wasn't going to rant at John and drag him into her misery. She looked up into his eyes. 'I'm not going to moan.'

'We've got a lot to talk about,' John said, 'but not now. Let's just be quiet.' He led her to the bench against the sunny wall. 'You're good for *me*, Jenny. Very good for me.'

They sat close, absorbing the ambience of Nan's garden, the scent of apples and crushed grass, the busy wings of bumble bees and tiny, flake-like butterflies with exquisite patterns on the underside of their blue wings. 'They've got wise little faces,' John said, studying one, 'and such black, bright eyes.'

'Lottie's so like you,' Jenny said. 'It's exactly what she would have said.'

'We're both grieving, in a way, for Lottie,' John sighed. 'Let's be quiet and think about her. She's staying in my London apartment with Olivia.'

Jenny put her head on his shoulder, her cheek pressed against the thick cotton smock he wore, her other cheek warmed by the golden autumn sun. They listened to the waves rolling in on Porthmeor Beach, the distant throb of a motorboat and the whirr of linnets' wings in Nan's garden. Out on the cliffs there were pockets of silence in the hot grass between rocks. Jenny longed for John to take her hand and lead her into one of those intimate places of deep quiet where you could hear the slim black pods of the gorse flowers snapping open and spreading their seed.

Lottie taught me that, she thought, *before I had polio*. Everything joyful had come before polio. Until John.

Jenny looked down at her iron leg and at the crumpled nightie she was wearing and the matted cream shawl with its tatty tassels. What was she doing sitting in the sunshine wearing grimy rags, her unwashed hair hanging in sullen tangles? How had she got into such a state? It wasn't only her clothes. Her mind ached with shame, and blame, and bitterness. Where was the bright, clear-minded, confident girl she'd always been? Who was she now?

She looked at John. He was watching her. Their eyes met and they both began to speak at the same time.

'I'm sorry, John ...'

'I'm sorry, Jenny ...'

'Go on ...'

343

'No, you go on,' John said firmly. 'I'm in better shape than you, Jenny. Talk to me. Let it out.'

A phantom smile wavered between them like a reflection in the harbour.

Jenny sighed. 'I hate myself, John. You've been so nice to me – and I'm ashamed of the way I look. I never meant you to see me like this.'

'Shall I go away?'

'No.'

'I was going to apologise for the upset my daughter has caused you, Jenny.'

'I hate myself,' Jenny said again. 'I did something dreadful. Matt told me about the baby and I gave him such a scolding. I was so angry. I felt like a thunderstorm and I marched up to the school – gave myself blisters! – and . . . Lottie was there enjoying her class. She looked happy and calm, John, and . . . oh, I can hardly tell you – I hate myself,' Jenny paused, a hot pain in her throat.

'Take your time. Slow down.' John gave her a squeeze.

'I've never hurt Lottie, never slapped her or anything, but I was beside myself with fury. I dragged her out of school. I called her terrible names. No wonder she's run away. I wish, oh, how I wish I could go back to live that day again. I'd give anything to have Lottie home and tell her I'm sorry – so sorry.' Jenny began to cry, hardly noticing the tears mingling with her confession. John kept still, rocklike, his eyes never leaving her face. 'I took Lottie straight to the doctor, John, and she tried so hard to tell me how she feels. She's being unbelievably brave and she wants to keep the baby.'

'She told me that too,' John said, 'and I didn't listen. I walked away and regretted it. I know how you feel, Jenny.'

'The worst thing was – oh,' Jenny sobbed, 'Lottie wanted me to hear the baby's heartbeat. You should have seen her face – like the face of an angel – when the doctor let her listen through the stethoscope. And I turned my back. On my own grandchild. John, I'm so wicked. Don't get involved with me. I'm a wicked, grubby old witch. And you're a decent, proper handsome man. Don't get involved with me. I'm a dishrag. I've driven all my children away and it serves me right ...' Jenny tried to get up and scurry back to the safety of bed with her face to the wall. She'd just lie there and die.

But John wasn't going to let her. He curled his strong, steady hands around her small wrists and made her look at him. 'Jenny,' he said, again putting such love into her name, gazing steadfastly at her.

She stopped crying and felt stillness gathering around her, stillness with dappled sunlight. It was a place of transformation. John had seen her at her worst and he was still there, holding her. Everything he wanted to say and all she needed to hear was encapsulated in the way he'd spoken her name, infusing it with healing love, as if the name was her whole being, the essence of her.

'It will be okay. I am here, and we will get through this – together,' John said.

*

Nan was on a mission of her own. She put her foot down on the accelerator and the Austin Seven flew along the winding hilltop road, backfiring at every sharp bend and groaning as it climbed the hills. Nan was getting tired, but she daren't stop in case the car never started again. She met only occasional traffic as she drove on between high stone hedges, the summer flowers now a mist of brown seed pods.

On and on she drove in clear autumn sunshine, winding through Camborne and Redruth, glancing up at the Carn Brea as she passed, wanting to go up there and see the giant stacks of weathered granite and remember its legends.

But there wasn't time.

A signpost loomed out of the hedge pointing towards the sea. It said PORTREATH.

Should she go down there and find Matt? Someone had to talk to him. But, no, she must focus on the task at hand; the reason she'd driven such a long way. The car seemed to be getting hotter and hotter.

Nan wasn't particularly worried about Lottie. In her opinion, Lottie was level-headed and wise beyond her years. She'd already coped with everything life had thrown at her. Lottie would sort herself out, even being pregnant. Social expectations like marriage and being old enough didn't bother Nan, and she'd no time for gossip. She felt sure Lottie would soon tire of London and come home.

It was Jenny who bothered Nan. Jenny would end up in Bodmin, a hospital for the mentally ill, and they were terrible places. Worse than prison. In fact, they were a kind of prison. Nan believed it was Jenny, not Lottie, who was seriously at risk. Mental illness was invisible, misunderstood and regarded as shameful. People would go on hiding it for years rather than face a doctor with it. There seemed to be no kindly treatment on offer. It was the loony bin or nothing.

So Nan's secret mission today was for Jenny.

The signpost to Truro was half hidden in a gorse bush and she almost missed it, braking sharply and steering the car wildly into the turning. At least it was a wider, straighter road and the countryside began to change from the granite moorland to a softer landscape, the fields greener, the cows fatter, even the sunlight seemed more mellow. Closer to Truro there were tall, dark conifer trees, pine and cedar, and houses with green lawns and gravelled driveways.

Money, Nan thought; *people with money live here.*

As she drove on through the outskirts of the city, Nan saw something that made her slow down. Parked in a grassy layby were three colourful gypsy caravans with three skewbald horses tethered in the thick grass. The caravans were impressively lofty and beautifully painted with birds and roses, elaborate scrolls and motifs, some painted in gold leaf. They glowed richly in the autumn sunshine.

Nan paused, studying them with interest. She'd always felt an affinity with the Romany gypsies, especially the women. The caravans were deserted. The women would be in town selling waxed paper roses, clothes pegs and bits of lace. Some would be offering sprigs of white heather and lucky charms, such as tiny brass Cornish piskies. Tired as she was, Nan felt energised by seeing the caravans. Finding the Romany gypsies was phase one of her mission.

She felt rebellious driving into the grand city of Truro in her battered Austin Seven. Most of its paint was back home in St Ives, scraped along the many sharp granite corners she had misjudged. The stuffing was bursting out of the back seat from where the chickens had been excavating with their sharp claws. The floor was damp under the seats with moss and even a few tiny toadstools.

Nan knew her way around Truro. She must get in there without hitting any of the expensive-looking motors. She mustn't hit the pavement either, or drive on it – and she mustn't forget to do the hand signals. She wound the window down and flapped her arm up and down, and by some miracle she managed to park neatly in a road close to the cathedral.

Exhausted, Nan sat for a few minutes and closed her eyes. She was boiling hot and so was the car.

It might catch fire!

She heaved herself out, struggling to unbend her legs after the long drive. She opened the bonnet with the intention of topping up the water tank. Heads turned as a whoosh of steam erupted from the engine.

'Don't touch it, madam.' A little man in overalls and a cap stepped between Nan and the car. He looked up at her like one of the seven dwarves. Probably Grumpy. 'You'll burn the skin off yer,' he said. 'Let 'un cool down first.' He looked her up and down. 'Looks like you need to cool down, yerself.' He peered into the back window. 'Proper old banger, int 'er.'

'If I want your opinion on my mode of transport, I'll ask for it,' Nan said imperiously, her voice rising above the hiss of steam. 'Kindly go on your way.'

He made a face, but walked on. Nan was relieved – she didn't want to start a conversation. She needed to be quiet and private and focus on her mission.

It was mid-morning and Truro was bustling with people: wealthy women shopping with their subservient daughters; men in suits looking switched-off and important; country folk like herself with willow baskets. A few streets away, the market was in full swing and she could hear the high-pitched babble of an auctioneer. Nan found cattle markets distressing, picking up the fear in the frantic voices of bewildered cows and sheep, and the terrified squealing of pigs. Avoiding it, she walked on towards the cathedral.

Nan was delighted to see a Romany gypsy woman making a beeline for her, carrying a basket laden with bunches of paper flowers. The dark-eyed woman's smile startled Nan. Didn't she know that face? Something about her was hauntingly familiar.

'Will you buy some paper roses, madam?' The woman looked at her knowingly. 'I could tell you something you need to know – if you buy one of my lucky charms for a shilling.'

Nan peered into the basket. 'Ah, you have some Cornish piskies!'

'Wait – let me pick one for you,' the woman said in a lilting, seductive tone, her eyes gleaming. She chose a brass piskie and put it into Nan's hand. 'That's a rather special one.

349

He's very, very lucky for you, especially today – you must have him. Keep him with you, always. Don't give him away. You were going to, weren't you?'

'Yes, I was going to,' Nan admitted. She'd intended the piskie for Lottie.

'Don't,' the gypsy said quickly. She reached into the basket, underneath the stems of the paper flowers, and drew out a small cardboard box of gemstones. 'If you want a charm for a child in your life, a little girl you love very much, choose a piece of Cornish turquoise. It's rare and precious. Only the Romanies know where to find it. And if you want a charm for a sturdy little boy, choose a piece of rainbow ore.' She took a piece out to show Nan the winking, rainbow colours in the sunshine. 'See how it glitters.'

Nan smiled to herself. She took the piskie, a piece of pale turquoise for Lottie and a rainbow stone for Tom. She gave the gypsy woman a florin. They stood looking at each other, Nan trying to understand why she felt so drawn to this warm, contented gypsy woman. 'I think we've met before, haven't we?'

'No, madam,' the gypsy said firmly, 'but we're going to meet again – many times.'

Nan nodded. 'Would you tell me your name?'

'Petronella. And yours?'

'Nan.'

A secretive sparkle came into Petronella's eyes. 'Nan! Nan indeed,' she said. 'I will see you again, very soon. Look after those charms.'

Petronella flashed her a radiant smile and walked on, hips swinging in her colourful skirt. She didn't look back, but the glint in her eyes stayed with Nan. *Where* had she seen those eyes before?

Nan forgot how tired she was and continued walking to the end of the street, which opened out onto the cobbled precinct of the cathedral. A weathered Celtic cross stood opposite the main door, as if guarding the majestic cathedral with its spires and rose windows. There were a few people strolling about or sitting, and there was a cart parked with a donkey like Mufty. A cacophony of music filled the precinct from various buskers: a man with a barrel organ and a pet monkey, an elderly tramp playing a harmonica and a young girl playing a fiddle, all of them far enough apart to be playing their own individual repertoire.

Nan stood listening intently to one particular tune.

The Ash Grove.

Her pulse quickened and goosebumps covered her arms. She stared towards the cathedral and lost all control of her emotions, not caring if people saw her crying.

For there on the steps sat a thin, dark-haired boy playing his heart out on a piano-accordion, its pearl buttons shimmering in the sun, his fingers flying over the keys, his face alight with a wicked grin.

She'd found him.

She'd found Warren.

*

Far away in London, Lottie let herself into the flat, her fingers trembling with excitement and trepidation. She wasn't sure how her birth mother was going to react to her news.

Olivia was already angry. 'Where have you been? And why are you dressed up like that? You're far too young to wear your hair in a bun.'

Lottie sat down and kicked her shoes off, rubbing her feet. 'I've walked miles and the London pavements are so hard.' She studied her mother's disapproving expression. John hadn't told Olivia about the baby and had advised Lottie to keep quiet about it. Olivia wouldn't be able to cope, he'd warned.

'Answer my question,' Olivia glared, her eyes red-rimmed under heavily pencilled brows. She drained the last inch of red wine from a glass on the table. Another glass stood half full on the windowsill, and another on the floor by an armchair.

'I've got a job,' Lottie said brightly.

'What?'

'I. Have. Got. A. Job.,' Lottie replied bluntly.

'Don't be ridiculous.'

'It's true. Whether you believe it or not, *Mother*, I'm starting work tomorrow morning at eight o'clock.'

'Doing what? And where?'

'As a nanny. Looking after a little boy. He's—'

'You're lying to me, Charlotte.'

'No, I am not. Why would I?'

'You are lying. You must be. How could you possibly get a job as a nanny when you're only seventeen?'

Lottie felt as if a door had been slammed in her face. Extreme disappointment at her mother's reaction was hard to swallow. She was proud of what she'd done. Earning some money would help her to keep her baby and bring her up – free of confrontations and disapproval. Facing Olivia was devastating. Her own birth mother didn't trust her, didn't *like* her, and apparently didn't even want her to succeed. 'Why are you so against me?'

'Aw, honey-child, it's not like that. I want to keep you safe and I want you to go to college – John does too. I can't believe you had the audacity to go out in London and get yourself a job when you're only seventeen. *Nobody* is going to hire a seventeen-year-old kid from Cornwall to be a nanny. It's a responsible, highly trained job. Explain it to me, please.'

'I will if you listen.'

'I am listening.'

'No, you're not. You're standing there with a shotgun, firing at me every time I speak.'

'Just explain about this so-called job. Without being a drama queen.'

Lottie sighed loudly. 'I have to be a drama queen to make you listen. Why can't you ever be pleased at anything I do? And I'm not going to talk to you unless you stop drinking wine. I shall go to bed, have an early night and go to my job in the morning, and you can't stop me.'

Olivia held her head in her hands. 'Oh God – how did I give birth to such a self-willed little madam?'

'Being self-willed is a quality. Nan admires me for it, and so does Daddy, and—' Lottie was going to say Jenny but her voice broke. She took a deep breath and searched Olivia's eyes. If she couldn't tell her about something as good and lucky as getting a job, how would she ever tell her about the baby?

'I need you to back me up,' she explained calmly. 'I lied about my age. He thinks I'm twenty-one. He's a nice, courteous, respectful man – and he's very rich. You should see the lovely house he lives in. It's got a curved staircase with a red and gold carpet and golden banisters, and a glittering chandelier.'

Olivia's expression began to change. She listened, wide-eyed. 'Go on.'

'His wife died and he's got a bright, bouncy little boy, Ben, aged three, to bring up. He had a proper, qualified nanny but she was taken ill. She's in hospital and he thinks it's going to be a while before she recovers – four to six weeks, he said – so it's a temporary job, perfect for me at the moment. He wanted a nanny urgently and he put a card in a corner-shop window and that's where I saw it. I told him I was well educated and experienced with children, like Tom and Warren. He looked so tired and desperate and he hired me on the spot.'

Olivia's mouth was open, her eyebrows arched. Lottie could see her attitude was changing by the minute. She remembered what John had said, scathingly, of Olivia: 'Money talks.'

'I'm old enough to leave school and work,' Lottie added, 'and don't try to stop me. You'll regret it if you do.'

Olivia's eyebrows met in a draconian frown. 'Are you threatening me?'

'Yes.'

'Then I am threatening you, madam. I can stop you going to this so-called job. I can have you made a Ward of Court.'

'No, you can't. You're not my legal guardian. Jenny is.'

They glared at each other. It was like a declaration of war.

Chapter 21

Lies

The moon in London was high up and far away, a tarnished shilling viewed through dust. It was three o'clock in the morning and Lottie had woken, convinced she could hear the sea. Filled with an unbearable longing, she went to the window seeking the healing power of fresh air and a clean, bright silver moon. She wanted the reassuring, eternal presence of the Atlantic Ocean, its white waves beating on the shores of home.

Matt, are you out there on The Jenny Wren, *dipping and rolling over the moonlit swell?* she thought, and the vivid memory was both painful and comforting.

Lottie felt she'd been managing her broken heart pretty well. Keeping busy. Standing up to Olivia. Finding herself a job, which she was looking forward to.

Ben was an appealing, lively little boy and Lottie felt confident in her ability to manage him. There was a garden at the back of the big house with a mature horse-chestnut tree. She planned to take Ben out there and share some of the magic Nan had taught her, the stories, games and legends. It helped her to focus on doing her best in her first job. Everything about her new life felt precarious, a driftwood fragment of her future being tossed about by the Atlantic surf. The great rolling tide was the ache of homesickness, the longing for Nan, and Jenny, and her father. And Matt.

Worst of all was the devastating belief that she could never go back.

Lottie went back to bed, still haunted by the sound coming through the open window. It wasn't the roar of the sea, she kept telling herself. It was the perpetual roar of London. Yet she still went to sleep imagining the surf thundering onto Porthmeor Beach.

In the morning, she quickly made herself look smart, ate a hasty breakfast of bread and butter with milky Camp Coffee. Olivia didn't appear, and Lottie let herself out of the flat at half past seven and set out on the long walk to Mountberry Avenue. She'd studied the map and found a quicker route, cutting through a magnificent park.

She arrived just as Mr Ford-Morgan was leaving for work dressed in the blackest black she'd ever seen. A majestic overcoat, a black umbrella and a black briefcase, his tired eyes peering out at the world as if trapped under the brim of his bowler hat.

Lottie managed to smile brightly, look him in the eye and say good morning. He looked pleased.

'Good morning, Miss Lanroska. I'm off to work as you can see. Mrs Rigby, my housekeeper, is expecting you. She'll help you settle in. And . . .' he stooped towards her, speaking in a low, conspiratorial tone, 'don't take too much notice of her. She likes to be the Queen Bee.'

Forewarned, Lottie found herself facing a pug-faced dumpy woman who looked her over suspiciously. It was unnerving, especially as she'd tried to keep her pregnancy hidden under a loose pinafore.

''Ow old are you?' Mrs Rigby asked with a frown.

'Twenty-one.'

'Hmm. And where are you from?'

'Cornwall.'

'So what are you doing in London?'

Lottie gave her a withering look. 'I was looking for a job. And, if you don't mind, I'd like to get on with it.'

'Yeah, you get on with it, dearie,' Mrs Rigby said huffily. 'Don't mind me. I'm a Cockney – born within the sound of Bow Bells. I speak my mind and I'm proud of my Cockney accent.'

'Bow bells? What are they?' Lottie asked, sensing a legend.

'Like in "Oranges and Lemons" – "*I'm sure I don't know, said the big bell of Bow.*"' Her face brightened as she sang the rhyme and her expression softened when she saw Lottie smile. 'We'll 'ave to rub along,' she said. 'If you get any trouble with young Ben, send 'im to me. 'E'll soon behave. 'E knows I'll smack 'im if 'e don't.'

'I hope that won't be necessary,' Lottie said. 'So where's his bedroom?'

'Up the stairs, first door on the right.'

Lottie set off, her shoes sinking into the lush red and gold stair carpet, aware of Mrs Rigby's shrewd eyes watching her.

There were twenty-three steps, each one of them painful, taking her on cushioned treads away from one life and into another.

A face on each step: Nan. Jenny. Mufty. Tom. All gone. Gone from her life, perhaps forever. There was only Matt whose eyes still burned in her heart. They loved each other and surely love would find a way to reunite them – wouldn't it?

She went eagerly into Ben's bedroom, expecting to see the bright-faced, polite little boy who Mr Ford-Morgan had introduced to her to. Instead she saw a pair of bewildered, hostile eyes looking up at her from the pillow.

'Hello, Ben. I'm Lottie, your new nanny.' She gave him a radiant smile. 'And it's time to get up.'

The little boy didn't smile back. His mouth pouted and his eyes filled with tears. 'I don't *want* a new nanny. I want my *old* nanny. Go away!'

Lottie sat down on the bed. 'Oh, you'll soon get used to me, Ben. We'll have lots of fun together.'

Ben stared at her in mutinous silence. Lottie wrinkled her nose. Obviously he'd wet the bed. She tried to reassure him. 'It doesn't matter if the sheets are wet, Ben. You couldn't help it.'

Ben's small face hardened. He climbed out of bed on the other side and crawled underneath it in his wet

359

pyjamas. 'I'm not coming out,' he yelled. 'I don't want you here. *Go away*!'

Back in St Ives, Matt waited outside the school gate, a white envelope in his hand. Inside was a letter he'd written to Lottie and he intended to ask Tom to give it to her. He sat on the wall kicking his sea-soaked boots against the granite. The day was quiet, St Ives muffled under a vast swathe of thick mist, the sea invisible except for its fringe of creamy white foam, the subdued waves whispering into the sand and sliding back like sheets of satin.

It was chilly and Matt wore his navy-blue fisherman's jersey, the last one Jenny had knitted for him, too small now and with holes in the sleeves. He felt cold waiting outside the school and wished he was back in *The Jenny Wren*'s cabin, bundled in a blanket, brewing tea on the Primus stove.

Weeks had passed since he'd last seen Lottie. He'd stayed in Portreath safely out of reach, wanting to be left alone to sort his feelings out, and he intended to go back there as soon as the mist cleared and he could take the boat back.

It must be December, he realised, seeing a poster outside St Ia's Church advertising the Advent service. Christmas was looming once more and the prospect of a family Christmas seemed even more remote.

Impossible, he thought. *Now I'm more isolated than ever.*

Matt had never written a letter except as an exercise in school. This one had taken hours and hours. He'd written and rewritten it umpteen times, the balls of screwed-up paper rolling around the cabin floor. He wanted it to be a love letter. Despite everything, Matt wanted Lottie back. Nothing else mattered. As for the baby, Matt still had his reservations. He wasn't ready to be a father, expected to protect the child until it grew up, and selfishly he didn't yet want to share his precious Lottie. He reasoned that his denial was based on an entrenched fear of motherly love. Would Lottie be taken over by its apparently awesome power? Would she love the baby more than him?

So Matt had struggled with the letter. He'd even gone into the library and searched for poems he remembered from school, and stories with love letters in them. None of it sounded Cornish. But he hoped Lottie would read it and forgive him. He hoped she'd come back to the harbour with magic in her eyes as she stepped aboard *The Jenny Wren*.

Once he let go of the letter, Matt knew he would be in a state of limbo. It would last until Lottie came back to him and the love would be sweeter and deeper than ever before.

Lost in thought, Matt jumped when he heard the school bell, soon followed by the voices and running feet of children going home. Tom came trudging out, his socks rumpled, his cap over his brow. For once his eyes didn't sparkle when he saw Matt waiting. There was something different about Tom, a sullen shadow around him. It made Matt uneasy.

Tom stood solidly in front of him, unsmiling. 'What do you want, Matt?' he asked bluntly.

'Will you give this to Lottie?' Matt held out the white envelope. 'It's important.'

'How can I?' Tom's eyes narrowed. 'Lottie's gone. She don't live with us no more.'

'*What?*'

'You 'eard,' Tom growled. His shoulders twisted and he tried to walk away from his brother.

Matt grabbed at his sleeve. 'Hey – don't just walk off, Tom. I didn't know Lottie had gone. Where is she? Tell me.'

Tom stopped reluctantly. 'She's gone to London to stay with her birth mother.'

'But Lottie doesn't even like that woman. And she won't like London – not after St Ives. How long's she been gone?'

'Dunno. A lot of weeks, Matt, and it's nearly Christmas, and Lottie's never gonna come home. I miss her, and Mum does – and Nan.'

Matt was shocked. His worst nightmare had come true. Lottie had gone to live with Olivia. And it was his fault.

'I wish I'd known. Why didn't anyone tell me?' There was a silence. He looked at Tom's eyes and thought, *'Cause I don't matter. That's why.*

'We didn't even know where you were,' Tom said, 'and Mum keeps thinking you're dead.'

'*Dead?*'

'Yeah, she thinks you'll get drowned, like ... like Dad.' Tom frowned, then looked straight into Matt's eyes. 'Mum wants you home for Christmas, Matt – and Lottie.'

He glanced at the letter in Matt's hand. 'Why don't you put it in a letterbox? You've gotta stick a stamp on it.'

'I don't know her address. Do you?'

'No.' Tom's frown deepened. 'And if I did, I'd go up there too and live with her, Matt.'

'Why? What's up with you, Tom?'

Tom slid down the wall and sat with his back to it looking at the billows of mist gliding up The Stennack from the sea. 'I know Lottie's having a baby,' he said in a low voice. 'Mum's so upset she's lying in bed day after day with her face turned to the wall – and Nan says she's ill and she'll end up in . . . in the loony bin, up Bodmin or somewhere, I dunno. Why should I care? Mum don't care about me no more, Matt. She don't even look at me or talk to me – all 'cause I told her she'd driven Lottie away.' Tom's chest heaved and he put his head down on his knees and sobbed.

'Tom!' Matt suddenly rediscovered his role as the elder brother. He forgot about the letter and sat close, his hand on Tom's shoulders. But he felt useless, unable to think of the right words to comfort him.

Keeping quiet, trying to send a wordless stream of empathy and love, allowed Matt a sudden, precious glimpse of his dad. A light shining in the mist, a pair of intense and soulful eyes, eyes that cared, a deep, rich Cornish voice; his dad's voice, and it said just one word: *Listen.*

Matt nodded. 'I'm listening, Tom. Talk to me. I'll walk home with you if you like.'

Tom shrugged and plodded on down The Stennack looking at the ground. He didn't speak until they both paused to lean on a wall and watch the waves creeping in through the mist. Tom fidgeted, then slowly turned his head and looked up at Matt. He shuffled closer to him.

'You're like my dad now, Matt,' he said in a husky voice. 'I miss you, and Lottie. And – and Lottie's baby is gonna be lucky to have you as a dad.'

Stunned, Matt studied his brother's candid eyes. Tom loved him! After all the bullying and fighting he'd done when they were growing up. The times he'd made Tom cry. Now Tom had set aside his own worries and made a simple, direct statement: *Lottie's baby is gonna be lucky to have you as a dad.*

Like a golden key, those words unlocked an undiscovered door in Matt's heart.

It changed everything.

He watched Tom disappear into Hendravean. Deep in thought, he headed back towards *The Jenny Wren*. When he came to the place where a bubbling stream crossed the lane, Matt paused on the bridge. He took the letter from his pocket and tore it into fragments, letting them flutter down into the water. His precious letter. He was glad it had gone, the tea-brown current whipping it away down a tunnel of bracken and bramble.

He'd have to start again. What he had to say was now very simple.

An uneasy truce had developed between Lottie and Olivia. A predictable routine turned out to be calming for both of them. Olivia liked to lie in bed until mid-morning and by the time Lottie came home in the evening, Olivia was already slightly drunk. It was Lottie who cooked their evening meal and cleared up afterwards, collecting the empty glasses her mother left lying around.

Olivia's shopping habits were erratic and some nights it was difficult to find the ingredients to make a meal. Lottie began to feel like her mother's servant, not her daughter. It was exhausting after a challenging day managing little Ben, then walking home on sore feet and swollen ankles.

On a Friday night Lottie hurried home, pleased to have her pay packet.

Three pounds. Three whole pounds.

She planned to pay most of it into her Post Office savings account, which John had opened for her. She carried the little book with her to work, safe in a secret pocket she'd stitched inside her apron. Olivia was not to be trusted.

The walk home was scary. Mr Ford–Morgan had looked at her sternly as he handed her the money.

'I don't like to think of you walking home alone with a pay packet,' he said, and he'd stood at the top of the steps and watched her go down the road.

Earlier he'd praised her work. 'You are excellent,' he kept saying, 'I heard you reading a story to young Ben and he clearly adores you – well done. I hope you're happy here; are you, Lottie?'

Lottie swallowed. *If only he knew!* 'Yes, I'm okay, thank you.'

Mr Ford–Morgan's eyebrows shot up. 'Okay? My goodness, that's an Americanism, isn't it? Don't teach it to Ben.'

'Sorry – no, I won't,' Lottie said, 'and it is American. I picked it up in New York.'

'You've been to New York? I thought you were a quiet little Cornish girl.'

'I am. Most of the time.' Lottie pursed her mouth and gave him a steely stare. She must be careful what she told him. Especially as he seemed keen to talk to her.

There was a hunger deep in his eyes, a hunger that seemed to get unnervingly stronger each time he talked to her.

She thought wistfully of Morwenna and her shrewd knowledge of men. What would Morwenna say about Mr Ford-Morgan? Probably: *"E's got a look in 'is eye. 'E ain't up to no good, Lottie. You watch out.'*

It felt strange having money pressed into her hand, feeling his thumb brush her palm. But the heady sensation of suddenly having three crisp pound notes tucked into her secret pocket gave her an unexpected energy boost.

But one Friday in early December Olivia was waiting for her, bright-eyed, and she'd made an attempt at setting out their tea. 'Hello, honey-child. Did you get your pay packet?'

Lottie felt caught in a net. She couldn't say no, but she didn't want to say yes, and she didn't want to start yet another row with Olivia. Lying didn't come naturally to her, but more and more often she was having to do it. She shrugged and sat down at the table. 'This cake looks good.'

Olivia gave a sceptical nod. 'Okay, honey-child, we'll talk about money later. It's Saturday tomorrow and I thought we'd go shopping. Wait 'til you see the shops in

Oxford Street. You need some smart clothes now you're a working girl.'

'I don't need anything – except a rest.' Lottie felt like crying from sheer exhaustion. She kicked off her shoes.

Olivia gasped. 'Look at your ankles, Charlotte! They're badly swollen. Oh my God, there's something wrong with you. You shouldn't have swollen ankles at your age.'

'There's nothing wrong with me.' Lottie took a slice of fruit cake and poured herself a cup of tea. She sat there eating, determined to screen out Olivia's rising panic. The baby stirred inside her as if she too was sensing the atmosphere.

'But Charlotte, you need to see a doctor.'

'No, I don't. Look, it's just London. I'm not used to walking miles on hard pavements.'

'Do you feel well?' Olivia asked with genuine concern.

'Yes, I do, there's no need to panic.'

'I'm not panicking, Charlotte,' Olivia said huffily. 'I wanted to take you shopping for clothes.'

Lottie sighed. 'I don't want to go shopping.'

'But you do need a change of clothes. You've worn that pinafore every day since you've been here. And Christmas is coming.'

Lottie continued eating her tea. 'You can't make me go and there's nothing more to be said.'

Olivia looked annoyed. 'I'm trying to be helpful, Charlotte.'

'*Lottie.*'

'Okay, Lottie then. I've been very tolerant and lenient, letting you go to this job where they think you're twenty-one. I don't know what your father is going to say.'

Lottie smouldered. She wanted to tell her mother she was homesick, missing Matt, craving the pure light of sea and sky. She'd managed to keep going and now the weekend yawned with emptiness. Two whole days away from home. How could she bear it?

Olivia was studying her with a hint of empathy in her eyes. 'I know what we can do – *Lottie*,' she said brightly. 'Why don't we go through my wardrobe? I've got a suit and a dress you might like. I've lost so much weight, they're too big and baggy on me now.'

That appealed to Lottie. Her bump was difficult to hide. Big and baggy was exactly what she needed but Olivia mustn't know why. John had warned her not to tell her mother about the baby. But talking about clothes seemed to be what made Olivia happy. So, tired as she was, Lottie agreed and followed her into the bedroom.

Angular slabs of rosy light shone on the walls and across the wide bed with its brown satin eiderdown. In the wardrobe mirror, Lottie could see the reflection of London's plum-coloured sunset.

Olivia had a lot of clothes. Her face came alive as she riffled through them, pulling out dresses and flinging them on the bed in a gale of eau-de-cologne and fustiness. She began to talk at top speed, giving Lottie a potted history of each garment; where she had bought it, when she had worn it and what had happened.

Finally, she said, 'Well, come on, honey-child – get that pinafore off and try something on. How about this one?' She held up a chocolate-brown velvet dress with an embroidered bodice.

'It wouldn't fit me.'

'Come on, try it. You'd look so good in it.'

Lottie touched the velvet. It reminded her of a dress she'd had as a child. 'It's lovely – but I couldn't wear it to work. It's too nice.'

'Well, you choose something,' Olivia snapped. 'There's no pleasing you, is there?'

'This one might do.' Lottie pulled out a red dress with a full skirt. She thought Matt would like it. She wished Olivia would go away and let her try on the dresses in private. And did she really want to wear something her mother had worn?

The pinafore she was wearing had been Jenny's, and that's why she loved it. She felt it clinging around her.

'I'm going to get a glass of wine,' Olivia said. 'You try it on.'

It happened so quickly. Left alone for a precious minute, Lottie struggled to get the pinafore off, pulling it over her head, hearing threads of cotton snapping as she wrestled with it. Annoyed, she finally emerged only to see Olivia in the doorway, wine glass in her hand, with an expression of shock horror on her face.

'Your stomach, Charlotte! You look – oh my God, you look pregnant!'

Silence twisted between them, tighter and tighter. Lottie felt her face burn with colour. A memory tore at her inner calm. Olivia's eyes were wild and furious like a painting of the mother she had once been, a mother out of control.

Lottie remembered being three years old, quivering with shock as Olivia shook her until the delicate bones in her neck sent cracks of pain needling across her skull and over her cheeks. A flash of insight told her it was the cause of her terrible headaches – that long-ago violent shaking.

'*Are* you?' Olivia demanded. 'Answer me.'

Lottie couldn't speak. What about the language of poetry, so eloquently promised by Dr Tregullow? It streamed past her like a shredded flag in a storm. Useless idealism.

'You are – aren't you?' The skin on Olivia's face shone like hard porcelain, her lips wire-thin. 'Answer me,' she spat. 'Is that what you've been up to with that sullen-eyed Cornish boy? You devious, dirty little *slut*.'

Nothing she could say would pacify Olivia, but Lottie's silence seemed even worse than the truth, driving her mother into a frenzy. Silence felt like the only safe option.

'Don't look at me like that, Charlotte.'

Lottie hardened her stare and, without warning, Olivia flung her glass of wine at Lottie's face. She blinked as it stung her eyes and its ripe-tasting fury ran down the side of her nose and into her mouth. The silence towered over them like a wave, growing darker as it burst into a torrent of rage.

'You're mad,' Lottie cried. 'Why can't you control yourself, you crazy, drunken witch?'

'*This* is what I'm talking about.' Olivia's arm shot out and landed an almighty slap on Lottie's tummy. 'This, this, *this!*' It was followed by another and another blow.

The pain and anger echoed through Lottie's womb. She screamed at Olivia.

'My baby! You're hurting my baby. Stop it. *Stop!*' Lottie curled her arms over her bump, her hands desperately trying to soothe the tiny child inside. 'It's all right, little one, little star,' she whispered. 'I won't let her hurt you ever again.'

Olivia stood over her, trembling. 'So there is a baby – a bastard. *His*, I suppose.' Her eyes glittered triumphantly. She picked up the cracked wine glass, which was rolling around the floor. 'A Cornish bastard.'

'Give me that.' Lottie reached out and took the cracked wine glass from her, surprised at how easily Olivia let go. She looked in her eyes; beyond the fury, there was fear.

'You sit down there,' she said, and Olivia sat on the edge of her bed, in amongst the dresses she had thrown there. Lottie sat down with her, still rubbing her hands over her bump.

'I don't care what you think, of Matt or of me. I've managed perfectly well without you all these years. We're not alike, thank goodness. Look at me, *Mother*, I'm a young woman now, not a child you can intimidate. First, you are going to sit there and listen, for once in your life, to how I feel about my baby. Then I am going to pack my bag and leave. I can afford to rent a room now.'

But even as she spoke those defiant words, desolation swept over Lottie. She couldn't go home to St Ives. She could never again live with the family she loved. The enormity of it welled up and she saw Olivia through a blur of tears. Her birth mother, staring at her with savage, bewildered eyes, her thin hand reaching again for the wine bottle.

Lottie squeezed her painful feet into her shoes again. She pulled her American bag out of the wardrobe and crammed a few things into it. The truth was she probably couldn't afford to rent a room, and didn't feel like trying. Deeply exhausted, both physically and emotionally, she needed a good night's sleep in a quiet bed. But where? And who cared?

She slung the bag over her shoulder and walked out, ignoring the harrowing sound of Olivia panicking in her high-pitched tearful voice.

'No, Charlotte – don't go, honey-child. Please – don't leave me. *Please.*'

Lottie walked away into the darkening evening, into the streets of London.

Desolate.

Chapter 22

Forgive Me, Honey-Child

After John's kindness and Nan's warning, Jenny managed to drag herself out of bed. She didn't know where Nan had been, or why. The car had arrived home, backfiring and skidding along the side of the chicken shed, sending a metal bucket rolling across the yard. Unperturbed, Nan had heaved herself out and waddled inside, straight into her armchair where she'd fallen asleep instantly, the basket on the floor beside her full of paper roses.

What has she been up to? Jenny had worried, thinking the old lady's behaviour looked sinister. *What if Nan has been to Bodmin? Was she secretly arranging for me to be carted off to the dreaded hospital?*

The next morning, Nan was up early sorting out Mufty and the chickens. Then she sat at her bureau writing what appeared to be a letter, dropping blots of dark blue Quink on the floor as she paused in contemplation.

Filled with foreboding, Jenny made a decision. She'd pretend to be pulling herself together, acting normal, even though she felt half dead and hopeless. She made Tom's breakfast: a boiled egg with bread and dripping. He looked at her in surprise. 'Are you feeling better, Mum?'

Jenny gulped. 'I'm trying, Tom.'

'Lottie's not coming back,' he said. 'We've gotta help Nan if we want to stay here.'

She nodded silently, trying to eat a slice of bread, feeling sick and not hungry.

'Why don't you brush Mufty, Mum?' Tom suggested. 'It's a nice job and Mufty is good for people.'

Jenny tried to smile. 'I might.'

She watched Tom go off to school. He'd spoken kindly. Why couldn't she respond?

Jenny confronted herself in the hall mirror. A dead-eyed, hollow-cheeked person stared out, ghost-like, empty. The urge to creep back to bed was overpowering. She fought it but it wouldn't go away. She made herself go to clear up in the kitchen, only to find herself standing at the window, a tray in her hands at a precarious angle.

Useless. You're useless, Jennifer.

'I'm going out in the car,' Nan announced, and Jenny almost dropped the tray. 'I'm glad to see you up and about.'

Pretend. Go on pretending. Once she's gone I can go back to bed, Jenny thought. She wondered what Nan had done with the paper roses, but didn't dare ask. 'Please be careful in the car, Nan,' she said instead.

Nan tossed her head. 'Careful? Me? When was I ever careful?' She cackled with laughter. 'If the damned thing starts, I shall get in and go like hell until I reach my destination. But first . . .' she tapped the blue envelope in her hand, 'I have written a letter to Lottie. I must go and get the address from John, then post it.'

Why couldn't I do that? Jenny thought, wincing as the Austin Seven careered out of the gate in a cloud of dust and leaves.

She wondered what kind of letter Nan had written to Lottie. A load of old Latin, probably. Whatever it was, Jenny realised Nan had spent a long time composing it. The close relationship between Nan and Lottie was something precious, but Jenny felt both envy and anxiety. Nan's forthright and often scathing manner might be deeply hurtful on paper. She imagined Lottie reading it in London, with Olivia sitting there.

The image evoked unbearable guilt and Jenny deliberately stubbed it out like a candle flame, leaving a trail of black smoke dispersing in her mind.

Alone at Hendravean, Jenny meandered around the house knowing she would end up crawling back to bed sooner or later. Sleep was the only way to cope.

Jenny picked up the sepia photograph of the Lanroska family and stared at it gloomily. She'd been the mother. The hub of the wheel. So much love and passion, and energy – gone. Forgotten. Why was she even alive?

But she *was* alive, and in that painful bramble bush of thoughts, something happened outside. A raucous, spine-chilling howl came from the yard, an echoing rhythmic scream going on and on, like someone being murdered.

'For goodness sake! What the heck is it?' Jenny dragged herself to the window, wide-eyed with alarm. The sound didn't stop, but went on and on in waves, resounding from the walls and rocks of St Ives.

Jenny shuddered with fright, then smiled when she realised what it was. Donkeys rarely bray. Some never do. But when they do, it is a gut-wrenching sound, more chilling than the howl of wolves in a forest. For some reason, Mufty was at the paddock gate, braying, his neck stretched out, his cavernous mouth wide open to the sky.

Even though she now knew what it was, Jenny still felt spooked by the deafening and relentless sound. She went to the door, which was open as usual, and called out to him. 'What's the matter with you, Mufty? Making such a din!'

The donkey quietened down instantly, turning his furry face to look at Jenny with bright black eyes. Then he turned his head and stared towards the lane, his ears pricked, listening. He seemed agitated.

'Don't start again, for heaven's sake,' Jenny said. She noticed something huge grinding its way up Foxglove Lane, something towering above the tall hedges. Only its scarlet and yellow roof was visible. It wasn't a farm wagon.

Jenny stared hard. It passed a gap in the hedge and she saw it had windows with pretty curtains. She could hear the rumble of wheels and the steady, scratchy plod of a horse's hooves along with a subdued clinking sound, as if pots and pans were being shaken around.

Gypsies! Jenny thought, and suddenly she was alive, fired up by a spark of anger. *How dare they come up here to Hendravean?*

Nan was out – and without Nan and her booming voice, Jenny would have to deal with it.

They needn't think they're going to set up camp here. She eyed the stretch of rough grass next to the yard.

Jenny pumped herself up and stepped outside. She could hear the creak of wood and the jingle of the horse's harness. She stood aggressively on the doorstep, arms folded, eyes challenging – a reincarnation of the old Jenny who'd lived proudly in the cottage in Downlong. A Jenny who would defend her family and home to the ends of the earth.

Obviously, the horse-drawn vardo would have to come into the yard to turn around. Jenny glanced down at Bartholomew, who sat majestically beside her, his neck lengthening as he watched the gate.

'We'll send them packing,' Jenny said to him and got an encouraging meow in return. 'Pity you're not a gurt dog.'

She watched, awed by the size of the vardo and the gleaming colours of the paintwork.

Romanies, she thought, and a tinge of nostalgia softened her anger. As a child growing up in Cornwall, she had loved the colourful Romany women who came swinging through the town selling clothes pegs and paper roses.

Paper roses! Jenny's hand flew to her mouth. *Has Nan set this up? I wouldn't put it past her*, she thought.

There was an odd kind of silence around the tall vardo and the obedient skewbald horse as it made the cumbersome turn into the gate of Hendravean. A young boy sat on the high driving seat, holding the reins, a cap pulled over his brow. Obviously he was concentrating on bringing the vardo safely in without scraping the gate posts.

Jenny put her hands on her hips, unsmiling and mentally rehearsing the confrontation to come. If they just turned around and went out, she'd keep quiet and breathe a sigh of relief. Despite her misgivings, she couldn't help admiring the elaborate pictures painted on the vardo. Vines and roses, oak leaves and acorns, and a flying eagle with gold-tipped wings.

Her heart thudded faster when she saw the gypsy boy steer the horse onto the patch of grass. They meant to stay. He loosened the reins and the horse relaxed and began to munch hungrily at the grass.

The boy climbed down. He looked small and oddly familiar, but she couldn't quite place him from a distance. Something shifted in Jenny's heart.

Who is he?

He stared towards the house. Then he threw his cap in the air and ran towards her. 'Jenny! Jenny!'

Jenny gasped. Her anger vanished and she held out her arms. '*Warren!*' His feet thundered up to her and Jenny hugged him tightly, smiling through tears of joy. 'It's *you*, Warren – driving that huge vardo. What a surprise.'

378

'I missed you, Jenny,' Warren said clearly. He looked up at her adoringly.

'I missed you too,' she breathed. 'But look at you! You're proper handsome now, Warren. You've grown so much. I can't believe it's you.'

'Nan found me,' he said. 'I were buskin' in Truro and she said me and Mum could come and camp here for a while.'

'Warren – you can *talk*!' Jenny said, amazed.

Warren looked up at her. 'You learned me,' he said, 'and I practised – and Mum helped me too. We've come to say thank you and make you better.'

'Your *mum*?'

Warren turned and looked at the vardo. 'You can come out now, Mum,' he called.

Jenny gasped in surprise as a radiant Romany gypsy woman emerged with a swish of embroidered skirt and came smiling towards her. She had the warmest, most loving eyes Jenny had ever seen. A pair of gold hoop earrings glowed from her thickly coiled black hair. Bangles clinked on her arms and a multi-coloured shawl was wrapped around her broad shoulders and reassuringly ample bust. She held out her hands to Jenny.

'Hello, my darling. I'm Petronella. Nan sent me to help you get well. I'm a Romany gypsy, dear, and proud of it.'

'And you're Warren's mum?'

'I'm Warren's mum. I want to say thank you for what you did for him, Jenny. He loves you for it. He told me how you rescued him – wonderful, wonderful kindness – and you gave him a lovely home, taught him to talk. He'd be dead by now if it wasn't for you.' Petronella looked down at Jenny's iron leg. 'You need a bit of help yourself now, don't you, darlin'?'

Jenny stood there, speechless. Her first impulse had been to resist, but Petronella's warm eyes and the radiance of her kindness were already melting her, offering her a way back. At the same time, Jenny was suspicious. Had Nan been up to her old tricks again? Folklore and magic and all the stuff Jenny hated. And what kind of mother would let her son live wild and get into such a state?

It was Warren who answered her unspoken question.

'Me dad's in prison now,' he said, 'and we're glad, aren't we, Mum?'

'Never mind glad, I'm celebrating.' Petronella's eyes changed, a deep sadness crossing through them like the shadow of a cloud across fields of corn. It passed swiftly and her eyes gleamed at Jenny. 'He were a bad 'un. Bad through and through. Left me and took Warren when he was five – wanted him to busk with the travelling fair. Broke my heart, he did, but I stayed with the Romanies – we're hard-working, peaceful folk. We don't hurt nobody. Warren was terrified of him. 'Tis no wonder he couldn't talk. He wasn't allowed to. His dad used to smack him round the head if he tried to talk. "Shurrup you," he used to shout.' Petronella shuddered with the memory and slipped her arm around Warren, who looked up at her with concern in his eyes.

'I ran away,' Warren said, 'trying to find Mum again, but I got lost on the cliffs and nearly drowned.'

'Good job I found you,' Jenny said.

Petronella gave her arm a squeeze. 'You were an angel,' she said, 'going out there with that leg.'

'It's only what anyone would do,' Jenny said, but the words had encouraged her.

'Then Dad kidnapped me,' Warren said. 'I were nearly home with some money for Nan. Then the police came and arrested him and they found Mum and took me there, to Chacewater.'

'We've still got the money,' Jenny said. 'You can go upstairs and get your jacket. John found it in the lane – we kept it for you, with all the money you earned.'

Warren darted upstairs and came down with his jacket, its pockets still bulging with coins. 'It won't fit me now,' he said proudly. 'But I'm giving the money to Nan. And she said I can keep the piano-accordion – forever!'

'A fair swap, don't you think?' Petronella laughed.

'We won't be no trouble, Jenny,' Warren said. 'It's just Mum and me and we live in the vardo. We only need water and a place to park.'

'There won't be anyone else arriving,' Petronella assured her. 'It's taken us ages to get here from Chacewater.'

'The vardo is so beautiful,' Jenny said. 'Lottie would love it.'

'Nan told me about Lottie. I'd love to meet her,' Petronella's eyes gleamed with enthusiasm, 'and you might need me – I'm a Romany midwife.' She leaned closer and looked into Jenny's eyes. 'Lottie will be coming home – believe me, I know. You wait and see.'

Jenny gasped. She clasped her hands in joy. 'Nan's not stupid, is she? How long can you stay?'

'We could stay for the winter – then we'll buzz off again in the spring, back to our Romany family. We do the flower and pea picking. I'd help you, Jenny, 'til you're better, then I'll look after Lottie and the baby for the first few weeks. And we'll live in the vardo.'

'It's our home,' Warren said, and his eyes shone.

'Nan set this up,' Petronella explained. 'She found Warren busking on the steps of Truro Cathedral. We got talking and she told me about you – and Lottie – and invited me and Warren to come and park here in return for helping you. You do look very run down – I understand 'cause I got like that when I lost Warren. Would you like us to stay for a while? I can do lots to help you in the house and garden.'

Jenny looked at her and instinctively trusted this beautiful, warm-hearted woman. 'I'd *love* you to stay – and Warren. I feel better already, I really do.'

'Nan said we can paint Mufty's cart,' Warren said. 'Romany style. Me and Mum know how to do it – and Tom can help. He likes painting.'

'Good idea. Tom will enjoy doing that,' Jenny said, suddenly seeing a new, happier time ahead. It was good to know what Nan had been up to. 'Where is Nan now?' she asked.

'We don't know,' Petronella said.

But Warren knew.

'Nan's gone to Portreath,' he said, 'to fetch Matt.'

Lottie sat on the bench watching the River Thames. The heavily silted river water kinked and swirled as it raced along, bringing floating rafts of driftwood jumbled with netting, rusting cans, bundles of straw and dead, unrecognisable birds. Rainbow patches of oil skimmed the surface in elongated shapes. The river smelled of tar and rotting wood. Barges with dark red sails came in on the tide towing strings of other barges. It was depressing, but oddly fascinating.

In her hand was the cream cardboard rail ticket; the return half John had given to her. Still smarting from the row with her mother, Lottie wanted desperately to go home. The special light of St Ives shimmered in her mind like a distant, tantalising vision of heaven. She wanted her baby to be born there on a starry night, not here in London. But how could she live among people who wanted to kill her baby? One by one, each person she loved and trusted had let her down.

Get rid of it, they'd said. *Babies are horrible. Termination. Adoption.*

Then what?

Then we will love you again, Lottie, now that you've murdered your baby.

Bitter thoughts, but true.

She'd had to be sensible. Tolerating Olivia. Getting a job. Pretending to be twenty-one. Building a future for her baby.

Was there a way forward? Returning to live with Olivia would involve a superhuman effort at being tolerant – for the sake of her baby.

It was nearly dark with rain clouds, and a northerly chill was creeping up the river. Lottie shivered. She had to sleep *somewhere*. She could feel one of her headaches coming on, the dreaded bolts of pain in her left temple, shooting through her eye and over her skull. She rubbed the back of her neck where a knot of pain was forming.

'You're a pretty girl sitting here on yer own.' A man who smelled strongly of beer and garlic sat down beside her, uncomfortably close. ''Aven't ya got an 'ome to go to?'

Lottie glanced at his red-rimmed eyes and thought of Morwenna. She got up and walked away, her bag over her shoulder. Rain began to fall and her headache was blinding. She needed to lie down, and she needed an aspirin, a cup of Nan's tea, and a safe, peaceful bed.

She stumbled back along the embankment, haunted by an alarming memory of Olivia. While Lottie was packing her bag, Olivia had been drinking glass after glass of wine. Lottie remembered the bottles of aspirin lurking in the cupboard and suddenly she was terrified of what her mother might do.

She had to go back – quickly.

A feeling of foreboding hung over Lottie as she let herself into the apartment. There was a smell. And a deathly silence.

Broken glass glimmered from the carpet, and wine was splashed up the wall in several places, soaking into the anaglypta wallpaper like an art form. Olivia's snakeskin shoes were splayed on the floor by the sofa, and on the dining table was a wad of papers tied together with a thin bottle-green ribbon. A broken doll sat there, her remarkably human eyes looking out from a porcelain face. It startled Lottie, but she brushed the memory away and headed for Olivia's bedroom.

'Mother?'

There was no response.

Terribly frightened, Lottie tiptoed to the bed and stood looking down.

Olivia lay on her back, her bare feet neatly together, her slim arms clutching a photo frame. Her eyes were closed, her skin pearly white. A dribble of foam trailed from her mouth and soaked into the pillow. On the bedside table was an empty aspirin bottle and a few of the pills scattered amidst the pools of red wine.

There was something husk-like about her mother's body; a sense of finality. She looked so small and so ... *discarded*. Like a dead seabird tangled in shoreline wreckage.

Lottie knew straightaway that her mother was dead. But her reasoning mind prompted her to seek for a pulse.

Olivia's wrist was cold, her fingers locked around the photo frame. Lottie told herself she could feel a thread of life faintly beating.

'Mother – Olivia. It's Lottie. I've come back. Please don't die – *please*.'

There was no response.

It was no good crying and pleading. She must stay calm and get help. She tucked a blanket over Olivia and picked up the telephone, not sure who to call.

'Number, please.' The voice was demanding and icily efficient.

'It's an emergency. I don't know who to ring. Can you help me, please?'

'Fire, police or ambulance?' snapped the voice.

'Ambulance,' Lottie said with a heavy heart. She gave the address and some brief details.

'Just stay with her. Someone will come,' the voice said, and added kindly, 'How old are you, dear? You sound very young.'

'Twenty-one,' she lied, determined not to risk being taken away by the welfare. Her head pounded as she waited for the ambulance.

It came quickly, its bell ringing, and two uniformed men lifted Olivia onto a wooden stretcher with a pillow and scarlet blanket. Lottie saw the look that passed between them. Negative.

'We'll take her to St Mary's, Paddington. They'll do what they can for her.'

'She . . . tried to take her life,' Lottie said and the stretcher-bearer nodded. He took the empty aspirin bottle from her. 'You'd best stay here, hadn't you?' he said, looking at her bump.

Lottie nodded. With a shaking hand, she wrote the phone number on a strip of paper.

'Stay near the telephone. They'll call you.'

'Okay.'

'Will you be all right?'

'Yes.'

Lottie stared at her mother's empty, shell-like face on the pillow. An uncomfortable blend of sadness, shock and relief filled her mind. *Is it my fault? I didn't like her, anyway. But did I love her? Daddy must have loved her once. How am I going to tell him?*

They took Olivia away so quickly, like a confiscated parcel whipped away and shoved in a drawer. Lottie stood by the window looking down at the roof of the ambulance, hearing its bell fading into the roar of London.

Gone. She was gone.

Only then did Lottie pick up the photo frame Olivia had been clutching so tightly against her heart. She turned it over and saw a framed poster – a photograph of a ballerina in a white dress. Under the picture the caption read:

OLIVIA DE LUMEN dances Giselle in London
An exquisite performance by this gifted young dancer

Tucked into the frame was a folded scrap of paper with LOTTIE written on it. Alone now in the flat, Lottie unfolded it with shaking hands. It said simply:

Forgive me, Lottie.
This is the me you never met. This is who I am and

who I was before I tried, and failed, to be a wife and mother.
Forgive me, honey-child. Fly free.
    Love,
    Your mother, Olivia

Stunned and deeply moved, Lottie took the framed photo into her bedroom. She pressed her face against the cold glass.

The excruciating headache kept her awake and she got up to swallow two of the aspirin from a bottle that hadn't been opened. Then she lay down on her bed with the photograph beside her on the pillow.

The eyes of the young dancer were the eyes she remembered so vividly. Eyes full of passion and light. Those eyes had welcomed her into the world when she was born and this was the mother she had searched for and never found. *Forgive me, honey-child. Fly free.*

Final words. Burned on her heart. Forever.

Chapter 23

A Lifelong Secret

Nan found Matt sitting on the beach at Portreath, chucking pebbles into the sea. She decided to skip the preliminaries and get straight to the point.

'I am calling a family conference,' she boomed. 'About Lottie. I think you should be there, don't you?'

Matt looked up at her, startled, his eyes momentarily so like Arnie's. Wild and unshaven, he quickly masked his true feelings and resumed the sullen stare. He continued chucking pebbles into the sea.

'It's not a meeting to criticise you, Matt. It's a chance for you to have a say in the decision we're going to make about your baby's future.'

He went on chucking stones.

'I have driven here in my unpredictable, dilapidated motor car to fetch you. I will take you home to Hendravean and

389

you can make your own way back.' Nan paused for a wheezy breath. 'I'm not going to stand here persuading you. I'm going now and I won't wait. Either come with me or stay here and throw stones.' She turned and walked off without looking back.

Nan had reached the car when she heard the crunch of Matt's long strides catching up. She pretended not to notice and began easing herself into the driver's seat.

Got you, she thought mischievously when Matt ran round to the passenger door.

'Wait, Nan. I'm coming with you.' Matt opened the door and got in, folding his long legs into the cramped space.

'*Nil illegitimi carborundum*,' Nan declared.

'What the heck does that mean?' Matt asked.

'*Nil illegitimi carborundum*?' Nan repeated it, her eyes twinkling with glee. 'It means don't let the bastards grind you down,' she cackled, pleased to see a grin on Matt's face.

She started the car. 'Prepare to be frightened,' she warned, and set off in low gear up the winding coast road, over the North Cliffs and Hell's Mouth with Matt, white-faced and silent, beside her. About an hour later, tired but triumphant, Nan swung the car into the yard at Hendravean.

Jenny and John were there, waiting in the sitting room, and Petronella was in the kitchen baking. Tom and Warren were in the yard cleaning out Mufty's stable, happy in each other's company. Nan felt hopeful, pleased that Matt was with her. He sat down, without looking at anyone, and stared out the window.

'Who is chairing this meeting?' John asked, a notebook and a brand-new pencil on the table in front of him.

'I am,' Nan said. She unfolded another wing of the extending table and sat down in the wide dining chair with arms. 'First, I have a confession to make,' she began, and a crippling bout of coughing and wheezing shook her body. 'Damned cough. Thank you.' She took the glass of water Matt had fetched for her.

'Are you all right, Nan?' Jenny asked.

'Of course I'm all right. I just sound like Richard Trevithick's steam engine.' Nobody smiled, so she embarked on the confession she had rehearsed in her mind. It would make a difference, she was sure – and it didn't matter now, what they thought of her.

'I have never told you this before. It's my lifelong secret and I would have carried it to the grave. It's hard for me to share, but I'm doing it for Lottie's sake. I think it may help us to understand one another.' Nan paused for breath, her storm-coloured eyes challenging each of them. She took a dog-eared photograph from her apron pocket and held it up.

'That's Grandad Vic,' Matt said, 'when he was young.'

'He lives in Newlyn now,' Jenny explained to John. 'He's Arnie's dad.'

'And as you know, Vic is my son,' Nan added, proudly. She took a deep breath and decided to just come out with it. She twisted her wedding ring round and round her finger. 'But see this ring? It's a lie – a fake. I was never married. Vic was illegitimate.'

The room went deathly quiet. Three pairs of eyes stared intently at Nan. Even Matt looked serious and respectful.

'I'm a fierce old thing,' Nan continued, 'and nobody's ever dared ask me about my husband. Well – there wasn't one. There was a boyfriend, Elliot. I ... I adored him. But he broke my heart. We were seventeen and in love, in secret, like *Romeo and Juliet*.' She looked at Matt. 'But when I found myself pregnant, my Romeo walked out of my life and never came back.'

'Aw, Nan!' Jenny reached across the table to give Nan's hand a squeeze.

'Don't be kind to me,' Nan warned, 'because I might cry.' She held on tightly to Jenny and was moved to see that Matt was gripping her other hand. John sat, wise-eyed, listening, twiddling his pencil. Nan felt the love and was encouraged to continue.

'I was terrified of my parents. Of course, they had to know I was expecting a baby – and all they could think about was how to get rid of it. They were in for a shock. I was stronger than them. I said no. I stood up to them and tried to explain how I felt. I loved my unborn child and honoured his life, his right to live. But they threw me out – onto the streets of London, and ... oh, you don't need to hear the rest of it, do you?'

Nan looked round at them, proud of the love and compassion, even in Matt's reluctant eyes. She'd always felt isolated and apart from her close family, but now she felt included in a secret circle of love. An empathy circle. It was a completely unexpected result of her brave decision to reveal her lifelong secret.

'We do, Nan – we do,' Jenny said warmly.

'All right – but to cut a long story short,' Nan continued, 'I earned my living by singing on the streets of London. I was lucky when my music teacher and his wife took me in, despite the pregnancy, and continued to train me for free because they believed in me. The rest is like a fairy tale. When Vic was born, I was in demand as an opera singer. I had plenty of work, enough to pay for a babysitter for the evenings when I was singing. I spent my days with my little boy and loved him. When he was five and old enough for school, I took a leap of faith and moved down to Cornwall, set up as a music teacher and made enough money to buy Hendravean – and here I am, wheezy and cantankerous but still going strong.'

Nan looked round at the spellbound eyes.

'What an inspirational story, Nan,' John said.

'The point of this meeting,' Nan said, 'is to bring Lottie home. She belongs here and she loves it. She loves us too, and . . .' Nan made her voice quiet, discreetly observing how it made everyone sit up and listen, 'I can't speak for the rest of you, but I intend to give Lottie my full support, and her baby will be a welcome blessing to this family and to this earth.' Nan noticed that heads were nodding. 'All we have to do is decide who is going to London to bring her home – unless she actually wants to stay with Olivia, of course.'

The telephone bell cut into the brief silence, making everyone jump.

'Damned, infernal cacophony.' Nan glared into the hall. She looked at John with fierce eyes. 'Would you mind answering the damned thing before it blows the dust out of my skull?'

'Okay.' John padded into the hall and picked up the receiver. 'Hello, this is John De Lumen speaking from Hendravean.'

'Daddy . . .' Lottie's voice sounded breathy and terrified.

'What is it, darling? I'm here for you.'

Lottie couldn't seem to answer. She was taking deep, shuddery breaths. John was instantly on alert. What if the baby was coming early? He made his voice low and reassuring. 'Try to stay calm, Lottie, and tell me what's wrong. What's happened?'

Nan, Jenny and Matt looked at each other in alarm. *Now what?*

He waited and eventually Lottie managed to speak. 'Daddy, it's Olivia – she . . . she's taken her life.'

Matt prowled up and down the platform of St Ives Station, a bunch of flowers in his hand for Lottie. He wasn't sure what time she would arrive. It could be a long wait but Matt was determined to be there.

It had been a big week for Matt. Apart from Lottie coming home, Ken had persuaded him to get *The Jenny Wren* out of the water for the winter. She was leaking and there were holes in the hull. He would have to spend the winter making her seaworthy again, an endless job but worth doing.

'Otherwise you'll end up with no boat at all, Matt,' Ken had warned.

So Matt was getting used to living on the land again, being warm and dry and sleeping in a bed.

He still resisted the idea of living at Hendravean when he still couldn't look at his mum. John offered him a temporary place to stay in the box room above the gallery. It gave him breathing space, and he felt at ease with John. But now, with Lottie returning, he'd be going up there to see her every day.

Nan's confession had given Matt a new perspective. He realised Jenny was trying to be kind and forgiving towards him, even managing to talk about the baby. It helped to have Petronella there, and Warren, and their fascinating brightly coloured vardo. It felt good to give Warren his old marble tin and watch him playing with Tom, rolling the glass marbles along the floorboards upstairs.

Matt had always been a night owl, and when everyone was in bed he spent satisfying time in Nan's extensive library reading and re-reading some of his favourites. One night, he dared to take out one of the heavy encyclopaedias and found the page on how babies were born. He pored over the diagrams and text until one o'clock in the morning. The information was an eye-opener for Matt; he tried to memorise it so that he could help Lottie and understand what she was going through.

Jenny left him alone. Relationships were fragile, like dew-spangled cobwebs in the dawn, clinging on in the salt sea wind. Another delicate strand would be added today, when Lottie came home, leaving John in London to deal with the legal issues surrounding Olivia's death.

Matt thought the train was never coming. Muffled in a scarf and his St Piran hat, he sat on the narrow GWR seat facing the sea. He found himself staring at the flowers in his hand. Flowers were hard to find in December, but Nan had led him into the tropical garden where the rocks were warm.

There were marigolds with burning orange sunray faces, a few precious late roses and spires of blue salvia. On the cold station, Matt soaked up their colourful presence thinking he must have lived his whole life and never actually gazed into the bright, deep face of a flower. He imagined doing paintings of hot marigolds against a silver sea.

Mesmerised by his creative vision, Matt jumped when he heard the train's hiss of steam burst under the bridge. He leapt to his feet, feeling overwhelmingly emotional. Was she there? His Lottie. His love.

Steam billowed over the platform. Clutching the flowers, Matt waited in the coal-flavoured mist. Doors slammed and hard shoes marched past him. The sea wind carved through the steam and Matt saw Lottie at the far end of the platform.

Small, straight-backed, she stood with her face to the sea, her hair a golden flame against a jet black coat.

She'd come home. Lottie was home.

It seemed to Matt like a miracle. A heaven-sent gift. When he didn't even deserve it.

Matt's emotions boiled over into pure joy. He wanted to dance and sing. But he couldn't move.

And Lottie wasn't moving. She was gazing at the sea.

What if she didn't want him? The thought fled from under him, a shadow vanishing.

Matt remembered that Olivia had died. Ought he to be smiling? Would Lottie be locked into grief and sorrow?

But he couldn't help standing there with a great big bucket of a smile on his face.

Lottie turned. She waved, almost dancing as she walked towards him and her face was radiant, not sad. Matt covered the distance between them in hungry strides. He held out his arms and everything blurred as they came together like twin flames.

Pulling her close, he sensed how eager she was to come to him. For the first time, Matt was aware of the warm, firm bump of the child in Lottie's womb. The vivid picture in his mind was stunning. He didn't see a horrible, screaming baby. He saw a star, a pure blue-white spirit of life.

Lottie looked up at him, a question in her dark blue eyes.

'I love you, Lottie,' he murmured, 'and I'll love our baby. I can imagine it in there, shining like a star between us – and I love you for being brave enough to keep it safe.' He noticed the shadows of tiredness under Lottie's eyes, but her smile was magical. It was his whole world and nothing else mattered.

'Those are the most beautiful words I've ever heard said to me,' Lottie whispered as their faces came close and they kissed blissfully, hardly aware of the train steaming backwards out of the station, leaving them almost alone on the windswept platform.

'That yours, sir?' Running feet interrupted their kiss. They moved apart, astonished to see the portly stationmaster sprinting past them in pursuit of a bunch of marigolds and roses, which the wind was whisking down the platform. He skidded to a halt, catching it on the brink of tumbling over the edge. Holding it triumphantly, he came rollicking back.

'Oops, I dropped it!' Matt said, catching Lottie's eye, and they giggled.

Breathing hard from his run, the stationmaster handed the flowers to Matt, a very Cornish twinkle in his eyes. 'Never a dull moment at S'nives Station,' he quipped, 'and you'll be moving on, the pair of you. Can't stay 'ere canoodlin' all day.'

All three of them laughed. Matt picked up Lottie's heavy bag and they walked out of the station, Lottie with her face buried in the fragrance of the roses. 'From Nan's garden?' she asked.

'From Nan's garden.'

'I shall keep them forever,' Lottie said. 'I'm going to press the petals in my diary. And when our baby is growing up, I'll show them to her and tell her about her kind, romantic daddy.'

Kind? Romantic? Me! Matt was actually feeling guilty. He was building up to saying sorry. Apologies didn't come naturally to a lad who had spent most of his life being defensive and rebellious. He'd hoped the flowers would say it for him, but they hadn't. And he'd dropped them.

In the past, his attempts to say sorry had merely invited further recrimination and the pain of not being forgiven.

Just say it, he thought, but the apology seemed stuck like a lump of grit in his throat. It wouldn't move and he longed to feel he deserved the candid, unconditional love Lottie was offering him. Despite everything life had thrown at her, she was carefree and radiant – in control, the way she'd always been, even from the first day when she'd arrived as a shipwrecked orphan with nothing to call her own except her endearing bossiness.

Together they leaned on the wall overlooking the moon-pale sand of Porthminster Beach.

'I've missed St Ives so much,' Lottie said, and her eyes sparkled in the afternoon light. She seemed aware of his silent struggle. 'Is there something you want to say, Matt?'

He nodded, his eyes downcast. He'd take a risk and just say it, but he couldn't meet the radiance in her eyes. 'I'm sorry,' he managed to say, and the word hurt across his shoulders. How many times? How many painful times must he say it before it finally vanished? 'I'm sorry, sorry, sorry, sorry.'

'Matt!' Lottie said tenderly. 'Whatever for?'

'The way I treated you when you tried to tell me about the baby – our baby.'

'It's okay, Matt. I've forgiven you.' Lottie touched his cheek and made him look at her. 'Let's forget about it. I'm so happy that you came to meet me. It means the world to me.'

Olivia's body was laid to rest in the St Ives cemetery overlooking Porthmeor Beach. The funeral was quiet and private with only John and the Lanroska family there. John chose the hymns he thought Olivia would have liked and, with Nan's help, Lottie chose a piece of music from *Giselle*.

A pair of pink silk ballet shoes, found in the corner of Olivia's wardrobe, were placed on the simple ash wood coffin. It seemed profoundly sad to Lottie that only six people stood dutifully around Olivia's grave.

A thick, luminous sea mist obscured the whole of St Ives, the ocean and the sky, and the wet grass glistened around their ankles. The seagulls were silent, the waves hushed and only a robin, the bird of winter, offered fragments of song to the memory of a girl who had danced with her soul in her eyes. In her final hour, there was no applause, no accolades, no tributes, and no love.

And nobody cried. Even Lottie was dry-eyed as she read the poem she had written as a eulogy.

> *I'll remember*
> *how you tried to love me.*
> *You were an angel, grounded,*
> *shackled to earth*
> *and wingless.*

Like a night lily
was your love,
its petals closed.
It never found the sun.

I'll remember
the way you died,
as you lived, alone and friendless.

I will pray
that you dance again
in the light beyond the bright river,
and I promise to carry forever
the words you have left for me:
Forgive me, honey-child. Fly free.

As she read the words in her clear voice, Lottie stood very straight in her black coat, a black velvet beret over the mane of golden blonde hair. The church of St Ia gave her its mystic space like a forest glade; the stone pillars and the polished wood, the empty pews, the glass faces, all steeped in sea salt and frankincense. When she'd finished reading, Lottie gazed at Matt, then at Nan, Jenny and John. She was happy to know they'd forgiven her and had accepted Little Star as a baby who mattered, a child who would bring love and light.

There was only the problem of Matt and Jenny. Would they ever be truly reconciled?

Chapter 24

Christmas and Candlemas

'*What* are you doing up that ladder?' Jenny yelled at Nan. She'd been watching from the window, hoping to catch Matt when he arrived to see Lottie. It was nearly Christmas and she wanted him home. After the heartache and the years of separation, a family Christmas was exactly what the Lanroskas needed.

Turning to look at the garden, Jenny was appalled to see Nan's huge bulk at the top of a rickety old ladder propped against the pear tree. She had to stop her. Grabbing her stick, Jenny hobbled out there as fast as she could. The ladder creaked and the tree shuddered with the old lady's weight.

'*Nan!*' Jenny looked up at the soles of Nan's shoes, her swollen ankles and the billowing skirt of the mottled blue dress she wore summer and winter. 'Nan, you could fall. You mustn't go up ladders.'

No answer.

Jenny peered into the branches, shocked to see Nan wasn't even holding the ladder, but reaching sideways, a pair of pruners open like a parrot's beak.

'Will you *please* come down, Nan? John will do that for you. The rung you're standing on is bending.'

'Stop kicking up a fuss,' came the tetchy reply. 'I've had this ladder forty years and haven't fallen off it yet. This ladder and I are old friends – we know each other's creaks and groans.' Nan gave a wheezy laugh, which didn't hide the fact that she was breathless and shaky. 'Calm down, Jennifer. I know exactly what I'm doing.'

'What are you doing?'

'Cutting mistletoe. Kindly don't distract me.'

The tree heaved and rustled as Nan wrestled with a clump of mistletoe growing out of the bark. Then she had a coughing fit. What if Nan fell out of the pear tree – at Christmas time?

Don't do this to me, God, Jenny prayed.

Nan hacked away at the tough stalk. 'Ah, success!' she boomed at last, and Jenny held onto the ladder, wincing to see the elderly rungs bending as Nan climbed down clutching her trophy. 'A perfect ball of mistletoe. Isn't that splendid? I thought we should have some this year, with two young lovers in the house.'

Almost crying with relief, Jenny disentangled a twig from Nan's thick silver hair. 'We love you, Nan. You're precious and we don't want anything happening to you.'

Nan gave her a reassuring pat. 'I'm a tough old bird. Now look at the berries on this mistletoe. They represent the sun.

And did you know the thrushes plant them? When they're eating the berry, they rub their beaks on the bark and the tiny seeds get stuck in a crack and grow.'

'No, I didn't. All I know is we need a new ladder.'

'I'll take this inside and Tom can hang it in the porch.' Nan looked at Jenny approvingly. 'You look nice.'

'Thanks.' Jenny had made an effort to look her best for Christmas. She'd brushed her long dark hair, and it looked good, flowing over her shoulders against her best crimson velvet dress. It might send a silent message to Matt: *Welcome. Come home. Home for Christmas.*

She remembered Matt as a leggy seven-year-old, how he'd loved her to wear that dress, how he'd creep close, stroke the velvet and look up at her adoringly. But that was before. Before it all happened.

Jenny thought nostalgically of Christmases when she'd taken Tom, Matt and Lottie to the church for the blessing of the crib, then the saffron buns and the tiny presents hidden in a barrel of bran. The tall Christmas tree bobbing with hand-knitted ornaments, peg dolls and tiny muslin bags of sweets. The happiness of singing carols with the children gathered around the tree, faces glowing in the candlelight. How she missed it.

Jenny followed Nan indoors. 'I'll help make the saffron buns,' she said. 'It'll take my mind off Matt.'

'Good idea,' Nan said. 'You spend far too much time agonising over him.'

*

Every day, in all weathers, Matt walked up to Hendravean to see Lottie and managed to avoid Jenny. He stayed away from the house, waiting outside in the barn next to Mufty's stable. He was making a cradle for the baby from sea-smoothed driftwood. Lottie sat with him, perched on a straw bale, and helped to sand the wood.

They'd spend precious time cuddling and talking quietly, but when they said goodbye, Lottie always said, 'Please Matt, I want you to come home. This is your home, with me. Won't you come for Christmas?' His only response was to kiss her and hold her close, both of them smiling when feeling the movements of Little Star between them, still safe in Lottie's womb.

With Christmas looming, Matt talked to John about his dilemma. 'It's Mum,' he said, and even the words stuck in his throat, the same old pain spreading into his shoulders. 'It's like . . . there's a stone wall between us.'

John was a good listener. He gave Matt his full attention, his dark blue eyes full of empathy. 'I'll tell you what we'll do,' he said. 'We'll chop wood.'

'Chop wood?'

'Firewood,' John said. 'Actions speak louder than words. I went up there one day and found Tom in tears out in the cold, trying to saw logs for the fire – he just isn't strong enough yet. But you and I could go on Christmas Eve morning and quietly get on with it. I can wield an axe any day.'

'Okay,' Matt agreed, 'but I don't see how it will help.'

'Give it a try, eh?'

Matt shrugged. 'Can do.'

'We'll do it quietly – sneak into the woodshed when they're all indoors making mince pies and painting pine cones.'

So, early on the morning of Christmas Eve, Matt and John set off in a bitter easterly wind. It was driving massive waves into the harbour and the air stung with beads of ice. Together the two men tackled Nan's chaotic pile of planks and branches, enjoying the work and the satisfaction of creating a neat stack of logs against the wall.

'I need a break,' John said, and Matt nodded, preoccupied with wedging the top layer of logs into place. He'd almost finished it when he sensed a presence. John had disappeared and someone else was there, behind him, watching.

He swung round. 'Mum!'

Jenny was in the doorway, leaning on her stick. Her eyes were bright and hopeful. 'Matt!' She looked at the stack of wood. 'You've done all this. Thank you – it's such a help . . . so . . . so kind of you.'

Matt looked at her silently. She seemed different – not angry, not afraid, but confident, the way she used to be. He couldn't remember her ever saying thank you to him before. The words shone in the air between them like a transformational light. *Thank you.*

He sat down on the straw bales, tired from chopping wood and suddenly emotional. Those words and their light, and the light in Jenny's eyes, had power to heal his pain. It was so simple. He tried to speak but couldn't, not while the pain was melting away from his throat and shoulders.

Jenny sat down beside him and he slipped his arm around her, remembering the feel of her hair and the hand-knitted shawl. She felt small and precious – and motherly.

'Look at me, Matt,' she said, and their eyes met in the dim light of the woodshed. Matt knew what she was going to say, but this time it sounded like music.

'Will you come home? Home for Christmas?'

He still couldn't speak.

'Come in by the fire,' Jenny said. 'It's cold out here.' She brushed the sawdust from his sleeve and gave him a little tug. 'Come on.'

He walked beside her in a dream, his arm still firmly around her shoulders, across the yard and into the warmth of Hendravean.

The smell of cinnamon. The cats curled up in front of a roaring fire. And Lottie hanging painted pine cones on the Christmas tree, her face radiant with joy. 'You've *got* him!' she said to Jenny.

Jenny grinned. 'That's right – I've got him. Now you sit down there, Matt, and I'll bring you a cup of tea and a saffron bun – with butter.'

Matt sank into Nan's voluminous sofa and managed to speak. 'I'd love that.'

Tea and a saffron bun, he thought, *the food of the Gods*.

He stared into the fire and felt its heat soaking into his bones, warming his face and the roots of his hair. Mesmerised by the beauty of the flames and the indescribable homeliness of Nan's room, he felt warmer than he'd felt for years.

Home for Christmas, he thought, dazed and softened with a new feeling – contentment.

He grinned at John, who gave him a conspiratorial wink. There was no inquisition. No recriminations. Only friendliness. Lottie snuggled next to him on the sofa, then Bartholomew on his lap, and Tom squeezed in on the other side of him.

The sound of the flames and the wind in the chimney, the scent of pine, the voices . . .

Matt looked at the clock. It was dark, and Jenny was drawing the curtains. He yawned and stretched.

'Ah, you're awake,' Nan said.

'Have I been asleep?' Matt asked, surprised.

'For three hours.' Nan actually smiled at him. 'You must have needed it.'

'I was warm,' Matt said. 'I haven't been warm for years.'

'We didn't disturb you. You looked so sweet.'

'Sweet?'

'You and Lottie – I wish I'd had a camera. She's still asleep.'

Matt looked down at Lottie's golden head on his shoulder. Had she slept for three hours too?

'We've been waiting for you to wake up, Matt,' Tom said. 'Me and Warren are starving.'

The saffron bun was a distant memory. Matt glanced at Nan's big dining table, which was laden with a Cornish Christmas feast. There were candles burning and a bottle of homemade damson wine.

'After tea we're having a sing-song,' Tom said. 'Wait 'til you hear Warren playing the piano-accordion.'

'Have you got a favourite Christmas carol, Matt?' Nan asked.

Matt nodded, remembering. He looked down at Lottie, who was now awake, her face glowing in the firelight. 'Yeah – I have. "The Bethlehem Star". The one where it says, "*Brighter than the brightest gem*".' He kissed the top of Lottie's head, "'Cause that's you, Lottie – you're my brightest gem.'

'Wait 'til the baby's born,' Lottie said, her eyes shining. 'You'll have two gems.'

Matt smiled, but kept his doubts to himself. The baby would be born in February and in the meantime, he was home. But how long would it last?

Tread carefully, he told himself, *don't spoil it*.

After Christmas the weather turned cold. Frost was rare in St Ives, but there were hailstorms and wild seas. In Nan's garden, sheltered from the gales, the first violets glowed purple in the hedges and stiff little snowdrops emerged from the carpet of leaves. By the end of January, the lane was bright with starry celandines and domes of pale primroses.

On the first of February, the rooftops of St Ives were alive with nesting pairs of seagulls. As always, spring had come early to the far west of Cornwall.

'What on earth are you doing, Nan?' Jenny asked.

Nan was preoccupied with a bundle of beeswax candles in her lap, picking them up one at a time and smoothing the pale golden wax. Her lips were moving as if she was talking to them.

'I'm impregnating each candle with a prayer,' she explained.

Jenny opened her mouth and shut it again. She had learned to keep quiet about Nan's unorthodox passions. She got on with her knitting, a soft white matinee set for Lottie's baby. It was the first of February and everyone was on edge waiting for the baby to be born. Dr Tregullow had threatened to send her to hospital if it didn't happen soon.

'To put it another way,' Nan said patiently, 'I'm blessing the candles because tomorrow, the second of February, is Candlemas. It's the turning point of winter, exactly halfway between the winter solstice and the spring equinox.' The firelight twinkled in her eyes and she looked at Lottie lying on the sofa. 'Candlemas is a very fortunate day for a baby to be born.'

'Why is that, Nan?' Lottie asked. 'Is there a legend?'

'Oh yes.' Nan placed the last candle into the basket on the table.

Everyone sat up and looked at Nan. 'Go on, Nan, tell us the legend,' Lottie pleaded, her eyes bright with anticipation.

'Oh please, Nan. Me and Warren will listen,' Tom said, and the two boys settled on the hearth rug at Nan's feet, carefully avoiding the cats who were blissfully entwined in front of the crackling log fire. Sensing a story, Petronella came in from the kitchen. She gave Lottie a sharp look. 'All right, are you, Lottie?'

'Fine,' Lottie said, but didn't mention the twinges of pain she was having. Nan and Petronella were both watching her. How did they know? It was like being part of an ancient, mysterious network of womanhood, and Lottie felt comforted, safe and at peace.

When she began to speak, Nan had an aura that turned everyone to stone. Nobody moved except Jenny, who made a furtive attempt to carry on knitting. At the first click of the needles, Tom turned on her fiercely. 'Shh, stop knitting, Mum,' he hissed. Jenny stopped.

'Hundreds of years ago,' Nan whispered, 'when dwarves and giants still roamed the earth – especially here in Cornwall – the three giants of winter came down to St Ives: one from Trencrom, one from Carn Brea and one from St Michael's Mount. The earth trembled with the thunder of their boots.'

Nan raised her voice to a boom and then went quiet again.

'They brought with them an almighty snowstorm, which swept down the valley and whirled around St Ives like an Arctic blizzard. The snow buried everything – the lobster pots, the upturned boats, the fishing nets – and it filled the streets with snowdrifts so high that people couldn't open their doors. No one could work. There was no firewood and no food. For seven long days, the snow was frozen solid, icicles hung from the eaves and even the edge of the sea was frozen, the waves crunching through globules of ice. The three giants laughed at the havoc they had created and rolled enormous snowballs down the narrow streets and into the harbour.'

Nan paused, her eyes looked piercingly at each of them. In the silence, Lottie heard the moan of the winter wind coming under the door, the purr of flames in the hearth and the dispassionate tick of the grandfather clock. She felt another pain in her back and low down in her pelvis. She wanted to get up and walk around, but she kept still, enjoying the comfort of Matt's hand on her shoulder.

'But . . .' Nan began again, her voice louder and faster, 'when the sun rose over the sea, a Celtic goddess came into St Ives along the golden path of light across the water. Her name was St Brigid and she is the Goddess of Poetry and Healing and Midwifery.'

Nan looked directly at Lottie.

'St Brigid brought with her a sacred flame, which shone so brightly that the three giants were dazzled. They turned away and left the town, never to be seen again, and as the thunder of their boots faded into the distance, the people of St Ives realised the snow was melting. They began to push their doors open and dig pathways and break the icicles. St Brigid brought with her a basket decorated with snowdrops, violets and celandine, and filled with beeswax candles, which she gave to all who were brave enough to venture out into the light. It was the second of February – Candlemas – and babies born on that sacred day are put in a cradle decorated with snowdrops, violets and celandine, and blessed with wishes for a happy life.'

And so it was, on the second of February, that Matt found himself alone in Nan's garden under the stars, a knot of deep anxiety inside him. Petronella, Jenny and Nan had closed ranks around Lottie and taken her upstairs in a mysterious huddle of crooning efficiency.

Lottie hadn't cried out. Not once.

All Matt could hear as he'd sat on the stairs was a low murmur and the creak of floorboards from upstairs, Petronella's brisk feet and the swish of her embroidered skirt as she bustled to and fro.

How long will it take? And why aren't I allowed to be there, holding Lottie's hand, watching our baby being born?

Matt wanted to rage at the sky about the injustice. He left the garden and padded back to the house into the living room, where the embers of the fire were still glowing. John was there and he didn't want to talk. He sat with his nose in a book, but Matt could tell he wasn't reading it. He seemed lost in thought and soon after midnight he was asleep in the armchair.

Matt worked on the driftwood cradle he'd been making until the wood had a silken sheen, not a splinter in sight. It smelled of sea salt and summer beaches and he was secretly proud of it. Lottie had helped him with the sanding. He touched the bits she had done, picked up the blanket she had knitted and held it against his cheek, feeling close to tears.

Don't let Lottie die, he prayed, *or the baby, God. Are you listening? We've had enough sorrow in our family.* The prayer drove Matt to the edge of an emotional chasm. A very unmanly chasm.

Yawning, Matt opened the front door and stood outside. The wind had dropped and the stars were diamond bright.

In the night garden, the clumps of snowdrops were luminous white in the dark grass. Behind him in the house, the relentless clock chimed three.

A door opened upstairs and he heard Jenny's iron leg tapping along the floorboards.

'Matt – Matt! Where are you? Come up here – quickly.'

Her voice sounded urgent. Doom-laden thoughts sped through Matt's mind. He charged upstairs.

'Shh – don't make a row,' Jenny whispered. 'You must see her before she goes to sleep.'

'See who?'

Jenny looked at him and bubbled over with happy tears, 'Your *daughter*, your little girl, Matt. She's just been born and she's gorgeous!'

Matt's heart exploded with joy. The bedroom door was open and the room flickered with the beeswax candles. But the brightest radiance was in Lottie's golden smile. Her cheeks glowed and her eyes sparkled like never before. She held out one arm to him.

'Matt! Darling Matt – look at our baby! She's perfect – just perfect.' She looked down tenderly at the bundle in the crook of her arm. 'Look, Little Star – it's your daddy. Your daddy's come to see you.'

The bundle made a cooing, gentle, humorous sound. Matt leaned over and, deep in the layers of lacy knitting, he saw a bright little face, unbelievably small, with sapphire blue eyes fixed on him in an unwavering gaze.

'Can – can I touch her?' he asked.

Lottie beamed. 'Of course you can. She won't break.'

Matt moved closer, hardly breathing, feeling a smile stretching his face. A tiny red fist emerged from the bundle. He offered a finger and the baby clasped it tightly as if she'd been waiting to meet him. The determined strength of her tiny fingers and the steadfast sapphire gaze seemed to be claiming him – for life. It was a moment Matt would remember forever. He mattered. He was Daddy. A new feeling billowed over him as if the clouds over his life had rolled apart and released a transformational stream of sunlight.

'She's wonderful,' he breathed. 'She's unbelievably beautiful.'

'Ooh, she likes you,' Jenny said, her hands clasped in joy.

'You can hold her, Matt, if you'd like to.' Lottie looked at him eagerly.

But Matt shook his head. 'No – no, I'd better not.'

'Okay,' Lottie said, but he could see she was disappointed.

'I'll sort 'im out,' Petronella said, gleaming with confidence. 'Let me 'ave her, Lottie.' She stooped and tenderly lifted the bundle. 'Let go of Daddy's finger.'

She turned to Matt, looking at him with her flashing dark eyes. 'Now then – you're gonna hold your daughter, Matt,' she insisted. 'You're afraid she'll cry, aren't you? Well, she might. But it won't be your fault, Matt. It won't mean she doesn't like you. Babies cry for all sorts of reasons – sometimes they're just letting off steam. If she cries, it's not your fault – have you got that?'

Matt nodded, grateful to Petronella for understanding what he'd been worrying about. She put the bundle firmly in his arms. 'It's like holding a cloud,' he said, still mesmerised by his little girl's intense gaze. It seemed natural to rock her gently and watch the sapphire eyes slowly close. 'She's going to sleep.'

Matt didn't want to put her down. A glow of contentment spread through him.

'We all need a good sleep now – especially Lottie,' Petronella said. 'I'll help you decorate the cradle later, Matt.'

'We're going to have a Candlemas naming ceremony,' Lottie said. 'I don't really want to go to sleep, I'm too happy. I've *never* been so happy.' And she closed her eyes. 'Her name is a secret,' she mumbled, 'until tonight . . .'

Candlemas day was blessed with a tranquil ocean and tall blue winter waves breaking satin-smooth under a golden sun. Lottie spent a blissful day sleeping, waking only to feed her baby and gaze at her, and talk about her with Matt. Nan came to see her and held the tiny baby for a long time, misty-eyed and emotional.

'She means so much to me,' she kept on saying. 'I can't believe she was born so quietly and she hasn't cried.'

'It's exactly how I wanted it to be for her,' Lottie said.

'You were a brave, brave girl,' Nan said, 'and you'll have a happy child because you love her – both of you. You're a shining, radiant family. Lottie and Matt and – oh, I wish you'd tell me her name!'

'Not until the ceremony, Nan,' Lottie smiled, enjoying the secrecy. 'We want to hold her up to the stars.'

'Well, the weather looks set fair,' Nan said. 'Petronella helped me decorate the lovely cradle Matt has made, and now we're going to make dinner and pudding pasties for tea. John has taken Jenny out. They're up to something, I think – and they are so thrilled with the baby.' Nan looked down fondly at the sleeping child. 'She's like a rose in a winter garden.'

John and Jenny returned to Hendravean in a taxi, with a new pram tied on the roof.

Nan looked at them shrewdly. 'And what have you two been up to?'

Everyone went quiet. Jenny blushed and looked at John. 'Go on then – shall we tell them?'

John's eyes sparkled. He took Jenny's hand. 'We do have something to tell you – and I hope you'll be pleased.' He looked at Lottie. 'I've grown to love Jenny. She's my perfect woman, and . . .'

'Even with my iron leg?' Jenny interrupted.

'Even with your iron leg,' John said patiently. 'Jenny is beautiful and courageous and I have asked her to marry me.' Jenny's face glowed. She held out her hand to display the ruby ring on her finger.

'Oh bravo!' Nan said, and tears ran down her wrinkled cheeks. 'That's wonderful news. I'm so happy for you.'

Lottie gave a cry of delight. 'I always knew you would, Daddy – and, Jenny, now you'll *really* be my mum!'

Only Warren looked uneasy. 'Are you gonna take Jenny away on a ship?' he asked.

Jenny shook her head. 'No, Warren. We're going to stay here in St Ives forever. We love it here – and you can come whenever you like.'

Warren grinned and copied Matt and Tom, who were both giving Jenny and John a thumbs-up sign. 'Shall I play me piano-accordion?'

'Not yet,' Nan said. 'It's too loud for the little baby. Later, when she's upstairs in bed we'll have a sing-song.'

'I'd love that,' John said. 'I've been waiting all winter for a Cornish sing-song. So, let's get on with the baby's naming ceremony. It's a clear, starry night.'

There were gasps of admiration as Matt carried the decorated cradle out of the scullery and put it on the table. The celandines had closed their golden petals for the night, but snowdrops glimmered and violets glowed in tiny posies, tied with curls of thin satin ribbon. Lottie stared at it happily.

'What an exquisite bed for our baby's first day on earth. It's lovely, Matt. You're so clever.'

She settled the baby into the soft nest of blankets. 'You, Little Star, are going to have a naming ceremony, just for you!' The baby opened her sapphire blue eyes and pursed her lips, looking up in astonishment at the bunches of flowers arched above her head.

The hall flickered with light from the beeswax candles and the heavy scent of honey and herbs filled the air. John held the front door open and everyone fell silent as the salty air from the sea wafted in and the wide vista of stars welcomed them outside. The Cornish night was cold and still, the full moon spilling its silver seeds on the dark water.

'I feel like a cloud,' Lottie murmured. 'So full of happiness that I could float.' Her smile filled the night as she looked down at her baby, her hair silvery in the moonlight, her eyes luminous. She didn't need to look at the family gathered around her. She could feel them. Their warmth, their faith in her. The old feuds and arguments were gone, swept away by the love that had flowed in like a velvet tide.

Lottie lifted Little Star out of the cradle. The baby was still awake, gazing up at her mother. Matt stood close and Lottie could feel his heartbeat as he wrapped his arms around them.

Nan was waiting, eagerly, for the name.

Lottie smiled at her. 'Thank you, Nan, for sharing your home with us. We will love you forever, you've been our guardian angel.' Lottie paused when she felt Nan tremble a little. 'And so, in honour of Nan . . .' she looked up at the stars, 'we name this child – Nanette.'

'Nanette! How lovely.' Nan moved closer. 'Let me have a cuddle.' She took the tiny, newborn baby in her arms. 'My great-great-grandchild, Nanette Lanroska. You, my darling, are a blessing to this family and to this earth.'

Acknowlegements

Thank you to the St Ives Archives and the RNLI for helping me with the research, and to Beth Emanuel for her meticulous typing and preparation of the manuscript. I've enjoyed working with a new editor, Bec Farrell, and I appreciate her care and skill. A warm thank you to my agent, Judith Murdoch, for her wise guidance.

The support and understanding from my family and friends has been wonderful, especially from Ted, my beloved husband and soulmate, who reads all my books and tells me he loves them.

Go back and read the beginning of Lottie's journey in Cornwall ...

A Cornish Orphan

A captivating Cornish saga set at the turn of the century, from the bestselling author of *The Boy With No Boots*.

Following a terrible storm, seven-year-old Lottie is rescued from a shipwreck by local Cornishman, Arnie Lanroska. Her clothing suggests she comes from a wealthy family, but Lottie's back bears the scars of a severe beating, and how she came to be on a cargo ship in the first place remains a mystery ...

Arnie and his wife already have two young children, Matt and Tom, but are desperate to keep Lottie. They decide to foster her, despite outcries from the local community, and though Matt appears hesitant to get close to Lottie, Tom quickly warms to the new sister in his life.

But when tragedy strikes the very heart of the Lanroska family, the repercussions could change the lives of everyone close to them ...

A nostalgic and heart-warming family saga, perfect for fans of Katie Flynn and Margaret Dickinson

AVAILABLE NOW IN PAPERBACK AND EBOOK

**SIMON &
SCHUSTER**